Insight

Tracey Hawke

Acknowledgements

Many thanks must go to my whole family for being so supportive and encouraging during the time it took to write, edit, and get this book to the point where I am happy with it. Thank you Mum, Dad, Antony, Nan, Susan, David, Debbie, Lesley, Stacey, Kim and Connie for having so much interest in it, and so much faith in me. I love you all.

Special thanks go to the best big brother ever, Antony, for the cover, layout and any and all graphic design. I know I've been a pain, but I love you for putting up with me.

For my mum, Carol, for always reading my stories and telling me you like them. Watching you getting lost in fiction inspired me to do the same, so I hope I have written a story you truly love.

I love you.

Prologue
Where It All Began

Technically, I didn't follow her tonight. When I found her this morning, I could feel her so intensely that her emotions and her mind were open to me. I felt what she felt, I knew what she was thinking, and I knew I'd see her dreams at night since distance wasn't an issue.

I knew she was coming here with her family. They were already seated when I arrived, so I definitely didn't follow her. She was with her mother and sister and they were celebrating, congratulating her, and I just wanted to see her happy and relaxed.

She doesn't know me yet. I should have introduced myself earlier today; I wanted to, but she was so distracted with nerves and anxiety, then relief after her exam was over, that I knew she wanted to be left alone. She didn't even see me, though I was only a few feet away from her, because her thoughts and her concentration were so internalised. She wasn't paying attention to anything around her.

I watched her. It was completely innocent, but I kept out of sight so I didn't alarm her. She left the restaurant completely sober despite the evening's festivities being centred on her achievement. The three women were walking arm-in-arm and she, the shortest of them by several inches, was in the middle as though the other two were afraid of losing her. They were chatting animatedly, but I wasn't listening to their conversation even though I could hear it perfectly, I was focusing on the feeling of contentment inside her; she had finished her degree and she was with the people who meant the most in the world to her. For that moment, everything felt perfect to her and I desperately wanted to be part of that, to be part of her world.

They had reached their vehicle, and I walked away back towards my own. I'd just got in and fastened my seatbelt when I felt her fear and panic, then I heard her scream. I was on my way back to her when I heard her gasp, then there was a shot, and then I felt pain. Jamie. She was in danger and she was hurt.

I was running back in the direction I came, covering the distance in seconds, only to find Jamie lying on the ground and bleeding from her left shoulder. She was alive, but unconscious; I was grateful to hear her heart beating. Her mother was dead on the ground beside her, and her sister was dead inside the car.

I knelt behind Jamie and cradled her head in my lap. Fear that I might lose her coursed through me and I hurt in ways I had never known before.

'Jamie!' I cried. 'Just hold on, baby,' I said, stroking her silky, dark hair off her face and fighting back tears. 'I'm going to get you some help.' I bent forward and kissed her soft mouth before scattering kisses all over her face.

The man with the gun had started walking around the car to where Jamie lay. He knew she wasn't dead, so he was going to shoot her again. Then he saw me.

He stopped, undecided whether to point the gun at Jamie, or at me.

'Stay right where you are,' I ordered with icy anger. 'Put the gun to your head.'

He hesitated for a barely perceptible moment, but I was very persuasive so he obeyed. I would have done it myself by force if necessary, but I didn't want to leave Jamie.

'Now pull the trigger.'

One

Beautiful Mystery

Surely a PhD student shouldn't have time for recreational reading, easpecially when studying for a doctorate in English literature and creative writing. However, I had exhausted the resources in my university campus library and several public libraries, so I was waiting for books I'd ordered to arrive.

I went to a bookstore, not an academic bookstore, just an ordinary high street branch selling a wide selection of general fiction. I was looking for something new to read, something that would have my required happy ending but whose story wouldn't be as predictable as the usual dross in brightly-coloured covers on offer.

I knew why I liked happy-ever-afters in the fiction I read: it was because I knew I'd never have one of my own. My life had recently been torn apart and I was just living in the fragments that were left. I made a promise to myself about seven or eight years ago that one day I would write a believable, cliché-free novel with a satisfying ending without making every female reader pine for their own Mr. Perfect, or worse, the fictional male character in the latest book they'd read, when the only men they had ever met made solitude seem like bliss.

I had a theory about the perfect man. I believed the closest it was possible to get to him was a man in fiction, specifically a vampire. I had read enough vampire fiction to know that a man who was made immortal at a young age is close to perfect as long as one happens to find him when he has been around for at least a century. That way, he would still look young and beautiful, but he would have had enough 'life' experience to know what is really important so he would not play all the emotional and mental games that mortal men play.

I decided at the age of fourteen that I wanted to spend eternity with a vampire. The idea of living forever appealed to me back then, and I used to be romantic enough to believe in there being one man I was destined to be with and I would love with my whole self. If I was being honest with myself, I was still romantic enough to want all that, I just no longer believed I'd ever get it.

That put the thought of vampires into my head, so I went over to the 'dark fantasy' section, always one of the smallest areas in every bookshop I'd ever visited, to look for any new attempts at my favourite subject.

I scanned the shelves and many of the books there I had either already read, or dismissed after reading the blurb on the back or a few paragraphs inside. I picked up one that I hadn't seen before, by a writer I hadn't heard of, and I was reading the back cover as I continued slowly walking along the narrow aisle. I collided with a man who I swore was not there until the instant I bumped into him.

'Oof,' I involuntarily uttered as I simultaneously stumbled and dropped the book on impact with him.

His hands reached out to grab my arms and steady me and, as I looked up at him, he was smiling warmly at me. My heart faltered under his penetrating gaze.

'Thank you. I'm so sorry,' I garbled in embarrassment. 'I was reading the back of that book rather than looking where I was going, so I didn't see you standing there. That'll teach me.' I grinned at him, then bent to pick up the novel.

'That's okay.' He was still smiling and there was amusement in his smooth, sexy voice. 'Are you all right?'

'Fine. I'm completely fine. I didn't hurt you, did I?' It wasn't likely; although he was slim, he had felt firm and toned as I'd fallen into him.

'No, not at all. I wouldn't read that if I were you,' he said, indicating the book. 'It's terrible.'

'I actually wasn't planning to. The description on the back didn't really appeal to me: I'm not into vendettas.' As disillusioned as I'd become with regard to romance, I still preferred a love story to anything else. 'You've read it, though, I take it?'

'Unfortunately. It's all rather gory, there's no real character development, and the writing is unimaginative and lacklustre. I swear some people will publish anything! It's wholly not worth the money you'd pay for it, and certainly not worthy of the time you'll lose reading it. You'll want your life back if you do, trust me.' He laughed once.

I laughed, too, and the shared intimacy made me brave enough to really scrutinise him. He was beautiful. Literally. His face was perfect: not a flaw, or an expression line, or a shadow where facial hair should grow. He had expressive, greenish eyes; rich, chestnut-brown hair which contrasted well with his porcelain skin; and he was tall compared to me: I barely reached his shoulders. Though, I am really short.

'Thanks for the tip.'

I wanted to ask him if he was into vampire fiction, too; he was in the appropriate section and he'd read a book I had dismissed, these were good indicators that he was. Basically, he was gorgeous, he seemed friendly, and I didn't want to let him go because I'd probably never see him again, but I didn't want him to think I was coming on to him and scare him away. However, there was something else, something other than simple physical attraction pulling me inexorably towards him, something he was emanating and something we were both feeling.

'Do you like vampires?' It was as if he had read my mind.

Some of my surprise that he had asked of me what I was thinking about him must have shown on my face, for he instantly seemed to regret it.

'Forgive me, I'm being intrusive,' he said gently, but still he looked at me intently.

'No, no, you're not. It's not that, it's just that I was debating asking you the same question.' I looked at him ruefully and tried not to let my painful shyness hinder me. 'But, yes, I do like vampires, very much. I'm severely tempted by the dark and forbidden. I don't like to abide by someone else's rules. How about you?'

'I don't abide by rules, either. And I'm not particularly drawn to vampires.' He had this expression that suggested his words had a secret meaning only he understood. 'I read most genres of fiction.'

'Oh. Do you have any favourites?'

'Not specifically. I like some novels from all genres,' he added vaguely. 'I'll bet you're a writer, aren't you?'

'Yes, I... How did you know that?' I frowned hard. Was I that easy to read?

'I just sensed it about you. You seem quiet and shy, and you're into books and non-conformity. That suggests to me that you're imaginative and creative and you like the escapism of it all.' He smiled, but didn't give me the opportunity to respond. 'I must go now. I'll be seeing you again, Jamie.'

The whole time we'd spoken, he'd never broken eye contact with me, not until he turned to leave.

'Wait. How do you know my name?'

He leaned in close. 'It's on your key ring,' he said softly into my ear, causing my heart rate to soar with nervous excitement.

He looked deep into my eyes, holding my gaze as though trying to communicate something telepathically to me, before walking away.

My key ring? I looked down and checked the pocket in my bag where I kept my keys. They were still in there, and I did have a key ring with my name and its meaning on it, but there was no way he could have known that.

I was confused; I knew that I had never met this man before, but he knew who I was. I put the book back in its place and hurried out of the shop to find him, but outside, the street was deserted.

Who was he and how did he know my name? Not to mention he knew I write. I desperately wanted to know who he was, after all, he said he'd see me again; he could have been stalking me.

Suspecting that I was possibly being pursued was quite an unnerving feeling. I could almost empathise with celebrities, but their jobs attract attention to them so it seemed feasible that they should have stalkers, but me? I had a very solitary life: I had a few close friends, but they were all married with families, I didn't have any family of my own anymore, and I'd given up my part-time job. I studied, occasionally visited my best friend and her family, but, essentially, my time was spent alone at home. I'd never done anything that would attract anyone's attention.

Still, whoever this man was, he'd been close enough to me at some point to see me use my keys and not only notice that I had a key ring with my name on it, but to be able to read it. I reasoned that I needed to be more vigilant and aware of who was around me; I'd always had a tendency to go off into my own little world and not look any higher than my eye line, which, considering I'm only five feet tall, isn't very high.

I stood outside the bookshop for a minute just in case he reappeared. I knew it was unlikely, that was why I only waited a minute and, as I was thoroughly uninspired by the books I'd looked at, I decided to go home.

I searched for him all the way back to my car. If he was stalking me, I was sure he must have been watching or following me, so I walked quickly, staying alert, got in my old car and locked the door behind me.

All the way home, I kept checking for a car following mine, but I didn't know what car I was supposed to be looking for, or even if I should have been looking for one at all, so I was searching the faces of the drivers. I didn't see him.

I was slightly perturbed that I was disappointed that he had completely disappeared. He had actually seemed really nice when I'd spoken to him, and like quite an intriguing man. I've always been a good judge of character, I read people well and, if a person is even a little bit questionable, I can feel it; I know it. This stranger made me feel warm inside, safe, and something more that I wasn't sure I could be right about, but it was strong. He wouldn't hurt me; I knew that for a fact. I'm never wrong about people, so although I didn't think he was dangerous, this man certainly owed me some answers.

When I pulled into my driveway behind my mother's car; which was in pristine condition, perfect working order, and which I knew I'd probably have to start using sometime soon because my little run-around was on its last metaphorical legs; I looked to see if he was anywhere around, hiding behind a tree or something. I recognised that I was being massively paranoid, but I couldn't help myself. It was all futile, anyway, because I didn't find him; I hadn't expected to; it was the mystery that was compelling me.

I locked the front door behind me when I got inside the house, as was my custom. I often went days without unlocking the door to go out and people never visited. When I saw my friends, I went to their houses or we met in public places. No one liked coming to my house, especially once I'd started living there alone, and possibly because I'd left everything the way my mother liked it. It was her house, after all. I wasn't offended. I supposed I'd have to make changes one day, but, until then, I was comforted by the familiarity and by Mum's personality being stamped everywhere.

Having nothing better to do, I picked up my favourite vampire book. I'd read it dozens of times and the words were as familiar to me as if I'd written them myself, but I couldn't concentrate on it because I couldn't get that mysterious, beautiful man out of my head.

I put the book down on the coffee table and dug out every photo album and every box of loose pictures in the house to see if he was in any of them and I was having an extremely unlikely memory lapse. I say 'unlikely' because I have an eidetic memory, so if I'd met him before, I would have remembered him. Still, I figured it was worth a try.

I pored over every single photograph, searching the backgrounds of shots from parties in case he was there, but just as I'd suspected, he wasn't. All I had successfully accomplished was to upset myself by looking at photos of when I was whole, when I was happier, when I had a family. My life hadn't been perfect then, nowhere near it, but it was better than this and I handled all the bad aspects that much better because I had my wonderful mum and twin sister to talk to, to seek advice from. Now it was just me.

I crawled into bed that night feeling like my barely healing wounds were wide open again; and I don't mean solely the physical ones; and I woke the next morning feeling drained, looking like the undead, and knowing I was going to have to use all my energy to hide it all from the friends I was going to visit. I knew I would have to try even harder to block what they were feeling to prevent it from affecting me.

Rather than appear totally deranged to them by telling them about my encounter with the beautiful stranger the day before, I decided to wait until I met him again before mentioning it to anyone. He did say he would be seeing me again and, whilst it was possible to interpret that to mean he would be spying on me, I chose to believe it was less sinister and I'd be able to talk with him, maybe ask him a few things.

I wasn't expecting anyone to get in touch and say, 'Hey, my friend such-and-such said he bumped into you in a bookshop the other day. Or should I say you bumped into him?' For some reason, because I knew that I had never met him before, I also knew that none of my friends would know him, either, and I didn't want to tell them about him. He was my enigma, my secret, something to take my mind away from what had become my everyday life and when the reasons behind it became too much to bear.

I knew that today I was going to have to hold myself together because I was going to visit my closest friend, Rachael. Rachael had just had her second baby, her hormones were still likely to be all over the place, so she would feel awful if she saw how much I was suffering. It would be even worse because she still felt guilty that she couldn't be there for me when my mother and sister died. She nearly miscarried six months into her pregnancy and was forced to stay in bed pretty much the entire time until she gave birth four weeks ago. I was going there to meet the new addition.

Rachael opened the door with baby Noah in her arms.

'Jamie! It's so good to see you.'

She leaned forward to kiss me on the cheek and, as she got close, I could see that there were tears in her eyes and I knew she was trying to hold back a whole flood of emotions.

We went through to the lounge where she put Noah in his straw baby basket so she could give me a hug. It was a big, squishy hug and she held me so tightly I knew she was trying to make up for not being around for a while.

'You're still glowing.' I couldn't help my mouth twitching upwards as I spoke my thoughts aloud and handed my oldest friend the teddy I'd bought for Noah.

'Thank you,' she said shyly, but smiling from her core. 'I feel wonderful. Noah is so well-behaved; he sleeps through the night and he's a happy baby who doesn't cry a lot. Tamara adores him so there are no problems with her adjusting to having our attention split between them. It has all gone perfectly,' she babbled.

She looked at me and her expression abruptly changed to horror at her perceived *faux pas*.

'Oh, God, I'm so sorry. That was a thoughtless thing to say. I'm so stupid.'

'No, don't worry, Rachael, it's okay,' I said quickly, trying to reassure her; something I had to do with most people. 'You're happy, your lives are perfect. Don't apologise for being happy.'

She shouldn't feel guilty that her life was good, and I tried not to be bitter when I saw my friends with everything they'd ever wanted when I had just lost everything I'd ever had.

'Speaking of Tamara,' her two year old daughter, 'where is she? And where's Baz?'

Her husband was unfortunately named 'Barrington' by his eccentric parents. He was good-humoured about it, but preferred being called 'Baz' regardless.

'They were doing potato prints, but Tamara managed to get more paint on her than anywhere else so Baz is cleaning her up,' she replied. The glint in her eyes made it clear that she was glad it wasn't her charged with that particular task.

'Oh.' I smiled back, imagining the scene.

'So,' Rachael began tentatively, 'I know I haven't been around for the last few months—'

'That couldn't be helped,' I interjected to prevent her saying something that would make me cry. 'It wasn't your fault.'

'Thank you for understanding, Jamie, but you should have come to see me more, you know, afterwards. You've lost some weight and you look exhausted. You should have talked to me,' she said with genuine concern.

I supposed I really shouldn't have thought I could fool Rachael into believing I was okay. She and I had been friends for fifteen years and knew one another too well. I wasn't really expected to be okay, but that didn't mean I wanted anyone to witness my torment. I didn't want my loss and pain to be the only things people saw when they looked at me. The rest of me was there, too, somewhere in the fragments.

'You didn't need any more worry when you were in danger of losing Noah,' I tried to deflect.

'But you talked to someone about it, didn't you?'

I said nothing. I hadn't wanted to talk to anyone about the grief, pain and guilt I felt. My silence exasperated her.

'Are you eating?' Her tone was curt.

'I haven't had much of an appetite lately,' I replied quietly. I barely ate at all these days.

'Sleeping?'

'Sometimes I dream about what happened.' I felt so uncomfortable talking about this, I couldn't look at her.

'You should see a counsellor,' Rachael deduced.

'I don't want to. It's only been a couple of months. I'm dealing with this in my own way.'

I was horrified at the prospect of talking to a complete stranger about how it felt to be the only survivor of the attempted robbery and subsequent shooting that had killed my family. It had been suggested by the doctors at the hospital and I declined the offer, but they weren't satisfied until I took some leaflets home with me. I threw them all in the recycling bin without even glancing at them.

Talking about it wasn't going to bring my mother and sister back. The pain of their loss was never going to leave me, so what, exactly, would it achieve?

'I think—' she began. I looked at her sharply to try to stop her, but Rachael didn't notice because Tamara had skipped into the room, peered into Noah's basket and, satisfied that he was asleep, headed straight for her mother.

'I'm clean, Mummy,' she trilled with a goofy grin, then climbed onto Rachael's lap.

'That's good, Tam.' Rachael kissed her daughter and her tone changed from remonstrating to patient. 'Aren't you going to say hello to Aunty Jamie?'

'Hello, Zamie,' she lisped, not having mastered the letter 'J' yet and either being intelligent enough to remember I hated the 'aunty' part, or just ignoring it.

'Hello, Aunty Jamie,' Baz mocked as he entered the lounge.

'Hello, Baz.' I laughed. 'How are you?'

'I'm great. I've been potato printing, you know,' he answered, winking at me. He leaned in and gave me a hug. 'You look tired,' he added bluntly.

'Bad dreams,' I replied, trying to smile and be light, but not quite managing it.

I swiftly looked away from him and caught Rachael mouthing 'Sorry' at me. I nodded my thanks to her.

'Have you thought about—' He stopped mid-sentence having caught the look Rachael was giving him, the discomfort which must have been evident on my face, and by my hands which were twisting together. 'Maybe it's too soon to think about that.'

A snuffling noise came from across the room, indicating that Noah was awake. As Rachael was happily holding Tamara, Baz scooped Noah out of his basket. He was wriggling to stretch out his sleepy limbs.

'Here you go, Jamie,' Baz said, handing the baby to me. 'Have a cuddle for a little while.'

'Isn't he due a feed?' I asked, panicking because babies usually screamed their heads off when I held them.

'No,' Rachael clarified, clearly amused. 'He was only fed about an hour ago. He should be fine for a while yet.'

I cradled Noah close to me so he could feel my heartbeat; I'd read somewhere that it comforts an infant after being so used to their mother's heartbeat during gestation. He seemed comfortable and, from the look on his serene face, he was happy enough to be held by me, which was more than could be said for how I was feeling.

I tried to relax so he wouldn't pick up on my tension and I smiled and cooed at him, stroked his face, held his hands and tickled his feet; all things I'd watched my mother do when holding babies, and she was a natural with them.

Tamara got off her mother's knee and came and stood beside me with her thumb in her mouth. She placed her other hand lightly on my knee and peered at Noah to make sure her baby brother was safe with me. Only when she was sure he wasn't in any danger did she return to her mother.

'Would you like me to make you a coffee, Jamie?'

'That would be lovely. Thanks, Baz.'

I waited for him to disappear into the kitchen, suspecting that Rachael still had more to say on the subject of me getting help.

'Jamie, I don't want to push you into anything you don't want to do, but maybe talking about how you feel would help. Even talking to me, not that I exactly know how to deal with the repercussions of that kind of traumatic experience. But I don't think you should just keep it all inside. You'll go mad,' she stressed.

'Thank you for the offer, Rachael, truly, I just don't see how talking about it will make me feel better. It won't change anything,' I emphasised.

'No, it won't change anything, but there are people who can help you cope with the grief so it doesn't incapacitate you. I wouldn't be surprised if you're feeling guilty for surviving, too. It's such an awful situation to be in. Don't get me wrong, Jamie; you're here, you're thinking of other people enough that you go out and see them rather than locking yourself away and swallowing handfuls of pills, and I don't for one second think that's easy. Just don't think that you have to sit and suffer; you don't. None of this is your fault.'

Just at that moment, Baz re-entered the room with drinks and he put mine on the low table in front of me.

'We don't want you to feel overwhelmed, Jamie,' he said kindly, indicating that he had heard what his wife had been saying, 'but Rachael's right. You do deserve a happy life.'

'How can I be happy with Mum and Carmel dead?' It was a brutal question, but it was valid. 'It's like saying it doesn't matter that they're not here, and it does matter.'

'Of course it matters.' Rachael leaned forward, frowning at me, eager to show that she understood. 'But what's the point in you going on living if you're not going to make the most out of the fact that you *are* alive? Don't waste your life, Jamie; you, more than anyone, know how fragile it really is. You owe it to Bea and Carmel to take the opportunities that were taken away from them.'

I was about to retaliate, but Baz quickly spoke first.

'That's not meant in a nasty way; you know we don't mean to be cruel. What Rachael is getting at—'

'It's okay,' I interrupted, defeated, but not bitter. 'I know what you both are getting at. It's just not as easy as that, or as straightforward. I don't mean this offensively, but neither one of you has lost someone you love, so you can't empathise. Until you can, you're just giving me platitudes. I appreciate what you're trying to do, but I need to grieve and move at my own pace. I'll learn to live with, and around, the pain and loss, but I won't waste my life.' I hoped that last part was true.

I knew that my friends meant well, but the pain doesn't just stop once the funeral is over. It had been eight weeks since I lost my family, but that's not exactly a long time. It can take many years to come to terms with loss and I may never fully accept it. I didn't expect it to ever stop hurting and I had to live the rest of my life, however long that may be, without my mother and my sister. I was still young, I was only twenty-eight, but I could live another fifty years or more and I knew I'd miss them both every single day just as much as I did right then. How is anyone supposed to live with that kind of pain?

Noah had been quite content to be held by me up until this point, but he started to grizzle. I became tense knowing how babies are never usually very comfortable with me, and I tried to soothe him, to no avail.

'You'd better take Noah,' I said as I stood up and gave him to his mother, 'before he really starts to cry.'

That went for me, too; tears of frustration as much as sadness.

Two

Empath

With new baby duty out of the way and still no books for me to be able to continue my research for my doctoral thesis, I decided I should use my free time to continue writing the vampire story I'd begun whilst I was recuperating from the bullet wound I'd received and organising the funeral for my only family members. It was the only thing that had stopped me from going mad.

I was the lucky one. My mother, my sister and I were out celebrating after I'd passed my Master's degree. I'd had my *viva voce* earlier in the day, been told I'd passed, so we were out having dinner at a nice restaurant. Unfortunately, we hadn't been able to park very close to it; we were at the far end of the vast car park and we were the only people walking to any of the cars in that area at that particular time of night.

Maybe that's why the bastard picked on us.

Carmel had driven that night. She'd had a nice little two-door Audi; it wasn't the newest or most expensive model, but she'd looked after it. She unlocked her door and got in, but for some reason, the passenger door hadn't unlocked, leaving my mother and I standing outside. We were just giggling about it when a man dressed in dark colours, maybe black, maybe navy blue, approached Carmel's door, opened it, and shot her straight through the heart.

Mum and I started screaming. He aimed the gun at me, but Mum knocked me out of the way, so I got hit in my left shoulder instead of my chest. I hit the ground, heard another gunshot, and Mum fell down next to me. She was dead. I passed out in shock after that, but I was told by the police officers who took my statement when I woke up in hospital that whoever that… there aren't words for what he was… shot himself after killing my mum.

I don't know how long it was before we were discovered, or by whom, all I do know is that he was male.

The thought crossed my mind that maybe that was who I met yesterday. Maybe the stranger knew me because he was the one who found me alive that night and asked the police or the hospital staff who I was, not that they should have told him. Then again, if it was him, why hadn't he got in touch sooner or why didn't he say something yesterday? Why be so cryptic? Besides, the man from yesterday seemed to know too much about me personally, and about my personality, and he didn't mention my injury. If he had found me that night, he would have known I'd been shot.

I hadn't asked about who found me. It had only been eight weeks and I had been trying to adjust and physically heal whilst at the same time throwing myself into my PhD. Thanks to my being largely incapacitated whilst my shoulder repaired itself, I was ahead of schedule for someone at the very beginning of their programme. Even if I had looked for the man who found me, I wasn't sure if I would have been able to look him in the eye: I might have seen pity there. When I was with my friends, I was subjected to a mixture of their regret, sympathy, and genuine concern, but they knew me. From a stranger, it was a bit discomfiting.

Then again, who knew how traumatised he was after what he saw? Not that it really mattered; I knew the police wouldn't be able to tell me his name because his information, statement, and everything else were confidential. If nothing else, though, it would have been nice to thank him; I could have bled to death if he hadn't found me. I considered writing a letter and asking the police to pass it to him. I doubted they would actually do it, but it was something to think about.

Before I went home, I dropped into the little coffee shop a few streets away from my house. I'd spent many hours ensconced in there with my laptop, typing up handwritten chapters of my Master's thesis and drinking endless cappuccinos. I got so friendly with the baristas that they advised me what cappuccino maker to buy for my house, showed me how to use it, and they even mixed up a special blend of coffee for me. I ran out a couple of days ago and I knew it was always productive to have a large cup of coffee to hand when I was writing.

I parked directly in front of the shop, locked my car, and stepped inside.

'Jamie!' Paolo, the owner and chief barista, immediately rushed out from behind the counter to wrap me up in a bear hug. 'I haven't seen you for nearly a month. It's good to see you've got your arm out of that sling at last.'

'Hello, Paolo. The nice people at the hospital told me I could take it off a couple of weeks ago. I'll be having physiotherapy for a while yet, but I was told I've healed really well. The bullet didn't do too much damage to the muscle as it went through, so I was lucky in more ways than one that night.' If you could call losing my family lucky, but that wasn't what I meant.

'Not that that's much comfort to you, is it?' His voice was thick with sympathy. He had such a kind, avuncular nature.

'Not really, no.' I tried to smile a small smile to show him I was coping.

'So, are you here for a cappuccino and a chat, or just a packet of coffee?'

He knew me too well. 'Just some coffee today, thanks. I've just visited some friends and their new baby, now I'm going home to get some work done where it's quiet. But it's just not possible without coffee.' This time I really did smile.

'Of course, Jamie. But you must come and see me properly soon,' he remonstrated lightly. 'We've missed you.'

'Thank you, Paolo. I've missed all of you, too. I'll be here, complete with laptop, to take residence at my usual booth in the corner soon. I've got some typing to do.'

He squeezed my hand before going back behind the counter to fetch a vacuum-packed foil package, which he always sold to me at a discounted price. Paolo was generous to his favourite customers.

I slipped him some money, gave him one last hug, and headed towards the door. I wasn't really concentrating on my surroundings or who else was on the premises, instead I was putting the packet of coffee in my bag. I looked up after closing the zip in time to see a tall figure slide effortlessly out of his chair nearest the exit and grasp the handle of the door to open it for me.

'Hello, Jamie,' the warm, rhythmic voice said.

Recognising it instantly, I snapped my head up to look into the breathtaking face of the beautiful man from the day before.

'Hello again...' I left the sentence hanging, hoping he would supply me with his name, but he didn't.

'They know you well here.' It wasn't a question.

'Yes, I used to sit in here for hours whilst I was working on my Master's dissertation. I spent a fortune on coffee.' I may not have ordinarily been so forthcoming with someone I didn't know, but I was inordinately proud of my Master of Arts by Research, and it didn't feel like he was a stranger.

He smiled back in a way that intimated I hadn't told him anything he didn't already know.

'And now they supply you with fresh ground coffee, too.' Again, not a question, merely stating something he knew to be true.

'Paolo and the rest of the team have always been very kind to me. Then again, I've been a good customer,' I explained.

'So you have,' he said, that same knowing smile playing on his lips. 'So, did you find a book to interest you yesterday?'

'No, I didn't. I resorted to reading one of my old favourites for quite possibly the hundredth time.' I half-laughed. 'How about you?' I asked, hoping to draw more information from him, though I knew full well he left the store directly after talking with me.

'I'm afraid not. I'll have to wait for you to finish your novel to read something decent.'

Of course, he'd told me the previous day that he suspected I was a writer, so it was only logical he would think I wrote novels not just short stories. I'd started several, planned several more, but never actually got very far when writing novels. I was hoping that would change with my vampire story.

'You seem to have a lot of faith in me.' I was still waiting for him to fill in his name, or tell me something about himself, but still he didn't.

'It's not unfounded,' he answered assuredly.

Unless he was psychic, or he owned a publishing company and wanted to give me a book deal, there was no way he could have known that for sure.

'Thank you, but that remains to be seen,' I responded, flattered he believed I was that talented, but unsettled because I had no idea why he thought so having never read anything I'd written.

He merely tilted his head to the side and looked at me with curiosity in his eyes and that same knowing smile.

'Well, I should be going,' I said, and took a step closer to the door.

'Work to do?' he asked, raising his eyebrows and pushing down on the handle that he was still holding.

'My bestseller isn't going to write itself,' I challenged him.

'Of course not.' He understood that I recognised he knew more about me than he should given our acquaintance, and his lips twitched. He opened the door, but, just as I crossed the threshold, he added, 'I'll see you soon, Jamie.'

I stopped and turned back to face him. His words were so similar to those from yesterday.

'How do you know me when I don't even know your name?' I gave in. I had to ask because I was getting nowhere.

'Take care of yourself,' was all he said as he let go of the door and returned to his seat.

Perhaps I should have been disturbed, or angry, but I wasn't. He didn't directly reveal anything about himself during that conversation, but I gleaned from what he didn't say, and from what I'd sensed from him, that he had known me longer than I'd originally suspected if he was already aware that I was a regular at the coffee shop whilst I completed my Master's degree, and that I was on first-name terms with not only the owner, but all the staff there.

I would have been worried if he was at all threatening, but he wasn't. He had a caring, soothing vibe that prevented me from panicking at the unusual circumstances. He wasn't controlling my emotional responses; he was exuding a reassuring energy from inside.

It only took me five minutes to get home and all I could think about as I drove was him. I wondered exactly how much of a coincidence it was that I'd seen him twice in two days.

Once inside my house, I headed straight for the coffee machine to make use of my recent purchase, satisfy my craving after being surrounded by the aroma of all those coffee beans in the shop, and ensure I was fully prepared when I commenced writing.

Though I'd started the story to escape into another world when the pain of my reality threatened to consume me, I often compulsively rewrote sections or was dissatisfied with my choice of words. That was when I could concentrate enough to write at all. I spent many hours merely sitting there with a notebook on my knees, a pen between my fingers, staring into space imagining the characters and their conversations, but not actually managing to write a word. It was a slow process.

After speaking with the pretty, green-eyed man whose name I still didn't know, I didn't have any of those problems. It seemed as though I knew the pertinent word in every instance and I managed to describe perfectly every scene the way I imagined it in my head. I suspected my sudden progress was a direct result of my beautiful stranger's belief that my writing was good and would be published someday.

I wrote solidly, not noticing how the afternoon crept into the evening, and how that changed to night. By the time I gave in for the day, it was approaching midnight and not only had I thought of the best way to develop my story idea into a longer narrative, I had also completed the first two, albeit still somewhat rough, chapters.

I had a bath before I went to bed to try to relax my mind and, as I soaked in the soporific heat of the water, I wondered if I'd get to sleep and have nightmares, or if I would lie awake until the sun came up, mentally exhausted but not able to shut-down.

At first, my body resisted sleep, but soon after I drifted off, my dream took a familiar, disturbing turn and I was back in that car park with my mum and sister. Just as I was about to be forced to mentally relive my ordeal, it changed. Instead of the killer approaching Carmel's car holding a gun, it was the man with the green eyes, brown hair and warm, wonderful smile walking straight towards me carrying a beautiful bouquet of lilies, roses and tulips in varying shades of pink.

From the time I got shot, I'd dreamt about it two or three times a week. Occasionally, I woke up screaming, and that was something I'd never done when I'd had nightmares before. However bad that was, I was relieved I didn't dream about it every night. Sometimes, I even dreamt I got shot in the head, but, no matter what, I was always the only one who survived. That night was the very first time I dreamt I was back in that car park, standing outside the car, but no one got shot.

In this dream, Mum, Carmel and I left the restaurant and walked to Carmel's car, just as we did the night they died. The driver's-side door unlocked, but the passenger door didn't, so Carmel got in, leaned over, and opened it from the inside. When it actually happened, the killer came from somewhere behind Carmel on her side of the car, but in my dream, the man with the green eyes came from behind me just as I was about to move the front seat forward to get in the back.

I didn't see him at first. He called my name, and I knew I'd recognise that voice anywhere despite only having spoken to him twice. When I turned around, there he was walking towards me, his eyes blazing as though he was looking at the love of his life, holding the flowers.

He came and stood directly in front of me, transferred the large bouquet from his arms to mine, then he moved in close, gently took my face in his hands and kissed me. As our lips touched, I woke up.

I don't know precisely what it was that woke me; maybe it was the shock of my dream deviating so drastically from its usual course, or maybe it was the surprise of being kissed; but as I opened my eyes, my lips were tingling. I assumed it was psychosomatic because the last thing that happened in my dream was our mouths meeting.

The thing was, in my dream, I could really feel that he loved me. Not only that, I loved him back, and those feelings stayed with me long after I woke which led me to question where they were really coming from.

Something none of my friends had ever known about me is that I'm an empath: I can discern what other people feel and I can feel it, too. I'd always been a bit of a hermit by choice because being in a crowd, enclosed by all the energy and emotion of so many people, can be unbearable.

The only ones who knew about my ability were my mum and sister. When Carmel and I were little, I'd get upset if she was even though nothing was bothering me. At first, our mother assumed it was because we were twins and were closely linked. However, when it became evident that I could feel my mother's anxieties, and when I went to preschool and hated being around all the other children, Mum knew it was something more.

Doctors and psychologists dismissed me as being 'sensitive' and claimed I'd grow out of it when I got used to being around other people. Dissatisfied with their diagnosis, Mum bought books about psychic abilities and suspected I was an empath. The older I got, the better able I was to interpret everything I was feeling and sensing, and we were able to confirm it.

Thankfully, I gradually learnt ways to deflect other people's energies away from myself when they were unwanted, but whenever I got upset, or my energy got low, I was unable to protect myself and I could wallow in melancholy for weeks. Hence my apprehension visiting Rachael and Baz, but that was nothing compared to Mum and Carmel's funeral. My grief was, understandably, overwhelming, but it was magnified by every other mourner at the service.

I wondered if my subconscious was telling me that this man believed himself in love with me, that really he was stalking me and his emotions were affecting me empathically and that was why I returned his love in my dream. Maybe I was just gratified by the attention of such a very attractive man, but, honestly, I knew that wasn't true. I felt it wasn't true because I'd felt something powerful and genuine emanating from him when I was with him, and something in me was responding to that.

I got nowhere trying to figure it out, and I was too disconcerted to go back to sleep. It was light outside and, on checking my clock, I saw it was seven-thirty: not an unreasonable time to get up even though I had no reason to get up early in the mornings. When I got shot, I gave up work, partly because I was injured and grieving and in no condition to do anything; not that my part-time office job was particularly mentally or physically taxing; and partly because I didn't need to earn money for a while.

My mother took out a life insurance policy when my sister and I were born and our father walked out on us. We'd had little other family at the time and she wanted to be sure we'd be financially secure should something happen to her. When she died, I got the house and the half-a-million pound life insurance payout as I was the only daughter named in her will who was still alive. I wouldn't have any money worries for years.

I hauled myself out of bed, not as well-rested as I should have been, and headed for the bathroom to make myself feel more human. After wrapping myself in my thick, fleecy dressing gown, I went downstairs to sit on the couch and lounge in front of the TV for an hour before... Before what? I didn't exactly have a demanding schedule. I could have stayed in my pyjamas all day and carried on writing, or I could have cleaned the house from top to bottom whilst my latest load of laundry went for a spin in the washing machine. Not that it mattered, anyway; there was nothing worth watching at that time in the morning. I was never partial to breakfast television, or daytime television for that matter, and just because I didn't have a job, it didn't mean I was suddenly obsessed with soap operas, celebrities, make-up and fashion.

Quickly giving up on the television, I picked up the notebook I'd left open on the coffee table and reread what I'd written yesterday. I knew it wasn't perfect, it was only a first draft, but I was pleased with it and I knew I could continue writing it to its conclusion; I'd lacked the dedication with my previous attempts at novels.

It had been a great source of shame to me that I'd been mentally fabricating and writing stories since I was a young child and I'd had so many ideas, made so many starts, but never yet completed a manuscript. I hoped that once I completed the first, once I proved to myself that I really did have it in me just as I'd always known I had, that writing subsequent books would be less of a struggle. It was the only thing I had ever wanted to do with my life. I wasn't like Carmel, who was more practical.

She trained as a beautician when she finished school, then she worked in various salons and spas until she found a partner with whom to open her own salon three years ago. Aaron was a hair stylist as well as a beautician, and they met at the health spa where they worked. They both wanted to have their own business, so they became business partners and made it happen. In the process, they also fell in love, and they got engaged on Carmel's and my birthday last year.

Aaron was supposed to be with us the night Carmel and Mum died, but his father had been taken ill so he was with his parents. I didn't think he would ever forgive himself for not being there even though I'd reassured him that the only difference, had he been there, was that he would probably be dead, too. He had argued that he would have driven so we would have used his car so the locks wouldn't have failed, or the fiend might not have targeted us because he was there so we weren't three women alone. Still, his father was ill and he needed to be with his family; that was more important than a dinner date; and that was the right choice because no one could have predicted what was going to happen that night.

I felt guilty for not going to see him more, but I recognised it wasn't easy for him to see me when I'd lived and Carmel hadn't. Equally, I saw it on his face that he felt awful for feeling that way when I had lost my entire family, and that was probably why he wasn't rushing around here to visit me, either.

I picked up writing from where I'd left off, determined to get something done rather than dwell on my dream from last night. If I did that, I'd obsess over it all day. Blocking the images of the mystery man from my mind, I concentrated on my characters and the next scenario idea I'd had, and I was so engrossed in it that the sound of the doorbell ringing over an hour later startled me back to reality.

I swiftly got up, retrieved the spare door key from behind a family photograph on the fireplace since my keys were still in my bag somewhere, unlocked, then opened the door. The man on the other side politely smiled at me.

'Ms. J. Kavanagh?' he asked, clearly amused that I was still in my pyjamas.

'Yes, that's me,' I automatically answered, slightly embarrassed at being caught like this.

'Delivery for you.'

He handed over a large brown box which I immediately knew held the books I'd ordered off the internet a few days ago.

'Thank you,' I said, and placed the box at my feet so I could sign for the parcel.

'Have a good day,' he said before sprinting back to his van.

'Thanks; you, too,' I shouted before he disappeared inside.

I admit it: I'm obsessed with books. My favourites are fiction, which none of these were, they were textbooks I needed for my PhD research topic. At least I had more options for what to do with my day.

I took the box through to the sitting room and ripped it open to check that all six books I'd ordered had arrived. Some had very pretentious, academic-sounding titles and had rather nondescript covers, but the rest looked approachable, even inviting, with quirky titles and illustrations, or some artistic photography, on the cover.

I wasn't lying, or exaggerating, when I said I'd exhausted the resources in my university and public libraries. I'd only enrolled on my course five weeks ago, but I'd already had my topic prepared before I finished my Master's degree. Three weeks after I got shot, I decided to get on with what I'd planned for my life. I went to see my supervisor, discussed my dissertation proposal with her, got it all agreed, and I officially enrolled two days later. I'd produced the written proposal by the end of the week, which was immediately signed-off, so I went about reading.

In four weeks, with a lack of social engagements, job, money worries, sleep due to the fear of nightmares as well as the nightmares themselves, or very much else to do, I had devoured all the relevant sources in the vicinity. In any other circumstances, I wouldn't have been anywhere near that organised, but it gave me something to aim for, to work towards and, most importantly, the hope of a future.

I put the books aside and went back upstairs to get dressed in my usual uniform of jeans and a jumper. I gathered up a load of clothes and bundled them into the washing machine before sitting back down on the couch with the second-least inspiring-looking of my new textbooks, and another notebook, to continue my research into sexism in contemporary female fiction.

Several hours, two painkillers to fight my encroaching headache, one bowl of cereal and numerous hits of caffeine later, I'd waded through the whole of the book. I knew it was potentially germane to my research subject, but something the stranger said to me when I spoke to him in the bookshop came to mind: I wished I could get the time back that I'd already spent reading it.

The washing machine had finished its cycle during the time I had been studying so intently, so I transferred the load to the tumble dryer and busied myself cleaning the kitchen and washing my bowl, cup and spoons.

I missed having someone to talk with. I was comfortable with my own company, but it could be tough going days without significant human contact, especially when I had been so used to sharing everything with my mum. I moved back home with her when I went back to university and only worked part-time, but before that, when I'd had my own flat, I'd drop in to see her every day and I'd speak to Carmel on the phone most days, too.

For the last few weeks, I'd had lots of free time to think about everything, and I missed the feeling of being in a relationship and having a partner to emotionally support me. With my last boyfriend, though, the idea of being in a relationship was better than the reality.

Hayden was a nice person who meant well, and we were supposed to stay friends after we broke up, but neither one of us ever contacted the other. The thing was, his idea of what a relationship should be came straight out of a teenage romance and it was suffocating. I thought I loved him at first. The level of adoration he showed me was flattering, but it became stifling when it became evident he didn't want me to do anything without him; or when every time we were out in public he had to have his arm around me as though I couldn't walk, or stand, unsupported; or when I got filthy looks, or snide comments, for looking at another man or wearing a revealing outfit. It felt like he was trying to control me and change me into someone else, someone who didn't think for herself.

I didn't want to be in a relationship so much that I'd tolerate that kind of behaviour. Not then, not now, not ever.

I did try to make it work. I persevered for nearly a year, but I was getting depressed. I was halfway through my Master's degree and it was affecting my work, so, much as I hated to hurt him, I had to end it.

I mentioned that I'm never wrong about people and I wasn't that time, either. I suspected Hayden could be slightly obsessive; he just kept the extent of his pathological side well-hidden for the first two and a half months. That was when it started to feel as though he wanted a girl from a fairytale rather than a real woman.

Taking a break from studying for a while, I flicked the television back on. There were usually dramas on in the late afternoon and I channel-hopped to an American programme about a mother and daughter in a small, close-knit community. It was innocuous and sufficiently entertaining to allow me to rest my brain for an hour, but I didn't really pay much attention to it because a few minutes after it started, the doorbell rang again.

'Jamie Kavanagh?' the woman outside asked as I opened the door.

'Yes,' I replied tentatively.

'These are for you,' she said with the tone of voice, and a smile, that said she thought I was a lucky girl.

'Thank you,' I blurted out, completely in shock, as I took hold of a large arrangement of roses, lilies and tulips in varying shades of pink, identical to the bouquet in my dream.

Three
Gabriel

I sat down with the flowers resting on my knees, and my hands were trembling as I searched for a card. Inside a small envelope with my name on it was a thick, cream-coloured card, plain apart from a thin gold border all the way around and a little way in from the edge, with a message in neat, flowing handwriting that read:

Meet me at the coffee shop,
10am tomorrow.
G.

I flipped it over, but all that was on the back were the contact details of the florist.

I didn't know anyone whose name began with 'G,' and none of my friends ever went to my local coffee shop. Besides which, none of them would send me flowers for no reason and, if they wanted to see me, they would call to arrange something. That had to mean that the flowers and note were from my mystery stranger.

This time he was actually scheduling a meeting as opposed to me just bumping into him, speaking for a few minutes, then one of us leaving. Maybe he was willing to answer some of my questions about him: his name for a start, but now I also needed to know how he knew my favourite flowers and that I liked them to be pink; how he knew what the bouquet in my dream had looked like in order to replicate it, indeed, that I'd dreamt of one at all; and how he knew where I lived.

As certain as I was that the gift was from him, I decided to call the florist to be absolutely sure so I knew I wasn't going to meet some psychopath tomorrow.

My heart was pounding as I called the number on the back of the card and waited for the friendly female voice on the other end of the line to finish her greeting spiel.

'Hi, my name is Jamie Kavanagh. I've just received a bouquet from your shop.' I managed to get the words out quite clearly considering how ridiculously nervous I was about the answer; it wasn't as though anything could happen from a telephone enquiry.

'Oh, yes, Miss Kavanagh,' she responded enthusiastically, 'I know exactly the one you mean. Do you like the flowers?'

'Yes, they're very beautiful, thank you. I was just wondering if you could tell me who they're from, the card doesn't say.'

'I'm sorry, but I can't give out any personal information; it's illegal.' There was regret in her voice and I could sense she would genuinely like to tell me.

Of course I knew she couldn't tell me anything, but most people were either ignorant of the fact that it was illegal, or they just didn't care. I wasn't asking for an address or telephone number, and she knew the flowers had been sent to me, so she must have taken some information from the sender.

'Not even a name,' I persisted, 'so that I can thank him or her?'

'I'm afraid not.'

'Okay, I understand. Could you tell me, though, did the customer specify the flowers and their colour, or were they your choice?'

'Oh, no, the customer knew exactly what he wanted. He chose every single flower himself.'

'He was there? Well, would you describe him for me, please? Or, I could give you a description and you could tell me if it was him.' I was getting hopeful.

'I really am sorry, Miss Kavanagh, but all information really is confidential. I'm sure the man who sent your flowers will make himself known eventually. Until then, just enjoy them; that's what they're for.'

'Thank you for your help,' I uttered, resigned to the fact this woman was not going to be of any use, and hung up.

Why was everyone being so evasive? I wasn't a conspiracy theorist, and I'd never been particularly paranoid, but it was impossible to get any answers about this man who had just appeared in my life, knew all kinds of things about me he couldn't possibly have known, was now starring in my dreams, and probably sending me flowers.

The bouquet had been beautifully arranged, so I carefully trimmed the very ends off the flowers' stems, put them in a vase of water, and settled them on the coffee table so I could admire them whilst I worked. I didn't have enough concentration to study or write anymore today after the surprise, and I was too excited about meeting 'G' tomorrow. The fact that he was initiating a meeting to specifically sit and talk with me indicated that he wanted us to become better acquainted with one another, which meant that I could find out exactly what he knew about me, and how he had discovered that information.

I sat for hours staring at the flowers in a sort of trance, imagining what he could want to see me about and the conversations we might have. He had obviously considered the most effective way to put me at ease about our meeting, so he'd chosen my regular coffee shop where I was well-known by the staff, as he commented himself. If at any time I felt threatened, we both knew I could ask anyone working there for assistance and I could be confident that they would help me. He was considerate. It all added to his mystique.

I finally snapped out of it when my eyelids started drooping and it felt like too much effort to stay awake. I got off the sofa and slowly trudged into the kitchen to get a glass of water, turning lights off as I went, and finally locking the front door with the spare key and taking it upstairs with me.

I couldn't even be bothered to wash my face or brush my teeth, I was so tired and my muscles were weighted with lethargy. I made sure I set an alarm to give me plenty of time to have a shower and do my hair in the morning and not be late to meet 'G' before I stripped out of my clothes and got into bed. For once, I fell asleep instantly.

I slept dreamlessly, which was unusual for me; I had always dreamt every night and the dreams were usually so vivid, and felt so real, that I often woke up more tired than when I went to sleep. I slept so deeply that the sound of the alarm shocked me awake. I leaned over to the bedside table to turn it off, blinking against the bright sunlight streaming through the thin curtains covering my window.

Once my eyes had adjusted to the light, I got up and padded naked to the bathroom. My mouth was dry so I reached for my toothbrush and toothpaste before I did anything else, and scrubbed my teeth and tongue clean. That helped to wake me up, but I wasn't fully alert until I felt the spray of hot water, like therapeutic needles, on my skin.

I usually took my time when I bathed, but I deliberately hurried, unconsciously aided by my anxiety, so I wouldn't be late getting to the coffee house. I wrapped myself in towels and checked the clock as I re-entered my bedroom. It was only eight forty-five, so I still had plenty of time to do my hair and get dressed before I needed to leave the house.

By the time I had dried and straightened my long brown hair, my stomach was squirming with nervous worry about the meeting and I was undecided about what to wear. I opened the window to get an idea of how warm it was outside. The sun may have been shining, but it was still March and there was a definite chill, so I opted for a pair of dark blue, bootcut jeans and a delicate rose-pink, slim-fitting jumper with a wide, round neckline which didn't dip too low, but nicely displayed the pale skin of my throat. I didn't want to look like I was deliberately dressing to impress, or tantalise, because not only was that not my style, it wouldn't have been prudent considering I didn't know what to expect from the man I was meeting.

Once I was dressed, I had nothing more to do than find the bag I'd discarded two days ago when I got home from the coffee shop to find my keys and ensure I had my purse and everything else I needed. I took the spare key with me downstairs and replaced it behind the photograph before locating my bag behind a cushion on the armchair nearest the door.

I still had twenty minutes until the appointed time so, instead of driving for five minutes and getting there early to worry and agonise over what this meeting could mean, I decided to walk, which would take me around fifteen minutes if I walked briskly. I put on my scarf and coat to keep the cold out, added my sunglasses against the bright sunlight, and stepped outside feeling a fluttering sensation in my stomach.

The streets were empty until I got to the corner of the block where the coffee shop was located. It wasn't a main shopping area as it was situated too far out of town, but there was a pharmacy, a shop that sold cute handbags, a beauty salon, a new-age bookstore that also offered tarot readings, and the coffee house all placed along a street of old Victorian buildings. It was still fairly quiet, but there was a young woman, aged about eighteen, in the handbag shop looking at a small lilac shoulder bag trying to decide whether or not she should buy it. I was tempted to go in and tell her to treat herself, but my heart was pounding hard against my ribcage and my legs felt weak due to my skittishness at being so close to meeting Him.

I stood outside the door of the coffee shop, put my sunglasses in my pocket, and inhaled deeply as I reached out to grasp the handle. I exhaled, then opened the door and hesitantly walked inside, surreptitiously looking for the stranger.

'You're back sooner than I was expecting, Jamie,' Paolo commented when he glanced up and saw me coming through the door. 'Have you got work to do?' He smiled at me as I walked up to the counter.

'Actually, I'm not here today to work. I'm meeting someone,' I answered cautiously.

'Someone tall, dark and handsome?' He flashed a knowing grin.

'Um, well…' I faltered.

'I wouldn't describe myself as overly tall,' the stranger remarked, his amusement evident in his smooth voice as he materialised at my side. 'Or particularly dark. As for the handsome part,' he smiled at me, 'I think that's for the lady to decide. Hello, Jamie,' he said as he took my cold left hand into both of his and held it.

'Hi,' I replied, looking directly into his beautiful eyes, and I squeezed his fingers, grateful for their warmth.

'Shall we get some coffee and sit down?' he suggested. I nodded and turned to Paolo to order, but he beat me to it. 'Can we have two of Jamie's favourite coffee, please?'

'Of course. Take a seat and I'll bring them over,' Paolo replied easily, and winked at me. I mouthed my thanks to him.

It felt to me as though Paolo was pleased I wasn't on my own for a change. He often commented on my solo status, not only because I went there alone, but also because I didn't have a boyfriend.

The stranger let go of my hand and rested one of his gently on my lower back to lead me over to a table. He held my chair out for me and made sure I was comfortably seated before pulling out the one next to me and sitting down himself.

I was bursting with questions as I removed my scarf and shrugged off my coat, but I knew I couldn't just start firing them at him; for one thing, it would be impolite, and for another, I was worried he would just leave if I did that.

'Thank you for the flowers,' I began. 'They're beautiful and they were such a lovely surprise. Did you know they are my favourites?'

'Yes, I did know that, and I know you like your flowers to be pink.' He looked at me earnestly and I could feel that everything about him was open to me.

We both had our hands in our laps, but we were leaning in towards one another with unconscious familiarity and I could see, now that our faces were so close, that his eyes weren't pure green; they were a mixture of blue and green, neither one nor the other, but they looked greener from a distance. We deliberately kept our voices low so that we wouldn't be overheard by any of the people at the other tables; people I had only noticed as I sat down.

'I dreamt that you personally handed me that exact bouquet of flowers the night before you sent them.'

I perused his face as I told him this to gauge all the nuances of his reaction; he merely looked down and his lips twitched, and internally I could sense his feeling of satisfaction, so I knew it wasn't a revelation to him.

'You already knew that, but how did you know? Do you know I still don't even know your name?' I felt exhilarated to be with him, but terrified of how he could have seen my dream. My heart was speeding again as he returned my gaze once more.

At that moment, Paolo came over with two large cups filled to the brim with foamed milk with chocolate sprinkled on top.

'I hope you're taking good care of our Jamie,' he remarked as he placed the cups down.

'Of course. I wouldn't dream of upsetting her,' my companion responded honestly, only briefly breaking eye contact with me to acknowledge Paolo.

As he walked away, Paolo put a hand on my shoulder and gave it an affectionate, yet gentle, squeeze, knowing it was my injured one. I smiled up at him in thanks, then looked back at the mystery gentleman; there was no other word for him taking his impeccable manners into consideration; to await some enlightenment.

'I'll start with the most fundamental detail,' he said softly. 'My name is Gabriel Castell.'

'Gabriel.' I thought about it for a moment. It suited him. 'It's nice to finally know what to call you.'

'What *have* you been calling me?' He gave me a quizzical look.

'I haven't spoken to anyone about you,' I answered quickly, worried that he thought I'd been gossiping. 'It's more that our encounters have been so extraordinary that I've thought about them a lot and, well, you've just been this mystery stranger. I feel less threatened finally knowing something absolute about you.' *Especially because you know so much about me,* I thought as I took a sip of my cappuccino and rested my free hand on the table. He gripped it tightly.

'Please don't be afraid of me, Jamie. I'm not stalking you.' I could feel his worry that I didn't trust him.

'Aren't you?' I queried. 'Then why is it that when I bumped into you in the bookshop you already knew my name, and that I had a key ring with my name on it when you couldn't have seen my keys? How did you know I'm a writer? I *know* I'd never seen you before that moment. Then, you turn up here, where I come regularly. I haven't seen you here before, so I can only assume you followed me. You sent flowers that I'd just dreamed about to my home, yet you hadn't asked me for my address. How could you know all of that unless you've been stalking me, Gabriel?' I tried not to raise my voice, or sound petulant, but it took all my effort to remain calm.

I watched him contemplate everything I'd just said and I could tell he knew I was too intelligent to believe him if he suggested he was an acquaintance of one of my friends. He knew I would have thought of that and realised it simply wasn't true. No one I knew would just give out information about me, and I would have been alerted to the fact that someone was asking questions. Never mind that it wouldn't explain the more peculiar occurrences such as finding me in the bookstore and the coffee house when no one knew I'd be there, or how he knew I'd dreamed of those exact flowers.

'I haven't been following you,' he insisted. 'I just sort of *know* where you are.'

'You're telepathic?' I didn't believe it was impossible; I had psychic ability after all.

'In a manner. I can't read people's thoughts exactly as they think them, like a running dialogue, or a series of mental pictures,' he qualified. 'I get a sort of overview so I can make out the subject of their thoughts. I'm essentially an empath and that enhances my telepathy.

'For instance, if your friend, Paolo, was having relationship concerns, I'd be able to tell by his thoughts that his partner was on his mind and I would feel his anxiety as he was thinking about her, so I would know there were problems in that area.'

My grip on his hand tightened.

'I'm an empath, so I can understand that. But with me it's more powerful for you, isn't it?' I could feel that and I believed it.

'Yes, Jamie, it is.' He leaned in even closer. 'Because you're also an empath, I can feel you more strongly, and I can tune in to you with much greater ease, than anyone else. Technically, it should be more difficult because you can protect yourself from other people's psychic attacks, but, for some reason, it isn't. I think it's because you have such very strong emotional reactions to everything. It also means the subject of your thoughts is clearer to me, too. I hope you don't find that too intrusive.'

His eyes were boring into mine, intensifying what I could already feel: Gabriel was telling the truth. Had he really been stalking me and meant to cause me harm, he wouldn't have gone to the trouble of introducing himself, and he could have hurt me at any time. After all, he'd known where I lived before I even learned his name.

'You do realise that most people wouldn't believe you?' I was sure he knew that I believed him, but I confirmed it regardless, albeit indirectly.

'I know.' He smiled slowly. 'But when have you ever been like most people?'

I laughed because it was true, but then I frowned.

'You talk as though you've known me a long time,' I observed.

He shook his head. 'No, it hasn't been a long time. I feel everything you feel as though those emotions were my own,' he said, delicately stroking my fingers in a soothing motion. 'I read you well and, unless you're blocking out my energy, you must be sensitive to what I feel, too. I don't shield anything from you.' His every word and action was designed to calm me and reinforce that I need not be afraid of him.

'I have so little contact with people these days that I seldom need to protect myself.' My voice was quiet because my statement made me sound somewhat pathetic and also because the light touch of his fingers on mine had set all my nerve-endings tingling, making my skin hypersensitive, and making me acutely aware of him. 'So, yes, Gabriel, I can feel you. I don't even try to block you out. I don't want to,' I admitted.

'And you know I won't, and have no desire to, hurt you?' Still the gentle caressing of fingers, so innocent, yet so erotic.

I nodded. 'But you knew me before I bumped into you in the bookshop the other day, didn't you? You already knew my name.'

'Yes, I knew you before then.'

'How long before then?' I held my breath in anticipation of how I might feel about his response.

'A while,' he answered evasively.

'How long of a while? Weeks? Months? More than a year?' I was panicking at the prospect he had been observing me for such a long period of time without making himself known and with me remaining oblivious.

'Not that long. It's nothing sinister, I promise,' he insisted. 'I happened to see you walking towards the university a couple of months ago. You were feeling anxiety bordering on terror and it showed on your face. It was overpowering. It gave me a sense of dread I'd never felt before, so I followed you; the only time I have ever followed you; to make sure you were going to be okay.'

'That must have been the day of my *viva*, just before I went in.' I remembered that day for other reasons, too. 'I thought my chest was going to explode because my heart was beating so hard and so fast. I'd never been that nervous before.' I half-laughed and Gabriel smiled.

'That's how I found out your name. You gave it to the university administrators in the office when you informed them you were there for your exam. It's also how I learned what you had been studying, and I knew from your thoughts that you're a writer, too.

'I waited outside until it was over to discover how you'd done and I thought that if it hadn't gone well, I could offer you a shoulder to cry on, but that wasn't necessary. You were so happy that you'd passed and you called your mother as soon as you walked out of the room. You were also really distracted, that's why you didn't notice me there. I didn't want to interrupt you, and you clearly didn't need me, so I didn't introduce myself. I wanted to, and I didn't intend to leave it so long…' His sentence trailed off and he looked away again, saddened.

After that, I became even more of a recluse. He must have realised that and so he must have known the reason why. How could he introduce himself to someone who'd lost her family and been shot after only seeing her once and been intrigued?

'I could have met you that day,' I said, more to myself, and I wished that I had. He felt it and wished it, too. 'Did you hear about what happened that night?' My voice cracked, as it nearly always did when I spoke about it. A lump formed in my throat and my eyes welled with tears.

'Yes, I know what happened.' He looked back at me. 'I am so, so sorry for your loss, Jamie. I know those words are completely inadequate, especially when I know how much pain you were in. You still are,' he added softly. 'I wanted to be with you, to offer you some consolation, but the doctors and a couple of friends were fussing around you; which you didn't like; and you were grieving so hard that the real you, the you inside, was barely there. It wouldn't have been a good idea to approach you then, but I was never far away.' I could feel his regret for not being with me.

'No, I understand. I didn't want anyone around, I couldn't endure it.' I needed to change the subject before I broke down, and I could feel that Gabriel recognised this and sympathised. 'What were you doing by the university that day?' I wiped at my eyes with the fingers of my free hand to dispel my tears before they could fall, and I forced some lightness into my tone and my expression.

'I'd been thinking for a while about enrolling on a postgraduate course. I was drawn there because of you, because you were there.'

'What would you study?'

'I was thinking literature or psychology. I have degrees in both.'

'You couldn't make up your mind?' I was captivated by him.

'I read lots of books and I'm interested in how the mind works. Mostly, I'm interested in the psychology behind fiction: why people write the things they write, the meanings of it all.' He looked at me with a challenge in his eyes: he was thinking about my stories.

'You mean what lurks in people's subconscious minds to fuel their imaginations?'

'That's part of it. Let's see, what are you writing about at the moment?'

'I don't want to be analysed.' I panicked, withdrew my hand, and turned my head away slightly.

In my peripheral vision, I saw Gabriel twist further towards me in his chair, then he reached out to place his hands on either side of my jaw and turned my face back to his with only the pressure of his fingers.

'Jamie, it's okay. I'm sorry,' he soothed. 'I said I wouldn't upset you and I promise I won't. Look, whatever people write is often fuelled by who they are, their personal tastes and their life experiences, whether they are from first-hand knowledge or things they have observed. You don't have to tell me what you are writing, but it wouldn't be surprising if it was quite dark considering what you have just been through. It would be perfectly understandable.'

He stroked my cheek once, then dropped his hands back into his lap, but he didn't look away.

'I'm sorry, Gabriel. I didn't mean to overreact like that.' My hands ached to take hold of his, and I moved towards them, but stopped, uncertain of myself. He noticed the slight movement, but let it go. 'It's just that I've had doctors, nurses, physiotherapists, and friends telling me I should have counselling, but I'm against the idea. I don't want to pour my feelings out about the loss of my mother and sister to someone who doesn't know the first thing about them, or me, only for that person to tell me it's okay to feel sad. I already know that. I don't know if you can identify with that, but I'm sure you can feel it.'

'I can feel it, but I've never been in that position myself, so I don't have personal experience. Your feelings are still so raw and you're still adjusting to the situation, so I can see why you don't want someone prodding into your mind like that.

I don't think I would want that in your situation, either,' he reassured me. 'It wasn't my intention to distress you.'

'You didn't. I'm so sorry if I gave you that impression. I hope I didn't offend you with my reaction.' My hands hesitantly reached out towards him again and this time he eased my awkwardness and took hold of them, lacing his fingers through mine.

'Not at all.' He brought our entwined hands up and kissed both of mine in turn.

It should have felt over-familiar considering I had only met Gabriel three days ago, but it didn't; it was fitting, and it made me blush, which made Gabriel grin.

'I am interested in what you're writing, though. I think I mentioned that to you the day before yesterday,' he reminded me as he set our hands onto the table and let go of one in order to pick up his cup and drink some coffee.

'I'm a little embarrassed to tell you about it,' I said, and bit my lip. 'I'm afraid you might think it's a bit ridiculous.'

'I could never think you, or your writing, is ridiculous. Never. Please believe me.' Even if I hadn't been able to feel it, his voice was infused with so much passion and sincerity it was impossible not to believe him.

'I believe you.' I hesitated before continuing. 'Whilst I was recuperating from my shoulder injury, and to focus on something other than my grief, I started writing a vampire story.' My mouth twisted in self-derision. 'It's about a girl called Freya who is ambushed, turned into a vampire, and left to fend for herself. She's angry that she has to leave her family, who assume she is dead. She tries to trace the history of vampires, searching through the various myths and folklore and going back to their origins to see if she can find a cure to turn her back to being human. And, yes, I do see the parallels with my own life; it's deliberate; it's to help me work through it all.'

'Do you think being a vampire would be that bad?' Gabriel asked, fascinated.

'I don't know. I think that it wouldn't be easy for someone who didn't have anyone to talk to about it, no one to help her or give her advice. In terms of having such a long existence, I think that seeing so much, watching the world change and discovering all the tiny facets of human nature, would definitely have an effect on a person's psyche.

'I think the only way to stop something like that from driving a person to insanity is not to contemplate eternity, but just experience it one day at a time. I can sort of relate to that; I try not to think about how long I'll live and that all that time will be without my mother and sister. I'm sorry; I've got maudlin, haven't I?' I flashed a wry smile at him.

'I don't want to sound like a therapist, but what you're feeling is understandable. I know I've already said that, but it is. I can see your point about not thinking about eternity when you can live forever, though at least you'd know that you've got time to do everything you could ever want to do,' he argued reasonably.

Before either one of us could say anything more, Paolo approached our table to clear away our empty cups.

'Would you like refills?' he asked, looking from Gabriel to me.

I looked at Gabriel to ascertain if he wanted to spend more time with me.

'How about we go for a walk, then maybe come back for coffee afterwards?' he suggested, eyebrows raised.

'I'd like that,' I replied, trying not to show just how delighted I was that Gabriel wasn't in a hurry to get away from me, even though I knew he felt it, anyway.

I sought some money out of my bag to pay for our drinks, but Gabriel had beaten me to it.

'My treat,' he insisted, and winked.

'Thank you. Next time it's on me,' I said as I stood up to put on my scarf and coat.

'Enjoy your walk,' Paolo said affably as we made our way towards the exit.

Four

Affinity

The sun was still shining and the temperature had risen, so I left my scarf untied and my coat unbuttoned as I made my way out the door and onto the pavement. Gabriel, I noticed, had also left his jacket undone.

'Gabriel,' I began, following in the direction he was leading, 'forgive me if I'm being too intrusive, but how is it you're with me today? Don't you need to work?'

He grinned before answering. 'No, I don't need to work. I'm one of the idle rich.'

'Okay,' I enunciated slowly, not knowing what to make of that.

'My great-grandfather was a physician, quite a radical one for his day, pioneering methods others wouldn't even consider. Some of those methods are common practice now, I might add. He was the private doctor of an extremely wealthy and influential family who paid him well for his exclusivity. He had three sons who all followed in his footsteps, worked for the nobility, and they invested their money wisely. No one in the family need ever work.'

'Was one of those sons your grandfather?'

'Yes, my grandfather was the youngest. My mother is his only child and she married the son of another rich family,' he said without cynicism, indicating his parents were really in love. 'Money loves money.' His mouth twisted on that last comment, however.

The slight note of derision in his voice made me deviate away from the subject of his family even though I couldn't feel a change in his good mood.

'Is that why you have more than one degree: because you don't need to work you have time for extensive study?'

'I wouldn't call it extensive, but I've been fortunate enough to have had the opportunity to pursue more than one interest to a higher level.'

'And what will you do with all that knowledge? Write a book on the psychology of fiction? Future literature students could quote you in their assignments,' I observed.

'That's an interesting thought.' He contemplated it for a moment. 'Who knows what will happen? I think those future literature students might be more interested in your fiction than anything I have to say about why you wrote it.'

'I don't believe that,' I said and realised, rather belatedly, where Gabriel was taking me.

A few streets away from the coffee house, still amongst the old buildings, was a public garden. Originally, it was the site of a large house with extensive grounds, but there had been a fire which ravaged the building to ruins. It was financially unviable to rebuild what was left in-keeping with the other houses in the area, so the wreckage was demolished and in its wake a beautiful garden was created, complete with its own duck pond.

As we got closer, I could hear ducks beating their wings, splashing water, and calling to one another, but there were no sounds from other people. As Gabriel and I walked through the trees outlining the perimeter, we could see that it was completely devoid of any human presence, though there were squirrels darting around, a few birds, and even a cat; probably from one of the nearby houses; ignoring the birds and bathing in the warmth from the sun.

'Let's sit in the shade,' Gabriel suggested, and he took my hand and led me over to a huge tree whose massive branches cast a wide shadow over the grass below.

He sat and rested his back against the large trunk and pulled me down beside him. The action was so unexpected that I lost my balance and, as I slumped to the ground, my head landed against his shoulder as though I were snuggling into him. I struggled, in my haste, to get myself into an upright sitting position and inadvertently placed my left hand on his chest and grasped his forearm with my right to stabilise myself.

'I'm sorry,' we said in perfect synchronicity.

'I didn't intend to tug your arm so forcefully.' He looked, and felt, slightly sheepish.

'You didn't; I just misbalanced. You cushioned my fall. Again. I'm not usually this clumsy,' I prattled, feeling utterly mortified so for a moment I wasn't able to meet his eyes, instead, I stared at his knee as he sat cross-legged on the grass. 'Sorry,' I reiterated, settling myself at an angle to him so we could look at each other whilst we spoke, my right knee touching his left.

'I'm not hurt, you're not hurt, so you've got nothing to be sorry for, okay?'

'Okay,' I said, and frowned. 'Have you always been like this?'

'Like what?' He tilted his head to one side, interested in any perceptions I had of him.

'Well, earlier, I said that living forever would give a person the chance to learn all the intricacies of human behaviour. Your whole demeanour suggests that you have that kind of knowledge, that you've witnessed the best and worst of humanity. It feels like there's nothing I could do that would surprise you; you've seen it all before.'

I thought I'd touched on something from the slight flicker of recognition in his eyes and the momentary acceleration of his heart, which I could feel as if it were my own, but it quickly returned to normal.

He leaned towards me slightly and looked into my eyes unflinchingly. 'Maybe you can't surprise me because I read you too well.'

'Possibly.'

'And maybe, once you've spent some more time with me and know me and understand me better, you'll read me as well as I read you. You've got the ability.'

I was thrilled that he'd said we would spend more time together, as though it were a foregone conclusion. It meant he *wanted* to see me more.

'So, we will be spending more time together?' I clarified.

'That was the plan. Don't you want to, Jamie?'

'Yes, I do. Very much. I just thought that maybe you were only meeting with me today to explain everything that had been going on and then I'd never hear from you again.'

'Why would you think that?' It was his turn to frown.

'Can't you feel the answer to that?' I challenged.

He was quiet and still for a moment, obviously analysing everything he could feel and discerning which of those emotions were his and which were mine.

'Abandonment?'

He wasn't asking for confirmation, he knew that was what I was feeling, he was actually enquiring about my reasons for feeling that way.

'My mother, my sister and I are very close. Grammatically, I should say "were," but I'm not ready to talk about them in the past tense, it doesn't feel right.'

'Take everything at your own pace. There's no right and wrong with grief, you know that,' he interjected.

'I know. Anyway, they are my world, the people who are always there. And now they're not. It's not by choice and it certainly isn't their fault, but they're physically gone,' I said sadly. 'My friends… Well, most of the ones I was at university with when I did my Bachelor's degree are scattered all over the country now. We're in occasional contact, but none of them even offered to come back to comfort me when I told them what had happened. As for my local friends, they're not really going out of their way for me. They fit me in, but they won't even come to my house.

'I'm tired of dealing with all of this on my own. I feel so alone. Unfortunately for you, you've met me now, when I don't even know if I'm the same person anymore.' That was difficult to admit.

'You're the same person you always were,' Gabriel said gently, but with absolute conviction. 'I encountered you before the tragedy with your family. I don't know if it's the same for you, I presume it is, but as well as feeling another person's emotions, I can both read, and feel, their soul and their personality.' I nodded; it was the same for me. 'It lets me know who they are inside.' He reached out and touched his fingertips to my heart. 'You're no different after all of this, just sadder at the moment, but the hope you always felt is still there, I can sense it. Please don't worry that you're losing who you are; you're not, and I'll be here to remind you, to help you. I promise.'

Tears slid down my cheeks and I tried to turn away to hide them from Gabriel, but he missed nothing. He reached forward, slipped his arms around my ribs to pull me off the ground, into his lap, and against his body. He held me tightly with one arm whilst he stroked my hair with his other hand and, for that moment, I felt I could let go, let someone be strong for me instead of holding it all inside.

'You don't have to be alone anymore,' he said quietly into my hair, his voice almost breaking with the heartache he felt for me, before kissing the top of my head.

I was sure that anybody other than me hearing those words, and the sentiments behind them, would have been alarmed; they were such intense feelings and declarations from someone whose behaviour could be perceived as resembling that of a stalker, but it wasn't odd to me. I felt the same instantaneous pull towards Gabriel that he clearly felt towards me, and I wanted him in my life. He was making me feel something other than sadness, grief and guilt, and maybe he could help me live again, not merely exist.

Gabriel had said that he didn't shield what he was feeling from me, so I analysed everything I was reading from him. He was being completely honest and genuine.

'I think I need you, Gabriel,' I choked out, desperately clinging to him and letting my tears fall freely.

'I'm here,' he affirmed softly. 'I'll always be here for you, Jamie.' He held me tighter and cradled my head against his shoulder to soothe me. It was pleasingly firm beneath my cheek.

When I was sure I had recovered, I lifted my head and leaned back to look at him, unsure of what to say. Gabriel met my gaze unswervingly, seeming to want to tell me something, but holding it back.

Neither of us could look away, I could feel our hearts start to beat faster, and our breathing became shallower and more erratic. With our arms still around one another, Gabriel leaned forward and softly pressed his lips to mine. The kiss was warm, tender, and lingered for a long moment before he pulled back to look at me again.

That kiss set my blood ablaze and my whole body heated. It was more than just a kiss; it was the expression of the need for one another that we both felt. We had no use for words at that moment; there was nothing we could say that we weren't already silently telling one another. Each of us was feeling a maelstrom of emotions: attraction, desire, the recognition of our souls' affinity; the air between us was charged with their intensity.

It was late afternoon, the temperature had dropped, and I shivered with cold only a few seconds before Gabriel did the same.

'Let's walk back to the coffee house. We'll get you a coffee to go and I'll drive you home so you don't have to walk in the cold,' he suggested as he pulled my coat together and buttoned it up for me.

'You saw me walking this morning?' I tilted my head to one side and waited for an answer.

He nodded briefly before getting to his feet and he held his hands out to me.

I placed mine in his and he pulled me up. I was disappointed because I didn't want to leave him yet and he obviously knew that.

'You can get some work done tonight and get something to eat; you must be starving by now. We can see each other again tomorrow.'

'I'm not hungry, but I can understand if you are,' I said, prepared to let him go since he made a salient point: I still had textbooks waiting for me at home.

Gabriel gripped my hand securely and we started walking back the way we came.

'You never eat because you feel a slight hunger pang and replace food with coffee.' He grinned at me. 'But I want you to be healthy. Try to eat something today, for me, please.'

'You really haven't been far away, have you?' It really was as though he had been watching my every movement.

He looked at me, but didn't answer. That said it all.

When we had walked to the garden earlier, we'd moved at a leisurely pace, not needing to hurry, just happy being in one another's company. However, our walk back was more brisk as it was now so cold I could see our breath in the air as we exhaled. It seemed merely a couple of minutes since Gabriel took my hand and then we were walking back through the entrance of the coffee shop.

'Have you had a nice afternoon?' Paolo asked as soon as he saw us.

'Wonderful,' I said happily, and squeezed Gabriel's hand.

'Good,' he responded with a gentle light in his eyes and a soft expression as he watched me. 'You deserve some happiness, Jamie.'

'Thank you,' I replied, holding back more tears.

'Can we get a cappuccino to go for Jamie, please?' Gabriel asked, and he looked at me indulgently.

I grinned back at him cheekily, then asked, 'Aren't you having one?'

'Not everyone is as addicted as you.' He laughed, so I stuck my tongue out at him, but I couldn't help giggling, too.

I felt a bit like a teenager again: carefree, light, hopeful. Being with Gabriel had reminded me that I was alive, and I started to believe that maybe there was some measure of happiness out there for me.

Paolo placed a lidded cup on the counter and, as I held some money out to him, he shook his head. 'This one's on me.'

Gabriel was still holding my right hand and he wasn't about to let go, but I leaned over the counter to hug Paolo with my left arm and kissed him on the cheek.

I picked up my coffee and was led out of the shop to Gabriel's waiting car. He unlocked it from the passenger side, opened the door, and switched the hand he was holding to help me into my seat. He only let go when he had to in order to close the door and make his way around to the driver's side.

He checked to ensure I'd fastened my seatbelt before starting the engine and pulling away. There weren't many cars on the roads as we were too late to get caught in the traffic from parents collecting their children from school and we were just ahead of rush hour, so the journey to my house took precisely four minutes; that was faster than I'd ever managed it in my beaten-up old car, disobeying the thirty miles per hour speed limit. It made me sad because it wasn't long enough. I'd have to leave Gabriel soon and the magic of our day would be over.

All too soon, Gabriel stopped the car outside my house. I glanced at the darkened windows and inwardly sighed before I turned to face him.

'Thank you for today, Gabriel. For everything. You were there when I didn't even know it and that means more to me than I can say. Really, there aren't enough words, even for me.' I smiled self-deprecatingly.

'I'm glad it didn't scare you, my telling you all that.' It was the first time I'd heard him sound, or feel, less than completely self-confident.

'Not even remotely,' I reassured him. 'It's comforting, like you've wrapped a blanket around my heart and it's warming every part of me. That doesn't put you off, does it?' I bit my lip in anticipation of his response.

'No, Jamie, nothing ever could. Thank you for the beautiful sentiment, and also for today.' He reached out and caressed my cheekbone with the backs of his fingers, tucked a lock of my hair behind my ear and traced its outline with his fingertips before dropping his hand to clasp one of mine. He lifted it and kissed it. 'Now go,' he said reluctantly. 'Get lots of reading done and don't neglect to eat something.'

I smiled and Gabriel let go so I could undo my seatbelt.

'Hold on a moment.' I wasn't the most logical person, but something just occurred to me. 'You said we'd see each other tomorrow, but how will we get in contact with one another? You don't know my phone number as well, do you?' I narrowed my eyes.

'No.' He grinned. 'I'm good, but even I can't read an eleven-digit number out of your head.' He pulled his phone out of his jeans pocket and pushed some buttons, probably typing in my name. 'What is it?' I reeled off the numbers and he programmed it all in, then returned his phone to his pocket. 'I'll call you tomorrow.'

I nodded and opened the door to get out. I didn't ask for his phone number because, much as I hated myself for it, I knew I wouldn't have the courage to call him if he didn't call me. Also, if he thought about it tonight and changed his mind about me, about everything he'd said, I wanted him to feel reassured that I wouldn't hound him and try to make him feel guilty.

Impulsively, I leaned over, before I could talk myself out of it, and kissed him on the cheek. As I pulled back to get out of the car, I saw the look of surprise on his face, but I could feel that he was pleased.

I searched for my keys as I walked down the driveway and I turned as I put the key in the lock. Gabriel was still there and waited and watched until I'd stepped inside before driving away.

I locked the door behind me and walked into the living room, turned on the light, dumped my bag on the chair and slung my coat and scarf over its arm. I walked into the kitchen, thinking about Gabriel's command to eat, and threw my now empty cup away.

I wasn't hungry yet, so I steeled myself for a few chapters of monotonous printed posturing from some white-bearded literature professor at an American university. I decided I would give in when it got too patronising.

I began a section of the book that seemed as though it would be relevant to my research topic, but after maybe fifteen minutes of skimming though several unhelpful chapters, I gave up on it entirely. If his book was anything to go by, the male perspective of feminist literature wasn't particularly well-informed. I tossed it aside in exasperation and, as it hit the floor, my phone bleeped, informing me I had received a text message.

The phone didn't display a name, only a telephone number, so I knew instantly it was from Gabriel. When I opened the message, it read:

> *I know you're worried, but there's no need to be. I'm not going to abandon you, I promise. Trust me. Gabriel. x*

He knew why I hadn't asked for his number, but he was reassuring me that everything about him was open to me, that I could trust him and he wouldn't let me down. I sent him my thanks in return, expecting that to be the end of the conversation, but almost immediately he sent another message.

Now eat something. x

It made me smile and I could sense the same concern in those words that he'd expressed earlier, though he had endeavoured to keep his tone light rather than scolding or accusatory so that I wouldn't feel as though I were being attacked and retaliate by getting defensive and refusing to eat at all.

I was feeling the initial stirrings of hunger, so, for once in my life, I was actually going to do as I was instructed, even though I hated it.

I couldn't remember the last time I'd done a big grocery shop; I just seemed to replace milk, cereal and bread as and when I needed. I opened the door to the freezer and inspected every drawer. All I found was meat and fish, which was completely useless to me as I was a vegetarian, but Mum had bought it for herself and to cook for Carmel and Aaron when they came to dinner, so, like everything else belonging to her, I'd left it where it was.

The refrigerator contained water, milk and orange juice, all perfectly fresh, but there were fruit, vegetables and salad ingredients which had seen better days, so I threw them all away and headed for the cupboard which housed my store of breakfast cereals.

The heating was on in the house to disperse the chill of a cool spring evening, but being away from Gabriel's warmth, to which I had been exposed all day, had left me feeling cold and empty, so I made oatmeal and added dried blueberries to warm myself from the inside. The memory of Gabriel's impassioned words, as wonderful as they'd made me feel, wouldn't physically sustain me.

I watched the bowl revolving around in the microwave and I decided to take a trip to the supermarket once I'd eaten.

I knew I needed to restock the freezer with vegetarian food, but it seemed wasteful to throw away all the meat and fish in there. I wouldn't eat it; there was no way I'd ever eat an animal; but maybe the homeless shelter in town would accept it.

The microwave pinged to signal that my cereal was done and I left it to cool for a minute or two whilst I searched through the telephone directory for the number for the shelter. I pulled my mobile phone out of my pocket and dialled the number in front of me before realising they might be too busy to answer. However, the phone was picked up after only a couple of rings.

'Good evening, Church Road Shelter, how may I help?' the man on the other end of the line asked.

'Hi, I was just looking through my freezer and I have quite a lot of meat and fish in there, but, the thing is, I'm vegetarian. It's still in date and I have no idea what to do with it, so I wondered if you might have use for it.' The shelter was, after all, largely run on donations.

Curiosity obviously overcame him because, instead of accepting or declining my offer, he blurted out, 'If you're vegetarian, why do you have meat and fish in your freezer?'

'Well, technically, it's my mother's freezer. She passed away recently and she's a carnivore. I completely forgot about the chunks of dead animal in the freezer until I opened the door to it a few minutes ago.' I spoke dispassionately, not wanting to betray my anger at his unwitting insensitivity. It wasn't his fault.

'Oh, I'm sorry, I didn't think. I couldn't have known...' he blustered.

'No, of course not. Would you like it or not?'

'Yes, thank you. That's very kind of you,' he sounded more contrite.

'Not at all. It would only have been thrown away if you didn't take it. I'd rather it benefited someone otherwise those animals were killed for nothing. I can drop it off in an hour or so if that's convenient.' My tone was curt.

'That would be fine. Thank you again.'

'Not a problem. Have a good evening.'

'You, too. Bye.'

I picked up my bowl and returned to the lounge to eat my oatmeal, but after only a couple of spoonfuls, I lost my appetite. The man from the shelter had really annoyed me. It hadn't been intentional; it was my fault, really, for telling him I was a vegetarian who had a load of meat to give away. It was only human nature that someone would ask why I was in possession of it at all.

The real problem was in having to explain that my mother was dead. It wasn't an easy thing to say, and it certainly wasn't comfortable. Along with the fact that admitting it always brought back memories and feelings from that night; the physical pain of getting shot and all the emotional pain of losing my family; there was also a part of me that was in denial. I *knew* that it was all true, but part of me was struggling to *believe* that it was true because it felt too unreal.

I dumped the remainder of my food into the bin in the kitchen, marvelling at how stomach acids and enzymes could break down such an inspissate, glue-like substance, then grabbed a couple of black refuse sacks and began unloading the unpalatable contents of the freezer into them, checking the date on each to be sure they were okay. Mum had meticulously written on every freezer bag the date she bought and froze whatever was inside, and the date by which it needed to be consumed.

I grabbed my coat and bag and headed out the door with two sacks full of food for the shelter. I decided to stop at the supermarket on my way back to restock with food suitable for me, for the time when I would be inclined to eat something more substantial again.

I turned on the stereo in the car; I hated driving without music when I was alone; and something suitably angry and angst-ridden greeted me. Since losing Mum and Carmel, I had preferred listening to loud, sometimes obnoxious, music rather than something sombre and melancholy intended to soothe or appeal to the soul whilst wallowing at the same time, or worse, something quirky or upbeat.

I didn't want to hear music which would bring back memories and upset me. I cried so often out of grief, sadness, loss, even self-pity, and there were times when I just didn't want to cry any more. I still felt the sadness, and whether I cried or whether I didn't, it wouldn't change either my feelings, or the situation, so I chose music that would encapsulate my anger and resentment that this had happened to me. It was easier to feel angry and want to scream than to cry and be left feeling drained, with sore eyes, dried-out oversensitive skin, and a headache.

The quick thump of the beat encouraged me to apply a generous amount of pressure to the accelerator pedal and I zoomed through the streets that led to the centre of town.

The shelter was established adjacent to a church hall which backed on to an imperiously beautiful church. I parked in the church hall's empty car park and hauled the bin bags, which seemed to get heavier each time I picked them up, the few yards to the shelter next door.

It was a little after seven when I arrived and, as I walked through the door, I could see that they were busy. There were half a dozen long tables; each of which could seat around twenty people; in the long rectangular room, and most of the chairs at them were filled. There was still a queue of maybe a dozen more people waiting to be served with an evening meal.

No one paid me any attention as I walked through the middle of the room, which was the most direct route to the kitchen.

'Excuse me,' I called as I opened the door with my elbow.

Several people in typical white kitchen attire turned to look at me.

'May I help you?' a woman who was spooning out mashed potatoes from a giant metal saucepan into serving tureens asked.

'I called a little while ago and spoke to a man about dropping off some frozen meat and fish. I didn't get his name, but he said it would be okay. It's all in date and it's not poisoned,' I added after a second when she didn't say anything.

'That's good to know.' She flashed a brief grin and came over to take the bags from me. 'Thanks,' she added, 'it's greatly appreciated.'

'You're welcome.' I smiled back at her. The rest of the staff nodded at me and I turned and left the kitchen.

A few people smiled at me as I walked back through the dining area and out the door, and I was rather pleased that in a small way I was able to do something for them. I knew Mum would approve if she could see this.

I got back in my car and drove to the supermarket. There were so few cars on the roads, and I bypassed inhabited areas, so I was able to drive at a comfortable sixty-five miles per hour; a little over the national limit on those roads; and I reached my destination within ten minutes. By the time I had parked my car, got a trolley and pushed it into the market, my arms were burning and a dull ache had begun in my left shoulder.

I had only got my arm out of its sling two weeks ago, so for the time being, I had to see a physiotherapist weekly and I was supposed to do special exercises and stretches daily. I'd forgotten about them entirely this week since meeting Gabriel. I quickly searched through my purse for an appointment card for the physio, hoping I hadn't missed it and assuming I would have received a phone call from her if I had. When I found it, it confirmed that I was booked in for tomorrow at noon. I calculated that I wouldn't hear from Gabriel too early since he knew I had reading to do. I promised myself I would get up early to work before I went for treatment so that if I did hear from Gabriel earlier than I anticipated, I'd still have made some progress.

I didn't linger in the supermarket; shopping for groceries for one person when that person didn't eat very much wasn't exactly conducive to an extended trip. I grabbed some fresh fruit and vegetables, but I loaded up mostly with frozen products which would last about a year so I could forget about them and not have to deal with rotted mulch the way I might with neglected fresh food. It wasn't as though I was a good cook; my culinary skills extended to toast and taking something from its packaging and putting it in the oven, and I had survived thus far.

Once back at home, I stored everything in its appropriate place and decided I ought to do some of my shoulder exercises before I saw the physiotherapist, especially because the slight pain I had experienced at the shop had intensified to a sharp pinching feeling. I hoped I hadn't done any damage to my weakened muscles, which still hadn't fully recovered from the bullet wound that had ripped them apart, by neglecting them and then putting strain on them this evening.

As I isolated my shoulder and rotated it forwards and backwards, then did the same with my arm extended, the pinching turned to searing and I winced with the pain. It was still bearable, however, and it had felt like that last week at my therapy session. The therapist said that was to be expected, but if it got extremely painful that would be the time to stop.

I worked through the list of movements I'd been instructed to practice, then took a couple of painkillers to subdue my protesting muscles and joints and waited for them to take effect whilst I soaked in piping hot bathwater.

Five

Rose Petals

I was dreaming again.

Gabriel had taken me to his house and we were sitting side-by-side on a big, comfy, cream couch in his lounge. I was wearing a clingy, thin-strapped, black dress that only reached halfway down my thighs, and killer heels which had to have given me an extra six inches in height. Gabriel wore black jeans and a soft, dark grey jumper which hugged his lean, toned body. On the glass table in front of us were two champagne flutes filled with a golden liquid that tasted sweeter than anything I'd tasted before.

Gazing around the large, open-plan ground floor, I could see that it had been artistically decorated with elegant, modern furniture. It suited him well; the furniture was exactly what I imagined he would have chosen for himself.

Gabriel leaned forward, looking deeply into my eyes as he took hold of my hands. He hesitated for a moment and glanced down at them.

'Your hands are like ice.' I could hear concern in his voice, and he caressed the backs of my hands with his thumbs. 'Are you cold?' He moved one hand up to stroke my arm.

'No, I'm fine.' My heart rate accelerated with his touch. 'My hands get cold when I'm nervous.'

'I can tell. There's no need to be nervous. I don't want you to feel anything other than completely happy and safe with me. I'll never push you to do anything you don't want.' He kept his voice low; I found it hypnotic and it set off sparks in my stomach.

I nodded. 'I know. You're not pushing me, Gabriel. It's not like I'm a naïve teenager, though try convincing my heart of that,' I said wryly. 'I swear sometimes it thinks I'm still about sixteen.' I exhaled heavily to calm myself down. 'I'm just a nervy person.'

'It's adorable,' he murmured, his mouth against my ear as he breathed in my scent. 'Do you trust me, Jamie?'

I nodded, biting my lip. Gabriel's hand came up to my cheek and he gently turned my face towards his. I held my breath as I saw the desire in his eyes that I could feel deep inside him; it mirrored my own; and he touched his lips to mine. I moved my hands up his body as I responded, tentatively stroking his stomach and chest as I went, then I slipped them around his neck and into his hair. His hands trailed all the way down my back, coming to rest at my waist, then he pulled me against him and held me more tightly whilst he intensified the pressure of his mouth. I felt as though we couldn't get close enough. As his tongue tangled with mine, I let out a moan and curled my fingers around handfuls of his hair.

Gabriel pulled back from me, took my hand in his and stood up, pulling me to my feet also, then he led me out of the lounge, up the stairs, and he came to a stop outside the closed door of what I assumed was his bedroom. He watched my face as he opened the door and he smiled as the surprise he had waiting in there for me registered.

The room was clean, tidy, and romantically lit, but I noticed very little else about it because my attention was completely focused on the large bed in front of me. The bedclothes were pristine ivory and scattered all over them were blood-red rose petals.

'Gabriel, I... don't know what to say,' I admitted. It was rare that I had trouble thinking of some kind of response.

'I wasn't assuming you'd say yes, and you don't have to say yes now, I just wanted this to be beautiful for you.'

'It is.' I stepped hesitantly into the room and trailed my fingers along the bottom of the bed, touching, but not disturbing, the petals. Gabriel stayed in the doorway watching me. I turned to him. 'Aren't you going to join me?'

He moved slowly, coming to a stop directly in front of me, and took my face in his hands to kiss me again. I reached my arms around his waist and pressed my body into his. He deepened the kiss and leaned me backwards onto his bed. Still not breaking the kiss, he lowered his body on top of mine, smoothing his hands down the length of me. I clutched his shoulders, holding him to me, loving the feel of the weight of him against me.

Gabriel brought one hand up to tangle in my hair and hold my head still as he kissed his way along my jaw, down the front of my throat, and around to the curve at the side.

'You are so beautiful,' he said, breathing my scent in deeply before giving the sensitive skin of my neck the lightest of kisses and a gentle stroke with his tongue, making me shiver with pleasure.

'Gabriel,' I murmured, my voice thick with longing, and I reached my hand into his hair once more.

Then I felt his teeth pierce into the skin he had just kissed and I gasped.

I opened my eyes with a start, my heartbeat sounded loud in my ears and I tried to focus on what had woken me. I wasn't sure if it was the shock of the dream, or a noise in the house. I strained to listen for any sound, scared that there might be an intruder. It was still dark outside, but the moon and the streetlights were providing enough illumination for me to see perfectly.

I pushed my duvet back and got out of bed, crept to my bedroom door, and grasped the butt end of a broken pool cue I kept for self-defence. I silently opened the door and stealthily made my way along the landing. I couldn't sense any movement, or the presence of another person up there, so I slowly descended the stairs hoping none of them would creak, and thankful the thick socks I'd worn to bed to keep my feet warm seemed to dampen the sound of my footfalls.

I held the cue ready to swing as I walked from the hall to the living room, from there into the dining room, and ending in the kitchen. There was no one in this house but me. Relieved, I dropped my arms and peeked out the windows and door at the back of the house to make sure no one was lurking in the garden. I got myself a glass of water as I retraced my steps back to the lounge. I looked out the bay window into the driveway, but there was no sign that anything had been disturbed, so I turned back to go to bed.

As I passed the vase of flowers Gabriel had sent me, I noticed a single rose petal had fallen from one of the flowers and was lying on the coffee table. I let out one short laugh and then giggled to myself as I ascended the stairs once more.

I woke up early the next morning and instead of rolling over and going back to sleep as I would ordinarily have done, I got up to begin one of the other textbooks I'd received a couple of days ago. I worked solidly until it was almost time to leave for my physio appointment.

I was just reaching under the sofa to retrieve the shoe I'd accidentally kicked under there the previous night when my phone started ringing. I pulled it out of my back pocket and I felt excitement zing through me when I saw it was Gabriel calling.

'Hi,' I said almost breathlessly.

'Hi, yourself.' I could tell from his voice that a grin was slowly spreading across his face. 'Are you busy working or can you spare a few minutes to talk?'

'I have been working this morning, I was just getting myself organised for a physio appointment. I've got time to chat before I have to leave, though.' *Please talk to me.*

The physiotherapist was probably running late, anyway; she had last week and I got the impression that was normal.

'Physio? For your shoulder?'

'I don't think I mentioned my shoulder, so how did you know?' Realisation hit me then. 'Oh, I forgot, you said you knew what happened and that I was in hospital. I'm not sure for how long I'll have to keep going for therapy, but it's my second session today and I forgot to do my stretches for a few days so I'm in trouble.'

'Jamie,' he remonstrated, concerned. 'Try to be more mindful of your recuperation otherwise you'll be left with permanent problems.'

'I know, I know, I haven't been neglecting it on purpose, it just slipped my mind. I'll see what the therapist says today and I'll do whatever it takes to recover.'

'Good. Now, I was thinking that I'd like to take you out to dinner tonight. You can get some more research done this afternoon, I won't disturb you, and I'll pick you up around seven. Would you like that?'

'Dinner at a restaurant?'

The last time I went to one, I got shot in the car park.

It sounded romantic, though, and intimate, which set my heart fluttering. I had never really had that kind of classic date with my ex: we tended to go to the cinema, or we spent time with his group of friends in their regular pub; that was where I got the pool cue.

'Not if you don't want to,' Gabriel began to backtrack. 'We could do something else, or I could cook?'

'No, a restaurant sounds lovely, just not the one—'

'I wouldn't take you to that one.' He made his tone as soft as possible.

'Thank you.' Unexpected tears formed in my eyes so I reached for a tissue to blot them away. 'I'm going to have to go, but I'll see you at seven, okay?'

'I'm looking forward to it.'

'Me, too.'

'Take care, Jamie.'

'Thanks; take care of yourself, too, Gabriel. See you tonight.'

We both hung up and I yanked my shoe out from under the sofa with my right arm so I didn't aggravate my left shoulder. I slipped it on and followed it with my coat as I made my way to the door.

My physiotherapy session was only supposed to last for an hour, but the patient scheduled for the appointment after mine had cancelled last-minute so Jill, my therapist, gave me a longer massage after discovering lots of knots in my back and tension in my shoulders. Though I felt internally bruised when I left her treatment room, I knew I'd feel a lot better by the time Gabriel knocked on my door to pick me up.

It occurred to me, as I was soaking in the bath in preparation for my evening with Gabriel, that the dress I was wearing in my dream the previous night would have been the perfect outfit for this date. However, not only was the weather too cold for a dress like that, I didn't actually own one. It was a good thing, though, because the thin straps would reveal the scars on my shoulder from being shot; the scars that I only just realised were missing in my dream. Instead, I settled for black trousers with wide legs and a high waist teamed with a dusky lilac top with capped sleeves and a scooped neckline. Thankfully, it looked feminine and pretty rather than plain, as I'd feared it might.

Gabriel's smile, when I opened the door and he saw me, lit up his whole face.

'Hello, Jamie. You look beautiful,' he commented, looking me over.

'Thank you.' I blushed. 'You look great, too, Gabriel.' He did; his black trousers and shirt looked as though they had been made for him, outlining the shape of his body perfectly without being too tight. His shirt was open at the collar, temptingly revealing the hollow at the base of his throat. 'Would you like to come in for a moment? I've just got to put my shoes on.' I grinned. 'I couldn't decide which ones to wear.' I stepped back to let him through.

Gabriel looked at my bare feet as he crossed the threshold and the grin he bore was slightly lopsided.

'I like your dark purple toenails,' he announced, raising his eyebrows.

'Thanks,' I said as I laughed, 'it's my favourite shade. Feel free to nose around,' I encouraged, leading him into the lounge.

I could see Gabriel surveying the room, taking in the flowers he sent me, the piles of neatly stacked books on the floor under the coffee table that I had been reading for my research, and the one sitting next to a writing pad with a pencil inside holding the page where I'd stopped reading earlier. His gaze was drawn to the photographs on the mantelpiece and he made his way over to them and picked up the one of my mother, my sister and me at my graduation.

'You look happy here,' he said with a tender note in his voice.

I went and stood beside him, still shoeless. 'I was. I was twenty-one, I'd just got my Bachelor's degree, and it felt as though the whole world was open to me. Little did I realise,' I commented sardonically.

'There's such a strong resemblance between the three of you; there's no mistaking the family connection. What are their names?'

'My mum's name is Beatrice; Bea to her friends; and my sister is Carmel.' I stroked the picture lovingly.

'Is your sister older than you?' he probed.

'Yes, by sixteen minutes, which she never lets me forget.' That really made me smile because it was as though I was saying it to her beaming image and she was looking back smugly.

'Twins?' I felt his surprise. 'I didn't pick up on that. I suppose because you're not identical twins it's not immediately obvious.' He looked at later photographs before turning back to me. 'You definitely seem to be the baby-faced one.' He brushed a finger along my cheekbone, making me tingle all over which, of course, he felt.

'I think that has something to do with Carmel. She always wanted to be a beautician so she's been giving me facials since we were about fourteen or fifteen. With all the products and techniques she's tried on me, my skin hasn't had the chance to age.'

That made us both laugh.

'You miss them,' he stated.

'Yes.' I didn't need to elaborate.

'So, what are your shoe choices for tonight?' Gabriel asked to lighten the mood.

I picked up two pairs; both black and made of faux suede; by their backs, one pair in each hand. 'These or these,' I said, indicating one pair then the other.

'Those are cute,' he said, pointing to a pair of shoes with chunky heels, 'but I think you should go with the shoe-boots; they'll suit that outfit. And they're sexier.'

'Good call,' I agreed, slipping my feet into them. They were actually my favourites and they had the added bonus of five-inch heels. Gabriel helped me into my black velvet coat. 'Ready,' I stated, picking up the matching bag.

'Let's go.'

I turned the lights off behind me and locked the door, expecting Gabriel to be waiting by his car. Instead, he was just a small distance behind me and he held his arm out as I approached him. I threaded my arm through his and he escorted me to the passenger side of his car.

Not only did Gabriel not take me to the restaurant where my family died, he didn't take me anywhere in that area, and there were several restaurants in different directions near it. My eyes opened wide when, instead, Gabriel entered the parking area of an exclusive hotel.

'We're going there?' I turned my head sharply to gape at him. Rooms in that hotel cost more per night than I used to earn in a month working full-time, and the chef there had a very good reputation. It wasn't as though money was a consideration, for either of us, but that was too much.

'Yes, I've heard it's very nice inside.' He kept a straight face whilst speaking, but his eyes flashed mischievously.

'Gabriel, I'm extremely flattered that you'd bring me here, but, really, you shouldn't have gone to this much trouble,' I said, feeling a little daunted.

'It's no trouble. I wanted to bring you here, specifically here, because I know that, for you, going out to eat will never be the same because of the memory of what happened in that restaurant car park. I felt your panic when I suggested it. I thought if I brought you here the atmosphere would be different and, if you felt uncomfortable, we could just sit in the bar instead.'

'What about our reservation? If we only went to the bar, I mean.'

'What about it? It's not important; I just want to spend time with you.'

'Only if you're sure it isn't too much trouble,' I insisted, and bit my lip nervously.

'Nothing is too much trouble.' He traced his thumb over the bottom lip I'd just sunk my teeth in to pull it free and looked at me intensely. I could feel his sincerity and that, added to the depth of his gaze, reassured me and I believed him. 'So,' he continued, 'it's your decision: dinner or drinks?'

He had invited me to dinner and I had accepted. He had booked us a table in the restaurant of a beautiful hotel specifically for me to avoid bad memories. He had dressed elegantly, behaved with nothing other than consideration and gentility, so I wasn't going to insult him.

'Having dinner with you would be wonderful, Gabriel. No matter what you say to the contrary, this took a lot of thought and effort, so, thank you. Truly, thank you.' I rested one of my hands on his as I leaned over to him and brushed my lips against his.

When I drew back, I could see, as well as feel, that my trust in him made him genuinely happy. It wasn't just a smile he gave me, it was as though he was lit from within and he looked like a little boy.

'Wait there,' he instructed and got out of the car, came around to my side, and opened the door. 'Would you do me the honour, Jamie?'

He held his hand out and I put mine into it, swivelled my legs out of the car with my knees together, the way a lady should, and stood up. Gabriel kissed my hand, shut the door behind me, and interlinked our arms as he guided me towards, and through, the entrance of the hotel.

Once inside, we walked straight past the reception desk and went in the direction of the restaurant and bar. The manager looked up as we approached and Gabriel gave his name.

'Mr. Castell,' the man said, and smiled. 'If you would like to follow me, your table is ready.'

I had to admit, I felt really intimidated by all the people in there, and I reverted to the shy, introverted creature I truly am once my impetuousness fades.

The manager weaved a path through huge tables with large, garrulous parties seated at them, towards the back of the room and up a few steps to a quieter, raised area where the tables for couples were situated. He led us to a table in the corner which would allow us some degree of privacy.

'*Madame*,' he indicated the chair he had just pulled out for me.

'*Mademoiselle*,' Gabriel corrected pointedly.

'Thank you,' I said, smiling politely as I sat down.

The manager looked across the room at a waiter who immediately came over to our table, handed Gabriel and me some menus, filled our water glasses, then discreetly disappeared.

'Your waiter will be back in a few moments to take your order. Enjoy your evening,' he added before departing.

I smiled at Gabriel before taking a sip of water, and I looked back up to find him watching me.

'What?' I asked.

'How was your physio session earlier?'

'Painful.' I grimaced. 'I confessed my forgetfulness, so Jill worked my shoulder harder to make up for it. I did get extra massage time, though.' I explained my longer session. 'I do enjoy the massage part.' I closed my eyes briefly in bliss.

'I learnt a few massage techniques once. If you have any problems between therapy sessions, maybe I could be of some assistance.'

'Thank you, I'll remember that.' My whole body suffused with heat at the thought of Gabriel's hands massaging my naked body, and then images from my dream the previous night invaded my reverie. Gabriel's lips twitched when he felt my reaction and sensed the direction my thoughts had taken, but he politely said nothing. 'So, tell me, what did you do with yourself today?'

'Actually, I've been on your university's website looking into postgraduate research degrees. I read through the profiles of the lecturers in both the English and Psychology departments.'

'Really?' I was pleased. 'What are your thoughts?'

'Well, I know which people to contact, the thing I'd need to do now is decide exactly what the point of my research is, which books I want to analyse, and whether to stick to one genre or look at examples from a cross-section of genres. There's still a lot to think about. I could also go into the reader's psychology: why she or he responded in the ways they did and why they chose a particular book in the first place. I'd have to conduct interviews and you, Jamie, will be one of my interviewees. I won't accept a refusal.' He took a lock of hair framing my face between his fingers, examined it, then returned my gaze.

'I wouldn't dream of it.' I smirked at him as I held my hands up in surrender.

I dropped my eyes to the menu to search for the vegetarian dishes, but, when I snuck a peek at Gabriel, he was still looking at me.

'Have you made a decision?' He was referring to the menu, of course, but it still felt like there was something more behind his words, another meaning with which I wasn't acquainted.

'The stuffed aubergine sounds nice. Most of the time vegetarians are only offered pasta, which is unimaginative, and I don't even like it. It's bland and slimy. What are you having?'

Just as I asked the question, the waiter reappeared.

'Are you ready to order?'

Gabriel's attention never wavered from me. 'How about a salad to start?' I nodded, so he tuned to the waiter. 'Two mixed salads and two stuffed aubergines to follow, please.'

'The aubergine is a good choice,' the waiter remarked, then noted it down and gathered our menus. 'And what would you like to drink?'

'I don't actually drink alcohol,' I said apologetically to both Gabriel and the waiter. 'Could I just have a Diet Coke please?'

'Of course, Miss.' He looked at Gabriel.

'I'll have a glass of Merlot.'

'I'll be back with those in a moment,' the waiter said, then disappeared again.

'A coffee-loving, teetotal vegetarian who's obsessed with vampires,' Gabriel observed with a grin.

'I guess if it wasn't for the vampires I'd be unbelievably strait-laced.' I smiled to myself in derision and looked down as I tucked some hair behind one ear.

'I wouldn't say that,' Gabriel disagreed. 'Sticking to your principles doesn't make you strait-laced. Besides, would a conservative person have had as many piercings as you?'

I looked up quickly. 'How do you know about those?' I asked, tilting my head to one side.

'I can see the little holes in your ear.' He leaned forward to run his finger around the outside of the ear I had exposed.

'Oh, of course, sorry. I used to have four in each ear, but I only wear one pair now so the others have begun to heal up. I could open them again quite easily; I've done so a few times. I liked piercings a lot a few years ago,' I explained.

'Do you have any others?' he asked, and raised his eyebrows suggestively.

I laughed. 'I still have my navel pierced; I love it and I'll never take it out. I used to have my tongue pierced as well; I kept it for a year before I took it out because it was annoying me. I miss it sometimes. I went to have one of my nipples pierced, but I was too nervous to go through with it.' I smiled.

Our drinks materialised before Gabriel could comment on that, shortly followed by our salads.

'So, are you a vegetarian, seeing as you ordered the same as me?' I asked as I picked up my knife and fork and started cutting into the vegetables.

'I don't believe animals should be killed for their meat, skin, fur, or anything else, which I'm assuming is how you feel, too?' I nodded enthusiastically. There was silence for a moment before a cheeky grin appeared on his face and he nudged my foot with the toes of one of his boots. 'You didn't ask me if I have any piercings.'

'*Do* you have any?' I arched one eyebrow.

'No.' He let out a strangled laugh. 'But should I decide I wanted one, which part of my anatomy would you suggest?'

'Nipple. Definitely a nipple,' I answered without hesitation. 'It's sexier on men.'

'Oh, so you were too scared to have it done, but it's okay for me to do it?' He started laughing.

'I wasn't scared, I was anxious,' I defended myself. 'What if something went wrong and I lost sensation in it? Women's nipples are more important than men's.'

'How have you reached that conclusion?'

Luckily for us, there weren't any couples at the nearby tables because, judging by how haughty most of the patrons looked, I suspected our conversation may have offended them.

'Women need their nipples to breastfeed,' I argued.

'But you don't have any children,' he countered.

'No, but maybe one day I will.'

'Hmm,' he responded cryptically, but said nothing more whilst we ate our starter.

I demolished most of mine, but Gabriel barely ate half.

I gestured to his plate as it was taken away. 'Didn't you like it?'

'It was just a little boring,' he said, taking hold of my upturned hand and placing it between both of his. 'The main course should be better.'

'Would you like something else?' I rested my free hand on the table.

'No, I'm fine.' He smiled. 'You haven't told me what your thesis topic is. Is it vampires?'

'I thought about it, but I decided to keep my pet obsession to myself. I thought I'd be exposing too much of myself if I wrote a hundred-thousand word dissertation on them and converted everyone into vampire fanatics so they wouldn't just be *my* obsession anymore.'

'I understand. So, what are you going to write about?'

'I'm looking at how women represent men and male-female relationships in contemporary women's fiction. I'm assessing whether female writers are sexist and rely on male stereotypes for their heroes and the behaviour of those heroes, and predictable situations in their relationships.'

Gabriel gave a low whistle. 'Impressive. Different angle; very original.' He moved one of his hands to pick up his wine glass.

'Thanks.'

'What about your Master's thesis?' He took a mouthful of his wine.

'I analysed erotic literature written by, and for, women.' I bit down hard on my lip because that disclosure always got a reaction. Gabriel nearly spat the liquid back out and leaned forward with laughter.

'Was your last relationship so bad that you had to resort to erotica?'

I laughed, too. 'No, my last relationship was so bad it drove me back into the pages of every vampire book I had ever read. Even the bad ones. Oddly enough, that partnership did end during my Master's degree.'

'Did you love him?' Gabriel's eyes were soft as he looked into mine for the truth in my thoughts and feelings.

'Not really. I thought I did, but the feeling disappeared rather quickly. I cared about him, though. It feels so unreal now; I can almost believe it never happened. I'd rather it hadn't.' I set my mouth in a line trying not to physically betray any emotion, even though Gabriel could feel what I felt. I looked back on that relationship and felt little but shame. It was one of the mistakes I'd made that I wished I could take back. 'I've never really been in love,' I confessed.

Gabriel seemed pleased about that; he didn't smile in satisfaction, but I felt something inside him that had been tensed suddenly relax. He released my hand so that our main course could be set down on the table.

I chewed delicately on a mouthful of aubergine for a moment and considered whether or not asking my next question was a good idea.

'So, as we've started going down this avenue of conversation, what was your last relationship like?'

'It was a long time ago, when I was still a kid, really.'

'I'd hardly say you were old now, Gabriel.' It was true, he only looked about twenty-three, or twenty-four at most, but I could tell from everything about him that he was older, more experienced.

'I'm older than I look.' He grinned. 'You should know all about that, Jamie. You could still pass for nineteen or twenty.'

I smiled because I was proud of that.

'Her name was Marta,' he began. 'Her family and mine had been friends for a long time and both were very wealthy, of course. We were the same age and grew up together, went to school together, and we were thrown together a lot by our families. Nothing was ever said about it, but our mothers were very keen for us to have a deeper relationship and, because we were good friends, we decided to give it a go. We got together on her seventeenth birthday, at the party her parents threw for her.' He spoke unsentimentally, and I couldn't feel any lingering emotions towards her, or their relationship, in him.

'Needless to say our parents were overjoyed,' he continued, 'and after a while, behind my back, they were planning our wedding. Marta never intended to work because, like me, she didn't need to, and she didn't see the point of going to university because she wasn't particularly academic and she knew she'd never use anything she learned. Her ambition was to get married to someone like me and have babies.

'By this point, I'd realised that I didn't love Marta, she was just a friend, and I told my parents that I'd been accepted at Oxford University. We lived in London and that was when they told me all about the wedding preparations they had been making and that I couldn't move away, I'd have to stay with my wife.' Gabriel stopped talking for a moment and pushed the food on his plate around dispassionately.

'Then what happened?' I needed to know the rest of the story.

'Then I broke it off with Marta and went to university. To say my parents were unhappy about it would be an understatement, but they came to accept it, in their way.' He pressed his lips together in distaste.

'What happened to Marta?'

Gabriel's mouth twitched upward as he said, 'She married my older brother.'

'I guess that's why they accepted your decision, then?' I laughed and he nodded. 'Hasn't there been anyone since?'

He shrugged. 'No one serious.'

I drank some of my Diet Coke as I began to process Gabriel's story. He was watching me.

'You're shocked and you feel bad for me,' he discerned. 'Not pity, but sadness for my pain.'

I couldn't deny it. 'Yes, I'm sorry that it happened to you.' I leaned forward and my hand shook as I reached out to touch the side of his face. He tilted his head into my palm.

'I was hurt because my parents weren't supportive and wanted to force me to be someone I'm not. Leaving them reinforced how different from them I was, and still am. Their only concern is the family lineage. I always wanted more than that, and the freedom to choose for myself. I've had a better relationship with them since things settled, though it's still not a good one, and I only go back for the occasional visit even though they're not far away. I don't belong with them; I'm happier this way.' He moved my hand and kissed, then squeezed, my fingers.

The waiter glided over to remove our plates.

'Would you like the dessert menu?'

'Not for me, thank you.' I smiled at him regretfully.

'You're not tempted by desserts?' Gabriel asked teasingly.

'Oh, I'm always tempted by desserts; I just don't have any room for one.'

Both Gabriel and the waiter laughed.

'In that case, may we have the bill, please?'

'Of course, Sir,' he replied and disappeared off to the kitchen to dispose of our plates.

I reached under the table for my bag and retrieved my purse.

'What's that for?' Gabriel asked, frowning.

'To pay the bill,' I replied.

'I invited you out tonight, I'm paying,' he said stubbornly, but not unkindly.

'Gabriel, I can't let you do that. At least let me pay half.'

'Jamie,' he said softly, appealing to me, 'I know you're independent and self-reliant. I understand that you're a feminist and you have no problems paying your own way, but, really, I'm insisting you let me pay tonight. When I ask someone out on a date, I expect to pay.'

'I don't expect you to.'

'I know you don't. You don't act, or react, in expected ways; that's part of why I like you.' He could see that I wasn't about to concede. 'Okay then, I'm asking you to let me pay.'

'It means that much to you?' I queried, wondering why.

'Yes. My parents instilled old-fashioned manners in me,' he explained.

'Okay,' I said reluctantly. 'I wouldn't want to offend you.'

The waiter returned with a small folder and presented it to Gabriel. He didn't even look at it, merely handed over a credit card which the waiter slotted into a portable card reader. Gabriel punched in a number and waited for the transaction to complete. He slipped the card and receipt into his pocket and got to his feet.

I followed suit and picked up my jacket, but Gabriel quickly came to my side.

'Allow me,' he said with a charming smile, taking the blazer out of my hands and holding it open for me.

I smiled back and slipped my arms in, but didn't button it up. I took Gabriel's hand and we walked out of the restaurant towards the reception.

'Would you excuse me for a moment?' Gabriel asked.

'Of course,' I replied and watched him walk towards the restrooms.

Whilst I waited, I plunged my hands into my coat pockets to see if I'd left anything in them the last time I wore it. I found a books returned receipt from the university library in one, and a packet of tissues in the other.

Gabriel was back within two minutes. He put his arm around my shoulders and we headed in the direction of his car. We were within a few feet of it when a male voice called 'Miss' and I heard footsteps rapidly approaching us from behind. A hand tapped me on the shoulder and I froze.

Six
The Whole Story

Gabriel felt the panic rise inside me, he felt my heartbeat accelerate dangerously and he felt me cowering inside myself, so he pulled me tighter against his side and turned us around to face the man who had accosted me.

'Excuse me, but my girlfriend,' he gestured behind him to a pretty blonde woman, 'noticed that your bracelet was hanging out of your pocket. She thinks it must have fallen off and you didn't realise. She didn't want you to lose it.' He smiled kindly at me.

I looked down and saw that my mother's bracelet, a simple silver chain with a miniature heart hanging from it, was dangling half inside and half outside of my pocket. I presumed it came undone when I fumbled around in them whilst waiting for Gabriel. I pulled the bracelet out and held on to it tightly. When I looked back up, I saw that the man's girlfriend had caught up with him.

'Thank you so much,' I said to them both. 'I'd have been devastated if I'd lost that. I didn't even feel it fall off.'

The couple walked away and I let out a big breath in relief as a measure to calm my heart rate. I could still feel protectiveness radiating from Gabriel.

He turned me to face him and looked at me solemnly. 'Jamie, are you okay?'

'I'm fine.' He didn't feel, or look, convinced. 'It's silly, but for a moment it felt like history repeating. It didn't happen like that when I got shot; the guy didn't say anything or touch any of us; but simply being approached by a stranger in a car park after I'd just been to dinner was spookily similar enough to momentarily freak me out.'

Gabriel nodded to let me know he understood, then took the bracelet out of my hand and fastened it around my wrist.

'It's pretty. It suits you,' he commented, tracing the blue veins on the inside of my wrist. The edges of his lips twitched with satisfaction as he felt the pulse there quicken.

'It's Mum's,' I said a little breathlessly due to Gabriel's touch. 'Carmel and I saved our pocket money for months to buy it for her birthday when we were six. We thought the little heart would be a reminder that she could wear of how much we loved her. Mum put it on me for luck before I left for my exam the day she died; she saw how nervous I was. I haven't taken it off since.'

'I'll bet your mother loves it, doesn't she?'

'She wore it every day from the day we gave it to her until my exam. She said it means more to her than everything else she owns.'

We'd reached Gabriel's car, so he unlocked the doors and opened mine for me.

He got in his side of the car and started it before he asked, 'Don't you have any other family? You said you and your sister bought the bracelet at age six. That's young to be financially aware.' He frowned.

'We had my mother's parents when we were very young, but they were middle-aged when they had her. They used to help Carmel and me buy presents for Mum for her birthday, Christmas, and Mother's Day. Their health deteriorated quite rapidly; between them they had several major illnesses; and they had both passed away by the time Carmel and I were five,' I explained unemotionally. I'd accepted their deaths a long time ago.

'Mum used to give us some money; twenty pence or fifty pence maybe; for helping her around the house. We'd do the cleaning and dusting, collecting the dirty laundry and separating it into light and dark-coloured loads, pairing up clean socks, or hanging up the clean washing after it had been ironed, little things like that.' I smiled at the memory even though it made me feel sad to remember. 'We were only kids so we didn't need to buy anything, so we saved our money to buy Mum's presents.

'When we went shopping, one of us would stand with Mum and make sure she didn't see what we were buying whilst the other went and got it. The people behind the counters would give us funny looks so we'd often have to point Mum out and explain we were buying for her. We managed it however we could.'

'Your mum sounds like a good woman.' Gabriel never used the past tense because he knew I didn't like it, and that meant so much to me.

'She is to me.'

'Both your mother and your sister will always be with you.'

'I can still feel them,' I admitted. 'I'm not religious, I never have been, so I don't believe in a Heaven as such, but I've got a feeling that Mum and Carmel are still around, so I'm not convinced that death is the end. Does that sound ridiculous to you?'

'No, it doesn't,' he said kindly. 'Religion has never been a part of my life, either, but I think it would be foolish to think that when a person dies that is the end for them. If you look at it scientifically, energy doesn't die, it has to go somewhere. That energy, the soul, the essential self, whatever you want to call it, still exists; I believe it's only the physical body that dies. I've never felt the presence of someone who's died, but I know of a reputable psychic who talks to them. Maybe you'd like to see her?' he asked tentatively.

'Maybe one day,' I said, taken by surprise. 'I think that now it's still too soon, but I'd like that.'

'Let me know when you're ready and we'll arrange it.'

I nodded. More than anything, I wanted to know that Mum and Carmel were okay. It was difficult for me to accept that they were dead, but it was more important that *they* accepted it. I hated the thought that they might be suffering, or lost somewhere.

I was so absorbed in thoughts about speaking to my family again that I hadn't noticed how close to home we were. I looked up as Gabriel was pulling into my driveway.

'Would you like to come inside for coffee?' I checked the time and it wasn't yet ten. 'It's still early.'

'I'd like to spend more time with you,' he said truthfully. He escorted me into the house, watched me turn on the lights and followed me into the kitchen before asking, 'Don't you have trouble sleeping after drinking all that coffee?'

'I drink decaff most of the time because I suffer on and off with insomnia. I've been experiencing nightmares since the incident, reliving it over and over, but I'm sure that's not uncommon for the victim of such a trauma. Do you want regular or decaff?'

'You look fairly wired so I think decaff would be a wise choice. I wouldn't want to be responsible for you not getting any sleep tonight.' His mouth curved into a wicked grin.

My eyebrows shot up in surprise, but I smiled widely at the innuendo. Gabriel and I had a strong emotional connection which was enhanced by our empathic abilities and, because we could each feel what the other person felt, it made our own feelings stronger, so, in turn, we feel that in ourselves and one another. However, our chemistry could not be denied and there was no mistaking the sexual tension between us.

Momentarily ignoring everything else, I narrowed my eyes at him and crossed my arms over my chest as I slowly made my way across the kitchen to stand in front of him where he was leaning back against the counter. 'You think you could keep me up all night?' I challenged, my voice pitched low.

'Honey, I could keep you up all night tonight, all day tomorrow, and all night after that and you would still be begging me for more.' His eyes were boring into mine and I could see the promise in them as much as I could feel the desire in him.

Desire was rising in me, too, exciting me, and I was confronting him by not backing away. I wasn't sure if I expected him to do anything or if I just hoped he would, but, either way, I wasn't disappointed.

Gabriel straightened up, reached out for me and hauled me against his body, wrapping his arms tightly around my waist as I grasped his upper arms to steady myself. I inhaled sharply in astonishment as I tilted my face up to look at him, but before I had the opportunity to protest, not that I was going to, he lowered his head and kissed me.

The kisses I'd dreamt between us the night before had been tame compared to the real thing. It wasn't that I lacked the imagination; I'd fantasised about kisses like this one; but my dream hadn't allowed me to experience it. My subconscious had obviously been holding back, waiting for the actual event.

Gabriel's mouth was urgent but tender, eliciting an equal response from me. He traced my lips with his tongue, so I opened my mouth beneath his; his tongue caressed mine and then they entwined. Loving the way he tasted, I slid my hands up to his shoulders and around his neck, pressing my entire body fervently into his as I stood on tiptoes to get as close to him as I could.

He hugged me to him even harder with one arm and brought his other hand up to cradle my head, both holding me steady and preventing me from breaking the kiss, as he spun us around to press me against the wall by the door. I moaned into his mouth and twisted my fingers into his hair, then Gabriel abruptly stopped kissing me, released me, and stepped back, putting some distance between us.

'This isn't right,' he rasped. 'It's not fair for me to do this with you when you don't know the whole story about me.'

'Gabriel, I…' I faltered. 'What do you mean "the whole story" about you?' Dread crept through me and I felt dizzy. He hadn't been lying to me, I'd have felt it, but what had he been keeping from me?

'You only met me a few days ago so you're still getting to know me, but I've known you for weeks. I've seen you in unguarded moments, and I know how wrong that sounds, but I don't mean it like a stalker or a pervert. I *know* you, Jamie, truly know you, inside and out. I watched you experience elation at passing your degree, then plummet to the depths of despair. I've seen you weak and strong at the same time. I love you, and I want to be with you more than anything, but before we go any further, you deserve to know everything about me. I *want* you to know everything,' he said passionately.

'You love me?' I repeated in a small voice.

'Completely. Unconditionally. Can't you feel it in me?' His voice cracked, and the hurt on his face and in his heart pierced me.

I sorted through everything I was sensing and there it was, suddenly enveloping and overwhelming me.

'Oh,' I gasped, my eyes wide. 'I've never felt anything like that before. It's so different from the love I felt from Mum and Carmel that I didn't recognise it. I wasn't looking for it, wasn't expecting it. Gabriel…' A tear slid down my cheek at the beauty of it.

He stepped closer, cradled my cheek with his hand, and gently wiped the tear away with his thumb before taking me in his arms and cradling my head against his chest. 'Shh,' he soothed. 'It's different from familial love.'

'I should have believed my dreams. They told me you loved me.'

'You knew, you just didn't trust what you knew,' he intoned kindly.

'I've made mistakes in that area before, with my ex-boyfriend.' Gabriel nodded and let me go. 'So, what haven't you told me that I should know?'

He exhaled heavily. 'Maybe you should make that coffee regular; this is a long story and you're going to have a lot of questions.'

We sat on the sofa in the living room, Gabriel's body was turned towards me with one knee bent, his ankle resting on the opposite knee, and I sat sideways on the seat, cross-legged, facing him. I'd cleared a space on the coffee table for a cafetiere, a jug of milk, and our cups.

'Jamie, I told you yesterday that I don't shield anything I'm feeling from you, and I don't. I'm not shielding anything now.'

I assessed that and I could feel that he was completely open to me. His heart and soul were full of love. I nodded to tell him I believed him and to indicate for him to continue.

'I've asked you to trust me, and I have been completely honest with you, but there's something I've refrained from telling you because most people wouldn't believe me,' he said warily.

'I'm not most people.' I narrowed my eyes; he should have known that.

'I do know that. Just keep trusting what you're feeling, okay?' I nodded. 'Tell me again why you like vampires.'

I frowned in confusion. 'What has that got to do with what you have to tell me?'

'I just need to clarify something. Please, it will make sense why I'm asking, I promise.'

'Okay.' I exhaled. 'Well, I'm fascinated by the possibility of it all. Vampires have the opportunity to really evolve mentally and emotionally and, because they experience so much, they learn what is really important. With that knowledge and self-awareness, they can live; or "exist" might be a more accurate term, since according to some mythologies they're not actually alive in the human sense; in a truer, happier way.

'Humans are so busy playing games, or trying to get whatever it is they're trying to attain, that they often only discover what's really important to them when it's too late.'

'Do you remember what you said to me yesterday about not being able to surprise me because I've seen it all before?' he asked, eyebrows raised. Again, I nodded. 'Think about that, and think about everything you just described, then apply it to me.'

I thought for a moment, then asked, 'Are you telling me you're a vampire?'

'Does the description fit?' he persisted, sensing my incredulity.

'Yes.'

'Then that's what I'm telling you. Jamie, you know I'm not lying.'

'No, it feels right, but maybe that's because you believe it's true. I mean, Gabriel, I'm a vampire fanatic, but I know they're not real.'

'Not in the way they're portrayed in fiction, no, they're not real, but I *am* a vampire. I was born a vampire into a pure-blooded vampire family. I don't have emotional or psychological problems, Jamie, it's the truth.'

'But, how?' I leaned over for my coffee cup, but Gabriel beat me to it and handed it to me.

'Real vampires are descended from a cannibal tribe that existed many millennia ago,' he explained. 'As evolution affected all mortal creatures, so it affected those cannibals and, instead of needing human flesh to survive, they only needed blood.'

'So you've evolved and are now born with immortality?'

'No, we're born mortal. We develop at the same rate as humans from birth to physical maturity. Vampire babies need milk as well as blood. Vampire children need food as well as blood, but, once maturity is reached, we only need blood, and that's when the ageing process slows down. A mortal vampire may only look around forty years old, but could really be well over one hundred years older. They're not susceptible to human illnesses until they're very old and frail; that's usually how they die.'

'They?' I queried.

'The ones who choose to stay mortal.'

'You're not mortal?'

'No.' He paused to assess my reaction. My silence and the calm I was forcing myself to feel satisfied him and he continued. 'Vampires can become immortal by making a kill, but we don't need to kill to survive. I get my blood from blood banks, and when one has family in the medical profession it's always easy to come by. Some vampires drink animal blood, but I've always disagreed with that: I think it's wrong to prey on innocent creatures. Others go to fetish places where people donate via a needle or enjoy getting bitten, but I won't elaborate on that because I think you get the picture.

'When a vampire reaches physical maturity, only then can he or she become immortal, only then does he or she have the strength to make the kill as it's not easy to overpower an adult human and drink all their blood. Killing a human child wouldn't work, incidentally: there's not enough blood to complete the change. Blood is a life-force,' he explained, 'and the vampire has to ingest all the human's blood, receive all of that particular person's life-force, into him or herself to become immortal.'

'So you've killed someone?' I was trying to comprehend everything Gabriel was telling me.

'Yes. He wasn't a nice person; he killed a young family. I was loath to take his tainted blood inside me, but I wanted immortality and I didn't want to kill an innocent human.' He implored me to understand.

'Why did you want to become immortal?'

'My parents are. They chose it after having my brother, sister, and then me. It seemed perfectly normal, and it is for my kind. I knew I'd have a long life regardless, but I was vain enough not to want to grow old. I want to go on living, go on experiencing and growing as a person. I would have done it when I was younger, but I'm like you and I looked younger than I was, even for a vampire. I didn't want to look like an adolescent for all eternity.' He grinned.

'How old were you?' I'd initially worried that I was older than him; I wasn't keen on the idea of a toy boy.

'How old do I look?'

'About twenty-three or twenty-four, no older than that.'

He seemed pleased. 'I was twenty-nine, and that was one hundred years ago as of next month.'

'You're one hundred and twenty-nine?' My mouth twitched in amusement. 'I've always been attracted to men who are older than me, but that's definitely some kind of record.'

He gave a short laugh. 'Well, technically, I'm only one hundred and twenty-eight; my birthday isn't until the thirty-first. Do you really believe me? It feels as though you do.'

'I think I do. I know you're not lying, and I've spent enough time talking to you to know that you're psychologically and emotionally stable, so the only conclusion I can make is that you really are a vampire.'

'I really am. I know it seems implausible, but I knew you would understand; you're open-minded and free-thinking.'

'So, was Marta from a wealthy, pure-blooded family, too? Is that why your parents wanted the two of you to get married?'

'Yes. They wanted pure-blooded grandchildren. They've got them now from my brother and Marta. Even my sister has a couple.'

'But not from you?'

'No. We can only have children when we're still mortal. It's not possible once we've become immortal because we're not alive in the same way. Our hearts still beat, our blood still circulates, our lungs still take in air, but reproductively we're dead; it's so we can't have an indefinite number of children and dominate the gene pool. I've never wanted children so I'm not upset that my chance has gone. Besides, I'm not interested in pure-blooded women.' He held my gaze so I knew he meant he was only interested in me.

'I'm assuming that there have been vampire and human couples.' Gabriel confirmed that there had with a nod. 'So what happens? Do the humans just grow old and die, or can they be turned?'

'They can be turned, but only by an immortal pure-blood,' he said unaffectedly. 'The vampire must drink the human's blood, assimilate their life-force, until the human is weakened, then the human must drink from the vampire to get their enhanced life-force back.'

'A human doesn't have to make a kill to make it complete?' I wondered.

'No, because the vampire has already done that. He or she is immortal, the immortality is held in their blood, which is stronger than any human's blood. The weakened human need only drink that.'

'And then the human would become an immortal vampire in the same way as you?'

'What do you mean?' He tilted his head to one side.

'Well, what you said about the heart still beating, blood still circulating, lungs still needing air, but reproductively dead. Is it like that when a human is turned, or are they dead?'

'Oh, no, they would still have a heartbeat, they'd still be alive. The only difference in that sense is that they wouldn't be born vampires. You have more questions, don't you?' He leaned back in his seat and smiled at me, feeling pleased that I'd accepted everything.

'Can't a born vampire be made immortal in the same way a human can be transformed, so that they don't have to take a life?'

'That would be nice,' he sighed, 'so that there was less killing, but unfortunately, no. A born, mortal vampire must take the human's life into himself, or herself, to reach immortality. It's different for humans because, as I mentioned, your blood is weaker, and when you drank the stronger vampire blood, it would have been mixed with your own as you would have been almost drained.'

I could sort of understand that. I thought for a moment, then asked, 'Do you have fangs?' I felt rather naïve asking him that.

'Not in the way you think.' He laughed. 'My fangs are longer and much sharper than a human's, but they don't lengthen in bloodlust or anything. Does that disappoint you?' he asked knowingly.

'I admit, I always found the fangs quite sexy, but I never believed vampires were real so, no, I'm not disappointed.' I couldn't believe I'd never noticed his fangs before, but then the rest of him was so beautiful that I hadn't really scrutinised his teeth. Now that I was paying more attention, I could see that they were longer than a human's, but it wasn't blatant.

I hesitated before asking my next question, not knowing if it was too personal for him, or how I might feel about his answer. 'Do you drink from people?'

'No,' he said immediately, and he felt my relief. We both realised I would have been jealous if he did. 'I have on occasion, from friends who were willing, but I have a contact at the blood service.'

'What about regular food? You ate tonight, what happens to that?'

'I don't need it and can't metabolise it. I tried to only eat a little so there was less to cough back up.'

'That's where you went before we left, to cough the food back up?'

'Yes.'

'Do you have stronger senses?'

'Yes, better eyesight and hearing, taste and smell are stronger, and I'm very sensitive to touch. It's much more intense, especially with you, Jamie. When you touch me, I feel sparks under my skin which spread through my whole body.' His voice was low and sexy, and I shuddered at the sound, the feeling, and the evocative image.

'Really?' He nodded and I blushed; I was pleased. 'I get sparks from you, too, Gabriel,' I blurted out. 'What do I smell like to you?'

'You smell warm and sweet, but it's subtle, not overpowering.'

'That's nice. I like that. Do you ever feel like you want to bite me?' My heart was thundering at the thought of him biting me. Not only did it seem like a sensual act, it reminded me of my dream.

'Yes, but not for sustenance, only for intimacy so I can be closer to you. And, yes, I have drunk from other women in the past, but it was with women I knew and cared about as friends, and they allowed me to feed from them. It was never romantic. I've never loved anyone before you, Jamie.'

'I... I...' I wavered. 'Thank you. It's a lot to take in.'

'I know,' he leaned forward to touch my cheek, 'and I can feel the tumult your emotions are in. I expected that.' He kissed the centre of my forehead, the exact place where psychics say the third eye is situated. 'I'll take my leave of you so that you can process all of this.'

'But—' I began.

'I know you have more questions, and I promise I will answer them truthfully, but it's very late and you should try to get some sleep.'

'Do you sleep?' I enquired, thinking back to a vampire myth in one of the books I'd read.

He grinned. 'Yes, I sleep. I am still alive so I expend energy like a human and I get tired.'

'Okay. I'm sorry, no more questions tonight.'

Gabriel stood up and helped me to my feet. My legs had seized and gone to sleep in my cross-legged position.

'One more thing before I go,' he said without letting me go. 'When you asked me if I ever felt like biting you, you were thinking about the dream you had last night.'

'We were kissing and then you bit me, it was then that I woke up.'

'I got that. I think that as well as being an empath, you unconsciously divine things telepathically from people and your subconscious tells you what you learned in your dreams. You said you have also dreamt that I was in love with you. You knew that was true, you felt it, and you knew that I'm a vampire already. Think about it,' he advised when I didn't immediately respond.

We were standing so close that it was easy for him to bend down and brush his lips against mine as he wrapped his arms around my waist. I wound my arms around his neck and kissed him back.

I walked him to the door and watched him grasp the handle. He turned back to me. 'If you want to see me later, give me a call. If you need more time to adjust to everything, I'll understand.'

I knew that he would, but I also knew that it would cause him pain. 'Of course I want to see you. This doesn't change anything.'

'You're sure?' I saw hope brighten his eyes, just as I felt it in his heart.

'Completely. It doesn't worry me that you're a vampire. Gabriel, you're you, and I want you in my life.' I knew I was falling in love with him, but I wanted to be sure. After I misinterpreted my feelings for Hayden, I didn't want to hurt someone else, or myself, again.

He nodded. 'Call me,' he said before swiftly kissing me, then walking away.

I waited in the open doorway until he'd driven away before locking myself in for the night. It was almost three in the morning and I was tired, but I knew that everything Gabriel had told me would keep me awake for a while, so, before I went to bed, I emptied the remains of the undrunk coffee from the cafetiere and washed up everything we had used. All the while, the same thoughts kept running through my head: Gabriel is a vampire, a *real* vampire, and he loves me. As impossible as it seemed, I knew it was true; I felt it, not like a gut feeling, but as a certainty, as something that just *is*.

I lay, not sleeping, for at least another hour, replaying everything Gabriel had told me and examining exactly how all of it made me feel. That vampires were real and Gabriel is one was undeniably a thrill; I'd had daydreams and fantasies about meeting one and being bitten since my early teens. It really didn't bother me, and it certainly didn't scare me. Gabriel didn't feed on people, he wasn't dangerous, he was still the caring person who had been secretly watching over me since my family died. Not only that, he loved me; he was in love with me.

I had no problems accepting how in tune with me he was because he's an empath, like me, but he also has telepathic ability. I read people better than most thanks to being an empath, and apparently my dreams fill in some more of the blanks, so a few conversations between Gabriel and me were all that was needed to establish a deep connection and bond. The thought of losing him from my life hurt more than the thought of losing Rachael, and she and I had been friends for years.

From the first moment I met him, and it was difficult to believe that was only four days ago, I'd felt something strong between us. I hadn't ever felt fear or caution despite having had reason to suspect he'd been stalking me; I knew I could trust him.

I held the knowledge that Gabriel loved me in my heart and I imagined myself telling him I loved him back. It felt special. It felt true. With that in mind, I fell asleep.

The sound of my phone ringing woke me up. I flung myself over to the bedside table to answer it, unsure who to expect calling, and was shocked to see Aaron's name on the screen.

'Aaron! Hi, how are you?' I tried to make myself sound fully awake.

'Hi, Jamie. I woke you up, didn't I? I'm sorry,' he said in a kind tone of voice, feeling both partially amused and perturbed.

'It's okay; it's about time I got up, anyway. It's good to hear from you. How have you been?'

'I have good days and bad days. I miss Carmel so much.' His voice was thick with emotion.

'I know; I miss her, too. It feels like she should be pestering me to come to the salon because she thinks my hair is overdue for a trim, I'm in need of a facial, or she wants to try something new on me.' I smiled sadly to myself.

'That sounds about right.' Aaron almost laughed. 'I was just calling because I received a letter from my solicitor this morning confirming that Carmel's share of the business is now mine. I just wanted to let you know and to thank you. I would have bought it from you, you know.'

'I couldn't have borne that, it was never mine to sell. Carmel's half only came to me because she doesn't have a will and I'm her next of kin because you two aren't married.' I still didn't use the past tense and Aaron didn't comment on it. 'I really had no rights to it at all in my opinion; I think it should have gone straight to you. I know when we approached the solicitor he insisted on a cooling-off period in case I changed my mind, but that was never going to happen.'

'Thank you again, Jamie. I know it has been difficult for you, losing them both. I miss your mum, too, you know. I miss her warmth and her sense of humour. I thought of her as my second mother,' he added wistfully.

'The two of you have always got on so well with one another, and she can see how happy you make Carmel; that's all Mum's ever wanted for her.' I hoped my words would eventually give him some comfort, at the moment they weren't really penetrating through his grief.

'Listen, I know Carmel didn't charge you for treatments—'

'I never expected that,' I interrupted. 'I was always willing to pay.'

'I know, I know, it's okay. She would never have taken money from you and she would've killed me if I hadn't respected that, or continued to respect it. I just wanted to make it clear that you're welcome to still come to the salon. That is if it isn't too painful for you.'

'It's my turn to thank *you* for *your* generosity. It won't be the same without Carmel experimenting on me, but I appreciate the offer.' I wondered if it would be painful being treated by someone else in Carmel's salon, in her treatment room.

'Oh, I've got to go; one of my employees is waving quite frantically at me so I think he might need my help. Look after yourself, Jamie.'

'You, too, Aaron. Call me if you ever need to talk, or if you just want to talk about Carmel. Promise me.'

'I will,' he choked out. 'Bye.'

'Bye.'

I hung up and felt a wave of despair and emptiness. Aaron. He'd lost the woman he loved and wanted to spend the rest of his life with. He and Carmel had been planning their wedding. They'd wanted a houseful of children and pets. He lived in the home they had bought and decorated together. He worked in the business they had built from dreams, and they'd put everything they had into it. Now he had to go on without her.

The pain of it hit me in the heart like a wrecking ball. I rolled over on the bed and curled myself into the foetal position, my body heaving with sobs that made no noise because I couldn't breathe. It felt as though my chest was being crushed, or perhaps everything inside me was imploding on itself until there was nothing left of me, just a tangled pair of pyjamas in a rumpled bed. Maybe it was just my sanity slipping away.

I had no concept of time, no awareness of anything other than this crippling anguish and loss, so I don't know how long I'd been in this state when I heard an insistent thumping on the front door.

'Jamie!' a voice called. Gabriel's voice. It was followed by more rapping on the door. 'Jamie, can you open the door?'

I couldn't respond; I couldn't get enough air into my lungs to speak. I was trying to draw in deep breaths, but they were uneven. I rolled to the edge of the bed and stood up, but I was hunched over, clutching at my chest, trying to hug myself with one arm whilst with the other I held on to walls, doorframes, anything that couldn't move, for support as I tried to get to Gabriel.

I was on my way down the stairs when the knocking turned to hammering.

'Jamie! Jamie!' There was a desperate edge to Gabriel's voice and internally he was frantic, but he was trying to keep it under control so his feelings didn't make me worse.

I had my keys in my hand, though I didn't remember picking them up, and both the thundering on the door and Gabriel's calling stopped when he heard me insert the key into the lock. I pressed the handle down, but before I could pull the door open, Gabriel pushed it and hurried towards me. He looked so beautiful even though his face was tight with worry.

I stumbled towards him, hugging myself with both arms and still not breathing well. He scooped me up into his arms, kicked the front door shut, and carried me into the living room. He sat on the sofa with me in his lap, cradling me close and encouraging my head to rest on his shoulder.

In his most soothing voice, Gabriel said, 'Jamie, I want you to concentrate only on my voice and what I'm telling you to do, okay?' I just stared at him, wide-eyed, scared, and unable to speak, and he realised that was my capitulation. 'Okay, breathe in slowly. Slower,' he commanded as I inhaled. 'Now slowly breathe out. Good,' he said as I immediately obeyed. 'Again.'

I had to work hard to force my lungs to relax, my ribs to stop constricting, but with each breath in it became easier.

'Keep breathing slowly,' Gabriel advised, rubbing my back to ease the tension holding my muscles rigid.

I hadn't registered how tightly I had been holding myself until I felt the warmth of Gabriel's hand on my back and the soporific effect his stroking was having. His other arm was draped across my body, his hand on my hip, holding me securely on his lap.

I relaxed all the muscles I had clenched, closed my eyes, and I leaned into Gabriel's body, subdued. My breathing had regulated, so I uncurled one arm from my chest to reach up and place my hand on his cheek.

'Thank you, Gabriel,' I breathed, not opening my eyes because I was embarrassed about what had happened. 'I've never had a panic attack before, and I'm not used to being a damsel in distress. I can't say I like it.'

I felt him laugh beneath me. 'I know. You hate it when you have to rely on someone for help.'

I nodded and lifted my head to look at him. 'I'm not *that* girl. I've always been fairly self-sufficient, and I like it that way. I like being able to cope on my own and knowing I won't fall apart if there isn't someone there to hold me together.'

'You don't want someone to make decisions for you, and you wouldn't let anyone do that, either. You know your own mind, Jamie, I know all this. What happened today doesn't make you weak and needy; I don't see you that way,' he reassured me. 'You're not *that* girl, baby, you'll never be her.'

'I just didn't want you to think that I need to be rescued. I'm pretty sure all of this is grief, both mine, and Aaron's. I could feel it when I spoke to him.'

'Who's Aaron?' Gabriel's eyebrows drew together.

'He's Carmel's fiancé. They started their salon together and they had their life together all mapped out.' I looked at Gabriel unhappily. 'Now he's got to cancel all their wedding preparations. If he hasn't already.'

'It's sad, of course it is, but, Jamie, you need to be careful,' he said solemnly. 'Combining Aaron's pain with your own was very dangerous for you. I know you don't want to be impervious to how someone else is feeling, particularly someone you care about, but you can't afford to feel it, too. In this case, you must not fully empathise with him, though you'll still feel sorry for him. He probably feels bad for you; he knows you lost your whole family. I'm assuming he still has his?'

'Yes, loving parents and two sisters. It's not the same, though.'

'No, it isn't, but he has more people around him, those close to him, than you do. I don't want to hurt you, but where's your support system, Jamie? You said it yourself: your friends won't even come to your house. They rarely call you. In the time I've spent with you, your phone hasn't rung once and you haven't received any messages. They know you lost everyone and they just want to palm you off to a counsellor so they can feel they've done something to help rather than actually comfort you.' Gabriel had clearly given it a lot of thought and he was seething with fury at everyone's apparent neglect of me.

'It's you,' I affirmed quietly, looking directly into his eyes. His expression was sad, and he felt sad for me.

'What's me?'

'You are my support system. You are my everything, Gabriel,' I stated simply, and felt all the love inside him. He said he'd always be there.

'I'll be anything you want me to be,' he replied, exhaling and momentarily closing his eyes in happiness at my sentiments.

And with that statement, I knew for certain that I loved him, because he wasn't pushing me to love him back; because he'd told me he loved me and was prepared to be in my life in any way I wanted regardless of how that might make him feel.

I sent the thought and the feeling out to Gabriel so he would know it, and feel it, too.

'When you're ready, you'll say it, too.' He brushed his fingers along my cheek and tilted my face up to his to kiss me.

Seven
Not To Bite

We sat on the sofa like that, me in Gabriel's lap with him holding me against him to keep me warm and give me comfort, for a while longer before I decided I should get dressed. When I padded back downstairs after cleaning myself up and finding some warm clothes, I found Gabriel in the kitchen making me breakfast. The aroma of fresh coffee had floated up the stairs to greet me, but I was astonished to find a bowl of oatmeal with sliced banana on top waiting for me.

'For me?' I asked, even though I knew Gabriel didn't eat. 'I don't usually eat anything for a few hours after getting up. It takes a while for my stomach to settle.'

'Please try to eat a little of it, Jamie. After your panic attack, your blood sugar is probably quite low, that's why you're still feeling light-headed. Besides, I got here over an hour ago so you've probably been awake for almost two hours,' he reasoned. 'And you're feeling nauseous.'

'Only a little bit.'

'Try a mouthful and see how you feel.'

I did as Gabriel suggested, chewing slowly and swallowing hesitantly in case my stomach decided to reject my offering. It tasted nice, creamier than when I made it, but not sickeningly so, and my stomach seemed to appreciate it as much as my taste buds. I smiled at Gabriel and took another spoonful.

He was pleased to see me eating. He picked up our two full coffee mugs in one hand and put his other one on the small of my back to guide me back to the living room to sit down. He somehow managed not to spill a drop of liquid, but I knew that if I had done the same thing, I would have inadvertently tipped most of the contents onto the carpet.

'This tastes really good. Thank you, Gabriel,' I said after my second mouthful. He inclined his head to accept my praise and my thanks. 'Do you know much about cooking? I assume you didn't eat food for very long.'

'I stopped eating food in my late teens. I was a vegetarian, like you, and I must admit my own cooking back then was terrible.' He was slightly embarrassed about that small failing. 'Do you remember in the bookstore the day we first conversed I said I didn't much care for vampires?' I nodded. 'Well, I've been involved with both vampire and human women, and I've always preferred humans. I learned how to cook because I knew I'd be with a human woman and I wanted to be able to cook for her. It just took me until now to find you.'

He could see that I was struggling trying to finish the cereal he'd made for me. 'Full?' he asked.

'Stuffed,' I replied, putting a hand on my stomach.

'Good.' Gabriel took the bowl from me, put it on the coffee table, and replaced it with my cup of coffee. I sipped at it, grateful for the caffeine.

A question had occurred to me and I wanted to ask it, but I was a bit nervous of the answer. Gabriel caught me biting the inside of my lip.

'What is it?' he asked. When I didn't immediately respond, he looked deeper into my eyes and said, 'You can ask me anything; I won't hide anything from you, or lie.'

'It's not that. I'm worried that what I'm about to ask might anger you, and that the answer might scare me.'

'You won't anger me, and you have nothing to fear from me, either. I won't do anything against your will, you know that, Jamie.'

I nodded slowly, looking into my cup rather than at him, then I took a deep breath and turned to face him. 'You said you always knew you'd be with a human woman. Well, when you found the one you truly loved, your soul mate, was your intention to turn her into a vampire so you could be together for all eternity?' I closed my eyes, glad I'd asked. He knew I'd been thinking about our future, but much as I wanted to see, as well as feel, his reaction, I felt so exposed looking him in the eye. It was futile, anyway; he could both feel everything inside me, and read my mind, that's as vulnerable as it's possible to get.

'Jamie, look at me,' he instructed softly. I opened my eyes to look directly into his, into him, and he looked into me. 'You are the love of my entire existence, and yes, I want to turn you to be with you forever, but not if it's not what you want, too. If you want a mortal life, I will respect that. I love you, Jamie, and I'll spend your life with you if that's how you want it to be. Then it will be me who experiences the devastating pain of loss.' His voice thickened with emotion and he closed his eyes and rested his forehead against mine as we both felt his sorrow.

There were so many emotions filling me and causing my heart rate to increase: hope, excitement, desire, but overwhelmingly, love.

'Gabriel,' I said quietly, and he opened his eyes to look at me, 'I love you. You're everything to me and I want to be with you. Becoming a vampire isn't something I've ever seriously thought about. I wanted it when I was fourteen, but I never believed it was possible. Now that I know that it is possible, that you are a vampire, and that it would mean being with you forever… I'm so tempted, but it's too soon—' He placed a finger on my lips to halt my words.

'You should get used to the idea before you make that decision,' he said gently. 'There's no rush, and no pressure. And thank you for saying you love me.'

My face was already turned up to his, so he adjusted the position of his head in order to kiss me. It was soft at first, but then he kissed me with greater need, stroking his tongue into my mouth to tangle with mine. I twisted in my seat, holding my cup between my thighs so I didn't spill the remnants of the liquid at the bottom, to reach my hands up and touch my fingers to Gabriel's jaw. He made a soft growling noise and broke away from me.

My eyes shot open and I wondered what was wrong, but Gabriel merely took the cup from between my legs and placed it on the table alongside his own before returning his mouth to mine.

I sucked his bottom lip between my teeth and bit on it gently, dragging my teeth along it as I released it, then I ran my tongue along it to soothe any pain I'd caused and continued the kiss. In response, Gabriel grabbed me around the waist and hauled me onto him so that I was straddling his lap. I sat forward on his thighs and leaned my body into him to kiss my way along his jaw and down his throat with my hands pressed flat against his chest. He growled again and, as well as hearing it, I could feel it beneath my lips, my hands, and my chest. It seemed to incite us both further.

Gabriel lowered his hands from my waist to my bottom to pull me hard against his body, and then they crept under my top to caress my back. I tilted my head back as pleasure and need surged through me. With my neck exposed to him like that, Gabriel fastened his mouth to it and sparks danced along my skin, through the veins underneath, and desire suffused me. I closed my eyes and thrust my hands into his hair, but I gasped, then froze, as I felt the graze of his teeth.

Gabriel disengaged from me instantly and held my face between his palms. 'I'm not going to bite you, Jamie. I don't feel a compulsion to bite: not when I smell you, when I'm around you, when I see or smell blood, or when passion is coursing through me. I only feel love and longing, and there's a choice, both for you and for me. Nothing against your will, remember?'

'Gabriel, I'm sorry. I know and I understand. It was just that when I felt your teeth, I was jolted by the possibility that you *could* bite me, and then I thought of my dream the other night, and I just wasn't sure I was ready. I hope I didn't insult or offend you by overreacting. I'm so sorry.' I felt so ashamed of myself.

'You did not overreact, you did nothing wrong; there's no reason why I would be either insulted or offended. You haven't had a single negative reaction to anything I've said or done; you've understood and empathised beautifully. I couldn't have wanted for better.' He smiled self-consciously, but he knew I could feel his sincerity.

'I'm not averse to you biting me,' I explained. 'I like the idea of being closer to you in a way that otherwise I'd never feel. Even with the both of us being empaths, I know that would connect us in a more integral way.'

'It's okay, honestly. Please stop worrying.' He smiled and pulled me against his chest. I laid my head on his shoulder and buried my face in his neck.

I was absolutely terrified of hurting his feelings and worried he would think I was rejecting him, but I knew it was just me being oversensitive. I'd been stripped bare by the loss of my family so all my emotions were close to the surface and delicate, and this had made me hyperaware of anything even potentially hurtful. By virtue of the ability we shared, I didn't have to explain any of this to Gabriel, he had recognised it and felt it for himself.

I was so comfortable, our bodies fit together so perfectly, that I didn't want to move, and though Gabriel didn't seem to mind, the fact was that I was still straddling him.

'I should probably get off your lap,' I said wryly, raising my head.

'Why? You're not heavy and I'm not in any discomfort.'

'Perhaps it's not really judicious.'

Gabriel grinned at me and tilted his head to one side.

'You're still shy with me, even after my confession, even after telling you I love you? You said you love me, too.'

'I do.' *Didn't he believe me anymore?*

'I know you do, I can feel it,' he reassured me. 'I just expected that to make you feel more comfortable with me.'

'You think I'm not comfortable with you? I'm worried something might go wrong, but I'm completely comfortable with you.'

'What are you worried will go wrong?'

'I don't know, something with us. I don't have a good relationship history; I rushed into my last one and that was disastrous. Everything between you and me is so intense and it's happening really quickly. I can feel you more strongly than I've ever felt anyone else, that's how I know for certain with you this is real, and I know it's right, but that doesn't stop me from agonising that I'm going to hurt you in some way. I hurt Hayden.' I was regretful about that.

'No, you saved yourself. You were unhappy, you were being smothered, and Hayden was trying to control you. The worse that got, the more miserable you would have become and you would have rebelled against him more which would have made him try even harder to control you. That spiral would have continued until he got really angry with you and possibly turned violent. You need to stop blaming yourself.' He kissed my eyelids. 'I don't have a good history with relationships, either, but, like you, I knew they were wrong and that this isn't.'

'You always know what to say to make my heart sing.' I blushed.

'It's nothing but the truth.' He smiled sweetly.

I leaned forward and placed a kiss on Gabriel's lips, and he held me there for a long moment.

'I was thinking,' I began, and my breath caught in my throat as Gabriel ran his hands up my thighs, under the hem of my jumper, to caress my sides. The skin there was so sensitive, I had to bite my lip to stop from screaming out loud in reaction to the extreme sensation.

'What were you thinking?' Gabriel asked, mischief dancing in his eyes at both my internal and external responses, and giving me a wicked grin.

'I want to make sure Aaron's okay. I thought about dropping in on him at the salon today.'

'I think that sounds like a considerate thing to do. After we go there, why don't you come to my house? You spend so much time here that I thought maybe a change of scenery might be nice. We could sit and talk, or discuss books, or watch a film whilst cuddled-up on the couch.'

'I'd love that.' I smiled to myself at the image.

He'd been in my house and he'd known where I lived for a while, but it felt as though he had so many more insights into me than I did into him. Seeing him in his own personal environment, furnished to his taste and amongst his own belongings, would reveal how he operated when in his comfort zone, when he could fully relax. I doubted he'd be any different, but I wanted to see him in his space nonetheless.

'Okay.' He rubbed my thighs. 'Let's go.'

I got off him and carried our cups and my bowl into the kitchen and dumped them in the sink.

'I've just got to get a few things from upstairs first. Come on, I'll show you around.' It had occurred to me that he hadn't seen the whole of the house. I held my hand out to him and he placed his in it and clasped it tightly, intertwining our fingers.

'I looked around down here whilst you were getting dressed. I had a good look through the photos on the wall and your books and films.'

'Those are just a few of the books in the house, as I'm sure you can imagine.' I led him upstairs and started at the far end. 'This was Carmel's room,' I said, indicating that he should walk through the open door.

The walls were still painted peach and her old bed was still there, but she had taken most of her other furniture with her to her new house.

'She doesn't mind that Mum and I brought in bookcases for the overflow of books and films that we couldn't fit anywhere else. She has stayed overnight a few times when she's visited and been too tired, or had too much to drink, to drive home.'

Gabriel looked at the titles of some of the books, noting that most of them were classics that I'd read for my Bachelor's degree.

'Do you have something against classical literature?' He raised an eyebrow at me.

'It doesn't impress me and it rarely holds my interest. I can tolerate Jane Austen, but I can't bear most of the rest.' I shuddered at the thought. 'In my opinion, literature that is old and outdated does not automatically make it good. It's like saying that contemporary writers need not bother writing anything because it will never compare to something written in a totally different era, when society was far-removed from what it is now, and is completely alien to most of us.'

'Well, you write better than all of them, anyway.'

'How do you know?'

'I just know. No doubt your work will be in your bedroom.'

That gave me an idea for a present for Gabriel's birthday, which was just a few days away.

'My undergraduate and postgraduate dissertations are, but my creative work is stored on my computer and a memory stick. This is my mother's bedroom,' I said, showing him into the next room, which had lilac walls apart from a block of dark purple at the head of the bed.

There were framed photographs of Carmel and me as babies, children, and adults on her bedside table, the chest of drawers across the room, as well as mounted on the walls. My mum is so proud of her girls.

Gabriel couldn't resist the urge to look at them.

'Do you mind?' he turned and asked.

'Not at all.' I went and sat on Mum's bed whilst he studied each photograph in turn. I looked around the room, picturing my mother choosing her clothes, or doing her hair in the mirror whilst looking at me in the reflection as I stood a little way behind her as we conversed.

'This is upsetting you,' Gabriel observed, coming over and sitting next to me.

'No more than usual. I come in here sometimes expecting her to be in here, too.' I shrugged. 'I wanted you to see this to give you a better idea of my mum because she's so important to me. She made me the person I am.'

'She did a wonderful job.'

'Thank you,' I said sincerely.

'So, are you taking me to your bedroom next?' That devilish quirk returned to his mouth.

I laughed and got to my feet, took his hand, and started walking backwards.

'Bathroom,' I indicated without taking my eyes from his. He didn't even glance at it. 'My bedroom,' I said, pushing the unclosed door open wider with my backside.

My room was delicate pink in colour and it glowed with the sunshine pouring in through the window. I saw Gabriel hesitate momentarily as he noticed the three full floor-to-ceiling bookcases, plus extra shelving crammed into every space which wasn't occupied by necessary bedroom furniture. I had my own small library. Gabriel was unsurprised so he only gave them a cursory glance before returning his attention to me.

My bed wasn't far behind me where I'd stopped a little way through the doorway, but Gabriel continued moving forward until we were body-to-body, and he walked me backwards until I could feel my mattress pressing against the backs of my knees. Circling his arms through mine and around my ribcage, he used his bodyweight to lower me onto the bed. I grabbed hold of his shoulders as I fell backwards, both for support and to keep him near me, as he positioned himself on top of me. Our chests were pressed together and our hearts were beating the same rhythm as we just stared into one another's eyes. I saw his pupils dilate and I knew mine must have done the same because we were feeling the exact same thing: we craved one another.

We stayed like that for a few seconds, both breathing slightly unsteadily, before Gabriel got up and tugged me up after him.

'Come on,' he said. 'Get what you need and let's visit Aaron.'

I found the little velvet bag I'd taken with me last night and transferred my purse to the bag I regularly used which held a condensed version of my everyday life. It had everything I'd need if I got unexpectedly stranded somewhere, from things like tampons and miniature versions of toiletries, to a pad and pen so I could write when I wanted, and even a book.

I rummaged through it, checking I had everything, and caught the amused expression on Gabriel's face in my peripheral vision when he saw what was inside.

'Yes, I *am* that much of a girl,' I admitted wryly.

Gabriel held his hands up as if in defeat, still smiling. 'It's part of what makes you who you are.'

Whilst I'd been searching for everything, he'd found my hardbound copy of my Master's thesis on one of my bookshelves, had flipped to the 'Abstract' and left it lying open there on my bed.

'What do you think?' I gestured to the book. 'Worth a read?'

'Naturally; everything you write is worth reading.'

I realised something then. 'You already knew the subject of my dissertation before you asked me about it, didn't you? If you were outside the room when I had my exam, you must have heard every word I said.'

'Yes, I already knew what you'd written about. I heard you discussing your thesis, but I'd already read the answer from you. I asked you because I wanted you to tell me yourself. I wanted to talk about it,' he explained. 'May I borrow it so I can read it?'

'Of course.' I was rather honoured that he wanted to read it, then I realised that he may actually be quite critical of it. I knew he had more than one degree, but not to what level he had studied. I hadn't asked before when I thought he was an ordinary human. 'One question, though. Your degrees: are they graduate or postgraduate?'

'I have a Bachelor of Science with Honours, a Master of Science and a PhD in psychology, and a Bachelor of Arts with Honours and a Master of Arts in literature,' he informed me.

'Damn, you're already a Doctor; you beat me to it.' I felt a little defeated. I didn't like feeling that I may have inferior knowledge. 'But you said you hadn't studied extensively. You don't consider that extensive?'

'Well, I'm one hundred years older than you for one thing, and it was over a century ago when I got my PhD; I was still mortal. I could have achieved many more degrees and doctorates in the time since, don't you think?'

'Possibly, but it's still an impressive accomplishment. And it's one hundred and one, by the way.'

'I beg your pardon?' he asked, momentarily confused.

'You're going to be celebrating your one hundred and twenty-ninth birthday in a few days and I turned twenty-eight in January.'

'Are you calling me old?' He faked hurt and indignation.

'If the shoe fits,' I remarked, trying to suppress a smile.

'Thanks,' he said humorously.

'I just thought I'd bring you back down to my level, *Dr. Gabriel*.'

He came and stood toe-to-toe with me and I was forced to tilt my head back to look up into his face.

'And how is the weather down there?'

'Warm: it's closer to Hell.' He laughed. 'Doesn't it feel like there's a certain discordance between us: age, experience, education, height?' I frowned.

Gabriel grabbed my shoulders and glowered at me. He was upset. 'Don't ever think that, Jamie. I don't believe myself to be in any way superior to you. I'm older than you, that's immutable and I can't help that, so, naturally, I've had the time to do more. But you're mature and wise for your age, you're extremely intelligent and an immeasurably gifted writer. I've seen what you imagine, what you dream, I know what you think, I feel what you feel, and as far as I'm concerned, there are no disparities between us. Well, except that you are short, but I like that because you fit perfectly against my body. Like this,' he pulled me into his arms to emphasise his point.

'That's reassuring.' I looked up at him. 'I was starting to feel somewhat ingenuous compared to you. I'm actually relieved to know that you don't think, or feel, that way. I would be mortified if you did.'

'Not even remotely.' His eyes penetrated mine, showing me everything I could feel inside him: all the pure, unconditional love.

I put my arms around him, snuggled my head against his chest, and I closed my eyes as I heard the steady, vital, thumping of his heart. I turned my face into it and kissed it.

'It's yours,' he said, and I looked back up at him. 'My heart. All of me. I've always been yours.'

'I have always been yours, too. I always will be.'

Eight

Gabriel, Meet Aaron

Gabriel insisted on driving me to Carmel's salon, so I sat next to him looking at his profile as he manoeuvred through the traffic.

'You're staring at me,' he stated, the corner of his mouth curving up.

'You're pretty; I like looking at you.' I smiled sweetly at him and saw him smile wider. 'Not only are you beautiful inside and out, you're intelligent, educated, well-mannered, loving, caring, compassionate, psychic, and a vampire.'

'Does that sound like your idea of the perfect man?'

'Frankly, yes.'

'Good, then maybe I can keep you.'

Something I'd neglected to ask occurred to me. 'I didn't ask back in my bedroom, Gabriel, but as a Doctor of Psychology, what area did you specialise in?'

'I focused on emotional disorders, particularly depression, which can often be traced back to bereavement or loss. It could be the death of a loved one, the breakdown of a relationship, or the failure of a lifelong dream.'

'Have you ever practiced?'

'No, it's all theoretical, but I understand emotions better than most. As do you,' he said, tilting his head towards me.

'I do. So, theoretically, you would be in a better position to help me than some counsellor, considering everyone seems to think I need to see one.'

'Technically, yes, but I've got an emotional attachment to you.'

'That's what makes me believe you would be the best person for it, should I need help.'

'You're right. I love you so I'll make sure you're okay. In all honesty, Jamie, you don't need help. I know what all your friends think, but they're wrong,' he said fervently. 'You're beginning to overcome the shock of what happened; you're still very upset about it, as you should be, but from what I've seen, you are coping wonderfully. You're making plans for your future, you're moving forward. You may start feeling worse and everything might feel like too much, but if that were to happen, you've got me to help you. Does that reassure you?'

'Very much. Thank you, Gabriel. I don't know what you see in me, or why you love me.'

'I love everything about you and I see the same things in you that you see in me: your love, your compassion, your intelligence, your imagination, your beauty, and I don't mean that just physically: beauty comes from within. But I like looking at you as much as you like looking at me.' He grinned.

'You're a smooth-talker, do you know that?' I asked fondly.

'As I said before, it's nothing but the truth.'

'I believe you; I can feel it. I love everything about you, too.'

'I know; I can feel it.' After a pause he said, 'So, why did Aaron call you this morning?'

'He'd received the paperwork for the transfer of Carmel's share of their business to him. It came to me by default and my solicitor wanted Aaron to buy it from me, but I wouldn't hear of it. I just signed it over.'

'It seems harsh, but your solicitor was probably just trying to look out for you and make sure you weren't doing something you'd regret.'

'I know. I just didn't want the money. I've made enough from Mum and Carmel's deaths,' I said with distaste, 'and it just seemed heartless to profit from something that shouldn't ever have belonged to me. Carmel would agree with that.'

'It's okay; you don't have to defend yourself to me. I support your decision.' He smiled.

A few minutes later, we pulled into the small, private parking area behind the salon. It was full apart from one gap: Carmel's reserved parking space.

'Park in there,' I advised. 'Aaron won't mind as it's me, but he'd kill anyone else who tried to leave their car there.'

I felt nervous as I got out of the car and my hands were trembling as I reached for the handle to the door of the salon. Gabriel grabbed the handle, and the concern he felt for me creased his features.

'This is the first time I've been here since…'

In response, he took hold of my hand and interlaced our fingers, holding on tight, and waited for me to go through the entryway.

I recognised the young woman at the reception desk. Her name was Melissa and she'd been there many times when I had come for appointments with Carmel. She gasped as she looked up and saw me, then her eyes slid to Gabriel and they opened wide with admiration.

'Jamie, oh my God, I haven't seen you for weeks. I'm so sorry about Carmel and your mum.' Her expression was sympathetic, and she was trying to be solicitous of my feelings, but she was bubbling inside with her attraction to Gabriel. 'How are you holding up?'

'It's difficult, really difficult, but I'm doing the best I can. Thankfully, I've got good support.' I squeezed Gabriel's hand tighter.

'So I can see,' she remarked enviously, hoping I wouldn't hear. 'I can't even imagine what it must be like for you. Are you here for treatments?' She looked between Gabriel and me.

'Actually, I was hoping to speak with Aaron. Is he here?'

'Sure, I'll just get him.' Melissa stepped out from behind her desk and her eyes lingered on Gabriel for a long moment before she left us.

We had drawn the attention of the rest of the staff who were working in the large room where hair was being styled and nails were being done. Or rather, Gabriel had. Every female, and a few of the males, were staring at him with either unsuppressed longing or unadulterated lust. Even those who knew me suddenly hated me.

I stood on my tiptoes, placing my hand on Gabriel's chest for stability, in order to speak to him under my breath. 'It seems I'm not the only one who thinks you're pretty to look at.' I half-smiled, feeling compunctious of the unnecessary stab of jealousy I experienced. Apart from a cursory glance at Melissa when she spoke to me, I knew his eyes had never left me since we'd walked in here.

'I don't care about them, or what they think,' he said, knowing what I knew about how they were feeling.

Using the arm that was holding my hand, Gabriel pulled me against him with our hands still entwined and held me with my arm behind my back. With his free hand, he gently touched his fingers to my cheek as he lowered his head and kissed me breathless. It was a gesture that told everyone in no uncertain terms, 'I'm hers and she's mine,' and I revelled in it.

Gabriel withdrew his mouth from mine, but my eyes were still closed and my hand was still resting on his chest as Aaron approached us.

'Jamie,' he said, giving me a hug, and I returned it with only one arm because Gabriel hadn't let go of the hand he was holding. 'I wasn't expecting to see you this soon.' He looked from me to Gabriel and then at our conjoined hands.

'No, I know, Aaron. It was sort of spur of the moment. I was just worried, after speaking to you earlier, that you weren't as okay as you professed to be.'

'What makes you think that?' He narrowed his eyes, slightly suspicious of Gabriel and me.

'It was a feeling I had,' I responded vaguely, and felt Gabriel move in even closer to me as a protective gesture.

'Come into the staff lounge, we can talk there.'

Gabriel and I followed Aaron past all the hair stylists, who paused from working on their clients to stare after Gabriel once more, and into the private area for employees. It was painted in a terracotta colour to give the room a Mediterranean atmosphere and it was a tranquil space away from the noise of the main business area. The only other quiet places were the treatment rooms. I had often come in here with Carmel for a chat after my facials and before her next clients. She always left time to sit with me and, as my complete opposite, drink her herbal tea.

Aaron, long used to my habits, automatically poured me a cup of coffee, then turned to Gabriel. 'Can I get you anything?'

'Oh, I'm sorry, Aaron, how remiss of me. This is Gabriel,' I said and sat down on one of the orange sofas.

'Thank you, Aaron, but no, I don't need anything,' Gabriel replied smoothly and politely, relinquishing my hand but sitting next to me so closely the length of our thighs were pressed together.

Aaron came over and handed me a mug before sitting in a chair opposite me, holding a cup of his own.

'We've parked in Carmel's space, I hope you don't mind. She always told me to park in yours if you weren't using it,' I babbled, not knowing how to begin now that I was there. 'How are you coping, Aaron, really?'

'Honestly? I feel like a zombie much of the time,' he said solemnly. 'I'm going through the usual routine but not feeling very much of anything. I'm not seeing clients at the moment unless it's unavoidable. I'm mostly here for supervision.

'I had to hire someone new to deal with the clients that Carmel or I would normally treat, but I make sure she treats in my room not Carmel's. I go in there sometimes and just sit there and cry.'

I moved to get up and comfort him, but he waved me to sit back down at the same time Gabriel grasped my arm to restrain me. I turned, in shock, to look at Gabriel and he shook his head.

'Please tell me you don't just sit at home all the time on your own,' I said, facing Aaron once more. I knew that was hypocritical because that's mostly what I had done before Gabriel entered my life, but I had always been introverted; Aaron was a very social person. 'Are you seeing your family and friends?'

'I stayed with my parents for a week or so because they were worried about me, and they drop in a lot to check on me. My sisters have been great; they've tried to distract me with their kids and their stories. I've been out with my brothers-in-law and some friends a few times, but it's hard to be enthusiastic about it. I just need time to… get used to it, I suppose. Learn to live with the pain.'

'That's all either of us can do,' I empathised.

'I'm sorry, Jamie, I don't mean to be inconsiderate; I know I'm lucky to have a family to support me. You lost everyone.' His expression as he looked at me was strange and I couldn't quite decipher what he was feeling.

I forced a tight smile. 'The pain has been unbearable. But I have Gabriel now,' I explained, placing my hand on Gabriel's thigh. 'He lets me cry on his shoulder.' Gabriel covered my hand with his to keep it there.

Aaron raised his eyebrows, but didn't comment. Gabriel had remained quiet, seemingly impassive, leaving me to question Aaron and assuage my trepidation, but I could tell he had been reading Aaron during our encounter and he was disquieted.

'Jamie, there's something I want you to have,' Aaron announced. 'The funeral director gave it to me and I've been carrying it with me every moment since then. It's Carmel's.'

He reached into his pocket and pulled out Carmel's engagement ring: a white gold band with a single princess-cut diamond. He held it out to me.

I felt Gabriel stiffen and I knew he was preparing himself to comfort me if I got upset.

'Aaron, thank you so much, but I couldn't possibly accept it. You should keep it; you gave it to Carmel.'

'What am I going to do with it?' he asked sadly. 'Who else would I give it to?'

'You don't have to give it to anyone. You could keep it in your pocket, or under your pillow, or on a chain.'

He shook his head. 'Carmel always said this was a "fabulous ring."' I smiled at the recollection, as did he. 'It's meant to be worn and who do you think she would want to have it? Certainly not me. She'd want to see *you*, her twin, wearing it.'

I took it from him and held it between my fingers without putting it on. It was too big for my ring finger because Carmel is taller and has bigger hands than me, but I knew it fit my middle finger because I'd tried it on before, when Carmel had first shown it to me.

'Put it on,' Aaron insisted in a gentle tone.

I slid it onto my finger on my right hand. It was a little loose, but not so much that it would fall off, just enough that it wasn't constricting or difficult to get past my knuckle. I saw the look in Aaron's eyes, which was both happy and sad at the same time.

'If you change your mind, if at any time you want this back, it's yours. I won't hesitate to give it back and I won't ask for a reason, okay?'

Aaron nodded and I sensed him getting restless sitting there with me.

'We'll go now,' I said to dispel his discomfort. 'I'm sure you'll be needed out there again soon.' I jerked my head in the direction of the salon to indicate what I meant.

The three of us stood up and I crossed the distance between us to give Aaron a hug. He held me tightly for a long moment.

'I meant it when I told you to call me if you need to talk.' I rubbed his back.

'I will.' He let me go and shook Gabriel's hand. 'It was nice to meet you, Gabriel.'

'Likewise,' Gabriel responded with a smile, ever courteous. 'We'll see ourselves out.'

Just as I got to the door to exit the lounge, Aaron called out to me.

'Jamie, why did you survive, do you think?'

I shrugged. 'I can only assume the killer thought I'd either been fatally wounded or I'd soon bleed to death. What was more likely was that he was disturbed. I was unconscious by that point.'

He said nothing more so Gabriel and I left, both of us knowing that wasn't what Aaron had meant. What he really wanted to know was why I didn't die and Carmel survive.

We were back in Gabriel's car, heading towards his house, but I was too despondent to speak or notice where we were. I knew Gabriel would drive me home again later, so I would pay attention then to get my bearings.

'Jamie, I'm sorry,' he said eventually.

I looked at him for a moment before speaking. 'It's okay, Gabriel. I knew it bothered him that I lived and Carmel didn't, but this was the first time I got the feeling from him that he thought it should have been me who died.'

'You know the five stages of grief: denial, anger, bargaining, depression and acceptance?' I nodded. 'Well, from what Aaron was thinking and feeling, he's experiencing some lingering denial and a lot of anger. Unfortunately, his anger is directed at you for living rather than at the man who shot you all, and that's not good. He's especially angry because you're with me: he's jealous that you have me when he lost Carmel. He knows he shouldn't be feeling that way, he's trying to be reasonable, but I think you need to be careful around him.' Gabriel's mouth set in a tight line and I sensed his distress.

I looked at my hands, at Carmel's ring, and I felt a tremor of fear.

'I'm hoping it won't come to this, but should he become more unbalanced and he tries to attack you, do you know any self-defence?'

'The basics: go for the eyes, the shins, the solar plexus, and the groin.'

'Or punch your knuckles into his windpipe,' he added grimly. 'This is really important, Jamie: does he have a key to your house?'

'No. Wait, yes. Gabriel, he's got Carmel's keys so he's got her house key,' I said tremulously.

Gabriel swore under his breath. 'Okay, stay with me tonight and we'll arrange for a locksmith to go to your house tomorrow and change the locks.' I was starting to feel panic rising in me. 'It's just a precaution. I want you to be safe and feel safe.'

'I know, I appreciate it, but I'm starting to feel like a helpless female and I hate it.'

'Don't feel like that.' He flicked his gaze to me quickly before returning his eyes to the road. 'You're far from helpless, and you're just taking preventative measures to ensure you are secure in your own home.' He turned a corner and slowed the car into a driveway. 'We're here.'

I looked up and saw a house which had to be at least twice the size of my mother's, in a neighbourhood which exuded luxury and elegance. It wasn't unexpected since I knew he had money, but it was surprising considering he lived alone.

'That's a very beautiful-looking house, and very big for one person,' I commented, smirking a little but trying to keep it hidden.

'Wait until you see inside,' he teased, then got out of the car, came around to my side, and helped me alight.

Gabriel placed his hand on the small of my back and led me up the pathway and into his house. The entrance was painted in warm, subdued colours: the tasteful neutral tones of cream and coffee. He guided me through to the lounge where the colour-scheme continued and, glancing at the furniture, I noticed it bared a remarkable resemblance to the way I had dreamed it all.

'I'll call a locksmith then I'll give you a tour of the house. You're dying to peek in all the drawers and cupboards, aren't you?' He grinned at me knowingly.

I nodded guiltily. There had never been anything hidden in my little family; we rummage around in one another's possessions borrowing anything from jewellery, to scarves, to bags. Mum and Carmel even borrow each other's clothes and shoes since they are the same size, but because I'm so much smaller than them, they can't fit in mine and theirs are too big for me.

'I won't, though, not if you don't want me to.'

'You can look wherever you want. You're just as free to explore my home as I was yours. I have nothing out of the ordinary, no weapons, nothing illegal or kinky.' He raised his eyebrows. 'I have nothing to hide from you.'

Gabriel disappeared for a moment and left me looking around the large, light and airy room. The cream sofas were as I'd dreamt them, and there was a glass-topped coffee table not too far away from them, all sitting on a pale mocha carpet.

On the far wall was a huge gilt-framed mirror which reflected light back into the room during daylight hours, but the sky was rather dull today.

Gabriel returned to the lounge with a telephone directory in his hands. He sat on one of the couches and absently pulled me down next to him. Whilst he searched for a decent locksmith in the book and dialled the number, I couldn't resist the urge to play with his hair.

At first, I twirled a single silken lock from just above his ear between my fingers and noticed the beginnings of a smile on Gabriel's face. He didn't look at me, merely leaned forward with his elbows resting on his thighs. Then, as he began speaking, I thrust my whole hand into his thick brown waves. He tilted his head into my hand and turned to face me. I paid no attention to the conversation he was having because I was falling into the depth of his gaze which reflected everything he felt: every little touch was as meaningful to him as it was to me.

I had never really been the touchy-feely type in a relationship, which had surprised me because I had always believed I would be. When I was with Hayden, I would never spontaneously reach out and touch him for no apparent reason; I never felt the need to; instead it was always him who would hold my hand even if we were just sitting watching a film. I would flinch away in discomfort, or, I'm ashamed to admit, distaste, if he tried to play with my hair. With Gabriel, I felt as though I couldn't keep my hands off him and I *needed* to be in constant physical contact with him, though it was only occasionally that I felt the sanguinity to initiate the touch.

'I love it when you touch me, but you're shy about doing so,' he observed after he hung up, his blue-green eyes blazing with warmth.

'I keep thinking you won't want me to touch you, like I might be irritating you when you just want me to leave you alone,' I confessed.

'After everything I've professed to you, you really think I wouldn't want you to touch me?' He raised his eyebrows. 'When I've waited for you my whole life? I can't get enough of you.'

Gabriel pulled me against him and into his lap, and my hand dropped from his hair to his shoulder, so I trailed my fingers along his collarbone, loving the feel of the smooth skin and the shape created by the bones underneath.

Our faces were so close that when I looked up, I saw that he was watching me, noting the way I bit my lip to hide a smile of satisfaction as his heart picked up speed, and knowing how much I loved and wanted him. I could feel all of that inside him, too, pulsing as strong and as deep as the love he felt.

I felt as though I shouldn't push things too far; I loved him, I wanted him, and I was staying with him in his house tonight, but he promised me nothing would happen before I was ready. The speed of meeting and falling in love with him was wonderful, and amazing, but I didn't want to rush everything. I wanted to fully know him before we made love.

'Your eyes never stop fascinating me,' he said softly, surprising me. 'They look different in every light. In artificial light, they can look dark green or light hazel, except up close when, in any light, it's possible to see that they're actually a mixture of greens and blues with a gold starburst around the pupil. From a certain angle, in natural light, they look the colour of a rain cloud; opaque, yet as reflective as polished silver. But they're always beautiful and they always express what you're feeling.'

'So do yours.'

'But only you can see inside me. I shield everything from everyone else, not that I've met anyone other than you anywhere near percipient enough to read me.'

'Not among us mere humans,' I mused.

He shook his head. 'Not at all.'

'I'm special.'

'Yes, you are,' he said significantly. He laced his fingers through mine and brought our hands up to kiss my fingers. 'By the way, the locksmith will be at yours at eight-thirty tomorrow morning, so you can set your mind at ease that Aaron won't be able to just walk into your house. Now, are you ready for the tour?'

'Ooh, definitely,' I replied, almost squealing with delight.

Gabriel grinned, wrapped his arms around my ribs, and pulled me up with him as he stood. That did make me squeal. When I was steady on my feet, Gabriel took my hand and led me out of the room.

Nine
To Bite

The whole house was painted in neutral colours, much like the living room. The kitchen was quite obviously little-used apart from to house and heat blood, but Gabriel also drank liquids; he still needed water for hydration, but admitted he enjoyed coffee, wine, and the occasional liqueur. Other than those two rooms, the rest of the ground floor was consumed by a massive library.

Gabriel watched my face as, walking backwards, he guided me into the room, turning a light on as he went. He was trying to contain a smile as I gasped and my eyes grew wide.

'And I thought I owned a lot of books.' I flicked my gaze at him, but only for a second before it was drawn back to all the spines facing me.

Each wall was lined from floor to ceiling with shelves holding volumes upon volumes of books, and there were ladders on casters on either side of the room. Running in smaller rectangles inside the room were tall, free-standing bookcases. Plus, there was still space for more.

There wasn't a window; not only would that have used space that had been filled with books, but the sunlight would have bleached the colour from the covers, some of which looked very old and extremely valuable. I looked up to see that the ceiling was covered in spotlights so that there was adequate illumination to read comfortably without causing eye strain, but it was not harshly bright.

I stood just inside the doorway, not daring to go any farther, instead just absorbing it all. In the centre of the room, I could see a large mahogany desk with a computer sitting on top, writing paraphernalia, and another stack of books. At a right-angle to the desk was another large, comfy-looking cream sofa, identical to the two in the living room, and a faux fur rug on the floor in front of it with a low table in the middle.

'Do you like it?' Gabriel intoned quietly.

I twisted to look at him and he was smiling. 'You already know,' I answered, tapping my heart, and then I paused to discern what he was feeling. 'But, like me, you like to hear it spoken as well.' His face softened even more. 'I love it in here, Gabriel. I think I could happily spend the rest of my life in this room. With you.'

He came and stood behind me, wrapping his arms around my waist and bending his head to breathe directly into my ear, making me shiver, 'If that's what you want.' He kissed my temple as he raised his head.

I turned in the circle of his arms so I could look him in the eye. 'Apart from having my family back, all I want is you.'

I saw his pupils flare and I felt the love he radiated towards me. I returned the feeling just as vehemently.

'So,' I asked, 'how are all these books organised?'

'I've got all the non-fiction, the psychology books and the literary criticism on the higher shelves; the ones even I need the ladders for; and all the ones within easy reach are fiction.'

'So you haven't hidden the good stuff where I can't get to it?' I teased.

'No.' He laughed, and I loved the feeling of the vibration of his chest against mine. 'I wouldn't torture you.'

I grinned back at him and turned around once again to face into the room. It had always been a dream of mine to have a library in my house, but that was when I imagined a career in literature: writing, teaching, or both; when I imagined buying my own house, choosing my own furniture, and fitting all the bookshelves and bookcases into their own room as Gabriel had. Now, I couldn't imagine selling my mother's house, nor could I imagine refurnishing or renovating any of the rooms.

Sensing where my thoughts had taken me, Gabriel pulled me out of the library.

'We'll come back in here later,' he promised. 'I want to show you the upstairs.'

The same thick, light mocha-coloured carpet from the living room continued in the hallway and all throughout the upper storey of the house. There were only two doors at the top of the stairs, and Gabriel guided me into the nearest one first.

'I have completely remodelled up here,' he said. 'This is the spare bedroom.'

It was a generously sized room with its own bathroom, not shower room, and a built-in closet for clothes. It was mostly furnished with a double bed, a small table to one side of it, a low chest of drawers, and a dressing table complete with a plush cushioned stool and a large triple-faced mirror on top.

'Pretty,' I commented. 'You've got good taste. Or a good interior designer,' I added.

'It's all me. Come on, one room left.' I looked at him archly. 'Don't get any ideas, Jamie; I won't let you corrupt me.' He grinned wickedly at me.

I laughed and followed him to the door. He stood to one side and left me to open it and go in alone. I turned the handle, pushed the door inwards, and stepped into a huge suite. It looked as though this had originally been a four-bedroom house; the guest bedroom and bathroom had been combined and the master suite was created from the other three bedrooms.

I inhaled sharply as I took in the beautiful wrought iron base of the bed and matching bedside tables with glass tops. There were two large wrought iron bookcases against one wall with a chest of drawers in between them made of a light-coloured wood.

The cream and coffee theme continued in here, but the wall behind Gabriel's bed was papered in cappuccino-coloured wallpaper with off-white swirling rune patterns on it, some of which were accented with deep espresso brown.

There was an archway cut into the adjacent wall and I walked through it into a large, luxury, black-tiled bathroom. It had a long, dark grey marble counter containing two sinks with lots of space for toothbrushes, toothpaste and all the other bathing and beauty necessities, and a mirror running the length of the wall above it. There was a free-standing, roll-top, Cinderella slipper bath in one corner and a separate shower cubicle in the other with the toilet in between. I couldn't picture Gabriel in that bath; it was too feminine; it was the kind of bath a woman would want in her personal bathroom.

I walked back out to find Gabriel sitting on one side of the bed waiting for me.

'Gabriel, your house is so beautiful. That word doesn't even begin to do it justice; it's a dream home, really.'

'Could you picture yourself living here?' he asked, narrowing his eyes and feeling slightly nervous.

Was he asking me if I wanted to live here with him?

'Sure, who wouldn't want to live here?' I prevaricated, avoiding giving a more involved response because of my feelings towards my mother's house. 'How long have you lived here?' I asked before he could press me further.

'Almost one hundred and four years, ever since I completed my doctorate. I renovated this house as soon as I bought it; I changed the upstairs to have this substantial master suite, which wasn't often done back then. I always kept the spare room even though I've never had guests to stay and I can't, and don't, have offspring, and of course the library was an essential. I could tell you approve of the décor.'

'I love the colour-scheme. It's warm and I feel like I'm in a huge latte.'

'That was my thinking when I devised it. I don't like cold colours and I wanted it to be neutral, elegant. I've updated the furniture as styles have changed and it has all been recently repainted to keep it looking clean and new.' He shrugged.

'I've got to ask you about that bath. It's not the sort of bath I imagine a man would usually choose.' Though I didn't actually ask a question, Gabriel knew what I meant.

One side of his mouth turned upwards. 'That's new. I had a relatively plain bathtub in there originally, but I changed it a couple of weeks after I encountered you at the university; around the time of your family's funeral.'

'Why did you change it?' I already knew the answer, but I needed him to confirm it.

'For you, Jamie.' Gabriel's voice was low and deep. 'I wanted this house to be somewhere that could be a home for both of us. I knew you'd love the library, the colour-scheme, and the feel of this house, but my bathroom seemed functional rather than beautiful and I knew it was the bath that was wrong. I pictured the most aesthetically beautiful bath I could think of and I bought it because it was the only one I could imagine you bathing in.'

'You've been picturing me naked?' It felt like my eyebrows rose into my hairline, and I tried desperately not to sound embarrassed. He ignored my question, just continued looking at me silently and steadily. 'You've been imagining me living here with you,' I said finally, not asking because he'd already told me that was the case. 'Gabriel, did you fall in love with me straight away?' My voice was shaky, breathy with nerves.

'From the instant I felt you,' he confirmed, exhaling. He got up, took my hand and pulled me over to sit on the bed next to him. 'I've been an empath all my life. I've always been able to feel people's emotions and their characters, but I always believed the person I would feel the strongest would be my soul mate, my one true love, the love of my existence, and all those other phrases that don't do what I feel for you justice.

'When I first felt you, it completely overcame me and I just knew that it was you, that you were that person for me. In amongst all your pain and sadness, didn't you feel the same when you met me? Didn't you feel me more strongly than you've ever felt anyone else?' he asked fervidly.

'Yes.'

'Exactly, but you were wary. Your dreams proved everything you felt was true. I know I've been rather intense ever since you met me, but I'm answering all your questions honestly, as I promised I would.'

'I know you are, and I want you to always be honest with me. I want you to know that I'm not worried about the intensity of this, of us. If I'm a bit hesitant, it's only because I was starting to believe that I'd never have this kind of relationship with anyone and, after Mum and Carmel died, I felt like I would never be happy again.' I smiled at him, but it was tinged with sadness.

Gabriel put one arm around me and hugged me to him. 'I wish I could bring them back for you, Jamie. Just keep remembering them, keep talking to them, and let me make you happy,' he said, looking into my eyes.

'I want you to,' I told him, and buried my face against the side of his throat where the skin was warm and the musky scent of him was strong. 'I want to make you happy, too.'

'You do. Being with you is the happiest I've ever been. I won't let you go now; it would kill me.' He was quiet for a moment and he stroked my hair whilst we both just let ourselves feel the love we had for one another. 'Let's go and get something to drink and maybe you can have a better look around the library. I know you'll want to investigate all the books eventually.' He grinned at me as I raised my head.

'You may even have some books that will help with my PhD,' I suggested as I stood up.

'Possibly,' he said, following suit, 'but if you've read everything in your university library on the subject, you may just find duplicate copies of some of those books. I've also got some old books, by today's standards, which may be worth mentioning, but you need to keep your research current.'

Gabriel and I went downstairs and back into the kitchen where Gabriel switched on the coffee maker. He opened his fridge to retrieve a bottle of milk and I noticed bags of blood on the shelves. As he closed the door, Gabriel saw what I'd been looking at.

'Does the sight of those bags unsettle you?' He felt the mixture of emotions inside me.

'No, I wouldn't say "unsettled." I just had a glimpse into your reality, but it isn't any different to me than you drinking any other liquid. That's all blood is when you think about it. There is something I wanted to ask you, though,' I said tentatively.

'What's that?'

'The blood you drink is screened by the blood service, but if you didn't get your blood that way and you drank from random people, they could have diseases or infections that you wouldn't know about. Can you be infected by them; by HIV, AIDS, or hepatitis, for example?'

'No, diseases like that don't affect us, even when we're mortal, unless we're very old.'

'Can you carry them in your system, though, and pass them to a human through sex or blood-sharing? That is if you can share your blood with a human without changing them.' I had been thinking about that since he mentioned biting me earlier.

'Yes, a vampire can share blood with a human without turning him or her if it's only a taste and the human hasn't been drained. And, no, we can't carry diseases. A vampire's immune system is so strong that it kills everything that tries to infect him or her. So, if a human drank the blood of, or had sex with, a vampire, mortal or immortal, the human couldn't be infected with a nasty disease or illness.' He knew why I was asking and it pleased him. 'Do you want to taste my blood?' he asked slowly. 'You know I want to taste yours.'

I could feel his lust, both sexual, and the desire for the intimacy and trust that came from the sharing of blood. My heart began to hammer with nerves, anticipation made my stomach clench, then the sensation travelled lower.

Gabriel could feel everything I was feeling and he knew I was going to consent without me having to say the actual words. He slowly came to stand in front of me, cupped his hands under my jaw to tilt my head up to his, and he bent his head and softly kissed me.

'I've never done this before,' he confessed breathlessly.

'Done what?' I asked, confused.

'Shared blood. I've drunk from friends, I've told you that. I *fed from* them, not *shared with* them. You're the only person who will ever taste my blood. I've been waiting for you to share this with,' he said ardently.

'Why?' I needed to know.

'I've always believed there's a distinction between feeding and sharing. I didn't want to give my blood to someone I didn't love, it would be giving that person too much of my self, and I didn't want to join myself to the wrong person in that way. I hope that makes sense to you.'

'It does,' I reassured him. 'And it means everything to me that I'm that person for you.' I pulled his head down to press my mouth to his.

Encouraged by my words and actions, Gabriel walked me backwards out of the kitchen and into the living room, kissing me the whole time. He held me tightly against him as he sat back onto one of the sofas, taking me with him so I was straddling him, and he deepened the kiss. I ran my tongue along the underside of his teeth and felt for the first time how sharp his fangs actually were and a shiver ran down my spine. Gabriel traced the movement with the tips of his fingers, causing me to shudder against him, and I felt his mouth grinning with pleasure beneath mine.

I was almost beyond coherent thought, but I was expecting Gabriel's mouth to move to the delicate skin of my throat. Instead, he held my head still, pulled my bottom lip between his teeth and nipped the smooth skin on the inside, ripping it slightly. He sucked on my lip more heavily to increase the blood flowing out of the wound, and he licked it away.

I loved the sensation of the blood being pulled from my body into his, of Gabriel's tongue caressing me as he tasted me whilst still kissing me at the same time. It was possible to forget, for a moment, every ounce of pain I'd experienced over the past few weeks and to only feel him, his love, and this.

When he couldn't get any more blood from the little tear he had made, he drew back slightly and languidly opened his eyes. I could see a ring of dark blue-green around his dilated pupils. I watched him as he took his own bottom lip between his teeth and bit into it, I looked at the smear of red and then back into his eyes. He didn't move, he simply watched and waited for me to react.

I leaned in and licked his blood from his lip, savouring the taste for a second before kissing him and sucking on the wound, as he had on mine, to draw more blood. I swallowed, feeling a deep sense of satisfaction knowing I was the first, the only, person to do this and know what he tasted like. He tasted the same as he smelled: warm, comforting, and just like Gabriel, and it felt like I was taking a part of his essential self into myself which would stay inside me permanently.

Sharing blood didn't increase our empathic, or his telepathic, abilities, but, because it was such an intimate act, it did enhance the sensation of being connected to one another that had always been there.

It wasn't long before the blood stopped flowing and Gabriel's lip began to heal, so I kissed him for a while longer before reluctantly pulling away.

'How was that?' I asked. 'Was it different?'

'Completely different, because I only tasted your blood to be close to you, not to drink from you. You tasting my blood made me feel closer still.'

'I felt that, too. It felt like we were joined and now we can't be separated.' That gave Gabriel a deep sense of belonging that I could read in his eyes as well as feel. 'You taste the way you smell, uniquely like you. It's so different from the taste of my own blood.'

'It didn't feel at all strange or unnatural to you.' He was making an observation rather than asking a question.

'No, I liked it. I like the taste of your blood.' I wasn't at all shy or embarrassed about it, and it didn't appear to worry Gabriel, either.

'I hope this doesn't alarm you, but I'm going to need to drink soon. I left the house in a hurry this morning to get to you, and I haven't had any all day. If you find it too disquieting to watch, you can go into the library and I'll join you after. Then, maybe we can get you some food if you're hungry.'

'Do you want my blood?' I reached up to move my hair away from my neck, but Gabriel reached out to stop me.

'Jamie, I love that you'd offer,' he said, squeezing my hand, 'and I know why. You are everything to me, but you're not a food-source. Please understand I mean that in the kindest way, not as a rejection. I love you for who you are; you sustain me mentally and emotionally and that's what matters, not me drinking your blood.'

I nodded, understanding. 'Come on, let's get you some blood,' I said as I dismounted from my perch on his thighs and pulled Gabriel up against me. I wrapped my arms around his waist and held on tightly, walking backwards so he would have to walk forwards with me still clinging on.

He grinned at me and played along with his arms around my shoulders, letting me guide him even though I didn't turn to look where I was going. Once inside the kitchen, I came to a halt in front of the refrigerator. He swung me around so I wouldn't be hit by the fridge door as he opened it, and removed a packet of blood. I looked at it for a long moment, slightly fascinated.

Gabriel gently removed himself from my arms to empty the blood into a mug and put it in the microwave to heat it to body temperature.

'I'm glad this doesn't appal you.' His tone was sober. 'I appreciate how far removed this is from what's normal for you.'

'But this is your reality, Gabriel. You've been drinking blood since you were born so this is normal for you, and I want to be included in that. I don't want to be sheltered from it because this could be my reality one day.' I saw the look in his eyes and could feel just how badly he wanted that.

'Only if you're sure you want it to be.' He was breathing faster and his voice was uneven.

'I know that I love you and I want to be with you for as long as possible. Forever.'

Was I saying that I wanted to be a vampire? The idea of being with Gabriel for all eternity was wonderful, but being a vampire? I'd only ever fantasised about them before, but if that's what it took to stay with Gabriel, to not get old and die…

If I didn't die, I'd never be with Mum and Carmel again.

'I understand your ambivalence, Jamie,' he empathised. 'If I turned you, you'd be with me forever, but more than a hundred years could pass and you'd still miss your family as much as you do now. If you remained human, you would be reunited with them in perhaps fifty years or so.'

'You sound as though you're not convinced I'd be happy with you,' I commented disconsolately. 'And I can feel that you're worried you'll lose me because you won't be enough for me.'

The microwave sounded so Gabriel retrieved his cup and set it on the surface next to me, then placed his hands either side of my body, forming a cage around me. I stole a quick glance at the warm red liquid before looking back up at him.

'I know that *I* will be happy with *you*, that you are more than enough for me, and I'll do everything I can to make you happy, but I can't replace your mother and your sister. I wouldn't even try to do that. Only you can decide if I'll be enough for you.'

'I'm sorry, Gabriel,' I said. 'This can't be easy for you, either. I'm adjusting to my new situation and, having always known my own mind in the past, I'm sure I'll know what's right for me once I've recovered from all the shock.' I smiled weakly at him and stroked one of his cheekbones. 'I know that you are enough for me.'

He closed his eyes for a moment, enjoying the contact and feeling the truth in my words, then he moved his arms to pick up his cup and took a drink of blood.

'I have an admission that will come as no surprise to you,' Gabriel said, taking my hand and leading me out of the kitchen and back into the sitting room. 'I don't actually have any food in the house. How do you feel about ordering in?'

'I know a place that makes good pizza. I'll give them a call.'

Whilst I dialled and placed my order, I watched Gabriel as he sat back in his seat and consumed his blood. It looked as though it could have been coffee in that cup as he drank unhurriedly, not gulping it down as though he were either starving, or in the throes of blood-lust. It was surreal, I had to admit that to myself, but I wasn't distressed by any of it.

Just as I was watching him, he was watching me, conscious of every nuance in my expression and every movement I made, assessing all my internal and external reactions.

'Does it taste nice?' I was strangely enthralled.

'*Your* blood tastes nice. Other than that,' he shrugged, 'blood is blood. I need it to survive.'

'But isn't drinking it supposed to be pleasurable? Or was that just something invented and glamorised by gothic writers?'

'Sure, drinking it from the vein is pleasurable: the feeling of the person's skin under one's mouth, hearing their heartbeat, seeing the rise and fall of their chest and feeling their struggle. That's how we were intended to live, but we have become more civilised. Drinking this way is much like consuming any other liquid.'

'So, drinking from a person is a sensual experience no matter who the donor is?' I was telling myself I wasn't feeling insecure, I was merely trying to better understand this aspect of him.

'No, it was sensual with you because I love you. When I drank from friends, it was pleasing because they trusted me. When I drank from the stranger to become immortal, it gave me a thrill purely because I felt powerful, indomitable.' He grimaced, ashamed of feeling that way knowing it resulted in taking a life.

My pizza arrived and I went to the door to collect it. Whilst I'd been gone, Gabriel had taken his empty cup to the kitchen and returned with two glasses of water.

'Is eating that pleasurable?' he countered after I'd taken a couple of bites.

'It tastes all right, but I don't get gratification from eating; it's just a necessary function. Food is fuel to me, nothing more.'

'And my blood?' he persisted.

'Your blood is the best thing I've ever tasted, but I don't need to drink it to live. Drinking it was sensuous and it connected us in an essential way. It didn't make your feelings any clearer to me because they're already as known to me as my own. I wasn't able to read your mind or anything, though I really wish I could,' I admitted wistfully. 'You know what's going on in my head as well as my heart and I envy you that ability. I have to wait until I sleep for the workings of your mind to become clear to me.'

'Maybe if you drank more of my blood you could connect to my mind. Maybe if I turned you, you'd have stronger ability. It's possible,' he mused.

That admittance was one more aspect of vampirism that drew me towards it.

I gave up on the pizza halfway through my third slice and drank down the whole glass of water Gabriel had provided before depositing the pizza box in the kitchen as I made my way, with Gabriel, back to explore the library.

Ten
Bed. Sleep

Inside the library, Gabriel sat on the sofa reading the copy of my Master's thesis he'd brought with him from my bedroom whilst I looked through the shelves. It would take me days to search through them all, so I just glanced quickly at the spines, only pulling out a few to read the covers, of those that had printed covers.

Gabriel hadn't exaggerated that day in the bookstore when he claimed he read most genres of fiction, if anything, he had understated how much he read. He had every type of book in this library, including works I doubted I would read even if I did live forever.

I found Gabriel's collection of vampire fiction, noticing the book he had advised me against as well as many that I owned myself. However, in amongst them was a novel I didn't recognise. I didn't recall seeing it in stores or online. It had been published only three years ago, but somehow it had gone completely unnoticed, except by Gabriel. I decided to read it since the description on the back cover indicated it was a romance, so I took it with me over to where Gabriel was sitting and snuggled in by his side.

'Hey, baby,' he said, looking up from my dissertation and putting his arm around me. 'I was getting lonely over here all by myself. What have you chosen?' I held the book up for his inspection and he grinned quickly before pouting. 'Am I not enough vampire for you?'

I slapped him lightly on the thigh with the book. 'Better than all the rest of them put together.'

'Even the sparkly one?' he teased.

'Especially the sparkly one,' I affirmed.

That pleased him so he returned his attention to my thesis and immersed himself in the world of erotic fiction written by, and for, women whilst I commenced reading yet another vampire novel.

Less than half a dozen chapters in, I put the book down. It was entertaining; competently written, but not outstandingly so; the characters were engaging and the storyline generic enough to appeal to lovers of the genre, but not challenging its boundaries in any discernable way. Ordinarily, I would have enjoyed reading it more than I had tonight, but since meeting Gabriel and discovering the truth about vampires, the fictional ones diminished considerably in my esteem by comparison.

'Don't you like it?' Gabriel asked, his mouth twitching because he knew why it wasn't holding my interest.

'You are most definitely, irrefutably, unequivocally, and without doubt, more than enough vampire for me.'

'I'm glad to hear that,' he said, self-satisfied but not arrogant. I looked away and traced the lettering of the title on the front cover of the book with my finger. 'I compare them all to you, you know,' he added and I looked up.

'Who?'

'Everyone. Every fictional female, every woman I've ever known or met, and none of them are anything compared to you.'

I hoped I'd never get used to Gabriel saying such impassioned and, admittedly, slushy and romantic things to me. He always made sure I knew how he felt about me and I hoped I let him know just as often, and as fervently, how much I loved him in return.

I covered my mouth as I felt myself about to yawn.

'Are you tired?' Gabriel asked as he traced the shadow underneath one of my eyes with his little finger.

'Mmm, it has been a stressful day. I am so grateful for your presence, your company, your support and, mostly, your love. I think I should stretch my shoulder, then go to bed.'

Gabriel closed the thesis and brought his hands up to my shoulders to give them a massage.

'How about you exercise your shoulder and then have a hot bath?' he suggested. His voice was tempered with concern as he said, 'You've been holding yourself rigid today and I can feel tension in your muscles.'

I made a barely audible sound of pleasure. 'That sounds good. And that feels amazing,' I said, referring to the massage. I got up and replaced the book I was reading amongst Gabriel's vampire collection, then moved to exit the library with Gabriel just a few steps behind me.

'I'll get you some towels,' he said as he opened the door for me and followed me out.

At the top of the stairs, he went into the spare bedroom ahead of me. The closet in there was so big because it was where all the linens were stored and Gabriel extracted two fluffy white towels for me. I'd already started to walk in the direction of the bathroom when I felt Gabriel's hand on my shoulder.

'Don't use that one.' I turned to look at him with a frown. 'Use the bathroom in my bedroom. I installed that bath for you; I want you to bathe in it.'

I nodded and retraced my steps. As I drew level with Gabriel, I reached out to take the towels from him, but he shook his head and motioned me out the door. I walked along the hallway, into Gabriel's bedroom, then went through the archway to the spacious bathroom.

Whilst I looked around, marvelling at how immaculately clean it was, Gabriel arranged the towels on the heated rail. I turned the tap until the water ran hot, then slotted the plug into place.

I picked up a bottle of bath foam. 'Can I use some of this?'

'You're welcome to everything in this house, Jamie.' He was a little pained that I'd even asked. 'We're together now, and you'll be spending a considerable amount of time here, so I want you to treat my home like your own.'

'I will now that you've given me permission,' I affirmed as I poured some of the foam into the running water. 'My mother taught me manners, too, and she would be mortified if I hadn't asked.' I smiled at him, and I felt the sting I'd caused dissipate in him. 'Would you help me with my shoulder exercises please, Gabriel?'

'Of course I will. What do you need me to do?'

Gabriel checked my posture and movements to ensure I fully isolated my shoulder muscles and didn't use my arm, and by lightly holding on to it, he provided more resistance to make my shoulder work harder. By the time I'd finished stretching, the bath was ready, so Gabriel left the room to give me some privacy.

I lay back in the bathtub and contemplated the likelihood of Aaron using Carmel's key to let himself into my house tonight. If he had considered it before, there was clearly a rational part of him that had prevented him from acting, but after the feelings he'd experienced in my presence today, even I, who had known him for years, couldn't predict what he'd do. Furthermore, should he go to my house, what would he do when he found that I wasn't there? He'd presume I was with Gabriel, which would increase his anger and frustration. Would my house be safe?

I heard Gabriel moving around in his bedroom; I hadn't realised he had come back. Overcome with modesty, I panicked that he was going to walk in here or that he would see me through the archway.

'How's the water?' He thoughtfully didn't dwell on my discomfort.

'Hot: I'm going a lovely shade of red which is just how I like it,' I answered happily and heard him chuckle. It then went quiet.

I tried to banish thoughts of Aaron setting fire to my house; or destroying everything inside; or tearing my books apart, ripping up all my notes, and demolishing my computer. I picked up a washcloth and a bottle of body wash and concentrated instead on the simple action of cleansing my skin to try to stop my mind from wandering.

I wasn't the type to sing in the bath or shower unless I'd got a radio playing; usually, my imagination would take over and I would invent characters, picture scenarios and add dialogue, or I'd have imaginary conversations with my favourite characters. On this occasion, however, I was trying not to think about the sleeping arrangements tonight. I assumed I would be sleeping in the guest bedroom.

I let out some of the water and used the showerhead to wash my hair, and then I used it to clean the bathtub after I'd got out and wrapped myself in the warm towels. I quickly brushed my teeth and applied face cream before padding out into the bedroom, ensuring the towel around my body was secure, when I spotted Gabriel reclining on his bed reading my thesis.

'Oh! I didn't think you were still in here.' I sounded nervous and I felt slightly self-conscious.

'I didn't mean to scare you,' he said, closing the book and standing up. 'I was just finishing your dissertation.'

'It's okay, you didn't scare me. What do you think?' I nodded towards my thesis.

'It's exceptionally insightful, well-researched, expertly argued; extremely well-done. It certainly enlightened me; I'm not particularly conversant with women's erotic literature.' He grinned.

'Of course not. I wouldn't imagine you'd have any interest in that specific genre. Thank you for your comments, though, your opinion means a great deal to me; as much as Mum and Carmel's.'

'That is an honour,' he said, standing directly in front of me. 'You look cute.'

I blushed and, feeling a little vulnerable, I moved my right hand up to cover my scarred shoulder, hiding it from Gabriel.

'It's okay,' he soothed, and gently removed my hand to look at the angry, still-red marks. He stroked his fingers over them.

'They're ugly,' I remarked. Inwardly I winced, not at Gabriel's touch on my scars, but at the reason those scars were there. 'Ugliness put them there and nothing will ever be the same.'

'The outward scars will fade, or you could see a cosmetic surgeon to find out what could be done to improve them if you wish, but the rest can't be changed. As difficult as it is to accept, you can only move forward.'

There had been moments during the past nine weeks; and they tended to just creep up on me when everything seemed to be okay, when I was feeling fairly neutral and I was just trying to get on with my life; when all I could feel was emptiness. I felt hollow, as though I used to be a person, but everything that made me who I was had gone and I was just a shell.

Those feelings assailed me now, but instead of feeling wholly empty, I felt a small amount of hope.

Once I'd stopped believing that I was dreaming, or hallucinating; once I'd ceased trying to find a way to make what had happened not happen, to undo it somehow; once I'd given in attempting to discover some method of bringing Mum and Carmel back; I focused all my energy on making some kind of future for myself. I threw myself into university research. I began writing what may be a story, what may be a novel, to work even harder for the career I was trying to carve for myself before I lost my family.

That sense of purpose, the need to fulfil my potential, was still present and I knew I would still feel a great sense of achievement once I had my doctorate. I even knew I would still feel Mum and Carmel's pride in me. However, I also recognised that my sense of joy would be diminished for not having them there to share it with me. Whilst I am complete within myself, it's nice to have someone to talk to, to share things with, for my own sanity.

I felt less empty knowing that I would always have Gabriel to share important moments with. It didn't take the ache out of not having my family, but it was reassuring that I'd have someone to tell who I loved, who loved me, and who genuinely cared, unlike the majority of my friends.

I looked up to find Gabriel watching me, his expression thoughtful, and emotionally exuding his love for me.

'Of course I care, Jamie,' he said, reading my thoughts as well as my feelings. He put a hand under my chin and kissed my forehead, right on the location of my third eye, which naturally caused me to close my eyes, and the contact gave me a sense of contentment.

I gave him a kiss and smiled. 'I know; I can feel it.' I looked around the room then. 'Where are my clothes?'

'I'm washing them now with some of my own. They'll be dry by morning, but I've got one of my t-shirts for you to wear in the meantime. He picked up a plain black shirt from the edge of the bed and handed it to me, then reached for the towels that had been underneath it. 'I'll go and have a shower and leave you to change.'

'Thanks, Gabriel.' I watched him disappear through the archway, heard the spray of the water, then crossed the room to the full-length mirror.

I mostly avoided looking at the scars on my shoulder, but I checked them in my reflection to see how they looked tonight when Gabriel saw them for the first time. No matter how much they faded, they would always be ugly to me.

I moved away from the mirror back towards the bed where I removed the towel I was wearing and slipped Gabriel's t-shirt over my head. It was only a size small, but it was still loose on me and fell to almost halfway down my thighs. It smelled of detergent and fabric softener, but I detected the faint scent of Gabriel from where he'd handled it.

I unwound the towel from my head and gently rubbed my hair to dry it as much as possible before detangling it with the hairbrush from my bag. I sat at the end of the bed to wait for Gabriel.

About fifteen minutes after he went to shower, he walked back into the bedroom. His hair was ruffled and still damp where he'd roughly tried to dry it, and a towel was loosely wrapped around his hips. He saw me sitting prudently with my knees together on his bed and he gave me an appraising look.

'There's something both cute and incredibly sexy about the sight of you in my t-shirt,' he confided, his voice deep and seductive.

'You're standing there in nothing but a towel and you're telling me I look sexy?' I rejoined, shaking my head.

He was slim and toned, he had muscle definition but he wasn't muscular. His skin was perfect: milky white, flawless, but with faint blue veins visible beneath the surface. His body was almost hairless apart from a line of fine hair that led downwards from his bellybutton and disappeared beneath the towel.

'Would you like me to remove it, or would you prefer to do that yourself?' he asked, one side of his mouth tilting up mischievously.

I stood up, walked over to him, and stroked my hands down his chest and stomach to hook my fingers inside the towel as though I were about to rip it off him. It was his turn to inhale sharply at my touch. I smiled to myself and, keeping my hands where they were, I kissed the side of his neck and felt his heart rate increase. Then I let go and stepped back, but continued to hold his gaze.

He reluctantly looked away and moved to the chest of drawers to get a pair of boxer shorts. They were black and stretchy, and he stepped into them and pulled them on underneath his towel. I picked my towels up and moved to take them into the bathroom to hang them up. As I was about to pass him, Gabriel whipped his towel off and held it out to me.

'Would you mind?'

'Not at all,' I replied automatically, taking it from his outstretched hand. I could feel his eyes on me as I walked away.

He was still in the same place, waiting for me when I re-entered the bedroom. His shorts clung to his body, to the shape of his lean thighs, and my pulse quickened at the sight of him.

'Am I still pretty to look at?' he asked, noting my heartbeat and searching my thoughts. 'Even without most of my clothes?'

'You're beautiful, Gabriel; nothing short of perfect. And I've already told you I don't mean purely aesthetically,' I said as I walked to stand directly in front of him.

'That's how I feel about you,' he replied softly. He pushed my damp hair behind my ears and tilted my face up to his. 'Would you prefer to sleep in the guest room tonight, or would you like to stay in here with me?' Gabriel's impeccable manners surfaced, giving me the choice of an option neither of us wanted, or felt the need for, but he asked out of innate politeness.

My heart was beating so fast with anticipation that I could feel a pulsing sensation at my temples, but I didn't even have to think about it, I knew what my answer was going to be. 'I want to spend the night with you, Gabriel.'

He kissed me briefly before moving away from me to turn off all the lights in the room and pull back the duvet. He returned to me and put one arm around my back whilst with the other, he swept my legs out from underneath me, carried me the short distance to the bed and placed me just off-centre in it before climbing in beside me. I rolled onto my right side so that I was facing him and he scooted closer, facing me, so that we were only a centimetre or so apart.

I reached my left hand up to his face and, with my fingers, I followed the line of his eyebrow around to his prominent, high cheekbone, down his slim, straight nose to his soft mouth. I felt him smile beneath my fingertips before he kissed them. I moved my hand into his hair and shuffled forward so that our bodies were touching and I wouldn't have so far to reach.

'I love you,' I said.

Abruptly, Gabriel snaked his arm around me, pulled me hard against him and pressed his mouth to mine. It felt like this was what I had been waiting for and I entwined my legs with his and kissed him back, opening my mouth to him and holding on as tightly as I could, never wanting to let go. As our tongues met, Gabriel rolled me onto my back so he was lying mostly on top of me, his right arm curved underneath my body, his hand between my shoulder blades. I clung to his shoulders with both hands as he trailed his other hand down the side of my face, my throat, down the length of my torso over the t-shirt to my thigh where, upon contact with my skin, he trailed his hand back up underneath the shirt.

My heart was thudding hard and fast against my ribs, against Gabriel, and I could feel his, every bit as strong, beating in synch with mine.

My skin was so sensitive to his touch that it felt like the lick of fire as he moved his hand up my thigh, over my bottom, around my side to glide over my stomach, my ribs and stroke my breast. I moaned softly into his mouth and arched against him as I trailed my fingers down his back, stopping when I reached the dimples just above the waistband of his shorts, making him moan into my mouth in return.

I felt Gabriel remove his hand from beneath my t-shirt and pull the hem back down to cover me. He ended the kiss, raised his head slightly, and stared down at me. His eyes were shining and he gently touched his fingers to my lips.

'I love you, too,' he said, and rolled onto his back, taking me with him so that my head was cushioned by his shoulder.

'Is something wrong?' I was breathless and disappointed.

'No, Jamie, no, of course not,' he reassured me. 'I just didn't want you to feel that because you're in bed with me that I expect us to make love. This about us being together.'

I snuggled into him, burying my face into his throat, closing my eyes and inhaling the warm scent of him which had quickly become so familiar to me and affected me so deeply; every time I smelled him, my heart lurched with recognition and longing for him. I absently stroked his taut stomach and he made a sound of pleasure at my touch. I smiled, and softly kissed the skin beneath my lips.

'I love your scent,' I confided. 'I think I'm addicted to it.' I tried to imagine how strong it would be if I were a vampire and all my senses were enhanced. The thought made my heart flutter.

Gabriel chuckled. 'So it's not me you want, it's my smell.'

'No, it's definitely you. All of you. I don't want to live without you, however long I live.' I looked up at him.

'I don't ever want to be without you.' He emphasised his statement by squeezing me tighter.

I felt a sense of peace and contentment so deep that I fell asleep in Gabriel's arms, my body curved around his with his shoulder as a pillow. It wasn't long before I began to dream.

In this dream, we were lying on top of his bed, sunlight was pouring in through the window and shining on Gabriel who was resting on his elbow above me. His skin was pure white, almost looking like it was glowing, the red tones in his hair were gleaming to almost a copper shade, and his eyes, as he looked at me, were dark and full of love.

He lowered his head to place a soft, lingering kiss on my unresisting lips whilst his hand swept my hair away from my neck and he raised my head slightly. He feathered kisses downward from my lips until he reached the skin he had just exposed, giving it one more kiss before sinking his teeth in.

I felt a sharp pain as Gabriel's fangs pierced my skin and my body stiffened, but he was holding me so tenderly that the shock quickly passed and I closed my eyes because all I could concentrate on was the divine sensation of Gabriel drinking deeply, the draw of his mouth against my skin, and my blood being pulled out of me. It felt so wondrous that he could have drained every last drop of my blood and I wouldn't have even tried to stop him.

My heart rate was slowing down and becoming fainter, like it was barely beating at all, and it was getting difficult to concentrate because I felt so light-headed. I opened my eyes, but I could not focus. I was still aware of Gabriel and what was happening, so some part of me realised I was dying. It was at that moment that he ceased drinking and pulled his mouth away from my throat. He shifted his body to cradle my head in his lap, bit into his wrist, and brought it to my mouth.

'Jamie, drink,' he commanded. I was dazed and weak and it took a moment to register what Gabriel was asking of me. He pressed his wrist against me insistently and I felt the warm wetness of his blood on my lips. 'Please,' he entreated.

I opened my lips and latched on, feeling Gabriel's blood filling my mouth, hot as it trickled down my throat. It seemed to instantly revive me; my limbs felt less heavy and I was able to move my arms to hold Gabriel's wrist in place. I locked eyes with him as I began to suck his blood from his wound. I watched his pupils dilate with the same feeling of pleasure I'd experienced when he was drinking from me, then his eyes fluttered shut, he bit down on his bottom lip and tipped his head back in rapture.

All my senses were alert, magnified, and I felt as though I was taking part of Gabriel, part of his essence, into me.

His blood tasted so good, and I felt so irrevocably joined to him, that I didn't want it to end, but, eventually, Gabriel disengaged his wrist and said with satisfaction, 'That should be enough.'

He stroked my hair whilst a fire burned inside me and I twitched in spasms of pain, but in minutes it was over. I opened my eyes, sat up on the bed, and knew I was a vampire.

I woke up before anything more could happen. I had merely opened my eyes, and my heart was beating a little quicker than normal, but Gabriel already knew I was awake.

He touched my arm and sleepily asked me, 'Are you okay, Jamie?'

I tipped my chin up. 'I'm sorry, Gabriel. Did I wake you? I didn't think I moved. I was just dreaming.'

'I know, I saw it. I woke up because you did.' He disentangled his limbs from mine to roll us onto our sides to face one another more comfortably, but, unable to be with me and not touching me, he wrapped one of his arms around my back, keeping our torsos in contact. I placed my hand on his shoulder.

'You saw my dream?' I frowned. 'Does that happen often?'

'I don't always see the whole of your dreams,' he explained, sounding more awake, 'but every night you dream, I catch parts of them. My telepathy is weird that way: I can connect to your subconscious mind and see your dreams.' He shrugged and my body sensuously moved with his.

'Don't you have dreams?' I didn't want his ability to see my dreams to deprive him of his own.

'Since meeting you, I've had dreams similar to the one you were just having. I dream of us being together.' He smiled shyly. 'For my whole life before I met you, my dreams taunted me, giving me glimpses of my life with my soul mate, but they were agonising because I hadn't found you and I could never see your face clearly. But as soon as I felt you and

I saw your face, I knew I had been dreaming of you. I could suddenly remember every dream I'd had and the face in my dreams came into focus. It was you.'

'Really?' He nodded and I smiled. 'That's beautiful. I love you so much, Gabriel.'

'I love you, too, Jamie.'

'The dream I just had, do you think it was prophetic or do you think it was just a result of everything you've told me about yourself?'

'You always have a choice. If you don't choose to become a vampire, the dream won't come true because I won't force this life on you, Jamie.'

'I was thinking along the lines of my subconscious telling me that I've made the decision already, that it's secretly what I want, but consciously, I haven't fully admitted it to myself. That isn't true, though, Gabriel. I don't want you to think that I've been trying to find reasons to stay mortal,' I clarified to reassure him in case he doubted my commitment to our relationship. 'It's just that, you said it yourself, it's a big decision and maybe it's still too soon to act on any decision I do make.' I was a little distraught that I wasn't explaining myself clearly. 'I'm still not fully awake; I have no idea if I'm expressing what I mean particularly well. I don't mean anything untoward, I promise.'

'Stop worrying.' He stroked my back and smiled to reassure me. 'We've had this conversation already and it's not a problem.'

'I know, I know, please forgive my insecurity. I promise I'm not usually like this and I'm sure it's only temporary.' I waved my hand in the air expressively, knowing he could see it, before replacing it on his warm shoulder.

'I don't think you're insecure. I think I would question you if, after knowing me less than a week, and so soon after losing your family, you'd decided you wanted to give up your mortality.'

I didn't respond. What he said made perfect sense and I agreed with him, so, really, there was nothing to say, not that I needed to with Gabriel.

'Try to go back to sleep,' he soothed. 'You were only out for a couple of hours.'

I'd guessed from the darkness in the room that it was still the middle of the night, but I wasn't sure I'd be able to get back to sleep after that dream. It hadn't frightened me or perturbed me; it had exhilarated me. The sensation of my life-force flowing into Gabriel and then him giving his back to me was powerful, even in my dream. It was thrilling and all-encompassing, and it made me forget everything else existed outside him and me. I felt really fidgety.

'Gabriel, I can't stop thinking about that dream,' I confessed after a few minutes. 'Is that what it would be like to be changed?'

'I haven't done it myself, nor have I witnessed it, but from what I've learned about the process, it is much like that for humans,' he explained. 'The transformation was less intense for me when I became immortal because I was already a vampire.

'Naturally, everything you and I felt, both in the dream and in reality, would be unique to us since no two people's experiences, perceptions, or emotions are the same because no two people are the same. Your imagination has drawn on the details from our blood-sharing earlier and amplified it as we both drank larger quantities of blood in your dream. That is probably what would actually happen if I were to transform you: the feelings from earlier would be the same, but much more intense.'

'And you're as enchanted about feeling that as I am.' I reached out and touched his heart before stroking his face. I wasn't accusing him; I was pleased by it in unfamiliar ways.

'More, because that would mean the rest of my dreams had come true.' He stretched forwards and planted a soft kiss on my lips. 'Let's talk about this more tomorrow. Are you able to sleep on your left shoulder? It wouldn't cause you pain or jeopardise its healing, would it?'

'I can sleep on it. I've often woken up recently to find I've rolled onto that side during the night and it hasn't been painful. Why?'

'Roll over,' he instructed mysteriously.

I did as he requested and he pulled me back against him, curving our bodies together, placing one arm under my neck and wrapping the other around me to hold me to him. He slipped his hand under my arm and around my ribs to support my upper body so my injured shoulder wasn't bearing all my weight.

Feeling secure and warmed, not only by Gabriel's body heat, but by his consideration and his love, I drifted off to sleep thinking the words 'I love you' over and over, knowing he could hear me, knowing he could feel it.

Eleven
Unwelcome

The following morning, Gabriel and I were back at my house just after eight and I was relieved to find that the door was still locked and inside nothing had been disturbed or damaged, so it was clear that Aaron had not been here. Gabriel and I conducted a thorough room-to-room check to make sure of that, and to ascertain that he wasn't here hiding somewhere. I was grateful that in just a short amount of time I could be certain that Aaron wouldn't be able to get into my house unless I invited him in.

At precisely eight-thirty, the locksmith arrived.

'Mr. Castell?' he queried, verifying he had the correct address, to which Gabriel nodded. 'I understand you need a new lock for your front door.'

'That's correct. It is just the front door isn't it, Jamie?' Gabriel swung towards me worriedly, eyebrows drawn together.

'Yes, just the front door,' I confirmed. 'Would you like a cup of tea or coffee?' I asked the locksmith as he set to work.

'Tea would be lovely, er…'

'Jamie,' I supplied. 'Do you take milk and sugar?'

'Milk and two sugars, thanks, Jamie.'

I wandered off to the kitchen to fill the kettle and wait for it to boil. Gabriel wasn't far behind me.

'Are you completely sure Aaron only has a front door key? Is there any way he could have a key to the back door as well?

It wouldn't be any trouble to have that lock changed also.' He spoke quietly and the concern he was feeling for me was evident in his eyes.

'There is absolutely no way he could have a key to the back door.' I whispered so I knew for certain we wouldn't be overheard. 'We only ever had two of those, one of which is on my set of keys and the other is on Mum's, which I have hidden in her underwear drawer.'

'Jamie, for my peace of mind would you go and check that those keys are still there in the exact place you left them, and that all your mother's keys are present? Please?' he added, tilting my face up to his. 'I'll take over with the tea.'

'If it makes you feel better, Gabriel, then of course I will.' Gabriel's disquiet was beginning to make me feel slightly anxious.

I bounded up the stairs, went straight into Mum's bedroom and opened the drawer. There wasn't a sock, a pair of underwear, or a bra out of place from how I'd smoothed them after hiding the keys in a rolled-up pair of thick, woolly socks at the back. I found them, unravelled them to find the keys still there, and checked every one. The back door key was still there, sandwiched between my mother's front door key and the key to her car, where it had been forever. I put them back and returned to Gabriel, glad I had no reason to worry.

'Everything was where it should be and there was no sign those keys had been touched.' Gabriel didn't look, or feel, convinced. 'I love you for worrying, Gabriel, but, really, in order to find those keys, Aaron would have had to ransack the whole house and it was clear when we came in that nothing had been moved. I hid the keys in a specific pair of socks at the back of Mum's drawer; they were still there, and none of the rest of the items in there looked as though they had been rummaged through or tipped out and put back.

'Besides, there was no way he could have got in, searched the house, tidied it, got a spare key cut and returned the original last night. Most places would have closed by the time he eventually found the key, anyway. And yesterday was the first time I've ever felt him have any hostility towards me.'

'You're right.' Gabriel exhaled. 'I know you are. His scent isn't even in this house. You are my only priority, Jamie, and I can't bear the possibility, no matter how remote, that you may be in danger from him coming into your home whilst you're here alone.'

He pulled me to him and held me tightly against his body. I could sense that he didn't like the idea of us not being together for long periods of time, particularly now he knew I felt the same way about him as he did about me, but he wasn't going to stifle me by not giving me time to myself.

'I know how to incapacitate an attacker, remember?'

'But could you actually go through with it and hurt somebody? Especially Aaron, considering Carmel's connection to him?'

'After my previous confrontation with an attacker, I'm fairly sure I wouldn't hold back no matter who that person was.'

'No, probably not,' he concurred.

Within an hour, the locksmith had completed his task. He wandered into the kitchen carrying his mug. 'It's all done, Jamie,' he said.

'That was fast,' I rejoined, smiling widely at him and taking the mug he proffered.

He laughed. 'I've been doing this job for over twenty-five years and I think I know every type of lock inside out. That makes it short work for me.' His eyes crinkled kindly as he smiled.

'I'm sure it does,' I replied. 'Thank you so much,' I said, handing over the fee he had agreed with Gabriel last night.

'Here are your new keys and my business card should you need my services again.' I took them from him and showed him out. 'If you don't mind my saying, he really loves you,' he whispered conspiratorially, tipping his head in Gabriel's direction.

'The feeling's mutual,' I whispered back with a grin.

Gabriel was still standing in the kitchen when I returned. He was leaning back against the counter, one ankle crossed over the other with his arms crossed over his chest, smiling at what he'd overheard at the front door.

I briefly inspected the two keys in my hand before coming to a stop in front of him.

'I want you to have this,' I said, handing him one of the keys and slipping the other into my pocket. He was momentarily taken aback, but he stood up straight and took the key I offered him. 'I want you to treat my home like your own and, should there be another incident like yesterday morning, you'll be able to let yourself in.'

'Am I your emergency person?' One side of his mouth twitched upwards and he twisted the new key on to the set with his others.

'Gabriel, you know you are my everything,' I said honestly and took his hand, kissed it, and held it against my heart.

Something flickered in his eyes as he stared into mine that I felt come from the depths of his soul; it was the actualisation of something he always wanted, but never thought he'd have. I felt exactly the same.

After a moment, he moved the hand I held to slip his fingers into the 'V' neckline of my jumper, down between my breasts, and he hooked his first two fingers around the middle of my bra and tugged me over to him. I stumbled forwards and he steadied me. He kissed me softly, then took hold of my shoulders and turned me around to pull my back against his chest. He wrapped his arms around my torso, walked us into the lounge, and urged me to sit down.

'Do you want to talk more about your dream last night?' Gabriel asked, seating himself next to me.

'Not about the dream itself, I understand where it came from, but what's your reaction to it?' I placed my hand on his thigh and he covered it with his own.

'As I mentioned, I've had many dreams like that since I met you. I've dreamt that I've turned you. I've dreamt of an endless life together. That's what I meant when I said all of my dreams would come true if you wanted to be turned.' Our gazes locked. 'I'm already so fortunate that you feel for me what I feel for you, I've dreamed of that and it has happened, but to have you and have your love forever is everything else I've ever wanted. You told me I am your everything; you're mine. You're everything I've ever wanted.'

I put my arms around him. 'Do you know how much I love you?'

He grinned, responding in kind, and said, 'Yes, it feels like it's as much as I love you.'

'So,' I said, pulling back a little and laying one hand on his sternum, 'maybe we should combine our lives a bit more. For two people who want to spend their lives together, we live in very separate spaces.' I sucked in a breath, suddenly nervous of what Gabriel might think about that. I knew how he felt, but not what he thought.

'Jamie, I'd move you into my house today, you know I would, but we both know you're not ready to let go of this one.' His tone was gentle, compassionate; just like the man himself.

'I wouldn't expect you to move in here, Gabriel,' I explained. 'I know it probably seems like a shrine to my mother to most people, so I realise you might not feel comfortable here.'

'I'm perfectly comfortable here. This house has your presence and your history stamped all over it because it's your family home. What if we move some of your things into my house and some of mine into yours? It's somewhere to start the combining process.'

'I'd like that.' I smiled. It was like easing gently into living together. Wherever we were, we could wake up with our own possessions nearby so both houses had more of a feeling of being 'ours,' rather than 'mine' or 'his.' 'Do you want to do that today, or do you have something else you want to do?'

'Whatever *you* want,' he replied indulgently, tucking my hair behind my ear.

'Will you help me sort out some clothes and things to take to your house? I'd like to do it today.'

It didn't take very long for Gabriel to transfer about half my wardrobe to his car, then he enjoyed himself immensely going through my lingerie. He flung items at me and I bundled them into a cotton tote bag. I'd just disappeared into the bathroom to find one of the new toothbrushes, of which Mum seemed to have an endless supply, in the cabinet when I heard my phone ringing back in the bedroom where I'd left it on charge.

'Would you answer that for me, please, Gabriel?' I called.

Half a minute later, I returned and heard Gabriel speaking in clipped tones to the person on the other end of the line.

'I don't see how that's any of your business, and if you had any regard at all for Jamie, you'd want her to be happy.' Gabriel heard me approaching and turned to face me. 'Hold on a moment,' he said into the phone before covering the mouthpiece to speak to me. 'It's Aaron,' he said, answering my expression and feeling of disquiet. 'Do you want me to deal with him? He's not stable,' he warned as I shook my head.

'Let me try to talk to him.' I took the phone from Gabriel and he watched me, his mouth set in a tight line, indicating the depth of his displeasure. 'Hello, Aaron. Is everything all right?'

'You're with Gabriel again!' he stated with a large measure of incredulity.

'Yes, I—'

'Why is he answering your phone?'

'It's on charge and I was out of the room so I asked Gabriel to answer it. Aaron, what's wrong? Did you call because you need someone to talk to?' I hoped he recognised the concern in my voice.

'I can't believe you've just forgotten about your mother and sister so quickly and moved on. Probably to the first man who'd have you,' he spat out.

'That's cruel! How could you accuse me of that? How dare you degrade me in that way?' I fumed. 'I haven't forgotten Mum or Carmel; I'll *never* forget them. Whilst you're grieving, you've got two parents and two sisters to comfort you. Why shouldn't I have Gabriel? And I didn't just throw myself at the first man who'd have me.'

I was looking at Gabriel who, with his heightened senses, had heard every word Aaron had said as perfectly as he'd heard my side of the conversation. He was struggling to control the anger that was raging inside of him.

'You're not the only one who's hurting, Aaron,' I reminded him. 'I'm devastated. I'll speak to you again when you finally remember that.' With that, I ended the call.

I drew in a deep breath in order to dissipate my own anger, and Gabriel took the telephone out of my hands and placed it back on the bedside table.

'I can't believe he just said that,' I uttered, unable to look Gabriel in the eye; instead I looked past him, not focusing on anything.

'Jamie, he's lost in his own pain and he's not thinking outside of that, which, as I mentioned before, makes him potentially dangerous.' My eyes slid towards him. 'We know he had hostile thoughts about you yesterday; today he has been verbally abusive. I don't want to alarm you, but I think it's going to escalate,' he opined grimly.

'You probably got a better read on him whilst you were speaking to him than I did, Gabriel. I didn't hear very much of your conversation, but what exactly did he say, and what was he really thinking and feeling?'

He gave me a pained look and I knew he didn't want to hurt me. 'He was being vulgar about our relationship and inside he was seething with jealousy that we've got each other. His feelings were much the same as they were yesterday, but discovering us together today has left him with utter distaste for me, which I hadn't detected before, but he is contemptuous of your behaviour. I hate having to say that, Jamie,' he added, pulling me to him.

'That's his problem,' I asserted, wrapping my arms around his waist. 'We've done nothing wrong.'

'Shh,' he said against my ear. 'Don't let him upset you, he's not worth it.'

'I know,' I answered softly.

He leaned back a little. 'Are you ready to go?' I nodded. 'Grab your phone, then.' He smiled. 'Can you feel just how much I like this?'

I nodded and grinned at him. 'I like it, too.' I slipped my phone into my pocket, then followed Gabriel downstairs with my bag of underwear over my shoulder. I picked our coats up from where I'd hung them earlier, handed Gabriel's to him and said, 'All ready.'

'Not quite.' Gabriel moved past me into the living room, picked up the photo on the mantelpiece that he had studied the night before last, the one from my graduation, and handed it to me. 'I want you to put family pictures up at my house, too.'

'Are you sure?' I watched Gabriel nod. 'But you don't even have any photos of your own family on display at your house.'

'That's because I've never been particularly close to my family, and I'm less so since I decided to live my life the way I want. When you speak about your mother and sister, and when I feel the love you have for them, I know I would have liked them.'

'They would have liked you, too. Maybe they do,' I thought suddenly. 'Wherever they are, maybe they can see me so they've been getting to know you.'

'I hope so.' Gabriel ushered me out the front door and locked it with his new key.

When he pulled into his driveway almost twenty minutes later, there was an expensive black saloon already parked and waiting for him. As Gabriel switched off the engine and opened his door to get out, a male and female who looked to be in their mid-thirties emerged from the other car.

'Mother. Father,' Gabriel acknowledged each of them tersely as he closed the door behind him.

I closely followed Gabriel out of his car, surreptitiously looking at his parents for family resemblance. Gabriel's soft features were quite feminine: he had large eyes, generously full lips, and high, sculpted cheekbones which he inherited from his mother. His hair colour and his small, straight nose echoed his father's, yet he was uniquely himself, not really looking like either one of them.

'Gabriel,' his mother said in cold tones, shooting a disapproving glance at me. 'Your father and I are here to persuade you to come home and visit your family. Your nieces and nephews have expressed a desire to meet you.'

'Well, clearly the family still knows where I live, so it wouldn't be too unreasonable for them to pay me a visit,' he responded emotionlessly. Inside, I could feel his displeasure at their intrusion and his lack of filial love for them.

Whilst this tense exchange took place, I leaned into the back of Gabriel's car to gather all my clothes up into one large pile which I just managed to tuck beneath my chin.

Gabriel looked at me grappling with my things and gave me an indulgent smile. 'I'll let you in, Jamie.' He opened the door to the house and marshalled me inside ahead of his parents. 'Go ahead and take everything up to the bedroom.'

I began to walk up the stairs as Gabriel took his parents through to the living room. I was certain, judging solely from the expressions on their faces when Gabriel told me to go up to his bedroom, that they had instantly disliked me. I decided from Gabriel's internal reaction to them to exclude everything they felt.

Once I was in the bedroom, I placed everything on the bed and walked over to the drawers and cupboards to see if there was any space for my things. As I suspected, there wasn't. Gabriel had masses of clothes. Just looking at all the shirts, jumpers, jeans and trousers, not to mention the underwear, made me smile to myself. Maybe I could get into the habit of wearing one of his shirts with a belt around my waist, or snuggling into one of his jumpers on a cold day.

I couldn't hear any voices coming from downstairs, but, as vampires, their hearing was so sensitive that they could speak in whispers in different rooms and they'd still be able to hear one another perfectly, so I wasn't all that surprised. I decided, however, to stall before going back downstairs, so I delved into my bag to find the new toothbrush I'd brought with me.

I walked through the archway, unwrapping the brush from its packaging as I went, and placed it next to Gabriel's in the holder between the two sinks. I made a mental note to go shopping for my regular toiletries to leave in there, too.

It was then that I heard raised voices coming from below. A male voice I didn't recognise, so I knew it was Gabriel's father, said my name, but the rest of his comment was unintelligible to me. I felt rather awkward, as though I were hiding up here, but, equally, it wasn't my place to get involved in the conversation between Gabriel and his parents even though my presence in Gabriel's life was the subject of their argument.

As there wasn't currently any space for my clothes in the master bedroom, I moved them into the guest bedroom where there was space in the linen closet. The only thing left was the framed photograph Gabriel had insisted I bring to keep here. I carried it back through to Gabriel's bedroom and stood it on the nightstand by what had been my side of the bed last night. I'd have two nice things to wake up to when I slept here from now on: my family photograph, and Gabriel.

Concluding that I couldn't stay up here indefinitely, I descended the stairs and made my way to the living room. Gabriel had considerately closed the door to prevent his parents' hurtful comments from reaching me, but standing outside the door, I could hear Gabriel's mother's voice clearly.

'Honestly, Gabriel, wasn't it enough for you to hurt and shame us by refusing to marry Marta and disappearing for years? Then you chose immortality and squandered your chance to have children, destroying our hopes for you entirely, and now you're having a liaison with a human. You're moving her in here!' she spat out contemptuously.

'How I choose to live, and with whom, is my decision not yours, Mother.' He said the word 'mother' with complete derision. 'The life you wanted for me was yours; it wasn't what I wanted. You never cared about my happiness, just about your precious bloodline!'

At that, I politely tapped on the door and entered the room to find them all standing glaring at one another. Gabriel instantly came over to me.

'Jamie, I'm so sorry about this,' he breathed. His face reflected the anguish he was feeling.

I reached out and touched his cheek. 'It's okay, Gabriel; it's not your fault. I think maybe it would be wise if I left for the time being; my presence is incensing your parents.'

'I'm sorry they've spoilt our afternoon and made you feel uncomfortable. I'll call you when I've sorted this out,' he promised, taking my hands in his and kissing them.

'Jamie,' his mother called. 'May I speak with you for a moment?'

'Of course, Mrs. Castell,' I replied civilly, and stepped further into the room. Gabriel stood warily beside me with one hand on the small of my back for support.

Her gaze swept over me and assessed my clothes and demeanour, and I wondered if, like their son, either she or Gabriel's father had any psychic ability. I hoped not.

'Gabriel has informed us you are studying for a PhD. What do you plan to do with it once it is complete?' she asked dispassionately.

'I like academia,' I began. 'I hope to remain within it as a university lecturer and, as a specialist in my area, I'm sure I'll write articles and books on my subject. I also hope to publish some fiction someday.'

I refused to fidget or break eye contact with this woman; I refused to do anything which could be interpreted as a sign of submission.

'Are you from a family of academics?' his father enquired.

'No,' I answered succinctly.

'What is your family background?' his mother continued.

'I don't wish to talk about my family,' I replied, endeavouring to end the conversation.

'Are you ashamed of them?' she asked with a disparaging sneer.

'Not even remotely.' She would have relished it if I was, it would have been more ammunition against me.

'Mother,' Gabriel warned.

'Then what is it?' his father persisted.

'I don't have any family anymore,' I informed them, trying not to sound bitter. 'My mother and twin sister were killed nine weeks ago.'

There wasn't a flicker of emotion on either of their faces.

'And your father?' Gabriel's mother wasn't giving up.

'He left my mother right after my sister and I were born. He has never been in contact, I have never met him, and I have no desire to.' Gabriel's mother was about to speak again, but I overrode her. 'Gabriel, I'll call for a taxi to take me home now.'

'No, you won't,' he replied, removing his whole set of keys from his pocket and placing them in my hand. 'Take my car, it's safer.'

'I can't take your car. What if I damage it?'

'As long as *you* don't get hurt, it doesn't matter; it's only a car.' He bent to whisper into my ear. 'I promise I'll resolve all this so you can drive back later and help me move some of my clothes.' He smiled reassuringly at me.

I smiled back and, like the gentleman he was, he walked me out to his car. He pulled me against him and kissed me before holding the car door open for me.

'Good luck in there,' I said sympathetically before closing the door. He waited until I'd driven away before returning inside.

Back at home, I parked Gabriel's car behind mine and, when I walked past it, I noticed several dents in the door and bodywork along the driver's side, as though my car had been repeatedly kicked. Then, as I got to the front of the car, I saw that the windscreen had been smashed. It was still intact in its frame, but there was a huge snowflake pattern spreading out from the middle. I was grateful that there was no glass to clean up.

I didn't need my next door neighbour's confirmation to know that Aaron was responsible for the vandalism. She had called the police to report what she had seen and, when I went into my house, I found a note left by the officers who had been called out telling me to contact them.

'Your bloody fiancé, Carmel,' I cursed out loud in the hope that she could somehow hear me. 'He used to be so nice.'

Twelve

Lingerie

When I called the police station to speak to the officers who had left the note, my call was immediately forwarded to Detective Inspector Jim Fordham. DI Fordham had investigated what happened to my mother, sister and me. He had felt sorry for me and had kindly checked on me with fatherly concern several times after the case had been closed and he had been alarmed when he'd happened to hear my name mentioned when the officers returned after inspecting my car.

I explained the situation, my concerns about Aaron after his strangeness when I saw him at the salon, and his irrational reaction on the phone earlier. I even explained that I'd changed the lock on my front door because I realised he was in possession of Carmel's key.

'Are you sure you don't want to press charges about your car, Jamie?' DI Fordham asked.

'It's an old car and it's unlikely it would have made it through its next MOT.' It had barely made it through its last. 'It's not worth the cost of the repairs. Do you think you could talk to Aaron for me, though, Detective Fordham? I'd really appreciate it; he might take notice of a warning from you.'

'Of course I will, Jamie. If he continues to give you trouble after that, don't hesitate to call me.'

'Thank you, Detective Fordham.'

If Aaron didn't respect me, or Gabriel, or our relationship, maybe the police would scare him.

It was difficult to take my mind off what had happened to my car. I was angry that it had been destroyed like that and frustrated with the knowledge that even if I pressed charges against Aaron for the damage done, it was unlikely that he would receive significant punishment; at worst he would probably get a fine. I knew I wouldn't be able to concentrate enough to write, I'd lose focus with a film, and I'd lose patience with fiction, so I opened the most anodyne of my new textbooks and began to read and make notes.

By the time Gabriel called, a little over an hour later, I had made reasonable progress with the book and I had regained my equanimity.

'How did it go after I left?' I asked with trepidation.

'I received the same tired argument from them that they have been throwing at me since I was eighteen,' he said with a trace of amusement. 'They tell me that I'm a disappointment to them and to my whole family, and that I don't respect them as I should, all in an attempt to make me feel guilty for not letting them dictate my life for me back then. I don't know why they still try that.'

I sensed that wasn't everything, that there was something he wasn't saying.

'I thought you said your relationship with them was better now.'

'It is; we have next to no contact for at least a decade, then they'll try to "appeal" to me out of some feeling of familial obligation.' He laughed humourlessly. 'Good old Lillian and Mordecai. What was making you so angry earlier? I was distracted and could only sense something about your car. I'm sorry I couldn't call.' He both sounded, and felt, remorseful. I recounted the afternoon's events to him. 'At least the police are aware that he's a nuisance, Jamie, and DI Fordham sounds as though he's prepared to act if this continues. I'll come over and inspect your car; I want to see it for myself.'

'But I've got your car. I'll come and get you.'

'No, stay at home. I'm a fast runner.' I could feel him grinning. 'I'll be with you soon.'

I had no idea how fast he meant by 'fast,' or exactly how soon he'd be here, so I moved one of the armchairs closer to the window and sat, with my books, continuing to read and looking up every couple of minutes to see if Gabriel was near. It was less than ten minutes after he called that I saw him approach the driveway.

I stood in the open doorway as he slowed to a stop in front of me, not even slightly out of breath, and there was no sign that he'd even broken a sweat.

I flung myself into his arms and pressed my mouth against his.

'I missed you,' I said as I drew back a little, and I grinned at him. I hadn't realised just how quickly I'd become accustomed to him being there until I'd had to leave him this afternoon.

'I missed you, too.' He smiled broadly, not letting go of me. 'But the welcome more than made up for it.'

'You probably got here faster by running than you do when you drive,' I marvelled.

'Except for yesterday morning.' I frowned and he explained, 'Ordinarily, I drive a bit closer to the speed limit, but I must have driven at motor sport speeds yesterday to get to you because I got here in about five minutes.'

'I'm very grateful, Gabriel, but please be careful.'

'I'm always careful,' he affirmed as he stroked my face from my cheekbone down to my chin.

I could feel all the love he was feeling for me. I always missed that when we were apart because, unlike him, I needed contact with a person to feel what they felt: I needed to hear their voice, or be in relatively close proximity to them, for their energy to affect me.

'So, tell me what happened with your parents this afternoon.'

'Later,' he promised. 'Let me look at your car first and then we'll go inside where it's warm.'

After a few minutes looking all around and underneath the car, he ushered me inside, closing the door behind him.

'He snapped your exhaust. He must have kicked it. Did you notice that, Jamie?' he said as we sat side-by-side on the couch.

'No. I wouldn't be surprised if he also tampered with the brakes in the hope that I'd get into an accident taking the car to the garage or something. It's definitely not worth the expense of the repairs now.' I sighed.

'We'll get a scrap dealer to tow it away. Will you use your mum's car?'

'Yes, I've already called my insurance company and changed my policy.' I'd never been the most practical person, but I was learning quickly. 'Are you okay after your parents' visit? Is everything resolved?' The concern I felt was evident in my voice.

'They are as unreasonable now as they have always been. I would have expected the centuries to soften them a little, actually, a lot, but not them.' He sighed wearily. 'Everything I've achieved means nothing to them; my degrees carry no favour whatsoever. They will be eternally disappointed in me for not marrying Marta, or some other pre-approved, pure-blooded female, and providing them with grandchildren.

'I brought shame on them when I didn't agree to their marriage plans for me. All the time they've lived, the changes they've witnessed in the world, and they're still stuck in the dark ages.' His beautiful mouth became a tight line at his remembered pain.

'Your mother mentioned the rest of your family wanting to see you. Are going to visit them?'

He sighed again before answering. 'I'll never hear the end of it if I don't; I'll keep getting visits like this one from them.

If I get it over and done with, that will probably be the last I see or hear from them for a long while. It will only end in arguments when I go, so I really don't see the point.'

'When are you going? Please don't say your birthday; I was hoping to spend that with you.'

He smiled, dispelling his sombre mood. 'Have you got something special planned?'

'Actually, I was going to dress up as a naughty fairy and grant you three wishes,' I quipped.

He laughed, grabbed me around the waist to pull me against him, and tipped me back onto the sofa. 'Well, it's a good thing I said I'd go tomorrow. That gives you the day to find the perfect outfit. Oh, and don't forget the wand.'

He pulled me upright with him and I asked derisively, 'So, did I exacerbate your parents' displeasure with you? It was glaringly obvious they neither like, nor approve of, my presence in your life.'

'They're not prepared to like anyone they haven't picked for me themselves. Don't let them upset you; they're not worth it.' He pushed some hair behind my ear.

'You are the only one who matters to me, you know that, Gabriel,' I said, reassuring him that I wasn't affected by his parents' dismissiveness. I reached over with both hands to stroke his hair out of his eyes and he pulled me onto his lap to kiss me. 'Are you coming back tomorrow or will you have to stay for a while?'

'I'm not spending any more time with them than I absolutely have to. I'll be back with you tomorrow afternoon at the latest.'

'Good.' I dropped one hand onto his shoulder and kept the other in the back of his hair.

'I noticed you put your clothes in the closet in the spare room.' Even if I hadn't been able to feel the guilt he was experiencing over what had happened earlier at his house, I would have been able to see it clearly written on his face and heard it in his voice. It was there loud and clear.

'They're only in there until we decide which clothes you want to bring here.' I grinned. 'You have so many there was no room for mine. Not even my underwear.'

'What I saw was not "underwear," that was "lingerie." Do you want to carry on from where we were so rudely and unwelcomely interrupted?'

'Do you even have to ask?' I stood up. 'I'll drive.'

I loved driving Gabriel's car. It wasn't even a year old and it had every convenience to make the ride and handling as comfortable and easy as possible. My car, on the other hand, was a pensioner in car years and it was fairly basic. It hadn't come with central locking or electric windows; the original stereo didn't even play CDs, needless to say I replaced that immediately; and as for power assisted steering… forget it. I never intended to keep it so long, I'd just never quite got around to upgrading.

'I can't remember the last time I was a passenger in a car,' Gabriel commented, fairly happy to be chauffeured for a change. Once or twice I caught him glancing at the speedometer. 'Why don't you like speed limits?' he asked wryly. He was conscious of the fact that I was aware he didn't obey them, either.

'I want to live my life the way I choose and do all the things I want to do, so I want to spend as little time as possible in a metal box on tarmac.'

'You must really hate traffic jams and slow drivers then.'

'Like you wouldn't believe,' I confirmed.

Once we were in Gabriel's driveway, I locked the car behind us and handed his keys back to him. He let us both into the house and I'd only taken a few steps along the hallway when Gabriel caught hold of my arm.

'Before I forget,' he said, sliding a hand into the front pocket of his jeans and holding whatever he'd removed from there out to me, 'this is for you.'

He pressed something small and metallic into my palm and closed my hand around it. I knew immediately it was a key to this house.

'Welcome home.' He kissed my closed fingers.

For the second time today, I flung myself at him and wrapped my arms around him as tightly as I could, not wanting to ever let him go. 'I love you, Gabriel. I hadn't said it today.'

He snaked his arms around my middle, pulling me closer. 'I love you, too, Jamie.' He buried his face into my neck. 'I have been able to smell the scent of you on my skin all day. It has been driving me crazy and it made me miss you even more whilst I had to endure my parents' visit.'

I pushed up one of my sleeves and sniffed my inner arm. 'Your scent is fading, but I like smelling of you, too'

No doubt Gabriel's parents, with their heightened sense of smell, had scented me on their son. It was one more reason for them to disapprove of me, as if they needed more. Not that I cared about their opinion of me, or that they could smell me on Gabriel, or what they thought about that.

'Come on, let's get your clothes,' I ordered, grasping Gabriel's hand and leading him, unresisting, and both looking and feeling happy, up the stairs.

Gabriel and I pulled out jeans, shirts, jumpers, socks, and boxer shorts from drawers and his closet until we'd almost halved it. I surveyed the large pile of clothes on his bed to assess how much was actually there.

'I'm not sure I've got enough space in my bedroom for all of this,' I gestured to the pile. 'Are you addicted to buying clothes? Is it a secret passion of yours?' I asked teasingly, narrowing my eyes slightly for effect.

'Actually, I detest clothes shopping,' he said, coming to stand beside me and putting a hand on my backside.

I responded in kind. 'Me, too.' I shuddered at the thought.

'All these clothes have just accumulated. I've never followed fashion trends, I've just bought what I like and think suits me, and it never really dates.' His mouth twisted. 'That just made me feel like an old man.'

'I don't mean to offend you, but technically, you are an old man; not physically, of course; and your attitude, your whole way of living, is so modern: you haven't entrenched yourself in the past. You've merely seen a lot and experienced a lot; you've *lived*.' I moved my hand under his jumper to the small of his back and rubbed soothingly with my fingertips. 'Does it make you feel mentally or emotionally weary?' I couldn't imagine the passage of all that time not having an effect on him.

Gabriel took me by the hand and led me over to the edge of the bed where we sat side-by-side.

'I've had moments when I've got depressed and felt as though I've lived enough, seen enough, and done enough. The concept of eternity is difficult to reconcile and it can get very lonely.' He gazed deeply into my eyes so we were looking into one another. 'I've known humans, watched them have careers, have families, grow old and die whilst I go on.'

'I thought you said you didn't have any experience of bereavement.' I frowned.

'Not in the way you have.' His voice was quiet and he smiled softly. He felt a little sad for me, and he smoothed the furrow between my eyebrows with his fingers. 'I've never been close enough to anyone, emotionally involved enough, to feel the tragedy of their loss. I only kept acquaintances for a short time to avoid too many explanations.'

'Apart from those you've drunk from, of course. You obviously cared for those friends.'

'Yes, I did, and I saw them all get married and have children. Some of them even have grandchildren, I believe. But there haven't been as many of them as you think, and none of them ever meant anything close to how much you mean to me,' he added ardently, taking my hand and feeling the desolation that was creeping insidiously through me. 'You have nothing to fear. You are everything to me, Jamie.'

I knew it was futile to feel jealous of the women in Gabriel's past; after all, he'd had a century of life before I was even conceived. I also knew that what I was experiencing was unreasonable since he'd told me, sincerely, that I am the only person he has ever loved.

I realised that I'd become quiet and unresponsive whilst I thought it all through because Gabriel's concern was growing in magnitude and I was so embroiled in my introspection that his disquiet did not immediately register. The instant it did, I squeezed his hand, looked up at him and smiled.

'I know,' I reassured. 'You are everything to me, too, Gabriel. I want you to know that and feel secure in it.'

'I do, I can feel it; but even if I couldn't, I'd believe it because you said so. I trust you.' After a couple of heartbeats, he lightened the mood by saying, 'Let's go and get your clothes out of the spare room and into their new home.'

'Ooh, does that mean I get my own drawer for my underwear?' I played along and chased him out of his bedroom.

'If you're *very* nice to me, I'll give you two drawers,' he teased, then came to an abrupt stop inside the other bedroom so that I would deliberately crash into him, and he clung on to me to steady us both.

'Cunning,' I commented cutely, and stood on tiptoes to place a kiss on his unsuspecting mouth.

'I thought so,' he responded, grinning. 'So,' he said, letting go of me and opening the doors to the linen closet, 'you take the clothes whilst I get better acquainted with your lingerie.'

I pressed the tip of my tongue against my top lip, eyebrows raised.

'Don't look at me like that,' he said, laughing. 'I'm not planning on wearing it, I'll just have fun imagining you in it.'

I laughed, too. 'I'm sure you'll be seeing me in my underwear quite a lot from now on.'

'I know I will. As you get dressed every morning, I'll watch you shimmy into it, and then I'll watch you parade around the bedroom in it for a few minutes before putting the rest of your clothes on.'

'You think I parade around in my lingerie before getting dressed? I hate to disappoint you, Gabriel, but I just get dressed. I don't even inspect my body in the mirror.'

'Okay, so no parading up until now, but would you do it for me?' He used his most charming voice and gave me his most endearing smile.

I thought about it for an instant, then, before I lost my nerve or reasoned myself out of it, I kicked off my shoes, pulled my socks off with the heels of my feet whilst I unzipped my jeans, pushed them down, and stepped out of them. Next, I pulled off my jumper and dropped it on the floor so I was standing in nothing but a lacy black bra and matching thong. I turned in a circle, slowly, so Gabriel could get the full three hundred and sixty degree view.

'Would you like me to parade around now?' I asked, somehow keeping my voice steady whilst my nerves were jangling inside me and my heart threatened to burst out of my chest.

I watched his pupils dilate and his eyes sweep appreciatively from my head to my toes and back up again to meet my own. 'Feel free,' he answered huskily, his heart thudding heavily with anticipation.

He stood there, his gaze trained on me as I sauntered around the room, turning his body to follow my movement and tilting his head as he watched. I finally came to a halt in front of him, our bodies only separated by a few millimetres of air.

'Was that as good as you imagined?' I asked, my heart skipping a beat as I saw the desire on his face and felt it wash over me.

'Better,' he replied simply, 'because I can do this.' He reached a hand out to the base of my neck, curling his fingers around the back of it to pull me closer and kiss me.

It felt as though something inside me erupted, and I took the last step forward to enable me to press the entirety of my body into his and kiss him back with everything I had.

Gabriel moved his hand from my neck into my hair to cradle my head, and wrapped his other arm tightly around my waist to hold me against him whilst my arms crept around his neck.

Whilst still kissing me, and not letting me go, Gabriel walked me backwards out of the room, along the landing and into his bedroom, coming to a stop at the foot of his bed. He broke the kiss and looked into my eyes, an unspoken question in the depths of his. In response, I tugged off his jumper and ran my hands up his taut stomach and chest as, using his feet, he removed his boots and socks. I looped my hands back behind his neck, sliding my skin against his as I stood on tiptoes to reclaim his mouth. He moaned, and his warm hands caressed my back and settled on my shoulder blades. My skin was so sensitised to his touch that I pulled my mouth away from his as I inhaled sharply.

We stood, both breathing unevenly and just staring at one another, but Gabriel tore his gaze away from mine to glance at the bed. I also looked at it and, reading one another, we both moved at the exact same moment to tip Gabriel's clothes off.

He drew the duvet back, then pulled me against him. He trapped my face between his palms and bent his head to kiss me, and my fingers went to the waistband of his jeans. I released the button at the top, gently tugged the zip down, then dragged my mouth away from his to ease the jeans down his legs to his ankles so he could step out of them.

I straightened, kissing him and deliberately brushing my body against his all the way up, causing him to shudder slightly. I put both my hands on his rear to hold him to me and he reciprocated by placing his hands on my back and spinning us so that the mattress pressed against the backs of my legs. He kissed my mouth softly, just once, then kissed his way down my throat. I tipped my head back to give him better access and, with his lips and tongue teasing and tasting the skin there, he lowered us into the centre of the bed.

Between us, our hands caressing one another and each of us kissing our way over the other's body, we removed the last remaining items of clothing separating us.

Gabriel settled himself between my thighs and I thought I might cry with how perfect it felt to have his weight on top of me, his whole body covering and warming mine, and how I wanted to always feel like this.

'I know,' he whispered, and I could feel the same emotions coursing through him.

Our gazes locked and he claimed me, uniting us together in the most intimate and natural way a man and a woman can be joined. His body worshipped mine, and mine worshipped his as our senses heightened, pleasure built, and muscles tightened until everything inside me exploded. I cried out Gabriel's name mere milliseconds before he choked out mine and his body shuddered through me.

He collapsed into my arms. Both of us were breathing heavily and our hearts were beating against one another's.

'I'm blaming your lingerie for this,' he said, dropping kisses along my collarbone.

'Really?' I laughed. 'It wasn't because you love me and find me irresistible? Because I love you,' I said in an innocent voice to make him feel guilty for his wry remark. I traced each of the vertebrae in his spine with the tip of my index finger and he gave a low groan which delighted me. 'And I find you irresistible. It's hard to keep myself from touching you.' I pouted.

He laughed and, because our chests were still pressed together, I felt my body vibrate with it.

'Nice try,' he said, and raised his head to give me long, lazy kisses. 'You know I love you and every millimetre of your body. You think I can resist you? How often am I with you and not touching you?'

'Never,' I admitted. I liked it that way.

'Exactly,' he murmured, responding to both my spoken comment and my unspoken thought. He brought his hand up to my face, but as he did, he brushed it all the way up my side causing me to quiver. I felt his smile of satisfaction against my mouth. 'But on this occasion, I'm blaming your lingerie, or rather, you parading around in it.'

'Hey, you said it was what you wanted,' I reminded him. 'I was just complying with your wishes.' Our legs were entangled and I stroked one of his calves with the inside of my foot. 'We should get back to those clothes. Mine are still in the spare room and yours are on the floor.'

I felt a momentary pang of worry pass through him. He slipped his arms underneath me, gathering me to him, and rolled onto his back so I was lying sprawled on top of him. He was concerned he was crushing me.

'They can wait,' he said indolently. 'It's not as though either of us has anything... Ugh, except I've got to go and visit Lillian, Mordecai, my siblings with their pre-approved spouses, and their pure-blooded offspring tomorrow.' There was unreserved contempt in his tone and I could feel it flowing through his body, too.

'I don't want you to go, either, Gabriel; not when they've always treated you with complete disregard for your wishes.' I could hear in my voice the anxiety I felt, and I knew Gabriel could hear and feel it, too. 'At least it's only for one day to appease them.'

'Less than a day. I'm not letting them keep me away from you longer than is absolutely necessary,' he said to reassure me.

'I'm all for that; the less time you're there listening to them trying to persuade you to end our relationship and making you miserable, the happier I will be.'

'I have no doubt they'll try, and I'm sorry about that, Jamie; they have no right to hurt you. You know that what I feel for you is real, it's permanent, and nothing can change or destroy it.'

'I know. I feel that way about you, too, Gabriel.'

'I know.'

'Come on, let's pick these clothes up and take them to my house.' I reluctantly extricated myself from Gabriel's hold and got out of bed to recover my underwear.

He pouted, but got up and dressed without complaining, then followed me back to the guest room to find the clothes I had discarded, taking the opportunity to watch me stroll around in just my lingerie again.

Once we had moved my clothes to his bedroom, we shifted Gabriel's from the floor. On our way to his car, I stopped him and asked, 'Aren't you forgetting something?' He looked at me, eyebrows drawn together, but before he could draw the answer from my mind, I answered my own question. 'Blood. You're going to need to keep some at my house.'

The look he gave me reflected exactly what he was feeling: relief that it didn't bother me, that I was comfortable talking about it, and had adjusted to it so easily that I'd broached the subject. And love; always love.

He handed me the clothes he was holding, opened the freezer door, and I saw that it was full of packs of blood. Finding another cotton tote bag, he transferred about a dozen IV bags into it.

Back at my house, after unloading and re-homing Gabriel's things, I pulled him into the shower with me, intent on getting clean and then curling up in bed with him.

I picked up our discarded clothes to dump them in the laundry basket, emptying pockets as I went. My phone slipped out of my jeans and Gabriel caught it before it hit the floor.

'You've got a message,' he said, glancing at it.

'Anything interesting?' I asked with a note of scepticism in my voice as I walked to stand next to him as he opened it.

It was from Aaron and had been sent hours ago, but I obviously hadn't noticed. In ominous capital letters it read:

YOU SENT THE POLICE OUT TO ME? YOU BITCH!

I tipped my head back to stare at the ceiling for a moment and huffed out a breath in exasperation.

'Why do I have the feeling he isn't going to leave me alone?' I massaged my temples to ease the tension I could feel encroaching in my head.

'You know I'll keep you safe, Jamie,' Gabriel said, pulling me against him. 'Don't let him intimidate you.'

'I won't,' I replied, and buried my face in the curve where his neck met his shoulder.

Thirteen
Gabriel's Birthday

I awoke the next morning to the sensation of fingers moving over my shoulder blades. I looked up to find Gabriel gazing down at me, a soft smile playing on his lips, and feeling perfectly content. When he saw that I was awake, his smile grew.

At some point during the night, I had abandoned my pillow in favour of Gabriel's chest. My legs were tangled with his, I was practically lying on top of him, and my arms hugged his sides.

'Hey,' I said, and pressed a kiss over his heart.

'Morning, beautiful,' he replied, stroking the lock of hair out of my eyes that had slipped forward as I'd kissed him.

'Have you been awake long?' I clambered up his body so that our faces were level and gave him a sleepily sexy kiss.

'A little while. I've been watching you sleep. You're so silent and still; you don't murmur, move, or even twitch. If it hadn't been for your breathing and your heartbeat, I wouldn't have known you were still alive because you weren't even dreaming.'

I didn't remember having any dreams last night, either. 'I don't need to dream when I've got you right here.'

'Neither do I.'

'You're going to leave to see your parents soon, aren't you?' I felt sad, and my wariness of his family crept in.

'Unfortunately, yes,' he said, feeling regret that he would be away from me, 'but I'll be back with you late afternoon. It's just a few hours. In that time, you can get some work done and find the perfect fairy costume.' He tilted my chin to look deeply into my eyes and he grinned.

'At least I'll smell of you all day, that's comforting. I think you'd better clean my scent off your skin, though; I'm sure it will only aggravate your parents into an argument if you don't.' I gave him a sad smile.

'There will be arguments regardless. I'm not going to wash your scent off my skin as though I'm ashamed of you. I don't care that it will infuriate them. They don't accept me the way I am, they never have, and that's why they're not a part of my life.' He knew I worried that this upset him more than he admitted and he shook his head. 'I don't feel any sadness about it. They are who they are, and my relationship with them is what it always has been. I don't miss them; we've never had what you have with your mother.'

I was grateful he hadn't used the past tense. I still felt close to my mother and sister because, occasionally, I thought I could sense their presence. I couldn't see them, or hear them, but it felt like they were in the room with me. If I visited a clairvoyant, I could find out if that really were true, or if it was just me hoping it was.

'It's time to get up now,' Gabriel said, his reluctance both palpable and audible. I pouted, and he pushed his hands through my arms and placed them on the backs of my shoulders to roll me onto my back.

He pinned me down, giving a soft growl, and smothered my face and neck with soft kisses that tickled and made me giggle. I hadn't really laughed in two months before I met Gabriel.

He released me with a grin, pushed the duvet aside to get out of bed, then disappeared to the bathroom for a few minutes. I sat and watched him get dressed, enjoying the show, before I got up and put on my dressing gown. I followed him around as he went to the kitchen, heated some blood for himself and made coffee for us both. I trailed him back up to the bathroom and hugged him from behind, my arms around his waist, as he stood at the sink to brush his teeth. He smiled back at me in the mirror, his eyes never leaving mine.

Finally, around mid-morning, Gabriel picked up his keys and moved to the front door. Before he could open it, I pulled him to me. 'Hurry back to me,' I breathed, my mouth against his ear.

He nodded. 'It's going to be a long day,' he remarked with a sigh. He kissed me goodbye, then opened the door and headed off to his car.

I waited until he'd disappeared out of the driveway before I closed the door, then I got dressed, got into my mum's car, and drove into town to get what I needed for Gabriel's birthday present. I also searched costume and toy shops for a fairy wand and found a girly pink, glittery one with a big star on the top.

When I returned home, I switched on my computer and printer. It occurred to me, when Gabriel mentioned that he had an upcoming birthday, that the best gift I could give him would be something personal. At one hundred and twenty-nine years of age, and being extremely wealthy, I imagined there would be very little I could buy that would mean very much to him. He had, however, consistently shown an interest in my writing, but so far had only read my Master's dissertation.

Whilst I was out today, I bought some thick, good quality paper and an A4 display book with transparent plastic pages in which to insert documents. I designed a cover page and wrote a few paragraphs of text as a dedication, an explanation of my writing, and my influences. I also told Gabriel how much I loved him and how much he had quickly come to mean to me as well as wishing him a happy birthday, stating that I hoped it was the first of many that we would share together.

I printed all my stories, the cover and dedication, and organised them all in the book. I wrapped and stuck a bow on it and hid it, along with the wand, in the now unused dining room. I knew it was unlikely Gabriel would spend much, if any, time in there before his birthday.

It had only been a few hours since he left; and it would have taken him about an hour to get there given the speed he normally drives and factoring in the traffic; but three hours in the company of his parents and siblings without a word from him gave me a queasy feeling in my stomach. It didn't matter that Gabriel had told me he'd never had an easy relationship with his parents, I couldn't help but feel a little bit guilty that they were likely to use me as another reason to castigate him. Mostly, however, it made me angry that they were so immutable and uncaring towards him. I would never understand why it mattered so much to them that Gabriel marry a pure-blooded vampire even if it meant he was desperately unhappy.

To take my mind away from a situation I could not immediately do anything about; I could merely ensure Gabriel knew he was loved, and felt loved, by me when he came home; I opened my notebook to the vampire story I had been writing. Printing out all my completed stories had been like giving myself a kick up the backside to write more, to feel like I had accomplished something, and to give Gabriel something more to read.

I'd been writing for a while when my phone began to ring. The display on the screen said it was Rachael.

'Hello, sweetie,' I answered. 'How are you? How's the family?'

'I'm great. We're all good, honey. Baz is at work, Noah is fed, changed, and sleeping, and Tamara is playing "Mummy" to her favourite doll.' I could hear the laugh in her voice. 'How have you been? We haven't heard from you since last week, so I hope we didn't upset you too much with the suggestion of seeking counselling.'

'No, you didn't. I know you're worried about me and, truly, I appreciate your concern; I understand it's difficult to know how to help in a situation like this. I think I'm managing, though, and I've decided that I'd like to see a clairvoyant. Maybe it will help me to know that Mum and Carmel are okay. I'm secretly hoping they'll have some kind of message for me. Does that sound ludicrous to you?'

'No, not at all, Jamie. I just hope you find a decent medium, one who can give you an accurate reading rather than generalisations and clichés. I think it's a good idea; I think it could give you some kind of peace of mind.' She really meant it; I could feel her honesty. 'It could be just what you need. You're already sounding more positive.'

'Well, I've met someone,' I confessed shyly. I wildly understated the circumstances because I knew the doubting reaction I'd get if I explained how far advanced the relationship between Gabriel and me really was. 'His name is Gabriel and he's wonderful. He's listened to me and has been really sympathetic, understanding, and supportive.'

'That's really nice, honey,' Rachael said, feeling uncertain about the situation, but trying not to sound that way. 'How did you meet?'

'I met him at a bookshop the day before I came to visit you. I accidentally bumped into him and we spoke for a few minutes about books.'

'You didn't mention anything when I saw you,' she pointed out. 'You exchanged details with a complete stranger and you didn't even tell me. This is hot gossip.' She warmed to the idea because she could hear enthusiasm in my voice; it made a change from sorrow.

'No, it wasn't like that.' I didn't know how to explain what really happened without making Gabriel sound like a stalker, or revealing too much about him, so I opted for half-truths. 'He recognised me from university. He's a postgraduate student, too, and he said he'd seen me there. I didn't tell you because I didn't think I'd see him again.'

'Well, it's still early, but it sounds as though he's making you happy.'

'He is.' That was putting it mildly.

'Good, you deserve it, but just be careful because you are still emotionally vulnerable. You are very intuitive about people, and you tend to be a good judge of character, so I'm sure he's a very nice person, but there are no guarantees it will work out between you. My advice is to take things slowly.'

I couldn't tell her that it was already too late for that.

In the background, I could hear Tamara calling for her mother.

'I'm sorry, Jamie, I've got to go. We'll speak again soon. Keep me posted on Gabriel. Love you.'

'Love you, too, honey. Speak to you soon.'

I ended the call and grinned to myself. Even without revealing that Gabriel is a vampire, I knew Rachael would have difficulty accepting both our empathic connection, and that what Gabriel and I have is real. She certainly wouldn't be happy that we'd moved in together, albeit in two separate houses, within a week of meeting. It was better that I edited the facts and told her only what she needed to know when she needed to know it.

After speaking with Rachael, I went back to my writing, but after about half an hour, I was disturbed by a knock at the front door. I knew it wasn't Gabriel because he would have used his key. I looked out of the window and saw Aaron's car before I saw him standing waiting for me to answer. I sucked in a deep breath and opened the door.

'Hello, Aaron,' I said coolly, keeping my expression neutral so I didn't provoke his anger. 'Aren't you working today?'

'Hi, Jamie. No, I'm not working after what happened with the police yesterday.' He had the decency to look uncomfortable and he was embarrassed that he'd been caught.

'I didn't call them. One of my neighbours saw you vandalising my car and called the police. She recognised you.' I crossed my arms, refusing to let him try to intimidate me. He caught a glimpse of Carmel's ring still on my finger as I moved my hand.

'How did she know my name?'

'She didn't, but she knew you were Carmel's fiancé. The police left a message telling me to call them to fill in the blanks. I did, and I told them I didn't want to press charges. I could have made things worse for you, but, out of respect for Carmel's love for you, I didn't.'

'If you didn't press charges, why did Detective Fordham come to visit me?'

'He's a DI actually,' I corrected. 'He was the one who investigated what happened to Mum, Carmel and me. He was very sympathetic towards me at the time because I wasn't in very good condition, if you remember. He's just looking out for me. He thinks I've suffered enough,' I added pointedly.

'Is Gabriel here?' Aaron asked suddenly.

'That's none of your concern.' I tried not to grit my teeth as I spoke, but I was really annoyed with him and this whole situation.

'Can I come in?' He put a hand on the door.

'No.'

He sighed in frustration. 'Look, how long have you known him? How well do you know him? What do you think Bea and Carmel would say about the way you've been behaving with him?'

'Not that this is *any* of your business, but the amount of time I've known Gabriel has absolutely *nothing* to do with how *well* I know him.' I was practically shouting. 'As for Mum and Carmel, they'd love Gabriel. He's intelligent, thoughtful, kind, and he makes me happy. They'd tell me to go for it. What you should be thinking about is what Carmel would think about the way *you* are behaving towards *me*.' I didn't give him the opportunity to reply. 'Would you please leave me alone now?' I closed the door on him without waiting for a rejoinder.

It was just moving into early evening and, although Gabriel said he would be back late afternoon, I still didn't consider him to be late. If he was on his way home, he could have got caught in traffic, or, more likely, he'd been delayed by his family. The suspense about what was happening had been increasing all day, but I was determined not to further aggravate the situation for him by continually calling or texting him.

I was agitated and restless after my conversation with Aaron, so I tidied all my textbooks and notebooks into a neat pile and began dusting. I started in the dining room. Nothing in there had been used since before Mum, Carmel and I were shot, but I had kept it clean and tidy. I swiftly flitted around with a cloth and furniture polish before moving into the living room. I dusted all the surfaces and then picked up the vase holding the flowers Gabriel had sent to me. I wanted to preserve them for as long as I could, so I emptied out the stagnant water, replaced it with clean water, and added some of the flower food Mum kept in the cupboard under the sink.

By the time I'd made it around the whole house, vacuumed the floors and cleaned the bathroom, almost two hours had passed. There was still no word from Gabriel so I finally gave in and called him. The phone just rang and rang until it eventually went to voicemail.

'Hi, Gabriel, it's Jamie.' I kept my tone light so I didn't worry him if he hadn't already felt my disquiet. 'I'm presuming you've been detained by your family. I hope they haven't exasperated you too much, or upset you,' I said sincerely, not knowing how he was feeling. 'I'm at my house at the moment, but I'm going to go to yours when I hang up because I need to get out of here. I'll explain everything when I see you. I love you.'

I put my phone back in my pocket and searched for some shoes and my bag. I picked up Gabriel's present and the fairy wand from where I'd put them earlier, a couple of textbooks and two notepads and, leaving a couple of lights on so the house didn't look deserted, I locked the door and made my way to my other home.

I was feeling paranoid about being in my mum's house alone after Aaron's visit. He'd presumed Gabriel wasn't with me when he'd dropped by and I felt as though if I stayed there, I was just waiting for Aaron to come back and harass me again because he suspected I was on my own.

Judging by the empty driveway and darkness from within Gabriel's house when I got there, he still hadn't returned. Once inside, I walked into the lounge but didn't turn on the light, I merely placed Gabriel's gift on the coffee table. I went into the library and deposited my books on the low table by the couch. I sank onto it and sat in the muted light, rested my head against the cushioned backrest with my eyes closed and I cleared my mind, feeling my earlier distress leave me. I didn't ever remember feeling trapped and unnerved by being in my own home, but here, engulfed by Gabriel's scent, Gabriel's possessions, and an environment so removed from my life before losing my family, I felt more like myself again. I could almost believe that Mum would be there when I went home again.

I felt mentally exhausted, and my left shoulder was beginning to ache, which was an indication that I had been holding myself taut with the stress of my encounter with Aaron and my frantic cleaning afterwards. I stretched my muscles to ease the tightness, then pampered them with a soak in a hot bath. The effect was more instant than taking painkillers.

It was still early, but, with my hair still damp, I climbed into bed. I'd kept my phone nearby all evening in case Gabriel called me back, but he hadn't, and the silence made me uneasy. I didn't for one second believe that whatever his family said or did would affect Gabriel's feelings for me, I was more worried about how angry they had made him and how demoralised they may have tried to make him feel. He didn't deserve that.

I quickly fell asleep, even though I didn't intend to, and a nightmare soon followed.

I was in the restaurant with my mother and sister the night we celebrated me passing my degree. We were eating slices of rich chocolate cake and joking that we would each be several pounds heavier the following morning as a result of our indulgence. Then, we were leaving the building and walking to Carmel's car where, in slow motion, Carmel was killed, I was shot in the shoulder, and Mum fell lifelessly to the ground after me. I was still conscious and the gunman knew I was still alive, so he came around the car to stand over me, pointing the gun directly at my head. Before he could pull the trigger, I looked up to see his face. It was Aaron.

My eyes flew open, my heart was hammering, and someone grabbed hold of me and pulled me into a sitting position. It happened so quickly that I didn't have time to scream.

'It's okay, Jamie, it's me. It's Gabriel.' He drew me against him, clamping his arms tightly around me, and I clung on to him desperately.

My face was pressed into his bare, damp chest and I forced myself to calm down; it was only a dream. I felt Gabriel kiss the top of my head and push the hair back from my face.

I pulled back slightly to look at him in the subdued light. I smiled as I took in his wet hair and the towel wrapped around his hips as he sat on the bed. 'How much did you see?'

'All of it. I was in the shower and I saw you with your family. I hoped it was going to be a pleasant dream, but, when I recognised where you were, I guessed it might be a nightmare.' The edges of his mouth turned down slightly. 'I hurried and I'd just got out when your dream turned nasty. I came straight to you.'

I stretched up and kissed him. 'Thank you. I'm glad you were here.'

'Are you okay?' He raised his eyebrows quizzically and I registered his concern.

I nodded. 'Aaron came to see me late this afternoon and it unsettled me.' I explained the conversation we'd had and how it had left me feeling uncomfortable to be there and that was why I had relocated. 'Are you okay? I was getting worried. What time is it anyway?'

'It's about nine. I know I said I'd be back hours ago, I'm so sorry you were worried.' He was full of remorse as he gently traced one of my eyebrows. 'Not only did we have all the usual arguments in between my six mostly obnoxious nieces and nephews bombarding me with questions, but I was just about to leave to be home by about four-thirty when both sets of my grandparents arrived. Then I had to sit through the same thing all over again.'

I could feel Gabriel's relief to be home mingled with his love for me, happiness to find me there, and annoyance at his family for taking him away from me.

'I couldn't even get a minute alone to call or text you,' he explained, 'but I got your message. I felt that you were overanxious so I hurried back, found you sleeping, and thought I'd wash the smell of my parents' house off me then cuddle up to you.' He stroked his cheek against mine.

'I was more concerned about the state of mind they'd put *you* in.' I frowned. 'I thought maybe they'd antagonised you, leaving you seething or completely disconsolate.'

'Oh, they did antagonise me, but it's more irritation that they can't just leave me be than anything else. They don't affect me emotionally; they haven't for a very long time.' He stroked his thumb between my eyebrows to remove my frown.

'Gabriel, I'm sorry you've got such an immovable and unaccepting family.' I touched his cheek. 'My mum and sister would have adored you. Actually, wherever they are, I'm sure they do. I hope that means something to you, gives you some kind of consolation.'

'It does. The feelings I get from you when you talk to me about your mother make me believe she's as wonderful as you esteem her to be. Though, what would she have thought when she found out I'm a vampire? We wouldn't have been able to hide my not ageing for very long, nor yours if I turned you.' He raised an eyebrow.

I laughed. 'My obsession with vampires has never been a secret. Mum joked once or twice that if they did exist, I'd find one and marry him. My mum isn't judgmental; where do you think I get it from?' I raised both my eyebrows.

'Still, do you think she could have accepted that? You don't think she would have been worried I'd try to kill you, or change you?' he challenged.

'She's my mum, she's always going to worry, but she'd get to know you for *who* you are, not *what* you are.' I pulled back a little further to look directly into his eyes as I elaborated. 'We would just have explained it to her the way you did to me. I think that would have been a better option than lying and saying that with your family's medical background, you're related to a very good cosmetic surgeon, or that someone is a genius scientist and had found a way to evade the ageing process.'

He stopped still and just stared at me, assessing. 'You're right, Jamie. I'm so sorry. I wasn't attacking your family, I promise. You know your mother better than I ever could, even if she were still alive, and she's nothing like mine. I'm just annoyed I lost a whole day being with my family when I could have been with you. Forgive me, please.' He reached for my hand and held it firmly against his heart.

My own heart melted. 'There's nothing to forgive. Honestly,' I said when he seemed unconvinced. 'You just said you trusted my belief in my mum, so I know you weren't criticising.' I shuffled closer and pulled his other hand to me to hold it against my heart.

Of course he'd question my mother's reaction to him being a vampire; it's not as though fiction had portrayed them particularly favourably. However, my mother would have understood once she knew the whole story.

'I just want to forget today ever happened,' he said.

'I agree with you there.'

'Are you tired? Judging by the time you called me and the time I got here, you couldn't have been asleep very long.' Gabriel moved our hands, interlacing our fingers together and bringing them to his lips to kiss first one set of my knuckles, then the other.

'I'm shattered; it wasn't very peaceful sleep.' I extricated one of my hands to immerse it in his hair. It was still soaking wet.

There was another towel just behind him which I hadn't noticed before. He'd obviously picked it up to dry his hair, but ran out to me before he could do very much with it. I pulled it towards me, knelt up in the bed, and gently rubbed Gabriel's hair dry whilst he ran his hands up my legs to my hips to hold me steady. When I was done, I dropped the towel and combed my fingers through his hair to remove any tangles, then I pulled him against me. He rested his head against my chest, listened to my heart beating, and gripped me tightly around the waist. I buried my face in his hair, inhaling the clean scent of shampoo.

'I love you,' I whispered into his hair.

'I love you, too,' he answered, giving me a squeeze. 'I'll get rid of these towels and turn off the lights,' he said, reluctantly releasing me and moving to stand, so I dropped my hands. 'Stay there.'

I remained kneeling on the bed and sat back on my heels as Gabriel quickly disappeared into the bathroom and re-emerged seconds later in another pair of snug-fitting shorts, turning the light off as he exited.

The lamp on my side of the bed was still on; I hadn't turned it off before I fell asleep earlier; and its soft glow allowed me to watch Gabriel's every movement as he stalked gracefully back over to me, my head tilted slightly to one side. He smiled, unselfconscious of my scrutiny.

'What?' he asked, grinning.

'I just like looking at you,' I replied innocently. He was so beautiful and I couldn't believe he was mine.

He got into the bed and knelt in the middle, just a small distance away from me. 'If you keep looking at me like that,' he said, grabbing me around the middle and pulling me down with him onto the mattress, 'you're going to get yourself into trouble.' He twisted so he was lying on his back and I was curled against him.

I giggled and he pulled my face to his to kiss me. I wriggled out of his grasp slightly and stretched over as far as I could to switch off the lamp. I'd just managed to brush my fingers against the base when Gabriel casually reached an arm out and beat me to the mechanism. The room went dark, but I could still see that he was grinning at me. I shoved at his shoulder, which only served to propel me backwards because Gabriel was cushioned by the bed, but my intention was clear.

He laughed, tugged me to him, and brought my head against his shoulder. 'Sorry, I couldn't resist,' he said as he smoothed his hands down my back.

'Hmm,' I muttered, then snuggled deeper into him, entwining my legs with his and dropping kisses onto his collarbone.

He moaned softly and I felt his heartbeat accelerate, then settle, as he began drifting off to sleep. Within moments, he was fully unconscious and breathing deeply, and the peace and contentment I felt within him eased the dream image of Aaron pointing a gun at me and I was able to sleep, too.

I awoke to the cold, grey light of a dull morning and opened my eyes to find that sometime during the night, Gabriel and I had shifted positions so that I was lying on my back with Gabriel on his stomach, half-sprawled across me, his face buried into the centre of my chest. I smiled to myself and lifted one of my hands to smooth his hair back out of his eyes.

I felt his breathing change and I knew that my movement had woken him. Gabriel's eyes fluttered open and he smiled lazily at me as he realised my fingers were still playing with his hair.

I smiled into his pretty eyes. 'Happy birthday, baby.'

'Morning, beautiful. Thanks,' he murmured sleepily, then pushed himself up so his face was level with mine and slowly kissed me, holding me down with the press of his body against mine.

'I've got a present for you,' I managed to say between long, languid kisses.

'You're my present,' he said before claiming my mouth again. 'I get you everyday, but it was pretty special to wake up on my birthday with you beneath me.' He looked at me and the expression in his eyes was the perfect reflection of what he was feeling: he had been so lonely and had waited such a long time for me and now he felt full, complete.

My heart ached for him and I wanted to give him everything, all of me. I wanted him to turn me right there and then so he could feel that way forever. I loved him. I'd do it for him.

'I know you would,' Gabriel said, reading me. 'And don't think I'm not tempted, but it's got to be for the right reason.' He slowly brushed the tip of his little finger along my bottom lip, making it tingle.

'It is the right reason, Gabriel: I love you,' I said emphatically, kissing his finger.

'As I love you, but this shouldn't be an impulse decision. We've got time.' He smiled softly.

'Okay, we won't act extemporaneously, but I really think I've made up my mind. We'll wait until we're both certain about it, and comfortable with it.' He nodded his agreement and I leaned forward to seal the promise with a kiss. 'I really do have a gift for you. Don't get up; I want to bring it to you.'

I grinned excitedly and it was infectious because Gabriel returned it.

I got up and ran downstairs to the living room where I'd deliberately left the wrapped parcel last night knowing that even if he saw it, he wouldn't linger over it if I wasn't there. I picked it up and hurried back to him, dragging my bag over to the side of the bed as I made my way back to him.

I hopped into bed and Gabriel hastily covered me with the duvet so I wouldn't get cold. I handed him the gift, complete with a red bow on top, with a feeling of expectation.

'There's nothing I want other than you,' he said, looking at the rectangle in his hands.

'In that case, I think you'll like this,' I responded obliquely. 'Open it.'

He pulled off the adhesive bow and stuck it on the top of my wrist to emphasise that I was his real present, then ripped off the paper. He opened the book, read the note inside and smiled, overjoyed.

'I'll bet there's a lot of you in these stories,' he agreed. He gathered both my wrists and placed them around his neck before wrapping his arms around my ribs and pulling me into him, pressing his forehead against mine. 'It's the perfect gift, really thoughtful. Thank you, Jamie.'

'Really? You're not just humouring me?' I bit my lip. 'It feels a bit egotistical.'

'Don't feel that way. I've told you I know you can write and that I want to read everything of yours. This is from the heart,' he said, placing his hand over my heart and giving me a kiss. 'Tell me, though, because I'm intrigued: why did you bring your bag over when this present wasn't inside?' He raised one eyebrow ever so slightly. I knew he'd already read the answer from my mind.

I tried to suppress a grin, then leaned over the side of the bed, unzipped my bag, and pulled out the fairy wand I'd bought yesterday. As I straightened up, I produced the sparkly pink wand for Gabriel to see.

'Don't tell me you forgot about the naughty fairy.' I raised both my eyebrows at him and waved the wand around.

Gabriel laughed and shook his head. 'No, I didn't forget about that. But where's the rest of the outfit?' he asked a little more soberly.

'I thought that you thought the wand was the most important part.' I hoped he wasn't too disappointed by the lack of costume.

'I told you not to forget the wand. I was also anticipating a frilly tutu, a transparent, lacy top, and gossamer wings,' he elucidated around a smirk.

'Oh, I didn't think you really expected me to take it that far. I assumed you knew I was only teasing.' I felt stupid for ever suggesting it in the first place. 'How about I parade around in some lingerie holding the wand?'

'It's okay; of course I knew you were only joking. I didn't really expect all that, you know I didn't, so please don't get anxious,' he implored.

I cast a worried glance at him, feeling a little inadequate; something I hadn't experienced since my involvement with Hayden.

'You definitely shouldn't feel that. Not ever.' He gently cupped my face and pushed me back against the pillows, feathering kisses all over my face.

'I'm sorry, Gabriel; I'm spoiling your birthday, aren't I?' I asked sheepishly.

'No, you're not.' He smiled into my eyes and I saw his glint wickedly. 'So, those wishes…' He took the wand from my fingers and examined it.

'Yes?'

'Can I have anything I want?'

'Anything,' I confirmed breathlessly.

'Well, in that case…' He dropped the wand, shifted onto his back and pulled me on top of him. 'Come here.' He brought my face down to his.

Fourteen
Restraint

Not only did I spend the rest of the day granting wishes; simple things like heating blood to provide Gabriel with breakfast in bed, snuggling together on the sofa whilst watching vampire films, at his insistence, and laughing at them; but his birthday turned into a week of me pandering to him. He confessed that he hadn't really celebrated any of his birthdays since his twenty-first as a university undergraduate, so I designated the whole week to make up for them, still acting as birthday fairy and granting wishes.

He taught me some massage techniques and I gave him a very amateur massage. He read all my stories; continually asking me questions about my narrative decisions; and analysing the psychology behind them all.

The week was also a welcome break from my research, which I ignored because my heart wasn't in it after such an intense and concentrated period of study up until now. I knew that a short break wouldn't impede my work, so I took the time to relax and just be with Gabriel.

When he'd read all my stories at least twice, he encouraged me to continue writing the vampire story I'd begun. He was so impatient to read it that he attempted the handwritten pages, complete with crossings-out and asterisks indicating insertions and additional narrative or dialogue, but he managed to make sense of it all with some guidance from me.

I requested that we stay at Gabriel's house. I felt more serene knowing that Aaron couldn't find me there and intrude on Gabriel's and my little lacuna. In fact, we barely left the house, though we did go to my mine a couple of times to ensure it was still secure and so I could take the flowers Gabriel had sent me, plus some food, back home with me. Gabriel even accompanied me to my physiotherapy appointment and proceeded to interrogate Jill regarding my healing, my progress, and paid close attention to her actions so he could minister treatment to me in the interim between my sessions with her.

I wished I could say that not being at Mum's house meant that I wasn't harassed by Aaron, but he still got to me by sending a couple of text messages spewing the same filth he'd said to Gabriel when Gabriel answered my phone that one time, and he attempted to call me, but when his name appeared on the screen, I rejected the call.

The need for human food eventually forced us out to the supermarket. I picked up a basket and Gabriel immediately took it out of my hands.

'Are those your old-fashioned manners taking over?' I asked with one of my eyebrows raised, not liking to be thought of as physically delicate just because I'm petite.

'Yes, but I'm also thinking of your shoulder. If this gets too heavy you could strain your injured muscles.'

'I'd carry it with my right arm,' I pointed out affably.

'But if it got uncomfortable, you'd be tempted to shift it to the other side. I'm removing that temptation.' He smiled sweetly and ran a finger over my pouting lips.

'If I hurt my shoulder, you could rub it better.' I smiled suggestively at him.

'I'll give you a massage any time you want; you don't have to hurt yourself, you only have to ask. Are you sure this basket is going to be big enough?' He regarded it uncertainly.

'It's fine. I don't eat a lot.'

'I've noticed,' he said, not nastily, but not pleased, either. 'I'll cook for you tonight,' he announced suddenly. 'You've pampered me all week; I'd like to do something for you in return.'

'I only want to be with you, Gabriel; you don't need to do anything.' I reached up and touched his face. 'I spoiled you this much because it was your birthday week. I don't want anything in return.'

He covered my hand with his and pressed his cheek into my palm. 'You said your birthday was January. I met you in January, but not until the end of the month. I missed it, didn't I?' There was a note of regret in his voice and he felt sadness for something else he couldn't change.

'Yes, it's the eleventh.'

'I'd like to make up for that if I could.'

'There's no need,' I reassured him. 'Having you is everything to me, and the only thing I'll ever want from you for the rest of my life, or forever if you turn me, is your love. You'll have mine forever.'

He knew I meant it. He pulled me to his side and put his free hand under my chin to tilt my face up so he was looking deeply into my eyes. 'I will love you forever, Jamie, you know I will.'

I nodded; I knew it. We felt it in each other as much as in ourselves.

'I'm still cooking for you, though,' he said decidedly. 'I want to see you eat something decent. Do you like goat's cheese?'

'I love it.'

'Good. I can make you a goat's cheese and cranberry tart accompanied by lightly steamed vegetables. How does that sound?'

'Actually, that sounds really nice.' He was about to comment, but I overrode him. 'That's as enthusiastic as I get about food. Do you know how to make vegetarian pastry?'

'Of course.' He flashed his teeth in a grin. 'In that case, I'm getting a trolley.'

He disappeared for a few seconds to exchange the basket for a small cart and I inserted myself behind it to push it whilst he selected what he needed off the shelves. We mainly bought items that wouldn't perish quickly; boxes of cereal and things that would last for a while in the freezer; but I also noticed Gabriel choosing things I couldn't believe he'd ever have a use for.

'What do you need caster sugar for?' I queried, suspecting that I already knew the answer given the amount of butter he had already picked up.

'I thought we'd make a cake. Are you any good at baking?'

'I'm a hopeless cook, but I *can* bake cakes. Okay, so it used to be quite possible for me to eat the majority of a cake to myself, but why would you want to make something like that when you can't even eat it? It's not worth it just for me.'

'You like cake, so it is worth it. I don't expect you to eat it all in one go; it will last for a few days, and if you don't finish it,' he shrugged, 'then you don't finish it.' Gabriel scrutinised me silently for a moment. 'You're human,' he began quietly, 'you require food to survive, so why do you think that needing to eat is such an inconvenience?'

'Because it is,' I explained, also keeping my voice down. 'Preparing and cooking food is so time-consuming in comparison to just heating some blood. It just feels so high-maintenance and I could be doing something else with that time.'

He grinned. 'High-maintenance? For something necessary for you to stay alive?'

'Yes, I know it sounds ridiculous, and I know the effects on the body of prolonged starvation: organ failure, osteoporosis, infertility, hair loss; the list goes on. I eat enough, I'm just not happy about it.' I started to cross my arms in front of my chest, then resisted the urge, because that would make it seem as though I were defending myself, and I had no reason to do that.

'How long ago?' he asked, eyes narrowed.

He was good.

'It started ten years ago and I was borderline anorexic for three years, throughout the time of my Bachelor of Arts with Honours. I got past it.'

'And recently?'

'It's not like that. I haven't regressed, if that's what you're worried about. Come on, *Dr.* Castell, you know it's not uncommon for someone to lose their appetite after suffering a bereavement. That doesn't mean I have an eating disorder.' I pleaded with my eyes and my heart for him to believe me, for him to understand.

'I do understand. I'm not accusing you, Jamie. I've told you before that I want you to be healthy. I'm going to cook for you tonight. It won't be an inconvenience for you or me, and you can work whilst I do. This afternoon, however, I want us to make a cake together. It will be silly and it will be fun. Please?'

'Okay.' I couldn't refuse him anything and he knew it.

'What type of cake do you prefer?'

'It really has been a long time since you've eaten food if you have to ask.'

'Chocolate?'

'Chocolate sponge, with chocolate filling, and chocolate topping. As far as cake is concerned, there is no such thing as too much chocolate.' I smiled at Gabriel, feeling the same way I did when I was a kid and Carmel and I used to bake cakes with Mum. We'd sample the mixture before it made it to the cake tins and we'd each have a spatula or a beater from the electric whisk to lick.

'You'd better get some cocoa powder then,' he instructed. 'Lots of it.'

I let go of the trolley and Gabriel took my place behind it, following me as I dashed down the aisle to find the cocoa powder. It was on the top shelf, just out of reach for me even on tiptoes. I was standing on the bumper rail that ran parallel with the bottom shelf, and I had just reached up to grasp a couple of containers of the powder, when a warm arm wound around my middle and I was pulled back against Gabriel's chest. He lifted me up off the rail and swung me back down onto the ground.

I giggled and looked up to find Gabriel smiling at me before he leaned in and kissed me. With his free hand, he picked up two pots of cocoa powder and handed them to me to put in the trolley.

There was a woman nearby, who looked to be somewhere in her sixties, who had watched this whole scene happen. She smiled at us as she walked towards us, pushing a trolley of her own. As she drew level with Gabriel and me, she stopped.

'I hope you don't mind my saying so, but the two of you look absolutely adorable together.' She smiled sweetly, first at me, then at Gabriel.

'Thank you,' I replied, a little surprised, but pleased. 'That's really kind of you to say.' Gabriel nodded his agreement with me.

'I hope you have many happy years together,' she added and, just as she was walking away, she turned back to us. 'From the looks of the pair of you, your children will be just as beautiful.'

'Thanks again,' Gabriel said as we shared an amused look.

I was silent for a moment, considering the older woman's comment. It wasn't as though I didn't know that being with Gabriel meant I'd never have children, and I didn't mind. I was twenty-eight now and I'd never felt the desire to be a mother.

'Don't be alarmed,' Gabriel said when the older woman was out of earshot. 'It's understandable that someone of her generation would look at a young couple and automatically think marriage and babies. That's what my parents thought when they saw Marta and I together more than a century ago. It's mainly your generation, and your mother's to some extent, that have begun to view parenthood as an option rather than an inevitability.'

'It's just disconcerting to be viewed that way. It was as though our identities didn't matter, just as long as we did our duty to procreate.'

'Tell me about it,' he agreed trenchantly. 'Only, in my previous experience, it was to cement a pure-blooded vampire dynasty.' He grimaced.

'Of course. I'm sorry, Gabriel.' I bit my lip and rubbed his shoulder. 'Have we got everything?'

'I think so. Is there anything you need before we go home?'

'No. Actually, yes. Would it be too much trouble to stop by my house so I can pick up my laptop? I've got a lot of typing to do with the vampire thing I'm working on, so I can do that if I get sick of research, or I can't write. You know, I'm not even sure I should continue that vampire story, or novel, or whatever it is,' I confessed uncertainly.

'Why not?' he asked, his eyebrows drawing together severely in bewilderment.

'Now that I know you, and I know the truth about vampires, anything I write about them is going to seem so unrealistic to me and probably completely ridiculous to you,' I explained. 'I would never write about what you've told me, though, Gabriel,' I quickly assured him. 'I wouldn't expose you.'

'I know that, Jamie, I'm not worried. As for what you're writing not being good enough, that is completely untrue. I like what you've written so far. I like the idea behind it: a vampire trying to regain her mortality rather than a human wanting to become immortal.' He put his hand under my chin and tilted my face up to look directly at him, and he held me there so I could both see, and feel, the truth in him. 'Your spin on vampire mythology isn't ridiculous because it's not the truth. It has come from your imagination; without you even knowing the truth, you wanted to move away from the tired myths and write something unique. Your imaginings are never dull; don't ever doubt yourself, Jamie.'

'You really don't think it's silly?' I bit my lip again. Gabriel noticed the movement and recognised it as a nervous habit of mine; something I did when I felt vulnerable or insecure.

He shook his head. 'I really don't.' He ran his finger over my bottom lip. 'I think you should finish it; it's too good not to.' He smiled sweetly at me.

'Okay. We'll pay for this then pick up my computer from home. It's not too much trouble, is it?'

'Nothing is too much trouble for you; you should know that by now.'

It wasn't until we were in the car on the way to my house that Gabriel turned the conversation back to my vampire story.

'So, is Freya going to find a way to become mortal again, or haven't you decided yet?'

I laughed. 'Do you really want to know? You really want me to spoil the surprise?'

He smiled. 'Even if you don't tell me, I'll know the ending before I read it on the page, anyway; I'll read it from you.'

'True. In which case you should already know the answer, Gabriel,' I countered.

'I haven't been looking for the answer. I thought I'd find out the old-fashioned way by asking.'

'I've got a few different ideas,' I admitted. 'At the moment, I'm not leaning towards any one more than another. My first thought was for her to find a way to reverse the vampirism, that maybe there's some clue in her blood: a difference between vampire blood and human blood. Then, if she were completely drained of her blood, to the point of death, and given a transfusion, she would be cured but it would be such a risky procedure the likelihood would be that she would die during the process.

'Another thought was that she would die attempting some kind of false cure, or it was the real cure but she died, anyway. I think you know why I had thoughts about her dying, or almost dying; it's not art imitating life at all,' I said sardonically.

'It's understandable,' he replied, his lips twitching.

'More recently, I've been thinking about her coming to terms with her vampirism; accepting who she is and that there isn't a cure. Her sire could find her, or she could find him, and he is remorseful for doing that to her against her will and leaving her. He had been desperate for a companion to share eternity with, had followed her as a human, liked her and chose her, but then hated himself for what he did and abandoned her out of guilt. He helps her accept it and they fall in love. That's the unlikely, soppy, romantic ending,' I added ruefully.

'So you'd seriously kill your heroine?' he asked, genuinely surprised considering he knew I was a romantic.

'Yes. What do you think?'

'They're all good. With what you've written so far, they'd all work.'

'I'll see which way the story takes me, then the right ending will make itself clear. Although, I've just thought of another alternative. Her sire could find her and it all goes as I've just described, but she also finds a cure. He doesn't want it, so she has to choose between mortality and him.' It was still similar to my own situation in a way, and we both recognised it. I thought about it for a moment. 'I think my idea of what the "cure" actually entails is a bit weak. I'd have to think of something else if I decided on that ending.'

'Your story is all myth, so your idea for a cure is as distinctive as your take on vampirism. The existence of vampires is largely secret, so few people believe we are real, anyway and, as there isn't a cure, your idea of blood being the key to both immortality and mortality is incredibly clever. Most people would think the concept of replacing blood is too simple to work so they would ignore using it; that's the beauty of it.'

Gabriel parked his car in the driveway of my family home, which had been completely empty since I'd had my old car taken away and my mum's car was now parked at Gabriel's house. I'd left my keys behind so Gabriel let us in, picking up a small pile of post as he protectively headed in before me to ensure it was safe; to ensure that no one had broken in and was either still in there, or had left a trail of destruction in their wake.

'I'll only be a few seconds,' I said as I headed in the direction of the stairs.

I climbed the first step, then twisted around to grab Gabriel's arm. He turned towards me and our faces were almost level. I only had to tilt my chin up slightly to press my lips to his, and I tugged his arm to bring him closer to me. He smiled against my mouth and reached his hand behind my neck, into my hair, to hold my head steady whilst he deepened the kiss.

I playfully stroked my tongue along his bottom lip before pulling it between my teeth and lightly nibbling it. Gabriel growled from deep within his chest, then I let go and pulled back slightly.

'Let me know if any of those are important.' I gestured to the envelopes in his hand and continued up the stairs.

'You want me to open them?'

'If you would.'

I hurried to my bedroom and found my memory stick on my dresser. I put it in my pocket and picked my laptop and its power cord up off the floor. Just as I straightened up, I heard the doorbell ring and, about two seconds later, Gabriel opened the door.

'I thought that if Jamie was home, you'd be here, too.' It was Aaron.

Annoyance flared inside me, echoing Gabriel's.

'What are you doing here?' Gabriel asked, sounding impassive even though I could feel rage beginning to burn inside him.

'I came to talk to Jamie. Where is she?'

I'd reached the top of the stairs and was wending my way down. Aaron looked up when I came into view, but Gabriel didn't move; he knew I was there.

'Jamie has made her point very clearly to you several times, yet you still continue to harass her. However much you're grieving, it's no excuse for what you're doing to her. Your pain is nothing compared to hers. I'm telling you to leave her alone and I suggest you get some help,' Gabriel finished coldly.

'Jamie,' Aaron began, and made a lunge forward to come into the house.

Gabriel thrust his arm out and braced it against the door frame, barring Aaron access. Aaron shot a baleful glance at Gabriel, then turned his attention back to me as he took a step backwards.

I got to the bottom of the stairs and stood by Gabriel. I could feel his protectiveness emanating from his core and he immediately reached over, put his hands on my hips and moved me behind him so he was a barrier from Aaron.

'What do you want, Aaron?' I asked, peering over Gabriel's shoulder and adopting his cool tone.

His gaze swept the driveway. 'Have you taken your car to the garage? I noticed you've been using Bea's.'

'No, it's not in the garage. I had to scrap my car.'

'But the damage wasn't that bad,' he protested.

'No, it wasn't, but the cost of the repairs was more than the car was worth.'

A look of shame passed over his face. It irked me that he was ashamed of damaging my car, but not of all the derogatory things he had said to me recently. He remained silent; he didn't apologise and he didn't even feel sorry for any of the pain he'd caused me.

'If that's all you came for…' Gabriel said, and he started to close the door.

He only got it halfway when Aaron shouted, 'Wait!'

I'd already turned to walk away, but I swung back around as Gabriel opened the door again. We stood there waiting, but Aaron didn't speak.

'What exactly is it that you want from me, Aaron?' I asked, my exasperation becoming evident. 'I voluntarily signed Carmel's share of the business over to you and I wanted nothing in return. Do you want Carmel's ring back? You can have it.' I clutched my computer to my chest with one arm whilst I slid the ring off my finger using the thumb and ring finger of the hand it was on and held it out to him. He didn't take it, so I put it in the pocket of my jeans.

'You've been nasty to both Gabriel and me on the phone,' I continued. 'You've sent vulgar text messages and you vandalised my car. How much more are you going to put me through? I know you hate it that I lived and Carmel didn't, but tormenting me isn't going to bring her back and I refuse to take any more of this crap from you. Go and get some help and leave me alone.'

I stormed away, silently fuming, and collapsed onto the sofa. Aaron didn't prevent Gabriel from shutting the door this time; I heard it bang and a second later, Gabriel was wrenching my laptop out of my hands. He set it down on the coffee table, sat in the space next to me, and pulled me against him and onto his lap. I buried my face into his shoulder and I felt him kiss my hair, then he stroked it all the way down my back.

'I think you should give DI Fordham a call, Jamie. He told you to let him know if Aaron continued pestering you, didn't he?' I nodded. 'Well, find out what can be done now before Aaron gets violent.'

'Did you sense violent feelings in him?' I raised my head to look at him. I had become too enraged with Aaron to notice if he'd felt that way.

'They're buried quite deep, but they're there, and I don't want to take the risk of him hurting you.' His mouth was pinched tightly with the worry I could feel exuding from him.

'Gabriel, can he hurt you?' I was suddenly aware that I didn't know what would happen if Gabriel got injured; if he could die.

'Only by causing you pain of any kind.' He kissed me on the forehead.

'Thank you.' I rubbed my palm over his heart, letting him know I thought it was a sweet sentiment. 'Can he harm you physically, though?'

'Not seriously. Any damage he did would heal within seconds if it's superficial, and minutes if it's a bit deeper. Even if he severed a vein or an artery, it would heal before I lost too much blood; of course, I'd have to drink to replace that blood.'

'But it would hurt, surely.'

'Yes, it still hurts just as much.' He smiled sadly.

'What about a bullet to the head or heart? Wouldn't that kill you?'

'A bullet could never penetrate my bones, even at point-blank range.' My eyebrows shot up. 'When a vampire becomes immortal, his or her bones harden, so a bullet to the head, for example, would pierce the skin but rebound off the skull. If the shot was to the chest, the bullet wouldn't make it through the ribs. I can't lose any appendages, and I can't break any bones, either.'

'So is there no way for an immortal vampire to be killed?' I asked, hoping that it meant he would never be in danger.

Gabriel monitored all my internal and external reactions closely. 'There is only one way immortal vampires can die. We can be beheaded, though only another vampire would have the strength to sever through the neck bones, which, incidentally, are the softest bones we have. It's as though we've been left an escape clause if we decide we don't want to live forever after all.' He gave a grim smile and shrugged.

'What about fire?' I asked, thinking of the traditional vampire mythology.

'If we received minor burns, our flesh would regenerate quickly, but severe, full-thickness burns all over the body would take much longer, and we'd be in excruciating pain.'

'Ouch.'

'Exactly. But we have quick reflexes and we can move swiftly, so the chances of that happening are slim.'

I put my head on his shoulder for a moment.

'I've got DI Fordham's direct line,' I said, returning to Gabriel's earlier suggestion. 'He gave it to me when he was investigating the shooting in case there was someone else involved and that person came after me to finish the job. He was really worried about me because I was on my own.' It was my turn to offer a sad smile.

'I like the sound of him,' Gabriel said enthusiastically, and he dug his hand into my pocket to retrieve my phone.

He handed it to me and I scrolled through the phone book until I came to DI Fordham's number and I hit the dial button. He answered after only one ring.

'DI Fordham,' the deep voice said.

'Hello, DI Fordham, it's Jamie Kavanagh.'

'Hi, Jamie. I take it your almost-brother-in-law is still being a nuisance if you're calling me.' There was a knowing smile in his voice; nothing got past him.

'I'm afraid so, Detective.'

'Please, call me Jim.'

'Okay, thanks. Unfortunately, Aaron's harassment hasn't stopped since you spoke to him. He's still calling and texting, saying similar things as before, both to me and to my boyfriend, but he's also been to my house: once last week when I was alone, and again just now.'

'Are you alone at home now?'

'No, my boyfriend is with me, thankfully. The thing is, Aaron hasn't been physically violent towards me, but I feel threatened and unsafe,' I said anxiously. 'After his last visit, I went and stayed at my partner's house with him because I felt so uncomfortable being at home where I knew he could find me. Is there anything you can do?'

'I'll arrange a restraining order, but if he comes near you again, call me directly and I'll come and arrest him myself.'

'Thank you.' I was so relieved I almost couldn't say any more. 'Do you need to see the text messages he sent for evidence? I have them saved on my phone.'

'That won't be necessary, I'll just take details of their contents, dates and times, plus what you can remember from his phone calls and visits. I'll also need to speak to your boyfriend about that, too.'

'Okay,' I replied, and relayed everything I could remember. I handed the phone to Gabriel. 'He wants to speak with you,' I told him.

Gabriel looked wary, but agreed to talk to him with a nod.

'Could you get me a glass of water please, Jamie?' Gabriel asked.

I nodded and, as I extricated myself from him and stood up to go, Gabriel put the phone to his ear.

'Hello, DI Fordham,' he said as I reached the doorway. 'Yes, I am Jamie's boyfriend.' I exited the room, but I could still hear Gabriel's voice. 'My name is Gabriel Castell... Yes, I am,' he said tersely. The pause must have been DI Fordham asking him a question.

Gabriel's voice was muffled by the time I reached the kitchen and, as I busied myself getting glasses and a bottle of water from the fridge, the sound of my movements drowned out even more of Gabriel's conversation so I only managed to catch the odd broken trickle of words.

'...bumped into her in a bookshop... recognised her...'

I thought that Jim must have been asking how Gabriel and I met and I wondered if that was for official purposes, or if it was him being both curious as well as cautious. He wasn't quite old enough to be my father, but he did have a slightly paternal attitude towards me.

There was another stream of words.

'…doesn't know… want… hurt her…' Gabriel must have been telling Jim about Aaron and his suspicions about what Aaron was capable of.

Both Gabriel's and my accounts of what had been happening should be more than sufficient to get that restraining order. Some of my agitation started to fade.

I realised then that having been at Gabriel's house for a week, I'd neglected the plants in my own. I found a jug in one of the cupboards, filled it with water, and gave my mother's plants a drink. The soil in each pot was bone dry and that made me feel guilty. My mum loves plants and I would hate myself if they died because I hadn't cared for them properly.

By the time I made it back to the living room, Gabriel was just finishing his conversation with Jim.

'I'll tell her, DI Fordham. I will,' he insisted after a pause. 'Goodbye.' He hung up the phone and passed it back to me. He ran a hand through his hair, blew out a long breath, then looked at me and smiled.

'Your water,' I said, handing him his glass. I took a mouthful from my own glass, then set it down. 'Is everything okay?' I sat down next to him.

Gabriel drained almost half the glass before he answered. 'Everything is fine,' he said, but I felt a brief flash of disquiet in him before he masked it with concern for my safety. 'DI Fordham said he'd organise that restraining order immediately. He also advised you not to answer your phone if Aaron calls. If he leaves voicemails, or sends text messages, let me check them for any threats to you, that way you won't have to listen to, or read them, if you don't want to.' Feeling my distress, he took hold of one of my hands. 'It's going to be okay, Jamie.'

I nodded and looked away from his gaze. I was worried about what Aaron might do next; this latest development was likely to incense him further. More than that, however, I was disturbed by that unease I had felt in Gabriel, what it could mean, and why he had hidden it from me when he said he never shielded his emotions from me. I had to ask him about it. I took his glass from him to set it on the table with mine, took hold of his hands, and looked at him firmly.

'Gabriel, I could tell that you didn't really want to speak with DI Fordham and, when you ended the call, you felt unsettled.'

'I was worried for you,' he said gently.

'No, you concealed it with solicitude for me, but you were feeling something else. Why did you hide it? You said you didn't keep anything from me.' I deliberately kept my tone inquisitive rather than accusatory. I had no reason to be suspicious, but my heart was beginning to beat a little bit faster.

'I know I said that,' he said, squeezing my hands tightly, 'and I meant it. I don't shield my feelings from you and you're right, I do have another concern. I won't keep it from you; I'll tell you all about it, I promise, but I really don't want to talk about it right now. Please understand, Jamie,' he beseeched. His eyes and his heart begged me as much as his voice.

'Of course I understand. When you're ready to talk, I'm ready to listen. You know by now that you can tell me anything.' I smiled to lighten the mood.

'I know.' He grinned back, gratitude radiating through him.

'So, do you still want to make that cake?'

Fifteen
Distraction

Our detour to my house had taken a little longer than anticipated, but, back at Gabriel's, we lost no time in getting started on the cake. As Gabriel switched the oven on to preheat, he laughed to himself.

'This is the first time the oven has ever been used,' he remarked.

I smiled. 'How long has it been installed?'

'Five or six years. Every time I modernise, I get rid of appliances that have never been used.' He studied me, measuring my expression and my feelings, and he discerned I was thinking about his past. 'I told you that you are the first person I have ever had in my house. I've never brought anyone else here for any reason.'

I nodded, conciliated. 'So, what happens to all those appliances? If they have never been used, it's such a waste to destroy them.'

'I don't destroy them; I donate them to under-funded centres: shelters, day-centres for the elderly, children's homes, anywhere that needs them. I pay for them to be fully checked for safety and installed where necessary.' One half of his mouth curved up when he felt how glad that made me.

I stepped up to him and put my arms around his neck, pressing my body into his. 'That is such a wonderful and generous thing to do, Gabriel.'

The other half of his mouth moved up and he leaned forward to place a lingering kiss on my mouth. 'I'm glad you think so. I know I live rather excessively, but I'm not so intemperate that I can't appreciate my situation and recognise that most people aren't so fortunate, and some are desperate for help.'

'Have I ever told you how much I love you?' I asked.

'You have, and I've felt it, but I always like to hear it.'

'I love you so completely and unconditionally that nothing could ever make me stop loving you.' I felt his heart skip a beat and I felt something that was an amalgamation of so many feelings; love, relief, hope; surge through him.

'You really mean that.' It wasn't a question; it was a statement he knew to be true.

'Of course I do, Gabriel. You never doubted me, did you?' I frowned; I hadn't felt any uncertainty in him.

'No, it's just that you know there's something I haven't told you and I was scared that might have put a barrier between us,' he said, feeling a little concerned.

'It hasn't, and whatever you have to tell me won't change how I feel about you.' I meant it and he knew it. I knew that whatever he wasn't telling me probably wasn't good, otherwise he would have told me already, but I knew that everything he had done for me he'd done out of love. I could feel that it was impossible not to love him back just as much, especially because he hoped and wished for it, he didn't just expect it.

'My love for you is unconditional, too, Jamie, even if someday you hate me for failing you.' I could feel the sadness that was evident in his eyes, and it pierced us both.

I wasn't sure where this was coming from, so I took his face between my palms to ensure he was looking directly into my eyes, into me. 'Gabriel, I could *never* hate you and you could *never* fail me.'

He closed his eyes but didn't respond to that; I knew he believed me. After a few long seconds, he opened them again.

'There are some weighing scales and a recipe book somewhere in one of these cupboards.' He gently removed my hands and let me go.

'Scales I'll need, but a recipe book I won't. I've made chocolate cake dozens of times and I know exactly what I'm doing.'

For someone who didn't eat, or have visitors to cook for, he had baking tins, roasting tins, pans, bowls and utensils in abundance. I avoided the electric mixer in favour of a wooden spoon; unlike Mum and Carmel, I always preferred mixing by hand. Gabriel thought it amusing that I picked the bowl up and held it at thigh level in order to beat the mixture because keeping it on the work surface made my shoulder and arm ache on account of my being so short. We took it in turns to mix; when my arms got tired, he took over.

We had just creamed the butter and sugar together and were adding the eggs when Gabriel softly asked, 'Jamie, in the time since you met me, why haven't you visited your mother and sister's grave? You'd been a few times before that.'

'I know.' My voice was barely audible. 'I'm ashamed of myself for not visiting more often. It's difficult not to think of them lying in coffins, deep under the ground, and it's more real when I'm standing next to where they're buried; I can't *not* think about them in there. It makes me feel panicky.' I wouldn't look up from the bowl.

'I don't mean this to sound crass,' he spoke in a soothing tone, 'but if you don't like the idea of them in their coffins in the ground, why didn't you have them cremated?'

'Because that would have been worse. I couldn't bear the thought of their bodies being burned.' My voice cracked.

Gabriel took the bowl from my hands and placed it on the work surface. Sensing how distressed I was by the idea, he took me into his arms and held me tightly before turning me around, pulling me back tightly against his chest, and continuing to attack the ingredients in the bowl with his arms through mine.

'No, it is a much more distressing thought. The mental images that cremation evokes are horrific. I understand, Jamie.'

I nodded. 'Thanks.' I leaned my head against his shoulder, then added some flour and cocoa powder to the curdling mixture.

Gabriel tilted his head forward and kissed me softly on the mouth. 'I was there at the funeral, you know. You were so strong.' He was still talking quietly, recognising I was feeling fragile.

'I knew that neither Mum nor Carmel would want a religious service, so I decided a Humanist one would be more appropriate,' I explained emotionlessly. 'It was difficult to hold myself together through that because it was so personal. It wouldn't have been like that if some priest or vicar had officiated; he would have droned on about God and Jesus and not really said very much about who Mum and Carmel are. I cried, but I didn't completely break down.

'I was determined to make it through my eulogy, though. I knew I could collapse afterwards just as long as *I* said what I wanted to say about them; to tell everyone who and what Mum and Carmel are to me. I couldn't *stop* crying after that.'

Gabriel added more flour and cocoa powder to the bowl whilst I stirred.

'I saw you. You sobbed at their graveside and I had to restrain myself from coming over to you and wrapping you in my arms. My heart was breaking for you, but you had no idea who I was so I had to keep my distance. People came and spoke to you, but no one was really there for you.'

'Rachael wanted to be there, but she was on bed rest until her son was born,' I informed him. 'Her husband, Baz, was there. He was there to support me, but he couldn't stay for long after the interment. I functioned on autopilot for the rest of the day, but it's all hazy; I don't remember the rest clearly.' I shrugged.

I didn't care that I couldn't remember much after the burial. My arm had been in a sling and I was taking medication for the pain and so I didn't get an infection. Carmel's friends were all friends with Aaron so they convened with him and his family. Many of my mother's friends knew each other so they also stayed together. Someone dutifully came over and spoke to me every now and then and tried to force me to drink cups of tea even though I hate the stuff.

I turned around in his arms. 'I want to go to their grave more often. I want to take care of it and make it look beautiful. It's all I can do for them now,' I said sadly.

'I'll take you tomorrow if you want,' Gabriel suggested. 'We'll get some flowers for them. I'll be there for you if you need me, and if you want to be alone with them, I'll wait in the car.'

I nodded. 'That would be nice. We've got to get daffodils; they're in season and Mum loves them.' I smiled slightly.

'Daffodils. Not a problem.' Gabriel smiled back.

I hugged him quickly, then we poured the cake mixture into the baking tins and, whilst they were cooking, we mixed up the chocolate buttercream for the filling and topping. Since Gabriel didn't eat, I got to lick the raw cake mix off the spoon and dip my fingers into the buttercream. He licked one of my fingers and I raised my eyebrows at him.

'It's close to liquid so it won't sit in my stomach undigested the way solid food would,' he explained. 'It still tastes as good to me as when I did eat.'

I swiped my finger back through the chocolate goo and held it out to him. He wrapped his lips around my finger down to the knuckle in the middle, and I felt his tongue stroke the tip. When the chocolate had gone, I felt him playfully nip at the flesh. I jumped slightly and Gabriel grinned at me, my finger still held between his teeth.

Impulsively, I said, 'If the cake is a treat for me, would you like some of my blood as yours? You can take more than you did last time.'

I thought it strange that during his birthday week, even though I'd told Gabriel he could have whatever he wanted, he could ask me for anything, he did not ask to taste my blood again.

He released my finger, but grasped my wrist in his hand and brought it to his lips to kiss the underside where the skin was thin over my veins.

'I love the feeling of closeness that tasting your blood brings,' he said, his pupils dilating with the desire that was growing inside him. 'And though I want to feel that as much, and as often, as possible, I don't want you to be covered in bite marks. You don't heal as quickly as I do and you could be left with scars, even after taking my blood in return; I don't want that. Even though you offer your blood willingly, for me to do that to you would be unconscionable; it would be bordering on abuse.'

'I think that's a bit strong, but I understand why you feel that way. I don't think I want to be covered in scars, either. I just thought that because you were already biting my finger, it wouldn't be much worse than cutting myself with a knife or something.'

'I hope you mean accidentally cutting yourself with a knife, not on purpose for me to drink.' He disapproved.

'Yes, Gabriel, I mean accidentally.' I tried not to smile at his stern expression: it was so cute.

He didn't say anything more and, without breaking eye contact, he brought my hand to his mouth and drew my thumb inside, closing his lips around it down to the base. He pushed the pad of my thumb, where my pulse was beating fiercely, against the sharp point of one of his fangs to puncture the skin, then he impaled me deeper so my wound would bleed more profusely and it would take longer for my blood to clot.

He eased my thumb away from his tooth and sucked deeply from the cut. He closed his eyes in pleasure as my blood flowed freely. It had momentarily stung when his fang pierced my skin, but the harder his mouth pulled at me, the more sensuous it felt. I moaned, and Gabriel briefly opened his eyes to pull me against him with his free arm and hold me there.

It fascinated me to watch him as he drank like this: not to satiate hunger, but to feel so viscerally linked to me. I'd been studying him for a while when he broke into my reverie.

'You're not clotting,' he stated, opening his eyes wide, and I saw they were etched with his concern.

'It's okay, I will. It just takes a while with me. Keep drinking,' I encouraged.

I felt him hesitate for a fraction of a heartbeat in fear that there was something wrong for the tear in my thumb to still be bleeding so effusively, but his trust in me overrode his worry and he compressed the flesh of my thumb between his teeth to force more blood to the surface.

It took several more minutes for my blood to finally stop flowing, but when it did, Gabriel released my hand and, with no thought of non-reciprocation, brought his own hand up to his mouth and bit deeply into the soft flesh at the base of his thumb. He held it towards me and I saw it was bleeding reasonably heavily. Without any hesitation, I reached for his hand and brought it to my mouth. Blood had begun to trickle in a rivulet down to his wrist and I licked it before fastening my lips over the bite and swallowing the warm blood as it flowed onto my tongue.

His hand continued to bleed for a couple of minutes and, whilst I drank from him, both of us were caught in the rapture of emotion the blood exchange provoked.

I raised my head when the blood-flow stopped and ran my tongue over the wound one last time before removing my mouth from his hand. I continued to hold it and watched as the puncture marks began to heal, sealing themselves over, and leaving him only with rapidly-fading pink teeth marks.

I looked up and pressed my mouth to his. I broke away only to say, 'I love you.'

'I love you, too,' Gabriel replied before he sealed his mouth to mine once more.

He increased the pressure, and I could taste my blood in his mouth just as he tasted his own in mine. We couldn't get close enough to one another and, when Gabriel pulled away, we were both breathing erratically.

'I promised I'd cook for you,' Gabriel said, and I watched the passion in his eyes recede, leaving warmth which echoed the smile on his lips. 'If I don't start now, you'll be eating this meal, complete with cake, for breakfast.'

Due to the generous size of the living room and the vastness of the library, there was no separate dining room in Gabriel's house and, though the kitchen wasn't used in the way it would be in a human home, it was still decently proportioned and had a table and chairs positioned off to one side. I placed my laptop on the table and sat in a chair facing Gabriel so I could watch him as he worked. I laid out the pages of handwritten copy and began to type.

Every now and then, I'd look up to see what Gabriel was doing, to watch him mixing ingredients for pastry together by hand, to view the deft movements of his long, elegant fingers.

'You're supposed to be typing, not looking at me,' Gabriel commented without looking up.

My eyes flew to his face and I could see that he was grinning. I started hitting random keys in a regular rhythm whilst surreptitiously still gazing at him. He still didn't take his eyes off his task, but I knew he wasn't fooled.

'You know I don't believe you're actually working,' he said, finally looking at me.

I grinned at him. 'I'm typing; I just have no idea *what* I'm typing. You didn't specify that it needed to be my story.' I gave him an arch look.

'You're in so much trouble later,' he purred sultrily.

'Promise?' I responded artlessly and was rewarded with the flash of his teeth as he gave me a sly smile.

'Do you think there is something wrong with your story?' he asked because I was so preoccupied. 'When I read it, I thought it was intriguing and you expressed yourself extremely well. You don't feel disappointed with it,' he observed.

'I'm not disappointed with it. I'm rather proud of it, actually. When I began writing it, I was in a delicate condition; both mentally and emotionally; and I just wrote, not even particularly certain how coherent any of it was. I'm pleased it reads so well.' I was contemptuous of my momentary lack of self-belief.

'So, why are you distracted from it?' he asked, knowing the answer.

'I think I'm writing a good story, and I've created a well-rounded character, but that's fiction. I've got you, Gabriel; you're living and breathing right in front of me, you love me and, much as I love my imaginary worlds, I'm living in this one with you which is a far better, not to mention real, experience. I don't need my fantasy worlds now I have you.'

'So, I'm distracting you?'

'In the best possible way, yes. I've actually got my perfect man in my life since losing my family, not someone I had to create in a story. I love my mum and sister, but I've always craved more than just familial love and, until now, I've had to imagine that. Even when I was with Hayden, I was imagining how I really wanted to be loved rather than what I got from him, and what I gave to him for that matter. So, please, keep distracting me indefinitely.' I smiled a lop-sided smile.

When I thought about it, I was actually rather pathetic and I was disappointed with myself for that.

Gabriel stopped what he was doing for a moment and looked me in the eye. 'You're not pathetic, and you have absolutely no reason to be disappointed with yourself, Jamie. Sometimes, you have to experience something that's wrong, or doesn't live up to your expectations, to fully recognise and appreciate the something that does, and is right. You don't always fully understand what you want until you endure something that's not quite right but has been masquerading as what seems right. I know that's a bit of a convoluted way of explaining what I mean, but you understand me, right?'

I nodded.

'So, I'll keep distracting you for all eternity, with great pleasure, and hope that it inspires your creativity. Your ambition is to write novels, so just keep writing. I'll always be here.'

'Thank you, Gabriel. What's your ambition?'

'To love you and to make you happy.' I blew him kisses and sent him love empathically and he smiled at me, sending love back. 'I've never had any real career ambition. I never intended to practice psychology, but my only other passion is books. I'm like you: I love them.'

'And you're a good critic. You've studied literature so you recognise good writing and a good story. You understand the psychology of fiction, and I still think you should write a book on that. How about editing my books?' I encouraged. 'I trust your judgment and opinion because you can see my vision.'

'I'm honoured. I'd love to.' He was genuinely touched.

'It would mean self-publishing because it's so difficult to get anyone in publishing houses to read manuscripts, and even if they did, and liked the story, they'd want one of their own editors to work with me. That person would probably instruct me to make changes that would fit their model of what they think my narrative should be rather than what I want it to be.'

'Basically, more of the same of everything else in the genre that they've published but with different character names,' he concurred.

'You've got it.'

'It's not a problem. We can set up a website and sell books directly from that, go to bookshops and ask them to distribute it for you, and you can advertise and sell on bookselling websites as well. It's not as difficult and as daunting as it seems at first,' Gabriel assured me.

'How do you know?' I asked, feigning suspicion.

'I've already looked into it for you.' I raised my eyebrows at him. 'I know you're not incapable, it was just something that crossed my mind when I discovered that you write. Self-publishing is a good idea; and you'll retain all of your rights.'

'I know. That's a massive draw for me; I want full control and ownership of my writing.'

'That's understandable. Just finish your manuscript and then I can start editing,' he said, inclining his head towards my computer.

I went back to it, deleting all the rubbish I'd typed earlier, but I kept peeking at Gabriel every now and then and he knew it; he was just too nice a distraction. I was working, though, so he didn't tease me and, secretly, he liked the attention.

After an hour of typing, my eyes were starting to glaze over and ache. I blinked a few times, gently rubbed them, and I got up to give them a rest from the screen and to stretch my legs.

I walked over to where Gabriel stood peeling and chopping vegetables, stepped up behind him pressing my body up against his, and I wrapped my arms around his middle. I slipped my hands under his jumper, over his hot, taut stomach, and I felt the hard muscles clench in response to my touch and he groaned. I grinned and pushed up onto the tips of my toes to kiss the side of his neck.

'Taking a break?' he asked. He turned his head so I could kiss him properly whilst my fingers were still lightly caressing his abdomen.

'Mmm-hmm,' I replied, my mouth against his. 'My eyes were starting to hurt, plus it's my turn to distract you.'

'No need. No matter where I am or what I'm doing, *you* are my priority, Jamie; you're the centre of everything and my reason for being. Nothing can distract me from you.'

Gabriel put the knife down and twisted around in my embrace. He leaned against the work surface and bent forward slightly so I didn't have to stretch up so far to meet his mouth.

'You really are perfect, Gabriel. I want you to believe I think that of you.'

'I do; I can feel it. I believe you're perfect, too.'

'I know; I can feel it.'

He indulged me for a few more minutes before ordering me back to work so he could cook, but, ten minutes later, he came over to me, placed a glass of water on the table, then swept me up out of the chair to sit in it himself with me on his lap. He pressed his chest against my back and wound his arms around me, enfolding me in his embrace.

'Don't stop,' he murmured into my ear. 'You've got a few more minutes until everything's ready.'

I picked up the glass and took a couple of mouthfuls of water, then I finished typing the paragraph I'd begun, with Gabriel reading over my shoulder. Literally. His chin was resting on my right shoulder so he didn't disturb me as my handwritten pages were on my left.

I saved everything, shut down the computer, and tidied everything away onto one of the spare chairs whilst Gabriel set a place mat, silverware, and napkin for me at the table.

He filled a glass with water for himself and brought it with him along with the plate of food he'd prepared for me.

'Thank you for this, Gabriel. There really was no need to go to all this—'

'Trouble?' he finished for me, eyebrows raised. He shook his head. 'It really wasn't any trouble at all.'

'Of course it was; you don't even eat.'

'But you do, and it's not an inconvenience to ensure you eat something nice rather than just something to make sure you don't starve.'

I cut into the goat's cheese tart and ate a mouthful.

'Good?' he enquired.

'Much better than good,' I corrected.

'High praise for someone not even slightly interested in food.' He grinned wryly.

I'd always felt a little self-conscious eating in front of people. It didn't usually apply to people I knew and trusted, but I was starting to feel this way with Gabriel watching me.

'I feel so greedy eating this whilst you sit there with only water,' I admitted.

'You're uncomfortable under my scrutiny because of your past eating disorder,' he observed knowingly. He looked at my face for confirmation that it was true. It was. 'We'll talk whilst you eat to ease your mind. I have a subject I'd like to discuss with you, but if it pains you, or angers you, we don't have to talk about it.'

'Gabriel, you can ask me anything. We can talk about anything.'

'Even your father?' he asked, deliberately quietly in case it upset me.

'Even him,' I confirmed.

'You've never really spoken about him.'

'That's because I've never met him,' I said without a trace of bitterness. I had no feelings for him. 'He saw me once, when Carmel and I were born, but that was it.'

'Literally, once?'

'Yes, literally only one time. He was with Mum when she gave birth to us; I think he even held us once, not long after we were born. Mum had to stay in hospital overnight and Joe, my father, went home and was supposed to pick us all up the following morning. He never came.

'After calling the house and getting no reply, Mum called her parents to come and collect us. When we all got home, Mum found that Joe had cleared out all of his clothes and left a note saying he couldn't handle it, he wasn't ready to be a father, and all those clichés.' My tone was even; Mum had long since got over her initial devastation.

'That's despicable.' Gabriel betrayed a note of disgust. I merely nodded my agreement as I had a mouthful of food. 'Your poor mother. What did she do?'

I swallowed and took a sip of water before answering.

'Joe's parents had moved to the south coast several years earlier, and Mum assumed it was possible he'd gone to them. He wasn't there when she called, but he did turn up a few hours later. His parents were appalled with his behaviour and they promised Mum they'd do what they could to make him go home and face his responsibilities, but he really wanted nothing to do with us.'

'But surely, if nothing else, he was financially obligated,' Gabriel pointed out.

'Oh, yes, of course.' I grinned. 'He did try to get out of that, but his parents and the legal system saw to it that he gave Mum money every month. My mother also sold their marital home, got a divorce as soon as she could, and moved us into the house she has now. Luckily, she had always worked. It wasn't easy for her, but she was determined.' Gabriel smiled at my pride in her.

'What about your paternal grandparents? Did you have much contact with them?'

'The Waites? That's my father's surname. Mum gave us her maiden name and she changed her name back. We didn't have a lot of contact with them because of the distance. They used to visit once or twice a year. Mum sent photos of us as we grew up, and they used to send cheques now and then to help Mum out.

'She actually liked them; she even got a little inheritance from them when they died. They were so ashamed of what Joe did to Mum, Carmel, and me. They still loved him, but their relationship with him was never the same.'

'Did Bea never remarry?'

'No.' That made me a little sad. 'She said she'd never fully trust another man that way again. She always had a large circle of friends, so I know she wasn't lonely for adult company whilst Carmel and I were still children.'

'What about you and Carmel? You must have been curious about your father.' Gabriel was intrigued.

'We were when we were young. We used to ask questions about him and Mum was relatively honest without being nasty about him. At least until we were old enough to fully understand what he did.' I smiled sardonically. 'She used to say that he wasn't able to be a daddy to us, implying that he was ill, or worked away, without ever actually saying that and lying, until she admitted what a bastard he was.'

'Evidently. Did he never try to have any contact with you and Carmel? Birthday or Christmas cards? Did he ask for photos?' Gabriel frowned. He knew enough about human nature to know people were capable of such heartlessness.

'No, nothing at all. Mum had no communication with him apart from financial support and divorce papers. After he walked out she didn't *want* to hear from him again.'

'And you?'

'Me? I want nothing to do with him,' I answered dispassionately. 'As far as I'm concerned, he doesn't exist; to me he never has.'

'That's fair,' Gabriel agreed. 'Finished?' he indicated my plate.

I nodded. 'Thank you, Gabriel, it was lovely. You're a very good cook.'

'Thank you. You're not surprised by that.'

'Of course not.' I gestured in his direction. 'What aren't you good at?'

'Nothing.' He grinned.

'Hmm, except modesty,' I said, laughing.

'Wait until you've lived this long and we'll see what you haven't become adept at.'

And there it was: the admission that he *was* going to turn me, that I *would* be with him for all eternity as a vampire. Not 'if' I lived to be as old as him, but 'when.' Gabriel's heart skipped a beat as he acknowledged what he had admitted; he wasn't talking about it as a speculative hypothetical anymore, but as an inevitability, and he was cautiously pleased.

My heart faltered, too, because I was definitely pleased, but also a little sad that I'd never be with Mum and Carmel again. That was my only hesitation, and he knew it.

'Are you ready for cake?' Gabriel asked as he rose and picked up my plate.

I massaged my stomach. 'In a few minutes. Let's clear this up first, then I'll make coffee to have with it. Would you prefer to wash or dry?' I asked as I stood up, and I followed him to the sink.

'I have a dishwasher,' he explained as he pulled open what I thought was the door to another cupboard. 'I use it to wash all the plates, cups and things when they've been sitting there for a while.'

'Okay.'

I was actually glad there was a dishwasher; I'd always hated washing up and we'd created quite a mess between us with all the baking. Whilst he loaded everything into it, I made coffee for us both. I set the cups down on the table and Gabriel came up behind me and laid a plate with a huge slice of chocolate cake on it in front of me. When I looked up at him, he was grinning shamelessly.

'Just because you can't gain weight, it doesn't mean I can't, either,' I said pointedly.

'I know, but you've lost weight the last couple of months.'

'Not much, only four or five pounds. And I don't want them back.'

His gaze swept me up and down, assessing, then he nodded, relenting.

'Do you think you'll be able to help me with this icing as it will melt to liquid?' I swiped the tip of my finger through the thick chocolate on top of the cake and held it up.

In answer, Gabriel leaned forward and sucked my finger into his mouth and caressed it with his tongue, driving us both crazy.

Sixteen

Approval

The next morning, Gabriel and I stopped at a florist on our way to the cemetery. He insisted we go to the same one he visited when he chose the bouquet he sent to me and, when we walked in, arm-in-arm, the tall, curvy woman behind the counter recognised Gabriel immediately.

'I remember you!' she enthused, stepping away from the dozens of stems she had been cutting and arranging and walking up to Gabriel. 'You were in here a couple of weeks ago. You created a beautiful arrangement of pink flowers.' She turned to me and smiled widely. 'I hope you're Jamie Kavanagh or this could be very awkward.'

I returned her smile; she was friendly and meant no harm. 'Yes, they were for me. Was it you I spoke to when I called to find out who they were from?'

'Yes, it was. I'm Joanne, by the way. I'm sorry I couldn't tell you anything, but I see it all worked out for you. I knew it would.' She wrinkled her nose affectionately.

'You were right; I'm just an impatient person.'

'I can't say that I blame you, he was rather mysterious,' she said, nodding in Gabriel's direction. 'So, what can I do for you today?'

'We're here for daffodils,' I explained. 'I'm assuming they're still around?'

'Yes, but probably not for much longer. Do you want anything with them? White roses, perhaps? They would work well together. Or chrysanthemums.'

'Thanks, but maybe another time. I just want a big bunch of daffodils. They look like happy flowers,' I added, picturing Mum's smile whenever she brought some home with her.

Thanks in part to our discussion last night, and thanks also to his innate ability, Gabriel sensed where my thoughts had gone. He slipped his hand inside my unbuttoned coat and under my jumper to make contact with the sensitive skin of my back. I felt the reassuring warmth of his palm seeping through my flesh.

Joanne made a big circle with both her hands around flowers whose buds were just beginning to open, and extracted them from their bucket of water.

'I'll just wrap them for you,' she said.

'There's no need for that. Could you just tie them, please?' I asked.

Joanne shot me a puzzled expression, but, to spare me saying the words out loud, Gabriel intervened.

'There's no need for wrapping or decoration because we're placing them on a grave.'

I could tell Gabriel was trying to explain as delicately as possible.

Joanne's hand flew up to her mouth in shock. 'I'm sorry,' she said, and then something seemed to occur to her. 'The flowers the other week: were they meant as a sympathy bouquet?'

'No, no,' Gabriel was quick to correct her assumption. 'Those flowers were simply to make Jamie smile.' He gave me a loving smile that I knew he had only for me, and which communicated the secret of the overseen prophetic dream, before turning to Joanne and smiling pleasantly.

Whilst I dug some money out of my purse, Joanne handed the daffodils to Gabriel.

'I hope to see you again,' she said amiably as we left her shop.

I took the large bunch from Gabriel's hands and I attempted to gently shake the excess water from their stalks so they didn't drip in his car. He opened the door for me and we passed the flowers back and forth whilst I got myself seated and buckled in.

It had been about four weeks since I'd last been to Mum and Carmel's grave. As soon as the doctor had said it was okay for me to take my arm out of its sling, I went and bought a glass vase and some pink roses and drove to the cemetery to half bury the vase in the raised earth.

Thankfully, it hadn't rained for a few days so the ground wasn't muddy, and I knelt on an old yoga mat so I wouldn't get dirt all over me. I kept some gloves, a small gardening shovel, some scissors, flower food, refuse sacks, and a large bottle of water in a canvas bag in the boot of my car. As I pulled on the gloves, Gabriel crouched beside me holding open a rubbish bag into which I disposed of the dead roses. I pulled the vase out of the mound of earth and tipped away the dirty, stagnant water. After rinsing it clean, I reburied it, filled it with fresh water and flower food, then cut the daffodils to neatly fit in the vase. When I was done, I tidied everything away whilst Gabriel threw the bag of deceased flowers into a large bin nearby.

I was standing staring at the two small metal plaques attached to the wooden cross at the head of the grave with Mum's and Carmel's names on them when he returned. He came up behind me and pressed himself into me as he wrapped his arms around my middle, settling them just underneath my ribs so he didn't crush them.

He pulled me back slightly to be closer to him, bent his head to kiss my ear, and almost whispered, 'I know I've already said this, and I know it's painfully inadequate, but I am so sorry, Jamie.'

I hadn't realised I'd started to cry until I discovered I was unable to speak. I just nodded, almost imperceptibly, to acknowledge him. Gabriel squeezed me tighter. I lifted a hand to brush away my tears and I found my voice.

'I'll be glad when the earth has settled so I can give them a headstone.' I sounded a bit unsteady. I felt it, too. 'There's something so forlorn about that cross.'

'You'll think of something beautiful to inscribe on it, and your mum and sister will be proud,' he said, still speaking intimately into my ear. 'May I ask why you buried them together? I mean, I don't understand how Aaron was amenable to that considering his recent behaviour.'

'I desperately wanted to keep them together. Aaron wanted Carmel to be buried separately from Mum, but in a double plot so that he could be buried with her when he dies, but I argued that it was possible he'd meet someone else, get married, and they would want to be buried together. I told him it would be unfair to Carmel if that were to happen and she was left alone. He said he would never marry anyone else, but, really, he knew he couldn't guarantee that.'

'Did you really believe at the time he would find someone else?'

'Yes. I know he loves Carmel, I didn't doubt that then and I never will, but he's only thirty-one. If he gets some help dealing with his grief, I think he could still be happy,' I said generously.

'But could you ever forgive him for what he's done to you?'

'Ask me that another time,' I replied ruefully. I leaned my head back against his shoulder to look up at him. He grinned in amusement at my response to his question and I simply gazed at him for a moment, feeling his love for me, and knowing he felt my love for him in return.

I made a sudden decision. 'Gabriel, I really want to visit a clairvoyant. It might still be too early for someone to be able to contact Mum and Carmel, but I need to try.' I turned in his arms to face him and I wrapped my arms around his waist. 'I miss them and it hurts so much. I just need to hear from them.' I silently implored him to understand, knowing he could feel every emotion and read every troubled thought inside me.

'I know how much it's hurting you,' he said as he rested his forehead against mine. 'I've got the number at home of a psychic who I think might be able to help you. Her name is Eloise and a friend of mine, named Abbie, was very impressed with a sitting she and her mother had with her.'

There were so many questions running through my mind, but Gabriel continued his story before I could ask him anything.

'About a year after Abbie's grandmother died, her mother wanted to see a medium but was anxious to go alone in case the psychic was a fake. Abbie went with her and told me all about it afterwards. She gave me Eloise's business card in the event that I ever desired to contact old acquaintances.' One side of his mouth quirked up at the thought.

'How long ago was this? Does Eloise still offer sittings?'

'It was only four years ago. Eloise offered all kinds of readings at her home and it was her full-time occupation. She had a very good reputation and was always busy, according to Abbie, and she was only in her early forties back then, so it's unlikely she would have retired.'

'So, I take it Abbie knew you're a vampire?' Gabriel nodded once, his eyes never leaving mine. I swallowed. 'Was she a donor? A girlfriend?'

I was curious and trying not to be jealous. Gabriel had a past; he would have had an extremely bleak life up until now if he didn't; but it was the past and I knew that he loved me and only me. I tried to tell myself that if Gabriel cared for her, Abbie was probably a very nice woman and I might even have liked her.

'Not a girlfriend; I wasn't interested in her in that way. She was just a friend,' he said with a slender smile as he took my face in his hands and traced his thumbs along my cheekbones.

'She liked vampires and she donated blood to me a couple of times, but we lost contact when she decided to frequent those vampire fetish bars I mentioned.

'I went to one out of morbid curiosity years ago, but it's really not my scene. Not only was it a little sordid, it was very gothic and stereotypical in both décor and costume.' He shuddered. 'Honestly, vampires are people, too; we change and evolve as individuals, just as humans do. What makes people think that even vampires who are several centuries old are so antediluvian that they haven't even updated their wardrobes?'

I laughed; his indignation was adorable. 'That's humans for you; not all of them are particularly imaginative.'

'You don't consider yourself human?' he asked, one eyebrow raised.

I realised what he meant when I reviewed exactly what I had said. I wasn't aware of it happening, but since meeting Gabriel, learning about his vampire nature, being with him and observing how he lives, I had been empathising so much with him that I had begun to feel more like a vampire than a human. It wasn't surprising.

'You're rubbing off on me,' I said with a smile and he grinned.

He put his arm around my shoulders and started to lead me towards the car, but, after a couple of steps, I stopped and swung back around.

'Bye, Mum. Bye, Carmel. I'll see you both soon,' I said, and I blew kisses in the direction of the plaques at the head of the grave.

I turned around again and Gabriel gripped me tighter.

'You know they're not really here,' Gabriel intoned, and I looked up into his face with wide eyes so I didn't cry. 'Their bodies are, but their souls are with you.'

'I feel them sometimes. You know the feeling you get when someone's standing near you, but just out of your peripheral vision?' Gabriel confirmed he knew what I meant with a nod. 'It feels like that, but when I turn my head in their direction, I can't see them. I know it's them: I recognise their energies.'

'Then you really know that they're with you,' he said fondly.

He held the car door open for me and, as I was about to get in, he bent down and pressed his lips to mine. It was a soft, sweet kiss and when we broke contact, I lifted my fingers to his cheek. He closed his eyes momentarily at my touch.

Back at home, Gabriel recovered Eloise's business card from one of the desk drawers in the library and handed it to me. It was cornflower blue with Eloise's name and contact details embossed in silver lettering on a picture of white, feathered angel wings.

With a little flutter of nerves, I leaned one hip against the side of the desk and dialled the number on the card. It was picked up on the third ring.

'Hello, Eloise speaking. How may I help you?' a friendly, soothing voice greeted.

'Hello, Eloise. A friend of a friend of mine came to you for a reading about four years ago,' I began. 'She was full of praise for you and I wondered if you still offered sittings, and if you do, could I book a session with you?'

'Yes, dear, I'm still in business, but I'm rather busy at the moment. I'm fully booked for the next three weeks, but, if you're available, I am free this afternoon.'

'That would be perfect. What time is convenient for you?'

'Can you be here for two o'clock?' she asked.

'I've got a four year old business card here, are you still at the same address?'

'Yes; I've been here for twenty years and I love it too much to move.'

'Then that's no trouble. Thank you, Eloise.'

'Can I take your first name, please?'

'It's Jamie.'

'Thank you, Jamie. I'll see you at two.'

I hung up the phone and started to feel excited that I might be hearing from my mum and sister soon. I was trying not to get carried away in case it really was too soon, or Eloise wasn't as good as Gabriel's friend had lauded her.

'Try not to be too disappointed if this doesn't work, Jamie.' Gabriel looked down at me earnestly. He'd heard the entire telephone conversation and felt what was going on inside me. 'It doesn't mean they're not around anymore if Eloise doesn't make contact.'

'I know, Gabriel,' I agreed. 'I just can't help but imagine the possibility.' I gave him a beseeching look and internally entreated him to understand and empathise.

He quickly pulled me to him and held my head against his chest. I could feel his heart thumping away beneath my cheek.

'I know how much it means to you to hear from them. I just don't want you to be too distraught if it doesn't happen today.'

I lifted my head and stood on tiptoes to press my mouth to his. 'I know,' I said, my lips brushing his as I spoke, 'and I love you for it.'

I sealed my mouth to his once more and Gabriel brought his hands up into my hair to cradle my head as he deepened the kiss, sliding his tongue against mine. I moaned softly and he responded with a quiet growl deep in his throat.

'I love it when you growl,' I informed him as I kissed my way down the front of his throat. When I reached the hollow at its base, I continued along his collarbone and up the side of his neck to lick the sensitive skin covering his veins. 'It's so sexy.'

I could see a line of blue clearly under his pale skin and I ran my lips along it before nipping it gently with my teeth. He growled louder and deeper and grasped my shoulders to pull me away from his throat. My gaze flew up to his face and I saw that he was grinning wickedly at me. His head swooped down and he captured my mouth again and, still clutching my shoulders, he walked me backwards to the sofa and eased me down onto it.

As I lay back, Gabriel covered my body with his and tugged at the zip that ran along the top of my jumper to expose my neck and shoulder. He began at my shoulder, kissing it and grazing it with his teeth as he travelled along it, then up my neck.

My hands crept underneath his jumper and my fingers were tracing patterns on the muscles in his back when his mouth connected with a particularly sensitive patch of skin and I clutched him to me tightly. When his mouth drew level with my carotid, he paused and, in the anticipation of what he was going to do next, I stopped breathing.

I felt his lips brush over the skin with a feather-light touch. My heart thundered irregularly and I clung to him, my fingertips digging into his flesh. Next, I felt his lips open, his teeth press against my flesh, and he bit down, but not with enough force to break the skin. A strangled cry of ecstasy escaped from my throat as I thought Gabriel was really going to bite me.

He made a noise of satisfaction at my reaction and his breath tickled my skin, but instead of sinking his teeth into me, I felt his tongue caress my neck where his teeth had been, causing desire to surge through me. I locked my arms around him, holding him tightly to me so he couldn't break away. He trailed his mouth back towards my own and he resumed kissing me.

His hands slid under my jumper, pushing it up with his arms as his fingers teased my sides, my back, my stomach, my ribs, until he reached my underarms. He pulled back slightly so he could tug the sweater off over my head and he dropped it onto the floor.

He was straddling my hips as he sat back, and my arms slipped from encircling him so my palms rested on his stomach. I twisted my hands around and brushed the backs of my fingers along the skin at the waistline of his jeans until I came to his pelvic bones where I turned them back around to stroke them with my palms.

Gabriel grasped the hem of his jumper, pulled it up his torso and off over his head, and threw it to join mine on the floor. I grabbed hold of one of his arms and pulled him back down to me. I lifted my head to meet his halfway and, as I sealed my mouth to his, he put his arms through mine to hug me, unclasping my bra as he gathered me to him and pulling me into a sitting position all in one motion. He manoeuvred us both so that he sat back on the sofa and I was then straddling him. I threw off my bra.

We both attacked the buttons and zips of the other's jeans with Gabriel pushing mine, along with my thong, down as far as he could. I stood up so he could slide them down the rest of the way. I kicked them off and pulled Gabriel out of his jeans and snug shorts before climbing back onto his lap and taking him inside me.

I smoothed my hands up his stomach, his chest, until I came to his shoulders and he sat forward, away from the back of the couch, so I could wrap my arms around him. At the same time, Gabriel's hands were travelling up from my bottom to the middle of my back and, as I began to rock my hips gently back and forth, he wrapped his arms around my ribs, holding me close against him.

I continued to move slowly, rhythmically, and Gabriel dropped his mouth to my shoulder to kiss it and bite it, taking his time, roaming up the side of my neck and down the front to its base. I felt him tease the hollow with his tongue and I moaned and tilted my head back to give him better access. Keeping my left arm around his neck, I moved my right hand into his hair, cradling his head and holding it against me whilst at the same time twirling locks of his silky hair around my fingers.

He lifted his mouth to my ear to murmur into it how much he loved me and exactly how I was making him feel, and his words and the sensation of him speaking so amorously into my ear forced me to cling to him even tighter. He sealed his mouth to mine and we both tipped over the edge.

Gabriel leaned back against the sofa cushions, taking me with him, and I collapsed against him, resting my forehead on his shoulder as we both tried to regain our breath and waited for our hearts to slow down.

'If your mother and sister do come through to talk to you when you visit Eloise, you'll have to ask them if they enjoyed the show,' Gabriel joked, lifting my face to kiss me briefly on the mouth.

I grinned at him. 'I'm sure they weren't watching. They probably saw what was about to happen back when we were by the desk, thought "Good for you," and made themselves scarce.'

He regarded me and, still holding my chin, traced my mouth with his thumb.

'They're happy that you're happy,' he stated.

'I think so.'

A shiver ran through me as I started to feel the chill of sitting there completely naked.

'You're cold,' Gabriel observed, and rubbed my arms. 'Let's get dressed; you'll have to leave for your appointment soon.'

I nodded and eased myself off Gabriel's lap. He hadn't asked if I wanted him to accompany me, and he hadn't assumed he'd come along. He recognised that this was private, something I wanted to do alone, and he knew I'd tell him all about it afterwards.

I picked up our clothes and handed Gabriel's to him, feeling slightly self-conscious.

'What will you do with yourself whilst I'm gone?'

'Actually, there's something I need to do so I was thinking I would drop you off, go where I need to go, and pick you up afterwards. That way, should you be upset after your sitting, you wouldn't have to worry about driving home.'

'That makes sense. Where do you need to go?' I asked, intrigued.

'It's a surprise. I need to look into something and, if it's suitable, I'll take you there some other time.' I raised my eyebrows at him. 'You'll like it, Jamie, I promise,' he said with a laugh.

I quickly disappeared to the bathroom to make sure I looked presentable and to ensure it wasn't evident what Gabriel and I had just been doing in his library.

Forty minutes later, I was greeted by Eloise. She had a serene face; unworried; which made her look younger than her years. She took me into a warm and bright conservatory where there was an oil burning, scenting the room with a delicate, clean fragrance.

'Take a seat, Jamie.' Eloise indicated a two-seated sofa parallel to a coffee table, so I sat down and she sat in an armchair opposite me. 'Let me take your hand for a moment so I can feel your energy.'

I put my hand in hers and she held onto it, closing her eyes to focus solely on what she was sensing.

'I can tell that you're hurting, that you've suffered a great loss very recently, but there's also some happiness that has come into your life since then.'

'Yes, I'm here about—'

'Your mother and your sister,' she finished, opening her eyes and releasing my hand. 'Bea and Carmel, right?' I nodded. 'They're here. They're eager to talk to you, actually,' she said with a smile.

'I'm so relieved,' I said, exhaling heavily.

'They want you to know they're okay, that they're still together and to thank you for keeping them together. Does that make sense to you?'

'Yes, I buried them together. It was fitting.' My voice was quiet because a huge lump had formed in my throat and my eyes had filled with tears.

'They've been worrying about you. Your mother is pointing at her shoulder. You had an injury there and she sends healing energy. She's not happy that you're not looking after yourself properly; not eating; but she says she's glad someone else is nagging you about this.'

'Yes, I've met someone. She's telling you about that?' I asked.

'Oh, yes. Your mother is showing me an angel.' Eloise frowned.

I smiled. 'His name is Gabriel.'

'That makes sense now.' She chuckled. 'She and your sister are saying he's gorgeous.'

'I think he is.'

'They think so, too. But it's not just his looks. They're saying he's not an angel, but he's perfect for you. He loves you for all the right reasons. They're really pleased the two of you have found one another because you're perfect for him, too, but you're scared of something.' Eloise's forehead creased deeply. 'They're being a bit cryptic with what they're telling me, so it's obviously a delicate matter, but you'll probably understand.'

She looked at me for confirmation and I nodded for her to proceed.

'Beatrice is saying that being with Gabriel is going to mean making a big decision, but you're afraid that if you take that big step, you'll never see her or your sister again. She's saying that whichever decision you make, they will always be with you; they're making that a promise; and you should do what will make you happiest.'

'Really? I mean, I know they want me to be happy, but I need to know I won't lose them.' Hope was efflorescing inside me.

'You'll never lose them. Do you ever feel them with you? That perhaps they're in the same room as you?' she asked knowingly.

'Yes, I just can't see them or hear them.'

'Well, they're there with you. You're feeling their individual energies. Carmel is saying that they have been trying to visit you in your dreams, but whenever you dream about them it's…' she trailed off. 'Oh!' she gasped. 'Oh, Jamie, I'm so sorry. Carmel is showing me what happened; how you got hurt and how they passed. Bless you both,' she said to Mum and Carmel. 'Your sister says that your nightmares are blocking them from visiting you, but don't be alarmed, it's not your fault and it's only temporary. Your nightmares will stop coming so frequently, Gabriel will help.'

Eloise took my hand briefly and squeezed it for support.

'I hope that happens soon, I'd like to see them in my dreams.' I squeezed back. My unshed tears spilled over and down my cheeks and I wiped them away.

'Who is Aaron?' Eloise asked abruptly.

'He's Carmel's fiancé,' I responded. I thought Carmel would have something to say about him.

'She's apologising for the way he has been treating you recently. She says she can't defend his behaviour and she is horrified. She's pointing to her ring finger and indicating you.'

'I have her engagement ring. Aaron gave it to me before he turned nasty,' I explained.

'Carmel's glad you have it. She wants you to look after it for her and she's telling you to be careful.'

'I'm being careful about Aaron, and with her ring,' I said for Carmel's benefit.

'There's one final thing your mother wants to say to you for today. There's something Gabriel hasn't told you. He wants to, and he will, but he hasn't so far because he didn't want your feelings about his revelation to pre-empt any other feelings you had for him.

'She says it's not a bad thing he has to tell you, so don't be worried that it will break your heart. She says don't be angry with him, not for anything. She and your sister are very grateful to him.' Eloise smiled beneficently at me.

'Thank you so much, Eloise. Your reading has given me a lot to think about, but I feel better now; reassured. It has given me some peace of mind.' I smiled back.

'I'm glad. I get so much satisfaction letting people know their loved ones haven't really left them and passing on messages that may help them in their lives. I wish you all the best, Jamie, my dear.'

'You, too, Eloise,' I replied, and handed over her fee.

She walked me to her front door and, as she opened it, I saw Gabriel pulling up in his car so I hurried along the path to get in.

I closed the door behind me and reached for my seatbelt, but Gabriel's hand on my arm stopped me. I turned to look at him and he silently scrutinised my face, noting that my eyes were still a little red from crying, but feeling that I was okay.

'How was… wherever it was you went?' I asked, breaking the silence and fastening my seatbelt.

Gabriel shook his head. 'That doesn't matter for the moment. Tell me about your sitting.'

I exhaled heavily and the words came rushing out as Gabriel pulled away from the kerb. 'Mum and Carmel are okay, they're glad I kept them together. When I told you I can feel them, I was right; it really is them, and they're trying to visit me in my dreams, but my nightmares are blocking them.'

Gabriel smiled, pleased for me. 'I'm glad they made contact, baby. What else?'

'Carmel is angry on my behalf because of Aaron. She said she wouldn't make excuses for him and she's pleased I'm looking after her ring for her.' I hesitated for a moment to draw breath. 'They know about you.'

'And?' he said, unworried, raising an eyebrow quizzically and the left side of his mouth quirking upwards slightly.

'And they approve.' I beamed at him. 'You'll be pleased to know Mum is happy you're badgering me about my eating.' This caused Gabriel to grin fully. 'They know you're a vampire.'

Gabriel darted a quick look at me, and I felt a brief flash of apprehension in him causing his pulse to quicken. I could also see it in his eyes and the set of his mouth.

'It's okay,' I reassured him. 'They were really cryptic so Eloise wouldn't suspect a thing. To indicate they were talking about you, they showed her an angel, so I told her they meant you because of your name. Then, they said that you're not an angel but you're perfect for me and you love me for all the right reasons.' I placed my hand on his leg.

'I do,' he affirmed.

'I know, and I love you for all the same reasons, Gabriel. They referenced the prospect of you turning me by saying I had a big decision to make and they know the thing that was bothering me was not being with them again if I became a vampire. They told me to make the choice that will make me happiest because, either way, they will still be with me.'

Gabriel looked, and felt, as though he might cry because he knew that was the one thing that was stopping me from making that leap. He knew I wanted to be with him forever, but I was worried about my family. Now I knew they supported the idea of me becoming a vampire, and they promised they would still be with me in whatever way they could so I would never truly lose them, he knew that I was sure.

He could feel it in me that I was certain of my decision: I wanted him to turn me.

Seventeen
Gabriel, Meet Rachael

'So, Gabriel,' I said when we were back at home, 'are you going to tell me what you were doing whilst I had my sitting?'

He shook his head. 'Where I went today wasn't suitable for my purpose, so I think we'll need to take a trip to London.'

'London?' I raised my eyebrows and he grinned. 'What for?'

'It's a surprise.'

He laughed when he saw the expression of exasperation on my face. It's always nice to be surprised; the perfect example being the flowers Gabriel sent to me; but to be told I was going to be surprised but I'd have to wait for it was frustrating, especially because I was quite impatient.

'When are we going?' I asked.

'I don't know yet. It depends on you, Jamie.'

'On me?'

'On your answer.'

'On my answer to what?'

Before he could respond, my phone rang. I checked the screen and it was Rachael. I immediately felt guilty for not calling her after I said I'd keep her informed about Gabriel. I answered the call.

'Sorry, sorry, sorry, sorry, sorry. I'm a useless friend for not phoning you.' I heard Rachael laugh on the other end. 'Forgive me?'

'Of course, babe. I'm just checking in. How are you? How is everything with Gabriel?' she asked ardently.

'I'm really good. I've just been to see a psychic and Mum and Carmel had a lot to say to me. As for Gabriel,' his gaze flicked to me, 'I'm with him now. He's fine, and everything is going great.'

'You're with him at the moment? Where?'

'I'm at his house.'

'Is he listening in?' she asked with a devious note in her tone.

'Of course.' I shot him an innocent smile. 'He's dying to know what I've told you about him.'

'Ooh, can I speak with him?'

'Rachael would like to speak with you,' I informed Gabriel unnecessarily.

'Is this where I get interrogated to within an inch of my life?' His tone was amused and he felt unworried about what she might ask him.

'Yes,' Rachael said, overhearing him.

'Rachael said "Yes,"' I repeated for Rachael's benefit.

Gabriel took the phone out of my hand and kissed me on the cheek before raising it to his ear.

'Hello, Rachael,' he said smoothly. 'Congratulations on the recent birth of your son.'

Gabriel drew me against him, so I wrapped my arms around his waist and began to nuzzle his neck whilst Rachael was talking.

'Yes, I saw Jamie at university back in January,' he responded to Rachael's grilling. 'No, I didn't have the opportunity to talk to her then, I just happened to bump into her in a bookshop a couple of weeks ago.'

It was Rachael's turn to speak again so I lifted my face to Gabriel's to give him a kiss. He was responding fervently, but broke off abruptly in order to answer her.

'Of course I know how devastated she is by the loss of her family,' Gabriel said as I kissed my way along his jaw, dropped a soft kiss just beneath his ear in the indentation by his jawbone, and inhaled the scent of him. 'I have absolutely no intention of hurting her; she's very important to me.'

He wisely didn't say he wouldn't hurt me because he loves me because although it seemed to me as though we'd been together for months, if not years, I had only met him a little over two weeks ago.

Whilst Gabriel listened to what Rachael was saying in reply, his free hand crept under my jumper to trace circles on my skin. I shivered slightly at his touch and he felt the movement against his body, which never failed to please him.

With the advantage of my position pressed up against Gabriel, I could hear the buzz of Rachael talking, but I hadn't really been paying attention to what she was saying. However, the words 'meet you' and 'come over tomorrow' filtered into my consciousness. My head snapped up.

'One moment please, Rachael,' Gabriel said and tilted the phone away from his mouth. To me, he said, 'Rachael wants to meet me and has invited us to her house for mid-morning coffee tomorrow.'

I sorted through everything I was feeling to discern which emotions were mine and which were Gabriel's. I was slightly anxious in case this was something Gabriel really didn't want to do, but my apprehension was completely redundant because he was in an affable mood. He raised his eyebrows, telling me it was my decision. I nodded.

'Jamie and I will see you tomorrow morning around ten. Is that a good time?' He waited for her reply. 'Perfect. I'm looking forward to meeting you, too, Rachael. I'll pass you back to Jamie now. Bye.'

He handed back the phone but didn't let go of me.

'Hello again, sweetie. You act fast,' I commented with a laugh.

'Well, I've got to meet the man who's been occupying so much of your time lately that you don't even text me,' she expostulated without malice. 'He has got *the* sexiest voice,' she added in an undertone.

He grinned mischievously. It was adorable.

'It gives me tingles,' I admitted, and Gabriel kissed me loud enough for Rachael to hear.

'Oh, God,' she said, mock-horrified. 'He just kissed you, didn't he?'

'Mmm-hmm.'

'I get it: it's new, you're in that soppy stage. Just don't rush anything,' she advised.

I couldn't tell her I wouldn't.

'I can't wait to see you tomorrow. Bye, Jamie. Love you.'

'Bye, Rachael. Love you, too.'

I pressed the button on the phone to end the call and then put it back in my pocket.

'"Soppy stage,"' Gabriel mused and tilted his head to one side curiously.

'The beginning of a relationship when each person thinks the other is completely perfect and they're forever kissing, holding hands in public, and having lots of sex in private. It usually lasts a few months. That's where Rachael thinks we are in our relationship,' I clarified.

'Oh, I know what she meant.'

'Well, we do kind of behave like that.' I gave him a sly smile.

'Yes, but it's not just a phase in a burgeoning relationship.'

'I know that, and you know that, but as far as Rachael is concerned, we have known each other two weeks, we're attracted to each other, but we're still getting to know one another. She's a very logical person, that's partly why I've never told her that I'm an empath. She thinks I'm perceptive and good at reading the signs people give off, but I've never elaborated and she's never asked, even if she has figured it out for herself.'

I waited to see if Gabriel had an opinion on that. He didn't say anything, but I sensed he was thinking about it.

'So,' I said, breaking the silence, 'I believe you've got something to ask me.'

'Have I?' He feigned an expression of confusion. He was good, but not good enough; he knew exactly to what I was referring.

'I haven't forgotten the conversation we were having before the phone rang. There's somewhere in London you're going to take me, but it depends on my answer. So, what's the question?'

He shook his head. 'It's a bit more complex than that,' he said obliquely. 'There's probably more than one question that needs to be answered, but I don't think we should go into that today. I think today you should just be happy about contacting your mother and sister.'

I sighed. 'I'm relieved to know they're okay, that they're not stuck somewhere unable to accept their situation.'

'I know that has been bothering you, and I can feel it has lifted now,' he said, sweeping my hair back off my shoulder. 'I have a gift for you,' he announced, taking me by surprise.

'A gift? What for?' I asked, bewildered.

'I didn't get you a birthday present.'

'You didn't know me then,' I pointed out.

'Or a gift for passing your Master's degree. I knew you that day.'

'But I didn't know *you* then, and I didn't expect anything from anyone for that.'

'I know you didn't, but I wanted to get you something special from me,' he said, reaching into one of the front pockets of his jeans and extracting a small rectangular box made of midnight blue card. 'I found a woman who sells her own jewellery. She designs and makes each piece herself, and each item can be personalised to make it special and unique.'

He handed me the box. I removed the lid and a layer of cotton wool and, lying there, was a belly bar for my navel piercing. It wasn't fussy, which I loved, it was a plain, silver-coloured bar with half a sphere at the bottom end. Engraved on the flat side of the sphere was the initial 'G' inside a heart. It was simple, beautiful, and elegant. I was lost for words.

'I could tell from your other jewellery that you like light-coloured metals, so this is white gold. You said you love your navel piercing, and your mother's bracelet has a heart on it,' he explained his choice. 'She engraved it right there in front of me. Do you like it?'

'I love it. Thank you, Gabriel. It's beautiful and perfect and so thoughtful of you. I'll always wear it.' I threw my arms around his neck and squeezed him tightly.

'I was a little worried the one you're wearing has some sentimental value: a gift from your mother or sister perhaps?'

'No, they've bought me earrings and necklaces before, but never a bar or ring for my bellybutton. This is extra special. I'll put it in now; I want to see how it looks.'

'Before you do, I suggest you sterilise it in something. The jeweller polished it with some kind of cleaning solution, but I'd feel happier knowing you won't get an infection from it.'

I wrinkled my nose at him. 'It's okay, Mum always told me the same thing.'

'Your mother is a wise woman,' he said with great affection.

'I know. I can only hope some of it rubbed off on me,' I said with a dose of self-deprecation. 'There's liquid antiseptic in the bathroom, so all I'll need is a cup and some boiling water.'

I gave Gabriel a kiss and disappeared to get the antiseptic. When I came back downstairs, he was in the kitchen. The kettle was boiling, three mugs were sitting on the counter, and he'd spooned ground coffee into a cafetiere.

'Are you hungry? I know I tried to force some breakfast into you this morning, but you didn't eat very much of it.'

'I am a bit. There's still a lot of cake left and I think I can hear it calling me.'

Whilst Gabriel cut a slice of cake for me, I poured a capful of antiseptic into one of the mugs and added some boiling water. I unscrewed the ball from the top of the bar and dropped both parts into the medicinal-smelling liquid to soak whilst I filled the cafetiere with the remaining water in the kettle.

We took everything through to the lounge and, as Gabriel poured coffee, I took a bite of the cake.

'You do realise your diet is appalling at the moment,' he observed, not unkindly.

'I could be tempted to eat a banana later,' I quipped, and he smiled. 'I had dried fruit in my cereal this morning.' He merely looked at me, saying nothing, with a patient expression on his face. He was only concerned for me. 'Okay, I'll eat more healthily tomorrow, but don't forget whose idea it was to make this cake in the first place. I've got to eat it.'

'Okay, point taken. I'll stop reproving you. So, prepare me: what is Rachael like?'

'Rachael is a very loyal friend,' I explained. 'We've known each other since we were teenagers and she's always the first person to offer help if I need it. When I was with Hayden, and we spent time with Rachael and Baz, she saw how possessive Hayden was. One time, we'd gone to Rachael and Baz's house to watch a film and she caught him seething at me because I'd commented to Rachael that I liked the lead actor.' My mouth twisted in derision.

'He thought no one could hear him because Rachael was in the kitchen and Baz was checking on their daughter, Tamara,' I continued. 'He started ranting that I wasn't supposed to look at any other men, I was supposed to love him and only notice him.

'I was about to give him a mouthful of vitriol in response when Rachael stormed back into the room, absolutely infuriated on my behalf, and beat me to it. She was livid.'

'You did speak up for yourself, didn't you?' Gabriel's eyebrows drew together slightly. 'I can't imagine you sitting there silently and letting someone else argue for you.'

'Oh, I argued for myself. Rachael leapt in with the point that all I'd done was say I liked an actor who I'd never even met, it wasn't as though I was going to jump on a plane, fly to wherever he was based, track him down and throw myself at him. She told Hayden that he was completely overreacting.

'That's when I said he couldn't seriously expect me to go through my everyday life not noticing other men when they make up roughly half the population. I had male friends and colleagues and I told him I couldn't, and wouldn't, avoid them just because of his irrational behaviour.

'Our raised voices alerted Baz to what was happening and he was incredulous. He couldn't believe what Hayden was expecting, and couldn't understand why I tolerated him.'

'Neither can I,' Gabriel stated honestly.

'I know. That was when he was at his worst and it wasn't long afterwards that I ended it.'

'Okay, that's the good side of her, but she wanted you to see a counsellor, didn't she?' he queried.

'As I said, Rachael is a logical person. She knows that not only am I grieving for Mum and Carmel, I witnessed their violent murders and, although I was injured, I survived, so I feel guilty. She also knows I have nightmares about it, so it makes sense to her that I should get help to reconcile and accept everything.' I shrugged. 'To me, it felt as though because she didn't know how to help me herself, she was pushing for me to see a professional,' I reasoned. 'I think I was a bit harsh, in thought, though not to her face, I hope. She just wanted to ease my suffering. I need time, but no one wants to see someone they care about in pain for a long time.'

'She obviously cares about you a great deal,' he said softly.

I nodded. 'Enough to keep calling me even when I neglect to call her.'

'Yes, but you go to see her, she doesn't come to see you. It balances itself out,' he asserted to make me feel better.

For the remainder of the evening, Gabriel told me about his closest friends: humans he'd known at university who'd died long ago, probably before I was even born. He also told me of some vampire friends, some of whom were settled with families, and some who lived peripatetic lives and travelled the world staying in far-flung places for short periods before moving on so no one would notice they didn't age.

That night, I slept wrapped in Gabriel's warm embrace. Though the days were slowly beginning to get warmer, the nights were still chilly, so I was ever grateful that Gabriel was perennially warm, the complete opposite of fictional vampires.

I had hoped to see Mum and Carmel in my dreams that night. After explaining to me they were trying to visit this way, I hoped that whatever occlusion preventing it would be cleared. Unfortunately, that wasn't the case, and I had my usual nightmare.

At first, everything in my dream happened exactly as it did on that night. When it really happened, I passed out quite quickly from the shock. It seemed like only a second after I saw my mother fall to the ground beside me that everything went black, and I wasn't aware of anything more until I woke up in hospital. In this nightmare, however, I saw Mum's face as she landed on the asphalt, then there was blackness, but, an instant after that, I felt my head being lifted and placed on something. It felt like my head was resting on a pair of human thighs.

I could feel the presence and energy of another person, and I could feel alarm, concern, and emotional pain coming from that person, but I couldn't open my eyes to see who it was. I tried to force them open, but they wouldn't move. I could sense the figure leaning over me, touching my face.

'Jamie!' his anguished voice cried.

I recognised that voice. It was Gabriel, and he was urgently shaking me to wake me up.

My eyes fluttered open and, as they focused, all I could see was his intense gaze.

'What's wrong?' I asked, my heart thundering from the shock of being woken up.

'I saw you having your nightmare and you didn't wake up. I was worried because you didn't initially respond when I tried to rouse you. I'm sorry if I scared you, baby,' he soothed, cupping my face and using his thumbs to trace my cheekbones.

'Did you see the rest, the part just before I opened my eyes? The person who found us, who found me alive, he was there. He lifted my head onto his lap. I don't know if that really happened or if that part was just a dream,' I babbled. 'I was sure I was completely unconscious.' Tears filled my eyes and Gabriel brushed them away with his fingertips.

'I saw it all. Please don't get upset, Jamie. You're here, you're safe, don't worry about what you can't remember,' he urged, lovingly. 'Don't worry about what you dreamt,' he added as he pulled me into his embrace and stroked one of his hands soothingly down my back.

'I thought I heard him say my name. It was your voice, Gabriel, but I'm not sure if that was just me hearing you calling me to wake me up.'

'Shh, don't think about it now.' Gabriel's fingers gently guided my chin up so our faces were level and he started feathering soft kisses all over my face. When he got to my eyelids, he said, 'Just sleep.'

At a few minutes before ten the following morning, I could feel the heightened anticipation thrumming through Rachael as she opened her front door to welcome Gabriel and me. She was cradling the awake and alert Noah in one arm with Tamara at her side, not wanting to be left behind and curious to see who was at the front door.

'Hello, my darling,' Rachael said warmly as soon as she glimpsed my face.

'Hello, honey,' I replied affectionately, stepping forward into the house and giving her a careful hug and a kiss on the cheek. 'You're looking well.'

'Thank you, Jamie. You're looking much better which, I assume, is largely due to you,' she said, turning her attention to Gabriel and smiling.

It was then that she really took him in and her eyes widened slightly in surprise and appreciation.

'It's a pleasure to meet you, Rachael,' Gabriel greeted unfalteringly even though he had read her reaction as well as I had. He held out his hand and Rachael took it, but he also leaned forward to kiss her cheek with perfect grace. 'I'm encouraging Jamie to take better care of herself,' he supplemented with a disarming smile.

'I like you already, Gabriel. Come inside,' she encouraged.

As Gabriel took a step inside the house, Tamara hesitantly stepped backwards, looking up at Gabriel with a wrapt, amazed expression. Noticing this, he flashed her a dazzling smile.

'That's Tamara,' Rachael informed him. 'And this little fella,' she said, slightly raising the baby in her bent arm, 'is Noah.'

As Gabriel crouched to Tamara's level to say hello, Rachael turned in my direction and mouthed 'He's gorgeous!' emphatically to me. I smiled happily back at her and nodded my head in enthusiastic agreement.

When Gabriel straightened up again, he raised his eyebrows suggestively at me, letting me know he hadn't missed what Rachael had said, or my concurrence with her. He took my hand and we followed Rachael and Tamara through to the sitting room, which had been tidied of all the little girl's toys apart from a brightly-coloured plastic tea set which had been laid out on a blanket next to the coffee table. A teddy bear and a rag doll were in attendance so she could have her own coffee morning alongside ours.

'I've got everything ready in the kitchen, I'm just waiting for the kettle to boil,' Rachael said as Gabriel and I sat next to one another on the sofa. 'If you'd just hold Noah for me, Jamie.'

She handed the baby to me and I tried to make him comfortable in the crook of my arm in my inexperienced, non-maternal fashion. He didn't cry. He looked at me with eyes wide open and eager to encounter new things.

'Hello, Noah,' I cooed at him. 'Aren't you a beautiful boy?' I smiled at him and was rewarded with a huge, gummy, baby smile in return.

'He's easily pleased,' Gabriel commented and reached for one of Noah's hands. Noah obligingly gripped Gabriel's index finger.

'Aren't all males?' Rachael proclaimed, coming in from the kitchen carrying a tray with cups, milk, sugar, spoons, a full cafetiere of coffee, and a lidded cup full of juice for Tamara.

She set everything down on the table, picked up the lidded cup, and handed it to the little girl. 'Remember, Tamara, the juice is only for you. Teddy and Dolly can't drink it, they just get wet.'

Tamara nodded, putting the cup in her mouth, and Rachael rolled her eyes at us.

'They've been splashed a few times when Tams has tried to make them drink orange squash.' She began to pour the coffee. 'How do you take it, Gabriel?'

'Just milk, please.'

'Like Jamie, then.'

'Not quite as much milk as that.' He smiled fondly.

'You know her well,' Rachel remarked, and handed cups to us both before settling back in her chair. 'So, what, exactly, is happening between you two? I'm not the most perceptive person, but I can tell from a mile off that the two of you are more serious than the average couple in their first few weeks of a relationship.'

Gabriel and I exchanged an expressive glance and I felt support and encouragement coming from him. Evidently, he had been reading Rachael, concluded that he liked her, and was happy for me to tell her as much as I was comfortable with.

I faced her. 'We are more serious than that. Rachael, would you believe me if I said it was love at first sight for both Gabriel and me?' I asked earnestly. 'Do you believe it's possible?'

'I've never experienced love at first sight. I've never even seen it.' She narrowed her eyes slightly at the pair of us. 'Though, I think I'm seeing it right now in front of me, aren't I?' she amended.

I nodded and Gabriel placed one of his hands on my thigh, an action which did not go unnoticed by Rachael.

'And just how advanced is your relationship?'

'We've each moved belongings into the other's house,' I informed her assuredly, not wanting to appear less than confident in our actions.

'Gabriel, forgive me for doing this in your presence,' she began with politeness and delicacy. 'Jamie has told me about you and you seem very nice, but I've got to ask her something. Jamie, are you sure about this?'

I could see concern etched plainly in her expression, and I could feel it radiating from her in waves.

'Completely. The psychic I saw yesterday said that Mum and Carmel know what's going on and they fully approve.' I felt a faint flicker of doubt from her. 'They brought him up. I deliberately didn't ask because that would have meant me giving the medium information rather than her receiving it from Mum or Carmel.'

'They're happy about you two?'

'They're more than happy; they think Gabriel and I are perfect for one another.' I grinned at her, then I looked to Gabriel and saw the love in his eyes that I always felt. I sensed he felt the same thing coming from me.

'Well, I'm not going to argue with them. They think more highly of you, Gabriel, than they did of Hayden.'

'Really?' he asked, eyebrows raised but feeling slightly smug.

'Oh, yes. They didn't dislike him, not at first, anyway. They tolerated him because Jamie had chosen him, he wasn't mistreating her, and they were willing to give him a chance. However, after he had his personality flip, they absolutely despised him. As did we all,' she added with a shudder.

I merely shrugged, unable to refute it, and turned my attention to Noah who had started making gurgling noises.

'I've got a bottle ready for him in the kitchen,' Rachael said as she rose to her feet. She slipped away for a moment and re-emerged with a bottle of milk, taking a swig to test the temperature. 'I think I'll give you to Uncle Gabriel for a while so Aunty Jamie can drink her coffee,' she said to Noah, taking him from my arms and placing him in Gabriel's.

This amused me, but Gabriel's pleasure was instantly replaced with discomfort, and his head snapped up to look from the baby straight into Rachael's eyes.

'You've only just met me, are you sure you want a virtual stranger handling your infant child?' he asked uncertainly.

Rachael narrowed her eyes again for a fraction of a second to consider her response. 'Jamie loves you, and you clearly love her and wouldn't do anything to hurt her. I trust Jamie and I believe in her judgement. She believes in you, and that's enough for me.'

Gabriel inclined his head in thanks and accepted the bottle Rachael held out to him. He proceeded to feed Noah and his discomposure at holding a baby eased a little.

Rachael laughed. 'I can see you're as natural with kids as Jamie.'

He smiled wryly. 'I have very little experience with them.'

'No nieces or nephews?' Rachael queried.

'I have several, but I only met them recently and they're far from babies,' Gabriel explained. At her puzzled expression, he continued, 'My older brother married my ex-girlfriend and, although I wasn't at all upset about it, they didn't feel comfortable around me. Their four children, and my sister's two, recently expressed a desire to meet me, so I went to see them a little over a week ago.'

'Did you meet them, Jamie?'

'No,' I replied cautiously. 'I have met Gabriel's parents, but only briefly.'

'What Jamie isn't saying, because she's considerate of my feelings, is that my parents weren't particularly nice to her. They're not nice people and I have as little to do with them as possible,' he supplied.

'Oh. Tell me more about your appointment with the psychic, Jamie,' Rachael said to change the subject.

I told her everything that I'd told Gabriel, withholding only that Mum and Carmel knew he was a vampire and that he should turn me so that I could be with him forever if that would make me happy. I also told her about Aaron and the restraining order.

'You poor thing,' Rachael commiserated when I had finished. 'At least the police are aware of the situation and will arrest Aaron if he comes near you. But your visit with Bea and Carmel sounds wonderful. Do you feel any better now?'

'A little, now that I know for certain they haven't gone away completely.' I frowned. 'I just want the nightmares to stop; not only so I won't have to revisit what happened over and over, but also because I might see them.'

Noah had finished his milk by this point so Rachael took him from Gabriel to wind him.

'Maybe you're still having those nightmares for a reason,' she suggested.

'What reason could that be?' I asked, but as I said it, I realised the obvious and knew what she was going to say.

'The person who found you and called the ambulance. Did you ever write to him?'

'What?' Gabriel asked as he turned to me, his eyes wide with alarm and a feeling of panic beginning inside of him.

I clasped his hand with one of my own whilst I put the other on his thigh. I interpreted what he was feeling as concern for me, for my safety, and for my mental and emotional health which could be jeopardised by contacting someone from that night.

'It was a thought I had once. I considered writing a letter to the person who found me to thank him for calling for help. I never quite got around to it, and I wasn't sure if the police would be allowed to pass something like that along.'

His hand squeezed mine hard. 'What do you know about him?'

'Absolutely nothing. The only thing I was told was that he was a man. Are you okay, Gabriel?' I was really starting to worry about him.

'I'm fine, Jamie. I'm sorry if my reaction scared you, I was just apprehensive about the idea and how it might affect you.' He smiled ruefully. 'That didn't come across as controlling, did it? I'd hate for you to fear I'm turning into Hayden.'

'You could *never* turn into Hayden, believe me, Gabriel,' I reassured.

'I agree,' Rachael opined. '*You* are concerned for Jamie's wellbeing. Hayden would have just felt threatened.'

Noah chose that moment to vomit up the milk he had just consumed, and he began to wail in discomfort. Gabriel and I said our farewells so that Rachael could concentrate on cleaning and settling him.

It wasn't until Gabriel was driving us home that I remembered my dream from the previous night. Rachael's suggestion must have jogged my memory.

Eighteen
The Last Piece Of The Puzzle

Until that moment, I had somehow managed to forget the addition to my nightmare the night before; the sensation of someone cradling my head on their thighs; but it all came flooding back. I knew I'd heard Gabriel say my name, the only thing I couldn't determine was if it was in my dream, or if it was him calling me to wake me up. The harder I thought about it, trying to figure it out, the more confused I became.

Gabriel's hand stole over to where mine were resting in my lap and he grasped them both tightly.

'Baby, I know you want to get to the bottom of your dream, but try not to think about it for now. You're not getting closer to an answer and you're just getting frustrated,' he said kindly, not wanting to sound condescending.

'Did it make any sense to you?' I asked hopefully, squeezing his hand back.

'I caught the part where your head was lifted onto someone's knees,' he said, his voice thick with the fear and hurt he felt at those remembered images. 'Then I tried to wake you in case it got nastier; like the time you dreamt it was Aaron who shot you and was trying to kill you.'

I nodded and looked at our entwined hands.

'I'm sorry,' he offered.

I shook my head and looked up at him again. 'There's no reason for you to be sorry. It was probably just a dream. I'm fairly sure I was completely unconscious from the moment I saw Mum die. The shock was just too much.'

'What do you think about Rachael's suggestion that you're still having nightmares because you haven't located the person who found you?' he asked warily.

I shrugged. 'I suppose it's possible. It's the only unresolved part of that night. I never expected to find him; I just thought I owed him a thank you.' My voice was a little bleak. 'The day I met you in the bookshop, I thought it was strange how you knew so much about me. The day after, the thought crossed my mind that it could have been you who found me,' I confessed.

I felt Gabriel experience a momentary flare of anxiety.

'Gabriel, are you okay? What's wrong?'

We had reached Gabriel's house, so he stopped the car and regarded me seriously without answering. Looking into his eyes, into him, I could sense the troubled thoughts and emotions that were intermingling and expanding inside him. We got out of the car and he took my hand and led me to the house.

'What convinced you that it wasn't me?' he asked once we were inside the front door.

'I thought you would have told me it if it was you,' I answered honestly.

He turned me to face him directly, his hands gripped my shoulders to hold me still and his eyes captured my gaze, not allowing me to look away.

'Jamie, what if it *was* me?' he asked a little nervously.

'Was it?' My heart was racing and beating hard. It was affecting my breathing: I could only take sharp, shallow breaths and I wasn't sure if I was excited or panicked.

He looked me in the eye unwaveringly. 'Yes.'

I didn't know what I was feeling at that moment, but Gabriel's confession pained him for some reason. I stood up on tiptoes, reached my arms around his neck, and pressed my lips to his. His arms moved around my waist and he pulled me tightly against him and he kissed me back as though his life depended on it.

He lifted me and carried me through to the lounge, setting me on my feet in front of the sofa. I took my coat off and sat down, and Gabriel did the same. We twisted to face one another.

'Gabriel, why didn't you tell me before now? And why are you so upset about it? You saved my life.'

'That's just it: I only managed to save *your* life.' He sounded so desolate. He felt so wretched. 'This is what I was reluctant to tell you the other day, the feelings I hid from you, and why I said maybe you'd hate me for failing you. You obviously read it from me telepathically, anyway, and your subconscious was trying to tell you in your dream. I woke you up because I wanted you to hear it from me.' He gently took hold of my hands and pressed them against his chest so I could feel his heart beating, and he covered them with his own to keep them there.

'The night you got shot, I stopped by the restaurant to see you with your family,' he began. 'I wanted to see you happy and celebrating your success, but I didn't want to intrude. I was going to find you the next day to introduce myself and try to build a relationship with you.

'I saw you leave the building with your mother and sister and go to your car, and I thought you'd be okay, so I went back to mine. I didn't know anything was wrong until I felt your distress and I ran back to you as quickly as I could. I'm fast, but I wasn't fast enough. I was too late for your mother and your sister, Jamie. Only you were still alive.' His own emotions were so raw, the pain and sadness he felt at finding me like that was overwhelming him.

'I'm sorry I didn't wait until you were all safe in the car. If I'd stayed, I could have stopped him, but...' He looked at me with anguished eyes and I could feel his self-recrimination. 'I'm so, so sorry, Jamie.' His voice cracked as he enunciated and he dropped his head into his hands, letting mine go. He couldn't bear to look at me.

'Gabriel, no,' I cried, moving my hands from his chest to wrap my arms around his hunched shoulders. 'I don't hate you, and you didn't fail me. Please look at me.' I put one of my hands under his chin and guided his face up with only light pressure from my fingertips. 'I don't hate you,' I reiterated, my eyes boring into his so he could see into me. 'I meant it when I said I love you unconditionally and that I could never hate you.

'You're not to blame for Mum's and Carmel's deaths. You were doing the honourable thing by leaving me to celebrate with my family. You had no reason to suspect the three of us wouldn't be safe. *I don't blame you.* You can feel what I feel; you know I mean every word I say.'

Both my hands were holding his face level with mine and his hands came up to grip my wrists, holding them there, as he gazed into my eyes for a long moment. He dissected each emotion I was experiencing for any shred of doubt, and I felt relief engulf him when he found none.

He hauled me into his arms and kissed me with all the love in him.

'But what about your mother and sister?' he asked when he had pulled back enough to talk, but not letting me go. 'You said they like me, but how can they? They must know I saved you but was too late for them.'

'Mum did mention that you had something to confess to me, but she told me it wasn't bad and wouldn't break my heart. If she and Carmel thought you could have saved them, or if they thought I should believe that, they know it would have devastated me. Instead, knowing what you did that night, and seeing how happy you've made me since, Mum said that she and Carmel are very grateful to you,' I said softly.

'I wanted to tell you. I never intended to keep it from you, but I was scared. I also didn't want to introduce myself to you as the person who loved you and found you that night. I wanted you to get to know me first, just as me. Can you understand that?' I nodded solemnly. 'I love you,' he said passionately.

'You saved my life,' I choked out despite the lump in my throat.

'I couldn't lose you, not when it took me this long to find you. Jamie, I've been waiting for you my whole life.' Tears filled his eyes and one slid down his cheek. 'I need you.'

'I've been waiting all my life for you, too, Gabriel.' I gently wiped away his tear with my thumb. 'You know how hard I've had to fight not to let my grief completely consume me, but, even on my good days, I never really felt alive, not before I met you. I was going through the motions, but I wasn't sure I'd ever feel anything again. You make me feel everything. I feel like me again.'

I drew his face towards mine and pressed soft kisses onto his eyelids and the lightest of touches to his lips.

'Will you tell me what else happened that night?' I asked hesitantly.

He sought my eyes and simply looked into them for a moment. Our gazes locked and we could see and feel that we were each completely open to the other, then he nodded.

'From the moment I first saw you, first felt you, I have been so acutely attuned to you that I can find you wherever you are. I can feel what you feel and I get a sense of your thoughts much easier and clearer than those of anyone else.' He smiled and lightly traced once of my cheekbones with his fingertips. 'So, even though I'd only met you earlier in the day, that night, I knew where you were.

'I couldn't resist seeing you with your family, not when I could feel how happy you were, but I didn't want to spy on you. I saw you in the restaurant, then I saw you leaving and, fully believing you were safe, I went back to my car. Everything happened so quickly and, from how it felt to me, you didn't suspect anything was wrong until you saw the man pull the gun. Then, in an instant, before I could even get out of the car, Carmel was dead.

'As soon as I felt your anguish, I knew you were in trouble and I ran,' he told me in a shaky voice. 'I felt it when you got shot. I was only a second away from you when your mother was killed. I could hear your heartbeat, and I could feel it within me, so I knew you were still alive and I rushed straight over to you. I sank onto my knees and cradled your head in my lap.' Tears flowed freely and streamed down Gabriel's face at his remembered distress.

'I kissed your face and implored you to hold on. The gunman knew you weren't dead, and then I was there as an added witness. He started to walk over to us and I knew he was going to shoot us, but I persuaded him to turn the gun on himself instead.' He looked at me pointedly.

'Persuaded him how?' I was certain I already knew what he meant.

'I looked directly at him and gave him an order. As a vampire, an empath and, to some extent, a telepath, I can easily persuade people to do what I want them to do,' he explained unemotionally.

Though I knew I had no reason to suspect he had ever used this gift on me, the thought popped, unbidden, into my mind.

'You know I haven't done that to you, Jamie. I wouldn't,' he confirmed, reading me. 'As an empath yourself, you'd know if I tried because you know which feelings and emotions are yours and which aren't. And, you know your own mind.' He smiled faintly, his tears having dried, and he pushed my hair behind my ears so it didn't occlude his view of my face.

'I know, Gabriel. I never thought you would do that to me, I have no idea why it even crossed my mind. I never doubted you. Please forgive me,' I begged, ashamed.

'It was a natural reaction,' he said, reassuring me he wasn't offended. 'You considered it was possible, but you trusted me not to have done that. Believe me, you would have recognised it immediately if I'd tried. The one thing I have always insisted with you is that you and I do nothing against your will. However, that doesn't mean that when I found you unconscious and bleeding I wasn't tempted to turn you to save your life. If that had been my only option, I would have.'

'Would I have healed if you'd turned me in that condition?' I frowned at him, considering it.

'Yes, faster, because you'd have had my blood in your system. You weren't dying, though, so it wouldn't have been right to turn you without it being your choice when I knew you were going to survive.'

'What if I had been dying and you'd turned me to save me, but I didn't want to be turned?'

He shrugged. 'If, after living as a vampire for a while, you decided you didn't want to be, that you would rather be dead, I would have killed you,' he answered brutally.

That didn't faze me. 'Could you have gone through with it? Could you have actually killed me?' I asked with extreme tenderness, caressing one of his cheekbones with my fingertips.

He closed his eyes briefly and expelled his breath in a rush. 'No. I love you too much. I couldn't do that to you, either.'

Gabriel eliminated the last little bit of distance between us and pulled me into his lap. He gently cradled my cheeks between his palms, pulling my face closer to his, and he pressed his mouth to mine and held it there. I brought my arms up and slid them between his forearms to place them either side of his neck, my fingers tangling in his hair. My lips opened to him and, as I felt his tongue slide against mine, all my feelings for him, everything I felt now that I knew it was him who found me, and finally finding out what happened after I lost consciousness overcame me and I began to silently cry.

Gabriel felt my tears when they landed on the smooth skin of his hands, but he also felt the tidal wave of emotion inside me. He released my face and held me against him whilst noiseless sobs shook my body. I clung to him and he soothed me with the loving touch of his hands stroking my arms as I held on to him, down my back, and then up to repeat the motion until my weeping subsided.

I abruptly raised my head as something occurred to me.

'When you spoke to DI Fordham on the phone the other day, the two of you already knew each other, didn't you?'

'I had to give him a statement because I found you and I witnessed the gunman take his own life. When I spoke to him on the phone and I told him my name, he instantly knew who I was and, because you didn't say anything, he assumed I'd tracked you down. I convinced him it was pure chance that I bumped into you in the bookshop.' He grinned mischievously at me, both of us knowing there was nothing coincidental about it. 'He was very anxious about you. He wanted to know if I'd told you, and then why I hadn't, and when he was sure I had genuine feelings for you and that it was only my concern for you that had prevented me from telling you, he informed me that I should tell you.'

'Now the parts I caught of your half of the conversation make a lot more sense.' I smiled to myself as I remembered the broken sentences I'd overheard.

'DI Fordham came to realise that what you and I have is real and the only danger to you is Aaron.'

I accepted his judgement of DI Fordham with a nod.

'I didn't thank you,' I said with a shy smile.

'Thank me for what?' he asked as he tucked a lock of my hair behind my ear and dropped a kiss on my lips.

'For saving my life,' I answered simply. 'Thank you.' It sounded so inadequate.

'I was saving my own life, too,' he answered. 'To have found you and lost you before we'd had the chance to know each other and love one another would have killed me.'

'Then thank you for saving both our lives. I wish you'd come to me sooner after it was all over, though. You waited eight weeks,' I remonstrated, a little hurt.

'I gave you time and space to mourn. I didn't want to confuse you with my sudden, and constant, presence in your life when everything had changed for you. It wouldn't have been fair to either of us because I wanted you and you just wanted your family back. I came to you when you had begun to reconcile everything; you didn't like it, but you were starting to accept it and you were trying to make a new life for yourself,' he explained honestly.

'I understand. It's just that I'd never been so lonely before, or so completely alone. It hurts to even think about it. I have you now, though, Gabriel, and I'm not letting you go,' I said, happiness suffusing me and then doubling when I felt the same in him. 'I love you too much to let go.'

'Then don't,' he said, locking his arms around my waist, and I laced my fingers together at the back of his neck.

'So, when are you going to turn me so that I won't ever have to let you go?' I held my breath in anticipation of his response.

His breath caught. 'You're mine and I'm yours forever, Jamie, regardless of whether or not I turn you.'

'I know, Gabriel. I know that you are, and always will be, more than enough for me, and I want us to be together forever. You told me that's what you've always dreamed of.' I could feel the need in him to do it, to bite me, to drain me and have me drink from him, to bind us together for all eternity. He wanted it. 'What's stopping you?'

His heart was beating harder and louder, and mine was echoing his.

'I know you're sure about becoming a vampire. I want us to be certain your mother and sister can get through to you in your dreams before I make you immortal and take away your chance to be with them again when you die because, as we've already established, I don't think I could kill you.'

'So you think that now I know it was you who found me, you who ensured the gunman killed himself, it might stop my nightmares from recurring and Mum and Carmel will finally be able to visit?'

His eyes narrowed. 'Possibly.'

'But once you know they can visit, you'll make me a

vampire?'

'With great pleasure. Literally.' He grinned.

'Then I hope they visit soon.' I grinned back and trailed my fingertips over his lips.

'So do I.' He moved his arms from around my waist to slide his hands up my sides, tickling me as they went, and causing me to shudder in reaction. He laughed. 'When you're a vampire, you're nerve endings, your skin, will be even more highly sensitised.' He moved his lips to my ear. 'Imagine how this will feel then.'

I shuddered again at the thought, and the sensual feeling of his breath in my ear, and I felt his lips curve into a knowing smile.

'Mmm, you smell good,' he murmured, inhaling deeply. 'I just realised I haven't fed today.'

I moved my head back and narrowed my eyes at him. 'What are you trying to say?' I asked with laughter in my tone.

'Not that. Come on, let's go to the kitchen.'

He patted my bottom and I released him and stood up. I grasped his hand, pulled him to his feet, then led him to the kitchen. He reached into a cupboard and retrieved a mug.

'You should eat something, too,' he suggested as he passed by me on his way to the fridge.

I dismissed the notion with a wave of my hand and saw his lips thin as he looked at me, internally debating something. He didn't say anything; he merely delved into the fridge and extracted a package of blood and a bottle of milk.

'I'm making you some oatmeal,' he said, his tone alone indicating he wouldn't accept any arguments.

He cut the bag open, poured the blood into the cup, and placed it in the microwave. Whilst Gabriel set the timer, I turned to the cupboard to find the cereal, then I heard the microwave quietly begin to whir. As I twisted back around with an oatmeal sachet in hand, the microwave exploded with a loud bang, and sparks flared inside which were visible through the door.

I screamed, then laughed at myself for being so easily spooked. Gabriel smirked at me and, when he was sure the microwave was safe, he opened the door and checked inside. The interior of the machine was blackened and the sparks had cracked the porcelain of his cup so blood was dripping out. He quickly poured the liquid down the sink, rinsed the mug, and threw it away.

It wasn't dark so there were no lights on; therefore, there was no immediate way of knowing if the microwave had fused the house. Gabriel switched the kettle on, but nothing happened. He went to turn on the light, and I heard the click of the switch, but the light stayed off.

I bit my lip to try to stop myself smiling, but Gabriel could sense I found the situation funny and he grinned even wider.

'Why don't I go and get the microwave from Mum's house whilst you play with the fuse box?' I suggested.

'Good idea,' he agreed, coming over to me, sliding one hand up my cheek and kissing me. 'Be careful.'

'I will,' I replied between kisses. 'You be careful playing with electricity.'

He smiled against my mouth, kissed me once more, then let me go. I backed out of the kitchen, smiling at him, to find my coat and keys. I automatically picked up the keys to my mother's car; for some reason, I still couldn't think of it as mine; rather than Gabriel's and headed in the direction of the door, but before I could get there, Gabriel beat me to it.

He opened it for me, walked me out to the car, and saw me inside. 'Lock your doors,' he commanded just before I got in. I complied, and he waited just inside the open front door until I'd driven away.

I'd just parked the car in the driveway at Mum's house, got out of it, and inserted my house key into the lock when someone materialised behind me.

'Really, Jamie, a restraining order?' the male voice said in a sarcastic tone.

Aaron.

My blood ran cold in fear. I was about to spin around and tell him to leave when he placed a heavy hand on my injured shoulder.

'Open the door and let me in,' he demanded.

'What for? I have nothing to say to you, Aaron.'

'But I have plenty to say to you. Now open the door,' he repeated viciously, giving my shoulder a remorseless squeeze which caused me to whimper in pain.

I did as he said and, once inside, he shoved me through the hallway and into the lounge. I put a hand inside the neck of my jumper and attempted to give my shoulder a one-handed massage.

'No Gabriel with you today?' he sneered.

'What makes you think that?' I countered, unwilling to admit I was alone.

'I saw you pull up. He wasn't in the car.'

'Have you been waiting for me? What do you do, come here every day?'

'I noticed you haven't been here lately,' he said, deliberately not giving me a direct answer.

'There's a reason for that. It's why I've got that restraining order on you. I honestly don't know what you want from me. I know you think I should have died instead of Carmel, but there's nothing you or I can do about that, so why are you doing this to me?'

I didn't care that I was possibly baiting the latent anger I could feel in him; I'd had enough of this from him. I refused to be intimidated, and that helped ease my panic, so I was much closer to being calm than I would have expected given the circumstances.

'Bea and Carmel both died. Why did you live?' he spat out.

'Mum pushed me out of the way when the gunman aimed at me and pulled the trigger. I still got hurt, but, thanks to her, not fatally. He'd already killed Carmel by then; he did that before we could even register what was happening. Neither of us could have stopped him. I've told you all this before,'

I asserted. 'He killed Mum and was about to shoot me again to kill me. It was only the arrival of the man who found me unconscious and bleeding profusely that stopped him.'

Aaron tilted his head to one side, disbelieving. 'If you were unconscious, how do you know that's what happened?'

'DI Fordham told me. He came to the hospital to get my statement. I saw nothing after Mum was killed. I asked him what happened after that. He told me that a man heard the gunshots and screaming and came to find out what was going on and to help. The man with the gun was already making his way over to me, but, when he saw the witness, he turned the gun on himself.' I shrugged, trying to downplay what I knew. 'The witness and I were both lucky that the gunman decided not to shoot him, too.'

By this point, I knew it didn't really matter what I said; Aaron was rapidly losing his grip on reason and was being engulfed by anger and hurt. He felt that if Carmel was dead, I should be, too. I needed to get away from him for a couple of minutes so I could send a message to Gabriel without Aaron seeing.

'Aaron,' I began, infusing my voice with as much compassion as I could even though I had none for him anymore. 'I know you're really hurting at the moment; so much that you can barely function. You're not yourself. You wouldn't want to hurt me if you were. I'm Carmel's twin, remember? She wouldn't want you to hurt me, would she?'

'But she's not here, you are, and that's the problem,' he said through gritted teeth, barely containing the urge to physically attack me.

'Look, calm down, Aaron. Please.' I took a step backwards towards the door. 'You said outside that you had a lot of things to say to me, so why don't you sit down and I'll make us some drinks? Then, you can tell me everything.'

His resolve wavered and he sank into one of the armchairs and nodded. I retreated to the kitchen, resisting the urge to hurry and look like I was scared. I tried to make my actions as loud as possible as I picked up the kettle, tipped the water inside away and refilled it with fresh water from the tap so Aaron wouldn't get suspicious. At the same time, I pulled my phone out of my pocket and was typing a message to Gabriel. I had almost finished the message when the phone was knocked out of my hand. I screamed in shock, and the kettle slipped out of my other hand and hit the floor.

Aaron grabbed me by the throat with both hands and began squeezing.

I could only hope that Gabriel had been paying attention and had felt everything I had been feeling for the last few minutes since Aaron approached me outside the house, and especially now that I was in so much danger and distress.

'He can't come and rescue you now, can he?' Aaron jeered.

I could feel his hands biting into the skin of my neck and the pain of my windpipe being compressed. I was struggling to breathe, wriggling to try to free myself from his grasp, and trying to prise his fingers off my throat. I dug my nails in, but he was physically stronger than me.

I groped behind me for anything I could grab hold of, planning to hit Aaron around the head with it to force him to let go. I wrapped my hand around the first thing I found and dimly realised it was the handle of one of the knives sticking out of its metal holder. As I pulled it out, I could tell it wasn't the biggest blade, but it wasn't the smallest, either.

I whipped my arm around and stabbed Aaron straight in the shoulder.

He yelled in pain and reflexively released me. I stumbled away, trying to drag in breaths, and headed towards the door to the hallway to get out and run to my neighbour's house for help. My legs felt weak and they didn't seem to want to obey as I tried to run, so I fell to my hands and knees in the kitchen doorway.

I quickly looked behind me and saw Aaron pull the knife out of his shoulder and take a couple of steps towards me, but at that moment, I heard a key in the lock of the door and swivelled my head around in time to see Gabriel bursting in, and he flew over to me.

I was still curled up on the floor, coughing and endeavouring to breathe normally. Gabriel put his hands under my arms to lift me to my feet, then swiftly placed himself between me and Aaron, one arm behind him resting on my hip.

'I've already called DI Fordham. He won't be coming alone so don't try anything even more stupid,' Gabriel warned Aaron with steely anger. 'And don't come anywhere near Jamie or I'll kill you myself.'

Responding to both Gabriel's tone, and his vampiric persuasiveness, Aaron let go of the knife and dropped to his knees, pressing his hand to his wounded shoulder to try to stem the bleeding.

Sensing that Aaron was no further threat to me, Gabriel half-turned and pulled me around and into his arms. I sobbed once.

'Are you okay, baby?' Gabriel asked, gazing deeply into my eyes, his voice thick with the worry I could feel surging through him.

'He was strangling me and I couldn't wrench his hands off... I stabbed him.' I was shaking with reaction, both from the attack on me, and because I'd injured Aaron. I'd never physically hurt anyone before. 'I was scared.'

'I got here as quickly as I could,' he said, stroking my hair back to examine my throat.

'I know, baby. I'm grateful.' I attempted a smile and I watched his expression harden as he assessed me.

He gave a dry laugh at my comment and kissed me. 'I think your neck will be sore for a while, and you'll have some bruising, but there's no serious damage.'

I pressed my mouth against his ear. 'Promise to kiss it better later?' I whispered.

'I promise,' he said into my ear, and I felt his lips curve into a smile.

I knew that we were speaking too quietly for Aaron to hear us, but seeing Gabriel and I together, embracing one another, made him feel sick with jealousy: Gabriel and I had one another, but Carmel was gone.

The front door, which had closed halfway, was suddenly pushed open and Jim Fordham stepped inside. The first thing he saw was Gabriel holding me close.

'Jamie, are you okay? What happened?' he asked.

Gabriel loosened his grip on me but didn't let go.

'Aaron had his hands around my throat. He was squeezing really hard and I couldn't get him to let go. The only thing I could reach was a knife, and I stabbed him,' I answered solemnly, feeling ill.

DI Fordham stepped a little closer and looked at the angry red marks on my neck, then strode over to where Aaron sat on the kitchen floor.

Gabriel was right about DI Fordham not being alone: several uniformed police officers entered the house and approached him awaiting instructions.

'Arrest him,' he ordered one of the officers. 'And call for a paramedic.'

DI Fordham took a statement from me, and then from Gabriel, whilst we waited for an ambulance. One of the paramedics went to aid Aaron whilst the other was assigned to look at my neck.

'You're lucky,' he announced with a smile, 'you've suffered some bruising, but there's no permanent damage.'

'That's what he said,' I nodded towards Gabriel.

'I come from a medical family; I know the basics,' Gabriel replied to the medic's questioning glance.

The other paramedic and a police officer led Aaron to the ambulance and, as they drew near, Aaron looked at me and said, 'I'm sorry, Jamie.'

I looked away without replying and Gabriel put his hands on my hips and drew me back against him in both a protective and possessive gesture.

Spotting us together like that, DI Fordham approached us before leaving.

'You shouldn't be hearing from him for a while, Jamie,' he said. His eyes flicked to Gabriel. 'Mr. Castell,' he acknowledged. 'I trust you've—'

'Yes, Detective, I've told Jamie it was me who found her the night she was hurt. She knows everything,' he said without inflection, but I know his remark held a deeper meaning only for me.

'Well, there are obviously genuine feelings between you so I suppose I have no reason to be suspicious.' Jim smiled at me. 'I'm glad you're happy, Jamie. After everything you've been through, you certainly deserve to be. Take care of yourself.'

'Thank you, Jim. You, too.'

Everyone departed, leaving Gabriel and me alone. I turned around and reached my arms around his neck, pressed my body into his, and kissed him. His hands crept to the small of my back, sealing me against him as his mouth roamed from mine, along my jawbone, and down to my throat, softly kissing the inflamed skin.

I tipped my head back so he had better access, and pushed my fingers into his silky hair. I let out a moan as I felt his tongue caress me.

'Is this making it feel better?' he asked between kisses.

'Much better. You know, Aaron also aggravated my injured shoulder. Do you think you could give me a massage later? At home?'

'Anything for you,' he said, and then he moved my jumper aside at the neck to kiss my shoulder, too.

A few minutes later, we cleared up the blood that Aaron had dripped onto the kitchen floor, picked up the kettle I'd dropped, mopped up the spilled water, and found my phone. Gabriel loaded the microwave I'd originally come for and my mum's plants into his car, locked the door, and we left. After today, I didn't want to come back here for a while.

Nineteen

In Dreams

If I had hoped that after the revelation that Gabriel was the man who saved my life in that car park when I got shot, and the knowledge that Aaron could no longer terrorise me, I would finally sleep, dream, and be visited by my mother and sister that night, I was disappointed.

I was still in a minor state of shock when we got home and, whilst Gabriel drank his blood, he insisted I ate something and drank a few sips of brandy to settle my nerves. It all tasted foul to me, but I obliged him because he loved me, because he was concerned for me, and because he had been scared he wouldn't reach me in time and would have been forced to turn me in front of Aaron to save me.

I felt mentally and physically drained and I wanted to soak in a hot bath, then curl up in Gabriel's arms to sleep. I invited Gabriel to join me in the bath since it could comfortably fit two, so he seated himself behind me, leaned back and drew me against his chest, encircling me in his arms and resting his thighs around mine.

'So,' he began, a smile in his voice and emanating a warm feeling, 'what do you think our chances are of spending the rest of eternity without any more traumas?'

I tilted my head back to look into his face and I smiled. 'My life used to be pretty mundane. It's only recently that people have been trying to kill me. One of them is dead, Aaron won't live forever, and I'm hoping I won't be mortal for much longer.'

Gabriel trailed a damp finger down my cheek. 'If it looks as though someone else is likely to threaten your life, I'll turn you before they have the chance to harm you and hope that your mother and sister contact you afterwards.'

'They promised they would,' I reminded him, reaching up to touch his jaw. 'Maybe there's no need to wait. I want to be with you forever; you know I'm sure of that.'

'I know,' he agreed, dropping his head to brush a kiss over my lips. 'Let's just give it a few days to see if they contact you whilst you're human. Maybe with the enhanced senses of a vampire it will be easier.' He shrugged. 'We'll see.'

Before the water could cool too much, Gabriel picked up a washcloth, poured a small amount of body wash onto it, and began to stroke it over my skin. When he was satisfied he had washed my whole body, he began on my hair, gently massaging my scalp to relax me. It was then my turn to do the same to him.

I wrapped my hair and body in towels, my limbs feeling heavy, and I slowly made my way out of the bathroom towards the bed with Gabriel only a step behind me. He had rubbed his hair dry and, once he was in the bedroom, he discarded the towel around his waist in favour of some clingy boxer shorts. Before I had time to get out of my towel, Gabriel placed his hands on my shoulders guided me over to the bed.

'Lie down on the bed, Jamie,' he commanded softly. 'On your front.'

I turned my head to look at him. 'What for?'

He leaned over to the nightstand, picked up a bottle and held it up between the tips of his fingers so I could see. 'Massage,' he said, lightly shaking the oil. 'You asked me to treat your shoulder, remember?'

'Only if you don't mind. I can still feel a dull ache from Aaron's vicelike grip earlier.'

'I definitely don't mind,' he said in low tones by my ear.

He stood behind me, softly pressing his body into mine and making me acutely aware of him. He reached around and pulled the towel open, holding it between us.

'Lie down,' he reiterated, brushing my cheekbone with a kiss.

I crawled onto the bed and Gabriel covered my lower half with the towel. He removed the towel covering my hair and combed the wet length of it through with his fingers before picking up a pillow and placing it beneath my head. He then poured some oil into one hand before rubbing them together to warm it and distribute it between them.

I felt him glide his hands up my back from the very base of my spine, right up to my neck, he firmly kneaded my shoulders, then he slid them back down.

I sighed in pleasure at the feel of his warm hands expertly moving over my body. I instantly relaxed, closed my eyes, and gave myself over to the sensation of being touched and healed so lovingly.

'How does that feel?' Gabriel asked after a few strokes.

'Wonderful. I'm tingling all over and it sort of feels like I'm floating,' I mumbled, my face partially obscured by the pillow.

He was pleased; I felt him warm a little in his heart.

'Good. You've got a lot of tension in your neck and shoulders so I'll have to use a bit more pressure. I'm sorry if it hurts; just think about something nice and keep your body relaxed.'

'I'm thinking about you, that's as nice as it's possible to get. You're perfect.' I sent him love empathically.

'I'm glad you think so. I think you're perfect, too,' he said as he sent love back.

It seemed a long time later that Gabriel's movements slowed to a halt and he lowered his head and kissed my back from one shoulder to the other, then up to nuzzle my neck, before lying down beside me. I opened my eyes and smiled shyly at him. He leaned towards me and softly pressed his lips against mine.

'You're too good at that,' I complimented. 'You'll have to tell me your secrets so I can return the favour a bit better than I did last time.'

He smiled. 'You look as though you're struggling to stay awake.'

I grinned at him. 'It feels as though my whole body has melted.' I also felt quite chilly, which was a natural side-effect from the massage.

Gabriel, on the other hand, was nice and warm, so I shuffled closer. He put his arm around me and gathered me against him. I tangled my limbs with his, revelling in his heat.

'I think we should get under the duvet so you can warm up fully,' he suggested.

He shifted us into a sitting position, threw the towel covering me onto the floor and helped me into one of his t-shirts, then he pulled the cover back and manoeuvred us into the bed. He reached over to turn off the bedside lamp before wrapping me in his arms again, not that I'd let him go: I'd clung to him around his waist the whole time.

I snuggled into him, burying my face in the heated skin of his throat and trying not to shiver. After a couple of minutes, my body temperature had returned to normal so I concentrated on the feel of Gabriel's body pressed against mine, on our hearts beating in a steady, synchronised rhythm, and I fell into a deep, dreamless sleep.

Gabriel was as surprised and as frustrated as me when, almost a week later, I still hadn't heard from my mother or sister. That didn't mean I wasn't grateful that I hadn't had any more nightmares. The dreams I'd had were glorious insights of the future I hoped to share with Gabriel; visions of Gabriel turning me; and several instances of us sensuously feeding from one another once I had become a vampire.

Not long ago, Gabriel had told me that he used to have dreams of us together, but it was as though his dreams were tormenting him because my face was never clear in them until he met me. His dreams gave him insights into what he *could* have. That was how I now felt. I was dreaming of the life I was eager to begin and the only thing delaying that was the final assurance I needed from my family.

It wasn't as though I couldn't sense that they were with me. I couldn't count the number of times I'd seen a flicker of movement in the corner of my eye, know it was them in the room, only to turn my head and find nothing but the furniture. Sometimes, I'd be on the brink of sleep, or I'd be reading a book, and I'd hear Mum or Carmel call my name, but nothing more. Every now and then, I'd be talking to Gabriel and something he said would make me laugh and I'd have this feeling that they were laughing, too. However, until I had direct contact with them in a dream, since I knew this was the easiest way for them to reach me, I couldn't make the leap that I was longing for.

'Gabriel, I think I'll go and visit Mum and Carmel and take them some flowers,' I informed him. I'd been reading one of my textbooks, but I was too agitated to concentrate. 'I need to talk to them.'

He looked up from reading the book I had dismissed a few weeks ago. 'You already talk to them all the time. You say some things out loud and, other times, I hear you whispering to them at night before you go to sleep,' he said kindly. 'You tell them everything.'

'I know, but maybe being physically close to where they are, to their bodies, will make a difference. I can't just sit and wait. I have to feel like I'm doing something.'

'Okay, I understand,' he said, feeling my disquiet. 'Go and talk to them. I'll be here when you get back.'

'I might be gone a while,' I said as I got to my feet.

'That's fine. Just be careful.' He closed the book, stood up, and removed the small distance between us.

'You can finish that book whilst I'm gone.' My lips twitched in amusement.

'I don't think so.' He raised his eyebrows expressively and I felt his internal distaste. 'It's complete drivel.'

I grinned. 'I know, that's why I discarded it after skimming a couple of chapters.'

He grinned back. 'Go, I've got research of my own to do.'

'Really? Research into what?'

'The surprise I promised you. I haven't forgotten about that.'

If only I could read his thoughts as well as his emotions. I hadn't had any dreams that gave me any clues to his surprise and he knew I wasn't a patient person.

'You won't have to wait much longer,' he promised, tilting my face up to his with the light pressure of his fingers. He bent his head and brushed his lips against mine. 'I don't want to wait much longer for this,' he added cryptically.

I wrapped my arms around his neck, pressed my body into his, and claimed his mouth for a kiss. His hands moved to grip me around the waist and he held me there even closer and more securely as I slipped my tongue into his mouth. My arms instinctively tightened as he sensuously tangled his own tongue with mine.

Slowly, reluctantly, I pulled my head back. 'I'm going,' I said a little breathlessly.

Gabriel nodded and released me. 'Be careful,' he repeated huskily.

As always, he saw me out and waited at the door until I'd driven away. I made a brief stop to pick up a bunch of red tulips; a symbol of my undying love for them; and, once at the cemetery, I made my way over to the side of Mum and Carmel's grave.

'Hey, Mum. Hey, Carmel. I've brought some more flowers for you. Pretty, aren't they?'

I knelt on my old yoga mat and changed the flowers, then adjusted my position to sit more comfortably to chat.

'I've left Gabriel at home. That is, at his house,' I clarified. 'I wanted to come here and talk to you alone.' I snickered to myself. 'I'm telling you all this as though you don't already know when I'm sure you're constantly watching me.

'I came here to be close to you and tell you that I love you and I miss you, and that I'm sad you haven't been to visit me now that my nightmares have stopped. I know that when I saw the psychic you said that you're always with me, but I really need to see you,' I said, my voice quivering. 'You also said that I should make the best decision for me, to become a vampire so that I can be with Gabriel for all eternity if that will make me happy. The thing is, I want him to turn me, I want to be with him and never have to leave him, but I know how painful it will be if I have to spend eternity never being able to see you both.

'If I don't let Gabriel turn me, I'll eventually die and be with you both again, but Gabriel will go on living unless he does something drastic. If I know you can visit me when I sleep, even if that's the only contact I ever have with you, at least I'll know we won't be eternally separated. I'm in a really difficult position. I want to be with Gabriel, and I know that if I don't become a vampire he'll support my decision, he'll still love me for all eternity, but I'll be hurting him, too, and I couldn't bear that,' I said, heartbroken.

The pain I felt at the thought of causing Gabriel to suffer was too much and I began to cry. The tears were silent at first, but they turned into sobs that shook my whole body. I knew that Gabriel would be giving me as much privacy as possible, but I knew it was impossible for him not to feel what I was feeling. I didn't want him to worry about me, but I was certain he anticipated that I would get upset coming here. I missed him now; he was always good at simply holding on to me when I cried over Mum and Carmel.

'I know that we can't change this. I can't bring you back no matter how much I wish, plead, or even pray that I could, but I'm begging you not to abandon me. Please come and see me, talk to me directly, let me know you're okay and that you're happy with my decision to be with Gabriel forever. Please. Please.'

I dropped my head into my hands and rocked back and forth until my tears dried up. I didn't care who saw me, heard me, or what they thought, not that there were many other people around. I blocked them all out, anyway, as I tried to detect energy and emotion from Mum or Carmel, but I was too overwrought to feel anything other than my own strained emotions.

I stood up to leave, gathered up all my things, then blew Mum and Carmel a kiss each.

'I hope I see you both really soon.'

I wandered back to Mum's car, but, before I left the cemetery, I attempted to tidy myself up so that it wasn't so obvious I'd been crying.

Gabriel knew the exact moment I returned home. Before I'd even brought the car to a halt he was standing at the open front door. I got out and ran straight into his waiting arms.

'I'm sorry you didn't feel anything,' he said, putting his arm around my shoulders as he guided me into the living room.

I looked at him sadly and allowed him to help me out of my jacket.

He sat on the sofa and pulled me onto his lap. 'Jamie, baby, I know it hurts, but all you can do is try to be patient. I truly believe they'll come to you.'

'When I saw Eloise, she told me they'd been trying to visit. My nightmares were preventing them from coming through then, but I'm not having those anymore, so I should be able to see them,' I reasoned.

'Maybe that's what they thought was blocking them, but maybe it's something else. I don't know very much about communicating with spirits, but I believe you had genuine contact with Bea and Carmel when you saw Eloise. You also believed it was real.'

'I still believe that. It just hurts so much that they're gone, and I need to see them,' I said quietly, knowing that Gabriel understood this didn't affect what I felt for him.

'I know.' He kissed my forehead. 'Maybe you're trying too hard. Just relax and let it happen.'

I looped my arms around him and snuggled in closer.

'How did your research go?' I asked after a minute or two. 'Did you find what you were searching for?'

'I think so. There are a couple of options and, when we go, we'll decide which is the most appropriate.'

'I have a choice in this, whatever it is?'

'Yes, several choices, all of which are vital.' He grinned at me.

'You do realise how oblique you're being, don't you?' He grinned wider and I smiled in response.

That night, as I got into bed, Gabriel pulled me against his chest, curved my body into his with my face pressed into his shoulder, and bent his head to whisper into my ear. 'Just relax. Don't try to force it,' he advised.

With him holding me, warming me, and making me feel loved and cherished, it wasn't difficult to get to sleep, and not long before I was dreaming.

In my dream, I was back in my family home, standing in the dining room. I didn't know what I was doing there; I felt strangely disorientated and, as I turned in a circle, I looked out the back door and saw my mother and sister in the garden.

I rushed to the door and tried to open it, but it was locked. The key wasn't sitting in the lock and I couldn't see it nearby. Mum and Carmel hadn't noticed me, so I banged the side of my fist against the glass to get their attention.

They swiftly approached the other side of the glass and tried to open the door from the outside. When it didn't move, they each checked their pockets for keys and found nothing.

'Jamie!' Mum was shouting, but her voice was barely audible.

'Try to find the key, sweetie,' Carmel finished for her.

'Wait there!' I yelled.

I searched the room, but couldn't find any keys. I dashed through the kitchen, only briefly scanning the work surfaces because I knew they wouldn't be in there. In the living room, I looked for my handbag, but there weren't any keys in there, nor on the coffee table. There were no spares on the mantelpiece, either.

I rushed back to Mum and Carmel who were still standing at the door. 'I've got to check upstairs,' I shouted. 'I'll be as quick as I can. Don't go anywhere.'

I ran as fast as I could, my heart hammering with panic that I wouldn't find any keys or that Mum and Carmel would be gone by the time I got back. In my bedroom, I searched every surface, in every drawer and bag, on every bookshelf, and even under my bed, but all my keys had gone missing. It was then that I thought of Mum's keys that I'd hidden in a pair of her socks. I rushed to her room and looked for the pair that I'd checked when Gabriel had the lock on the front door changed. They'd gone. I looked around the rest of the room, and in Carmel's old bedroom.

By the time I got back downstairs, I was frantic.

'All the keys have gone missing! Do you know where any of them have gone?'

They looked at me with expressions of complete despair. I felt my heart clench.

'Maybe we can break the glass,' I suggested, but Mum shook her head. 'What about a window? You could climb in.'

This time Carmel shook her head.

I put both my hands flat on the glass. 'Please,' I entreated. 'There's got to be some way to break the door. We've got to do something.'

Mum and Carmel each put a hand level with mine so they would be touching if it weren't for the barrier separating us. We stood that way for a moment before they began to fade until they disappeared completely.

I called out to them, but they didn't come back and I stood there, immobile, too shocked to cry or react in any way.

I forced myself to wake up so I didn't have to feel so alone. I opened my eyes and reached my hand up to touch Gabriel's cheek with the tips of my fingers. He opened his eyes and, feeling what I was feeling, he bent his head to kiss me and he clutched me tighter.

I buried my face in his shoulder as a few tears escaped. Gabriel stroked my hair away from my face and down my back.

'It's okay, Jamie,' he soothed. 'You saw them, so that's a start. You know they've found a way through.'

'I know. I wonder if there's something more I can do. The locked door and no key must mean something.'

'It might just mean that they haven't fully figured out how to talk to you. Don't agonise over it; it will resolve itself.'

Gabriel rolled onto his back, taking me with him, and he encouraged me to rest my head on his chest. With his heart pounding strongly and reassuringly beneath my cheek, and his hands lovingly caressing my back, I curled my arms around him and fell back to sleep.

It didn't take long for Mum and Carmel to visit me again: it was the following night. I dreamt that the three of us were in the library of Gabriel's house looking at a framed diploma that he had on his desk. It had my name on it and it was awarding me a PhD.

Mum and Carmel were wearing the same clothes as in the photograph from my graduation that was on my bedside table. I was in the same gown, and I could see the tassel from the cap swinging in my peripheral vision.

'Congratulations, darling,' my mother said, giving me a hug and kissing me on the cheek. 'You've worked so hard for this.'

'Yeah,' Carmel agreed, squeezing me tightly once Mum had let go, 'but just because you're *Dr.* Jamie now, that doesn't mean you won't still be my little sister.' She grinned at me.

I wrapped one arm around each of their necks to gather them as close to me as I could and I held on tight. For the moment, I ignored that I was still almost three years away from finishing my PhD, and that we were in Gabriel's house but he wasn't with us. I was with my mum and sister; I could see them, hear them, touch them, and I could even smell their individual perfumes. That was all that mattered to me in that moment.

'You made it through this time,' I stated. 'How? What was wrong last night?'

'We don't know why, but, whilst you were having nightmares about what happened the night we died, we couldn't reach you at all,' Mum informed me.

'But what about last night?' I persisted.

'You've always been the one with the psychic ability, Jamie,' Carmel continued. 'We've never had to try to communicate with you via your gift before, it was always you reaching out empathically to us. We just didn't quite get it right last time.' She had a sheepish expression on her face, but everything else told me she was so happy they had both reached me at last.

'We used this memory to get through,' Mum explained. They were taking it in turns to speak. 'You spoke fondly about your graduation when Gabriel was admiring the photograph. As he insisted you take it with you to his house, and you put it on your side of the bed, we knew you'd have looked at it before you fell asleep. It was the easiest way in for us, inexperienced as we are at this.'

'But the certificate… I don't have my PhD yet.'

'You will,' Carmel assured me, 'you know you will. You're going to do lots of things, which isn't surprising considering you're going to have all eternity to do them.'

'You mean with Gabriel.' I wasn't asking.

'Yes. You've found your vampire and you love each other with your whole selves. I always told you if vampires existed you'd find one.' Mum winked at me knowingly.

'But, if he turns me, I'll never be with you again, not the way the two of you are together,' I said sadly.

'No,' Carmel agreed, 'but you can't give up what you'll have with Gabriel. You love each other too much, and we love *you* too much, to let you grow old and die when you could be with him and stay young forever.'

'And we'll never leave you,' Mum quickly added to give me as much comfort as she could. 'We'll always visit. You'll always feel us once you've got the hang of feeling our energy now that we don't have physical bodies. You're an empath, and you're going to become a vampiric empath, so you'll learn to feel us emotionally again, I just know it. I feel it.'

'Me, too,' Carmel concurred.

'But I don't want it to be like this. I want you back.' Tears started flowing down my face.

'We don't want it to be like this, either,' Carmel said, choking back tears of her own.

'But,' Mum continued, 'this is how it is and we can't change it. Make the most of whatever happiness you can get, Jamie. You'll still have us, not in the way we'd all like, but we're here. You have Gabriel, too. Don't let him go.'

'I was never going to.'

'Good,' Carmel said. 'You want to be with him forever, so get him to turn you as soon as possible. Don't wait; there's no reason to.'

I nodded. 'I love you, Mum. I love you, Carmel.'

'I love you, too,' they each said in turn.

We hugged again, and I clung on as tightly as I could, but it was then that my dream changed.

I was at my graduation ceremony, wearing a different cap and gown, having my photograph taken with Gabriel. My arms were flung around his shoulders and his were gripping me firmly around my waist.

Twenty
Change

'I have never felt you at such peace before,' Gabriel commented as he regarded me over his blood the following morning. He was sitting at the kitchen table wearing nothing but a pair of pyjama bottoms.

He had made breakfast for me, too, but I was pushing the cereal around with my spoon rather than eating it. There was too much going on inside my head and my heart to feel hungry.

'You saw what I dreamt last night. I feel happy now that I've seen Mum and Carmel and they've told me themselves, in person, that they support my choice.' I looked him directly in the eye. 'I'm as certain as I can be that I want you to change me. I love you too much to risk ever being separated from you. So, the only question is, when do you want to do it?'

I felt his heartbeat accelerate, echoing my own. We both not only wanted this, we needed it. We needed each other.

Gabriel shot out of his chair, dropped to his knees in front of me, and grasped my hands to place them against his heart. I could see the fervent hope and need in his eyes that we were both feeling.

'How about right now?' he asked.

'There's nothing else I'd rather do.'

He put one arm under my knees, the other behind my back, and lifted me out of my chair. He moved quickly, taking me upstairs to our bedroom, and laid me gently on the bed.

'Gabriel—'

'I know when you dreamt about this happening it was on the bed, but that's not why I'm doing it here. It makes sense: I'm going to be draining your blood and you're going to be weak, so this will be more comfortable for you.' He smiled down at me as he joined me on the bed. I knew he could hear and feel how fast my heart was beating. 'I promise I won't hurt you,' he said as he positioned his lower body between my thighs.

I loved the feel of him pressing so close against me and I wrapped my arms around his torso to hold him there, but I kept them low so that they wouldn't obstruct his access to my throat.

'It took me so long to find you,' he murmured quietly, reverently, before softly brushing his lips over mine. 'The instant I felt you, I knew I wanted this.' I could feel the truth of his words inside him. He trailed light, tantalising kisses over my cheekbones, then he moved my hair aside as he made his way to my ear and whispered into it: 'I'm going to love you and keep you for all eternity, Jamie.'

'You'd better,' I managed to choke out, 'because that's what I'm going to do to you.' He could feel the truth in my words inside me, too. My breathing had become fast and shallow, making it difficult to speak, and it felt as though my heart was going to explode.

I felt his mouth move down the side of my throat, giving me tiny kisses which made me tingle, as he tilted my chin slightly to one side. His lips formed a smile against my skin before teasing it with his teeth, then I felt his tongue trace the vein in my neck which sent sparks racing through me. I was nervous that it would be painful, but I needed him to do it.

'Gabriel, please,' I implored.

He growled low in his throat, put one hand behind my back, between my shoulder blades, to lift my upper body slightly off the bed whilst, with the other, he supported my head. I felt the graze of his teeth and I moaned in ecstasy at the feeling.

'I love you, Gabriel, and I will for all eternity,' I whispered.

I felt a slight pressure, then a mild pricking impression that was more pleasurable than painful, as Gabriel's fangs pierced my skin and my vein. Then he began to drink, sucking deeply, and drawing me inside him.

I clutched him tighter, thrilling at the sensations flowing through me. When I'd dreamt of Gabriel turning me, my subconscious had drawn on my experience of having Gabriel taste my blood and magnified everything I'd felt. However, I didn't imagine the reality, which was so much more. It felt like my essence was flowing into Gabriel and I was giving him a part of myself to keep forever. I felt my love for him surging into him as I felt his enveloping me, keeping me warm, and I felt my desire rising along with his.

Then, everything began to dim. I could feel Gabriel drinking still, but all my perceptions became less powerful. My muscles felt weak and, instead of clutching Gabriel against me, my arms were wrapped limply around him. My head felt fuzzy, so I couldn't form a coherent thought, or speak an intelligible word.

My consciousness was threatening to slip away from me and my eyes slid shut, but I still felt Gabriel lower me back onto the mattress. He removed his hand from my back but kept hold of my head, and I fought against the darkness to open my eyes and watch him bite deeply into his wrist. He pressed it against my mouth and, somehow, managing to move my arms to hold on to his, I fastened my lips over the bleeding wound and began to drink.

Gabriel closed his eyes and tipped his head back as he experienced everything I had just felt when he was drinking from me. I sucked harder, causing him to purr deeply with pleasure, and I felt a deep sense of satisfaction and completion in us both.

All the love he felt for me was there in his blood, which was pouring onto my tongue, into me, as our souls combined, and I could feel my strength returning until, eventually, Gabriel touched my cheek.

'Jamie,' he rasped, 'I think that's enough.'

I could sense Gabriel was feeling weak, so I ceased drinking and let go of his wrist. He momentarily collapsed against me before rolling onto his side to give me space whilst my transformation from human to vampire took place.

I had no idea what to expect and neither did Gabriel, having never turned anyone before, though we both believed it would be more painful for me than it was for him since I was being turned from a human into a vampire, whereas Gabriel had been a vampire already. As I lay there with my eyes closed, it felt like fire was in my blood, spreading out from the centre of my body, pervading my veins, my organs, behind my eyes and into my brain. I had prepared myself to be in an excruciating amount of pain, but the burning sensation wasn't as bad as I'd feared.

I could feel myself heating from the inside out until I was sure that I'd scorch anything that I touched, and I was fearful that Gabriel would touch me and I'd burn him. Just when it felt as though I was about to burst into flames, the feeling began to recede, leaving a tingling sensation in every part of me.

'Jamie? Baby, are you okay?' There was a hint of fear in him. He was worried that I was in pain, and scared the transformation hadn't worked.

I still had my eyes closed, but I knew that Gabriel's hand was hovering less than an inch away from me. I could sense it. He desperately wanted to touch me to make sure I was all right, but he was frightened it would hurt me.

I opened my eyes, turned onto my side, and there was an expression of profound relief on Gabriel's face which I also felt radiating through him. What was shocking to me was how everything looked brighter, the colours deeper, and everything was more sharply in focus. My eyesight as a human had been perfect, so I didn't think it was possible for my vision to be any clearer or more precise, but it was. Gabriel's face was so clearly defined; I could see every fleck of colour in his expressive eyes, every eyelash surrounding them, every hair in his eyebrows. All my senses were amplified: I could hear his heartbeat, feel it resonating more strongly within me; I could feel the whisper of his breath on my face like a caress; I could smell the sweetness of his skin; but I could also feel his apprehension.

'The night you told me you're a vampire, you said that all your senses are more intense. I'm just trying to adjust to that. It's incredible to me, yet it has been this way for you your whole life.' I looked at him in wonder and his expression softened.

'There's one very important sensation you must experience as a vampire.' His smile widened and he reached his hand out to stroke my cheek.

I gasped at how sensitive my skin was now, and how my whole body reacted and clenched in response to one small touch.

'That's how I feel every time you touch me,' he confessed. 'And then there's this,' he added as he tilted his head forward, stroked my bottom lip with the tip of his tongue, then pressed his lips to mine.

Every nerve ending in my body zinged as though they had been touched by a live wire. I pulled Gabriel against me and shuddered as he stroked his tongue into my mouth.

'Your fangs have grown,' he said, grinning against my mouth.

'Good; now I'll be able to bite you,' I replied, and felt *him* shudder in response.

He peeled off the pyjamas I'd only put on in order to go down to breakfast and stilled above me.

'Gabriel, what's wrong?' I asked as his heartbeat tripped.

'Your shoulder,' he said quietly, and touched his fingertips to it.

I turned my head to see what he meant. The jagged, pink

marks of my scars had disappeared, leaving perfect, milky-white skin.

'Your blood did this?' He nodded. 'Did you know it would happen?'

'I wasn't sure.' He bent his head and kissed my unmarked skin. 'I knew that if I'd turned you right away, that is, at the scene to save your life, or even a few days or weeks afterwards, you would have healed and there wouldn't have been any indication you had been injured. The longer a person has a scar, the less likely it is to completely disappear, though it might fade a little. You've had yours three months; I guess that was still recent enough for my blood to have worked.' He smiled faintly, uncertain of my reaction.

'Well, I said that ugliness put them there, now love and beauty have taken them away.' I smiled back at him and reached a hand up behind his head to gently pull his mouth back to mine.

Gabriel had bound us by blood, now he joined us by body for the first time with us both as vampires.

Much later, I was snuggled up against Gabriel's warm, firm body, running my fingers over his chest.

He pulled me tighter into him. 'Do you remember I told you that you have choices with regard to your surprise?'

'Mmm-hmm,' I replied, looking up into his eyes.

'And that they depended on your answer to one question?' I nodded. 'It all depends on whether you decide to say yes or no.' He stroked a finger along my jaw to keep me looking at him. I could feel the tenderness inside him that just being here like this evoked in him. 'Will you marry me?'

Without any hesitation at all, I said, 'Yes.' A lump formed in my throat and tears spilled over. 'You've got me for all eternity and I want us to be joined in every way possible.' I stretched up to kiss him, placing my hand on his cheek to hold him there. 'I love you, Gabriel.'

'I love you, too, Jamie. Tomorrow we'll go to Hatton

Garden to find a jeweller to design and make a ring for you; something unique, just like you.'

Ever since I was a child, whenever I'd imagined getting engaged, I'd wanted a ring to be made especially for me. Even though for a good many years I never believed I'd be lucky enough to find someone I could love enough, or would love me enough, to marry, I occasionally still looked at rings when I passed jewellery stores and I didn't like any of them. I couldn't picture any of them adorning my hand as a symbol of love and commitment. Gabriel had obviously read this from me.

'Yes, I knew that. I also don't think any standard engagement ring would come small enough to fit you.' He smiled at me.

I grinned back. 'We should get wedding rings, too. I think we should get married as soon as possible. I don't have any family, and you don't care for yours, so it won't be a big wedding. It will just be the two of us and a couple of witnesses; perhaps Rachael and Baz; and a small, private ceremony. I'll be in a gorgeous dress and you'll be in an immaculate suit. What do you think of that idea?'

It sounded perfect to me, and the thought filled me with happiness that suddenly intensified and I knew it was Gabriel feeling the same, wanting the same thing.

'I love it. If your mother and sister were here to be our witnesses, it would be perfect,' he said softly.

'They'll still be there,' I asserted confidently.

The following morning, Gabriel guided me around the exclusive streets of Hatton Garden. He'd discovered a couple of jewellery stores that he thought might be suitable to design and make my engagement ring since he knew I didn't want anything fussy or old-fashioned.

In the end, the decision was easy; one of the stores stood out from all the rest. It was bright, modern, with glass displays of unset gemstones, and huge, freestanding rock crystals. It had a friendly feel that I noticed as soon as I walked through the entrance, and I knew it was right. I looked at Gabriel and he nodded his agreement.

We were guided over to sit at a table, and when the jeweller asked what kind of ring we were thinking of, Gabriel was ready with an answer.

'What I was thinking was a slim platinum band cradling a heart-shaped diamond, but I want a small teardrop-shaped, blood-red garnet embedded in each of the shoulders enclosing the diamond with the rounded ends facing the heart and the pointed ends facing out towards Jamie's other fingers. Unless you'd like something different, Jamie?' He looked at me, eyebrows raised mischievously.

I shook my head. 'That sounds perfect.' I smiled shyly, absurdly happy at such a small thing.

'It sounds beautiful,' the lapidarist, Cindy, agreed.

Whilst she began sketching the ring as Gabriel had just described it, he whispered so quietly that only he and I, with our enhanced auditory abilities, would be able to hear. 'A diamond heart to represent my eternal unconditional love, and blood-drop garnets; your birthstone; for commitment, fidelity, and soul mates.'

There really wasn't anything I could say in return to that, not that I needed to since he could feel within me how much I loved him, so beneath the surface of the table, I squeezed his hand.

When Gabriel mentioned wedding rings, Cindy told us that my ring could be curved to embrace the contours of the pointed end of my engagement ring so they would nestle together. Gabriel agreed with her and, though he didn't mind that his platinum wedding band seemed unembellished in comparison to my rings, I did, so I suggested that our names were engraved on the inside, just so Gabriel and I knew it wasn't completely plain. He insisted my wedding ring was engraved to match.

There was a lot of work involved in making our rings and Cindy couldn't guarantee they'd be ready in less than six to eight weeks, which meant Gabriel and I wouldn't be able to get married before mid-June. Gabriel used a little extra persuasion to make our rings her first priority, so we were told they'd be ready in four to six weeks instead.

Since we didn't have a clear idea of a date, we set about the mundane tasks of acquiring a marriage license and researching registrars. We wanted it to be legal, but not in any way religious, so no churches, but not a registry office, either. There was also the necessity of asking Rachael and Baz to be our witnesses.

Gabriel and I went to visit them one Sunday afternoon. Baz had immediately liked Gabriel, especially after we detailed everything that had happened with Aaron. It was obvious he was happy for me, so when I posed the question, he instantly said yes and Rachael followed, but with a slight reservation.

'Don't you want to do it, Rachael?' I asked, a little hurt.

'It's not that, Jamie. It's just that it's so soon. I do like you, Gabriel,' she clarified, switching her stricken gaze to him, 'so please don't be offended by what I'm about to say. Jamie, I know you said Bea and Carmel approve of Gabriel, and I said I wasn't going to argue with them, but you've made the decision to get married three months after losing them and you've only known Gabriel for what, a month? I'm worried you're not in a stable enough position to be sure about this.'

'Rach,' Baz intervened before Gabriel or I could respond, 'I haven't seen Jamie for a few weeks, not since before she got to know Gabriel, and I can see she's so much happier. She's genuinely happy, not just feeling a bit better than she did then. It's your decision, guys,' he said to us, 'and I support it. That's what friends do.'

'You're right,' Rachael agreed, and I felt her resolve to put aside her concerns for the rest of our visit.

'So, I noticed you asked us to be witnesses, not best man and matron of honour,' Baz commented with a knowing smile.

'Well, it's not really the kind of wedding that requires bridesmaids and a best man,' I explained. 'The two of you will pretty much be the only guests, along with Tamara and Noah.'

'And Paolo,' Gabriel added. 'I thought it would be nice to invite him, too.' He winked at me and, as always, I could feel how much he loved me and he could feel how much I loved him in return.

'I'd like that.'

'I think he would, too.'

'Anyway, as I was saying,' I continued, 'there will be limited guests and we're just having a small ceremony and that's it. Neither of us has family to please or entertain, so we're pleasing ourselves.'

'As you should,' Baz remarked.

By the time we left, Rachael had accepted that I was making the decision that was right for me, but it didn't stop her sending me a message as Gabriel was driving us home. I opened it and smirked to myself, seeing the humour in the situation.

'Rachael says that if our marriage doesn't work, she'll be there for me.' I smiled apologetically at Gabriel, feeling awful, but he was amused rather than offended. There was no way that Rachael could know that Gabriel and I would have each other forever.

Gabriel had asked Cindy to keep us informed with regard to the progress of our rings so that we could book a date to get married, and three weeks after our initial trip to the jewellery store, whilst I was busy with research, Gabriel received a call from her.

'She said she has been working flat-out on our rings and they should all be ready next week,' Gabriel informed me with a massive grin.

'We can book a date!' I could feel the excitement bubbling up inside me.

'Perhaps we'd better book it for two weeks afterwards,

just in case any adjustments need to be made.'

'So, three weeks' time.' I put the textbook I was reading aside. 'I'd better go shopping for a dress.' I grinned back at him.

I could tell he was imagining me in something white and slinky, and liking it very much. 'Let's arrange the venue first.'

The venue we had decided on was an old manor house that had been converted into a wedding hotel with beautiful rooms and gardens for the service and photographs. The whole house could be booked so the bride, groom, their parents, the bridesmaids and groomsmen could stay overnight before the ceremony. There was even a spa and a salon for the members of the wedding party to pamper themselves.

The establishment accommodated for ceremonies of all different faiths, as well as those who didn't subscribe to any religion, so they could arrange for the appropriate celebrant. However, the person on the end of the line when Gabriel called was evidently a little shocked when he asked to book a room for a service, a non-religious officiate, and nothing more: no hotel room, no reception, no elaborate decoration, no music requests.

I could hear both sides of the conversation, and the woman to whom Gabriel was speaking stuttered when he announced that we wanted a date for three weeks' time, or as soon after that as possible.

In her haughtiest tone, she informed him, 'Wedding dates are usually reserved at least a year in advance, Sir. I'm afraid every weekend is currently booked for the rest of the year.'

'It doesn't really matter what day of the week it is, or what time of day it takes place, we just want to get married,' he enlightened her, beginning to lose patience. 'We simply want a short ceremony with a minimum of fuss with a maximum of five guests in attendance.'

I heard her tapping her computer keyboard with rather too much pressure and, forcing a measure of pleasantness into her voice that she clearly didn't mean, told Gabriel they had an available slot on May the twenty-ninth at noon.

I sent Rachael a message with the details and a promise to call her later, but I knew I'd have to go and buy a gown before I did anything else.

I wrapped my arms around Gabriel and murmured into his ear, 'Do you want to come and help me choose a dress?'

'I'm not supposed to see it, or see you in it, until the ceremony,' he observed. 'It's bad luck.'

'You're going to know what it looks like before you see it, anyway. I've never known you to be superstitious before.' I frowned.

'I'm not. I thought you could go and have a look in a few bridal shops to see if there's anything you like whilst I organise a photographer and find something suitable for me to wear,' he reasoned, gently smoothing the crease between my eyebrows with his fingertips. 'If you don't find anything, or if you need my opinion, give me a call and I'll come and meet you.'

'Okay. Any preferences or dislikes?'

'It should be your choice; something you're comfortable in and happy with. That said, I beg you, nothing pouffy. Not only are dresses with hundreds of layers of netting hideous, you're so small it would look ridiculous on you.'

'I agree with you on both counts there. Okay, I'm going, but I'll go and see Paolo first and tell him the good news.'

I managed to park right in front of the coffee shop and Paolo saw me get out of the car. He was heading towards the door as I opened it and stepped inside. I grinned at him as he met me, arms wide, to give me a hug.

'Jamie! It has been weeks since I last saw you. I was getting worried about you.' He kissed me on both cheeks.

'I know, Paolo, I'm sorry. How have you been?'

'I'm very well. How are you? Does your lack of patronage recently have anything to do with your new man?'

I laughed. 'Yes, it has a lot to do with him. Do you have a

few minutes to talk? I'll explain everything.'

'Of course. Take a seat and I'll bring coffee over,' he replied, and returned to his position behind the counter.

A couple of minutes later, he came and sat in the chair opposite mine. He placed a large cappuccino in front of me and he had one for himself, too.

'Well, my "new man," as you referred to him, is called Gabriel. We've been spending a lot of time together recently, and the reason I haven't been here for a while is that I've moved in with him.'

Paolo didn't comment, but his eyebrows shot up as he regarded me over the rim of his cup.

'It was going to be a gradual thing,' I clarified, 'but my sister's fiancé was terrorising me. I had nasty phone calls and messages, and once or twice he dropped by the house. I got the police to speak to him, but it didn't make a difference, and I felt uncomfortable at home knowing he could knock on the door at any moment.'

'Jamie, you poor girl. So you've been at Gabriel's house so the fiancé couldn't find you?'

'Yes, only I happened to go home to pick something up and Aaron, that's his name, found me there and forced me to let him in. He tried to strangle me,' I said solemnly.

'Oh my God! Are you okay?'

'I'm fine, really. I picked up a knife and stabbed him in the shoulder.' I smiled grimly. 'The police arrested him. It's all over with now.'

Paolo looked relieved. 'And things between you and Gabriel?'

'We're fantastic. We're getting married. I came here to invite you.'

'You move fast.' He laughed. 'I'd love to come. When is it?'

'It's on the twenty-ninth of May at midday. It's not a big wedding; it will just be a short ceremony followed by a few photos. A couple of friends, and possibly their kids, are the only other guests.'

'And how long ago did you set the date?' He winked at me.

'About half an hour ago.'

'A rushed wedding. Are you expecting?' He looked pointedly at my stomach.

I laughed. 'No, I'm not pregnant. We just don't see the point in waiting and neither of us has to worry about pleasing family. We want a small, quiet service with no fuss. Please say you'll come.'

'Of course I will. One thing, though: why aren't you wearing a ring?'

'It's with the jeweller. I can pick it up next week.'

'Well, best wishes, my dear. You love each other and he makes you happy?' I nodded. 'Then that's all that matters.'

I gave him the rest of the details, finished my coffee, and dashed off after explaining my shopping trip.

'Good luck with the dress,' he called as I left the shop.

An hour later, I was approaching my third bridal shop having found nothing I liked even remotely in the previous two. None of the dresses in the window particularly appealed to me, though they were pretty enough.

No sooner had I stepped inside than the assistant stood up from where she was perched behind the counter, flipping through a magazine.

'Hello there,' she said in a pleasant voice. 'How may I help you?'

'Hi. I'm looking for a wedding gown, but, so far, I haven't found one that just screams at me that it's the right one.' I smiled courteously.

'What sort of dress are you looking for? Strapless? Corset bodice? Sleeveless?'

'Nothing strapless, that's not really my style. Neither is a corset.' I considered it for a moment. 'I don't think I want sleeves, either. I'm looking for something simple and elegant, nothing lacy, frilly, or pouffy; I don't like things that are too fussy. I'd like the material to have shimmer to it, like satin, so it doesn't look flat, and I want it to be figure-hugging.'

'Were you planning on wearing white?' she asked, narrowing her eyes slightly.

'Well, yes,' I answered, and frowned. 'Isn't that the tradition?'

'White would contrast well with your dark hair, but with your pale skin, I think it would make you look a bit ill. I'm sorry, I didn't mean to offend you,' she added, sounding contrite.

'No, no, I appreciate your honesty. What would you suggest?'

'Well, one designer recently sent me this one dress which, so far, no one has bought. I think most brides are looking for something extravagant and this one is beautifully simple. It's still white, but it has got a subtle hint of pink in it which will really flatter you. I'll go and get it because I don't think my description would do it justice. You need to see it for yourself,' she said enthusiastically.

She darted away and I had a quick look at a book that was lying around, which turned out to be a portfolio of dresses. They were all beautiful, and on the tall models they looked fantastic, but none of them would suit me at all.

Five minutes later, the assistant returned with a long, zipped, garment protector on a coat hanger. She opened it up and the first thing that struck me was the gentle lustrous sheen of the material. It was very subtly pink-tinged, had thin straps, and a low neckline which lightly draped over the bust. It had a pale pink ribbon stitched around the waist which tied at the side and flowed down to the pointed end of a diagonally-slashed hemline. I loved it.

She saw my expression. 'Would you like to try it on? I think it will be a little big on you, but I can order the correct size and alter it to fit.'

I nodded. 'It will have to be done quickly. I'm getting married in three weeks.'

'You've either left this to the last minute or it's a short-notice wedding.' She grinned.

'The latter. My fiancé proposed three weeks ago and we set the date this morning.' I shrugged. 'We're not particularly conventional.'

We went into the changing room and I undressed so the assistant could help me into the dress. It zipped at the side so it didn't spoil the look of the back of the dress and I wouldn't need someone to help me on the day. Once it was on, I could see it was a size too big, but Andrea, as she told me her name was, pinned it to fit so I could get a better idea of what it would look like.

It would fit like a second skin once I had the right size. I didn't look frumpy, and the hemline wouldn't emphasise how short I was. Naturally, the dress was also too long, but the hem would start just above the right knee and finish at the left ankle.

Now that I was a vampire, my empathic abilities were enhanced and I could feel Gabriel's emotions wherever I was, the way he had always been able to with me. I think it was a result of sharing so much blood that he could also read my mind easier, though I still couldn't read his. My telepathy, on the other hand, was still unconscious and revealed to me in my dreams. I could feel that he loved the dress, too.

'This is the dress. It's perfect,' I said earnestly, eyes wide, as I looked at myself in the full-length mirror.

'There are shoes in the same material as the dress, but dyed the same colour as the ribbon, to match,' Andrea said, holding up a pair of round-toed heels. 'The designer has even given the bride a choice of heel height.'

'What's the highest?'

'Four inches.'

'I'll take those in a size three,' I said with a laugh.

I took the dress off, but before I put my own clothes back on, Andrea took all my measurements. She explained it was for the dressmaker's mannequin she would use to alter my gown.

I didn't want a veil, and I'd decided against a headpiece, but I noticed a delicate tiara with hearts amongst the scrolling, and pale pink crystal hearts, and I couldn't resist it.

At the counter, I gave Andrea my contact details and paid half the total.

'I'll order your size dress and shoes now and they should be here in a week. I'll give you a call to come in for a fitting which will give me two weeks to make the alterations, though it shouldn't take that long, and then we'll have a final fitting. I promise I'll have it done in time for you, Jamie.'

'Thank you so much, Andrea. I'll see you in a week.'

Now that everything was actually happening; we had a date, a venue, hopefully a photographer, my dress was on order, and our rings should be ready in a matter of days; I could feel the anticipation growing inside both Gabriel and myself. We were actually getting married.

Twenty-One
I Do

I was still becoming accustomed to the greater sensitivity to energy I had now that I was a vampire, so instead of calling Gabriel's name to find out where he was as soon as I walked in the door when I got home, I concentrated on the energy I could feel. I made my way to the library, where I sensed Gabriel was, and I found the door ajar.

Pushing it open, I could see that he was sitting on the sofa with his back to me. He knew I was there, naturally.

'Hey, beautiful,' he said, without looking up from his book.

'Hey, yourself, gorgeous,' I replied, stepping up behind him and pushing my fingers into his hair to play with it, tugging it ever so lightly.

He tilted his head back to look into my eyes and he smiled. 'I love the dress. You'll look even more beautiful in it when it fits.'

I leaned forward and kissed him. 'You should have just come with me.' I moved my lips from his mouth to his jaw, then down the side of his throat where I gently grazed my teeth along the skin covering the vein.

He gave a soft growl low in his throat that I could feel against my mouth and, in response, he pressed his own teeth into the side of my neck; not enough to draw blood, but enough to make me shiver.

He put his book aside, reached up to grab me under the arms, and hauled me over the back of the couch and into his lap.

'If I had come with you, I'd have been shoved out of the shop by the assistant. Even those who aren't superstitious think the dress should be a surprise for the groom when he sees his bride wearing it when she makes her entrance.'

'Our wedding won't be like that, for one thing. For another, it's not possible to surprise you.' I wrinkled my nose at him as I thought about the fairy wand. He knew about that before I pulled it out of my bag, otherwise he wouldn't have teased me about the rest of the outfit.

'I know.' He grinned wickedly, both at the memory of the wand, and in delight that I couldn't surprise him. 'We have a photographer, by the way. He said this will be the easiest wedding he has ever worked considering he'll only be needed for about twenty minutes.'

'I don't care if we only have one photograph of us on our wedding day, just as long as it's a good photo.' I stilled for a moment. 'Gabriel, can you feel that?' I asked suddenly.

'Feel what?'

'It's Mum and Carmel. They're excited about the wedding and they're really pleased we're getting married. I just wondered if you could feel them, too.' I was overjoyed that I could feel their emotions. It was the first time I'd felt them clearly since they'd passed away.

'I think my empathic abilities only extend to the living, Jamie. I'm glad you can still feel what they're feeling, though.' He stroked my cheekbone.

I hadn't had an actual visit from Mum and Carmel since the night before Gabriel transformed me into a vampire. They had appeared in my dreams since, but I'd only seen glimpses of them, as though they were just letting me know they were still here. I also still caught flashes of movement in the corner of my eye which I was fairly certain was them, but I'd never consciously been able to see spirits before I was turned, so I wasn't surprised I hadn't seen anything more than those flickers now that I was a vampire.

A week later, Gabriel and I returned to the jeweller's to collect our rings. All three were ready and Cindy was proud to hand them over.

'I'm extremely pleased with how your engagement ring has turned out,' she said, presenting it to me. 'I can't wait to see how it looks on you. Try it with the wedding ring first to make sure they're a comfortable fit together.'

Gabriel picked up my wedding ring, checked the inside, and slid it onto my finger, then followed it with the diamond heart. As expected, they were a perfect fit and they nestled together smoothly. Neither Gabriel nor I said anything, we simply looked at one another and the love and happiness we both felt, and could feel in one another, was evident in our gaze.

I looked at Gabriel's ring, checked the engraving to ensure our names had been spelled correctly, as he had done with mine, then slipped it onto his finger.

'Thank you, Cindy,' I said, turning to her and seeing her big smile at our obvious pleasure. 'You've done a wonderful job for us. These rings are exactly how we wanted them.'

'And thank you for getting them made so quickly,' Gabriel added, winking at me.

'I love creating pieces that are so special to people. It's clear the two of you can't wait to get married. Have you set a date?'

'We're getting married in two weeks,' Gabriel told her, 'on the twenty-ninth.'

'Wow.' Cindy laughed. 'You were just waiting for your rings, then?'

'Pretty much,' I answered.

Gabriel took his ring off and I followed suit with both of mine. Cindy placed our wedding rings in a velvet box, but Gabriel kept hold of my engagement ring. He took hold of my left hand and placed it on my finger. He kissed my fingers and kept hold of my hand as he handed over his credit card to pay the balance.

'I wish my husband was more like you,' Cindy said as she processed the payment. 'He's never been particularly romantic, and he's certainly never showed his devotion to me the way you two do to each other.' She sighed to herself and handed Gabriel his card and receipt. 'Well, have a lovely wedding, and maybe I'll see you back here for an eternity ring when your first child is born.'

Gabriel and I merely grinned at her. 'Thanks,' we both said, and Gabriel handed me the box of rings to put in my bag.

That afternoon, Gabriel sat with me and watched a film whilst I continued with my research, which I was being careful not to neglect, and that night, I had a visit from Mum and Carmel.

We were in the living room of my mother's house, Mum and Carmel were sitting side-by-side on the sofa and I was kneeling in front of them holding my hand out so they could look at my new engagement ring.

'Oh my God, it's so beautiful,' Carmel gushed. 'I know that size and cost aren't important, but that's a substantial diamond, it's completely colourless and absolutely flawless, and a lot of work has gone into that ring. I think Gabriel would quite happily have spent his entire fortune on a ring for you.'

'Carmel, don't,' I reprimanded. 'Gabriel insisted on the rings. I'm happy just having him,' I gushed.

'Carmel's right, though, Jamie,' Mum corroborated. 'There's nothing that Gabriel wouldn't do for you.'

I blushed, and I know my face must have turned bright pink. It was at that moment I realised we weren't alone in the house. There was an obviously married couple in their thirties walking in and out of the room. Sometimes, they were trailing after a small child and, at others, being followed by another, slightly older one. They didn't pay any attention to our presence, and I had no idea if they could even see us.

'Who are they?' I asked with a frown.

'That's the family who lives here now,' Mum answered. 'You're getting married and you'll be living in Gabriel's house which, let's be honest, is much more spectacular than this one.'

'But—' I began.

'I know you don't want to let go of the way things were, but, even if Carmel and I were still alive, you'd move into Gabriel's home. You would have come back to see me, of course, but maybe I would have bought something smaller and sold this house once I was alone.'

'I wasn't going to move Gabriel in here and make him sell his house,' I said defensively. 'I mean, his library is bigger than the whole ground floor of this one so he wouldn't even have enough room for his books, let alone anything else. But I hadn't really decided what to do with your house, Mum,' I confessed.

Then, everything changed and that was the last I saw of my family that night. I had other dreams, but all I could recall of them were disjointed and indiscernible images of which I couldn't make sense.

'So, what are you going to do with your mother's house?' Gabriel asked on our way to the bridal shop, referring to the dream he'd overseen the previous night.

'Well, I don't really want to sell it, so I think we should contact an agency about renting it out.'

'Before we do that, we might want to stay there whilst we have renovation work done on our house,' he said with a devious smile.

'What renovation work were you thinking about?' He'd never mentioned any of this before, and I hadn't foreseen it, so it took me by surprise.

'We don't need the spare bedroom and bathroom, so I was thinking of moving the linen closet into our bedroom and extending the library upwards. We'd have two floors connected by an internal spiral staircase. What do you think?' His grin widened as he felt my pleasure increasing at the prospect. 'We've got all your books to house as well as mine, and I'm sure we'll add to the collection.'

'I think it sounds like a fantastic idea. I'd really like that.'

'I thought you might.'

As Gabriel and I entered the store, I saw Andrea glance at me and then her eyes widened when they encountered Gabriel.

'Hello again, Jamie,' she greeted me politely. 'I see you've brought someone with you this time. Is he here to give you his opinion on the fit?'

'Hello, Andrea, I hope so; this is the groom, Gabriel.'

Her smile only slipped by a fraction, but I felt her excitement at seeing him drop through the floor. She was hoping Gabriel was related to me in some way so that she could ask him out herself.

'Yes, she was definitely hoping that,' Gabriel confirmed quietly, and I tried not to let my amusement show.

'Well, it's lovely to meet you, Gabriel, but you know it isn't customary for the groom to see the bride's dress before the ceremony.' She tried to remain professional despite her disappointment.

'No, I know, but we don't follow custom or abide superstition,' Gabriel informed her dryly.

'It's just that I would have expected your mother to accompany you, Jamie, or a sister, or even a friend as the chief bridesmaid.'

'I don't have a living mother or sister anymore, and there aren't any bridesmaids. There's just Gabriel and me.'

'Not even a future mother-in-law?' she enquired.

'Not who matters,' Gabriel interjected amicably before I could reply.

'Oh, I'm sorry,' she uttered, chastened. 'It really isn't any of my business. Jamie, I've got your dress and shoes waiting for you in the fitting room. Why don't you go and change into them?'

I disappeared to change, quickly shedding my jeans and top and sliding into the dress. I could hear Andrea trying to dissuade Gabriel from seeing me in it on the other side of the door.

'But don't you want to be surprised by how beautiful Jamie looks when she appears by your side after walking down the aisle?' she insisted.

'Jamie always looks beautiful,' he stated. 'We're not having that kind of wedding, and we certainly aren't the "traditional" type,' Gabriel replied with the barest hint of mirth.

'Gabriel,' I whispered, knowing only he would hear me. 'I think she just wants to get rid of you because she's annoyed you're unavailable.'

'You're right,' he agreed with me under his breath.

'I only hope she doesn't take her frustration out on my dress.' I finished zipping it up and had a look in the mirror. 'It's a bit long, fits nicely at the bust and hips, but it's a bit loose in the middle,' I informed him.

'But still…' Andrea began to protest.

'All right,' Gabriel barked impatiently, reluctant to use extra persuasion for fear she really would take out her feelings on my dress once we'd gone. 'I'll wait at the front of the store. The dress needs to be taken in at Jamie's ribs, waist and thighs only. Of course, it's much too long, even with Jamie wearing the heels. The slash should begin three-quarters of the way down her right thigh and end three-quarters of the way down her left calf.'

I could sense Andrea's bewilderment at Gabriel's instructions considering she had yet to see me in the smaller-sized gown.

'I'm going to wait at the front, Jamie,' Gabriel called out for Andrea's benefit. 'I love you.'

'Okay, if you're sure. I love you, too, Gabriel.'

'You're going to look even more stunning in that dress when it's done,' he finished.

I felt him move away from the fitting area towards the front of the shop.

Only when she was sure that Gabriel had gone did Andrea open the door and join me by the mirror. She took a long look at how the dress fitted from every angle and frowned.

'He's right about what needs altering. How did he know? Does he have x-ray vision or something?'

I shrugged. 'He does things like that a lot. And in case you were wondering, he is always right. He's very insightful.'

'Doesn't that get annoying?' she enquired, narrowing her eyes at me.

'What, having a man who truly understands me?' I shook my head. 'Never.'

Andrea worked quickly to pin my dress in accordance with Gabriel's instructions and informed me she'd have the adjustments made by the end of the day, but to give her an extra day to be sure.

True to her word, I returned two days later and Andrea had completed the alterations. I tried the dress on for a final time before the wedding to ensure there weren't any problems, but there weren't. The dress was perfect. I left the bridal shop with my dress, shoes, and tiara to store in Gabriel's spare bedroom.

A few days before the wedding, Gabriel and I had a meeting with the registrar for a rehearsal and to discuss our vows. We considered writing our own, but everything we composed seemed trite and the promises were the same as the traditional vows: to love and cherish one another regardless of circumstance, and to be faithful to one another. Besides which, there was nothing we could write in a vow that we hadn't already promised one another over and over again.

We made it clear that as long as all religious references were removed, we were happy with the standard vows. However, we specified that instead of saying 'Till death us do part,' we preferred 'For as long as we both shall live.' Since we were going to live forever, we felt it was more appropriate.

When Gabriel and I awoke on the day of our wedding, the sun was shining brightly and it already felt warm and humid. It didn't take long for us to get ready; I'd never been a high-maintenance person so I simply straightened my hair as usual and, though I never really wore make-up, I added a little definition to my eyes and a natural pink lip gloss, mainly for emphasis in the photos.

Gabriel managed to surprise me in that his shirt, like my dress, had a subtle hint of pink in it, and his tie was the exact same shade as the ribbon around my waist and my shoes. His black suit was obviously made-to-measure by an expert tailor, and it delineated his lean physique.

'You look beautiful, Gabriel,' I remarked, looking at him in awe. 'You *are* beautiful.'

'Thank you; as are you. You are simply breathtaking, Jamie. And you're mine forever, as I am yours,' he added, pulling me close for a kiss.

A little over an hour later, Gabriel and I were standing facing one another in a large, airy, cream-painted room decorated with white flowers, in front of a registrar, with a view out onto the gardens. Sitting watching us were Rachael, who was holding Noah, and Baz. Tamara sat in between them on her best behaviour. Next to Baz was Paolo, who was smiling broadly and unconsciously emitting waves of affection and happiness for us. The strength of feeling from Baz was practically the same, and even Rachael was feeling more positive than she did the day we broke the news.

I could also feel a wealth of love from Mum and Carmel who, I could sense, were standing a little way behind me.

Naturally, everything everyone was feeling was nothing in comparison to Gabriel's and my emotions. Even if we couldn't communicate telepathically back and forth, we could emotionally, and our emotions said more than words could have at that moment.

I had removed my engagement ring and placed it on my right hand for the ceremony. Gabriel had my wedding ring in his pocket and he had given me his ring just seconds before the proceedings and I tied it to the end of the ribbon around my waist.

We gazed at one another, unable to conceal our joy, as we exchanged vows and took turns to place the rings on one another's fingers. Then the registrar pronounced us husband and wife.

Gabriel surreptitiously replaced my engagement ring and then he drew me to him to seal it with a kiss.

'I'll love you forever,' I whispered into his ear, my voice infused with all the love and devotion I had.

'We'll love each other longer than that,' he corrected.

It was soppy. And romantic. And true.

Epilogue
Full Circle

I was back at the university where I first found Jamie. I was drawn there that day three years earlier by her and the overwhelming strength of her emotion. When I felt her, and when I felt just how nervous and scared she was, I was compelled to follow her to find out what could be causing her so much distress and I was relieved to discover her anxiety was due to nothing more sinister than an exam.

I could feel those nerves in her again, though there was less fear in her this time. After everything she had endured after her last *viva voce*, this one didn't scare her so much.

She was only in the next room, and I could hear every word she said. I could hear her giving her presentation in defence of her dissertation. Her heart pounded hard and fast; I could always feel it as strongly as my own. She rushed it a little.

'Calm,' I advised her, knowing she could hear me, too. 'Take a deep breath before your next sentence and slow down.' I was encouraging her rather than upbraiding her, and she could feel the sincerity and love in me, just as I could feel her love and gratitude for my support.

Once the presentation was over, I listened to her expertly answering all the questions put to her by her examiners. Her confidence grew with every response she gave until I felt relief suffuse her that it was over.

I could sense her move into the waiting area whilst the examiners discussed everything they had heard. I was in the hallway, as I had been the last time, only this time, we could both hear the judgements of the examiners and their final decision.

Jamie went back into the exam room for her result and I waited impatiently for her to return to me. Those few minutes seemed longer than the hours of the *viva* itself until, at last, she met me in the vestibule.

'Congratulations, Dr. Jamie Castell,' I said, tugging her into my arms.

'Thank you, Dr. Gabriel Castell,' she replied before sealing her lips to mine.

We had been back to the jewellery store where we had our wedding rings made in order for them to make a diamond eternity ring to fit around Jamie's engagement ring. Again, Cindy made it for us.

I told Jamie I'd give her an eternity ring when she got her doctorate or when we published her first novel, whichever came first, as we would never have children, but the two events coincided. She had written the manuscript in the first two years of her PhD and during the third, whilst she completed her dissertation, I edited her novel rather than undertake another degree of my own. We finalised the book in the interim between her handing in the thesis and her exam, and she decided her heroine should have a happy vampire eternity with her sire, just like we were having.

Jamie protested against the ring, saying she didn't need another one, but I wanted to give her a gift and an eternity ring seemed to say it all.

I reached into my pocket and pulled it out. Taking Jamie's left hand in mine, I slid the ring onto her finger.

'Forever,' I promised, loving her with my whole self and knowing she could feel it.

'Forever,' she agreed, loving me with her whole self and knowing I could feel that, too.

Printed in Great Britain
by Amazon.co.uk, Ltd.,
Marston Gate.

5008415R00185